Praise for *The Birthing House*

Kathy Taylor is a literary force to be reckoned with. Her ability to seamlessly blend intricate storytelling, vivid imagery, and deep emotional resonance is awe-inspiring. Her works transport readers to different cultures and periods, immersing them in richly woven narratives that leave a lasting impact. A true wordsmith, Taylor's talent shines through every page.

- Literary Review Magazine

The Birthing House pulled me into its quicksand of moving, overlapping stories. Its unusual structure spins a fresh narrative from the confusion of deep grief and numb ache, as this little family creates webs of connection despite their outsider status, emerging into spacious radiant hope for the future. Kathy Taylor's book took my heart for a wild ride!

-Adrienne Hoskins

Kathy Taylor's writing is a breath of fresh air in the literary world. Her ability to explore complex themes with nuance and sensitivity is unmatched. Her characters come alive on the page, their struggles and triumphs echoing in the hearts of readers. Taylor's work is a testament to the power of storytelling and its ability to bridge gaps between cultures and generations.

- Bookish Connections

The Birthing House reflects Kathy Taylor's intense emotional connection to the unique charm of the German town of Marburg. This book creates insights into the history and culture of a multitude of ancient and typical characteristics of a town the author knows very well and that has been alive in her heart from the first moment she saw it. *The Birthing House* is an authentic and magic documentary of her love for Marburg and the people she met there.

- Jochen (Marburg)

The Birthing House by Kathy Taylor is a treasure trove of thought-provoking ideas and heartfelt storytelling. She takes readers on a journey of self-discovery, exploring universal themes of love, loss, and resilience. Her writing is captivating, drawing readers into immersive worlds where they can truly connect with the characters and their experiences. Taylor is an exceptional writer whose works deserve a special place on every bookshelf.

- Bookworm's Haven

The Birthing House by Kathy Taylor is a brilliant book that weaves the stories of a woman during two phases of life and of birthing, both in reality and metaphorically, with the common threads among women through time. Amidst the wide cast of characters in the book, the elder man Johann's personality and story will stick with me for a long time. A truly enjoyable book!

- Leslie Bishop

Kathy Taylor's literary voice is a rare gem. Her prose is eloquent, lyrical, and infused with an indescribable magic that captivates readers from the very first sentence. She effortlessly captures the essence of human emotions, weaving them into narratives that touch the soul. Taylor's ability to create intricate and authentic worlds is unparalleled, making her an author to watch. Her works resonate deeply and leave a lasting impression.

- Literary Wanderlust Review.

Kathy Taylor's book is in essence about human adaptability. The two timelines deal with profound losses. In the 1980s Clare grieves the loss of her unborn child; twenty years later, she experiences the pain of her father's death. While she wrestles with the challenges she faces in a new land, she learns about the hardships of others having to flee their home countries or make horrific choices in their lives. Taylor's writing expresses her sensitivity to people's journeys and consequently moves her readers. It makes them think about their own life stories, adaptability, and losses. I highly recommend this beautiful book!

- Majka Jankowiak

The Birthing House

Escribimos para darnos a la luz.

We write to give birth to our selves.

-Catalina Sastre

Kathy Taylor

This is a work of fiction. I have tried to make the setting authentic to the very real town of Marburg, Germany, but the story required me to invent some details and disguise others. Family and friends may recognize themselves in some of the characters, but they, too, have been fictionalized and many of the specific events were imagined. Fiction is not untrue, but rather, like all writing, it is a weaving of the threads of real experience and the filaments of the imagination.

Songs

"Wenn unsere Flöten" and "Alles ist Eitel" copyright with schott-music.com. All other songs are in the public domain.

References

Bakhtin, Mikhail. *The Dialogic Imagination*, translated by Michael Holquist and Caryl Emerson. Austin: Univ. of Texas Press, 1981.

Barthes, Roland. "The Death of the Author" in *Image, Music, Text"* Translated by Stephen Heath. New York: Hill and Wang. 1977

Borges, Jorge Luis. *"Las Ruinas Circulares" Ficciones,* Buenos Aires: Emecé Editores, 1944.

Costa Lima, Luis. *"Documento e ficcão."* In Jara, *Testimonio y Literatura,* Minneapolis, Institute for the Study of Ideologies and Literartures. 1986.

Derrida, Jaques. From diverse readings, lectures and references.

Iser, Wofgang. The Implied Reader. Baltimore & London: Johns Hopkins Univ. Press, 1974.

Kermode, Frank. *The Sense of an Ending:Studies in the Theory of Fiction.* New York: Oxford Univ. Press, 1967.

Murdock, Iris. *The Sovereignty of Good.* London: Routledge. 1970.

Nietsche, Friedrich. *The Birth of a Tragedy* in Hayden White, *Metahistory.* Baltimore: The Johns Hopkins Univ. Press, 1973.

Ortega y Gasset, José. *Meditaciones del Quijote,* 1914.

Sacks, Oliver. "A Matter of Identity" in *The Man Who Mistook his Wife for a Hat.* Harper Perennial / Harper Collins: New York, 1987.

Yorukoglu, Ilgin. *Acts of Belonging:Perceptions of Citizenship Among Queer Turkish Women in Germany.* Phd dissertation, City Univ. of New York, 2014.

Midwifery:

Hebammen in Hessen: Gestern und Heute. Hessische Landeszentrale für politische Bildung, 2022.

Metz-Becker, Marita. *Drei Generationen Hebammenalltag.* Gießen: Psychosozial-Verlag, 2021.

Dedication

To the fairytale town of Marburg
and to midwives everywhere.

Table of Contents

1
Déjà Vu

October 2005

Life is an eternal becoming, Clare mused as she waited backstage under the cover of darkness. Each time she walked out into the light, it was like she was giving birth to herself, penning with dark ink the first words on a blank page. She had done it many times, but it always felt new.

She watched as the woman approached the podium. Here we go again. Clare took a deep breath as the woman began to speak.

"Ladies and gentlemen, it is my honor and privilege to introduce our distinguished speaker for this month's graduate forum on writing. She is not a stranger to you, since you have all read her book and her bio that I sent out. Right?" Most in the crowd nod, a few sheepish chuckles from the back. "And welcome to all those who are joining our forum today. Professor Muller is well known for her work in literary theory and linguistics, but you may not know that she has also published a novel, short stories and poetry. Her recent book has made quite a splash in academia and beyond. So, without further ado, please join me in welcoming Dr. Clare Muller!"

Clare stepped up to the podium to polite applause. "Thank you. Thank you so much." She waited, nodding and smiling at individual faces that caught her attention. That was her trick for calming herself before a talk.

"Thank you so much for inviting me. I am honored to be here today and share with you my love of words and ideas that are the *materia prima* of our art." She paused for a moment and looked around as the silence settled on the earnest attention of the students. A page turned in her mind. She was getting tired of her own story.

"First, I want to make a confession," Clare began slowly. "I brought a carefully crafted speech to read today." She held up a small stack of papers as she spoke. "But I just realized that is not what I want to say to you. The biggest trap we professors can fall into is teaching our own books.

"So, thank you for reading mine. You can draw your own conclusions about it. Today, I just want to pose a few questions: Why do we write? How do we write? What do we write about?

"We are all writers, you know." The words were coming faster than her thoughts. "Not just those of us who claim to be, but every one of us. Each moment of our existence is an intersection of stories that inhabit us and connect us. As the present constantly unravels, we weave a future out of the threads of our past, inventing a narrative to make sense of things. We spend our whole lives rewriting that narrative so it can hold the complexity of who we become."

2
Timelines

June 2000

Clare arrived with full suitcases and an emptiness too heavy to carry. The Frankfurt *Hauptbahnhof* train station, as huge and busy as she remembered it, was a major hub for national and international travel. She sat on their pile of bags and looked around, feeling dazed and exhausted.

"I'll go get the train tickets. You wait here," Stefan said. Clare nodded gratefully, letting her husband take charge. She was usually the organizer and leading energy of their trips, but this time she felt like one more piece of luggage. Bits of conversations streamed by—a soundscape of tones and languages that normally would have fascinated her. A few words of German penetrated her fog, but she didn't let them in. Not yet.

"Hello, Frankfurt," she whispered, "I'm back," and she flashed back to twenty years earlier when she had sat in the same spot, with a suitcase of baby clothes and the memory of a miscarriage. They had planned so well for that year. Stefan had a Fulbright grant to do research for his dissertation and Clare would take time off from her graduate studies to work on a baby. It was perfect. They could afford to have another kid in Germany, where medical care was excellent and mostly free. Stefan had gone over first, and Clare had followed a couple of weeks later with their six-year-old son, who would be in first grade and would quickly become fluent in German, as only young children can.

"*Kann ich dir helfen, mein Schatz?*" a familiar voice asked. Stefan had returned with the tickets and in a teasingly formal tone said, "May I help you, my dear?"

That phrase took Clare back to the image of the white-haired angel, who had appeared to rescue her as she sat on a pile of luggage with 6-year-old Willy in a moment of despair and confusion. "*Kann ich dir helfen, mein Schatz?*" The woman had asked with such a sweet voice that Clare had choked on her tears and just nodded.

August 1980

Nothing had gone right or made sense since they arrived at the Frankfurt airport early that Sunday morning, after a sleepless night from New York on an economy flight. The airport was nearly empty and the machine to buy tickets for the local train to the *Hauptbahnhof* train station was out of order. The complex instructions in German had kept her trying for quite a while until a man came by and tried it himself, unsuccessfully.

"Es muß außer Betrieb sein," he said, shrugging his shoulders. "Out of order," he clarified, seeing the blank look on her face. He walked off before she could ask him what to do. One thing she did know was the penalty for *Schwarzfahren,* to travel without paying. She had read about that before leaving home. The stores in the airport were closed, and there was nowhere to change money or buy food. Even the escalator down to the tracks was not working, and she'd had to ferry the eight suitcases (they had packed for at least a year) down the stationary steps in several trips while she kept an eye on little Willy who sat wide-eyed at the bottom as the pile of bags grew.

"Okay, Willy, I need you to be my helper. Sit here and watch over the bags while I bring the others down."

The guidebook said that you didn't hand a ticket to a conductor when you got on a train. You just boarded and later someone would come by to check tickets. Maybe. But if you were caught without one, the fine was heavy. It wasn't clear to her which track to go to and there was no one to ask. "Doesn't anyone travel on Sunday here?" she shouted in her mind, but it came out in a muffled complaint to the sleeping escalator.

After walking in circles, she waited at what she hoped was the right track and soon heard the whooshing sound of an approaching train. Suddenly she panicked. The train would stop only briefly, and it was up to her to get all the bags and her son on before it took off again. Should she load the bags first and then jump on with Willy, or put him on first and hope he could help her with the bags?

The train pulled up and there was no time to resolve her dilemma. Adrenaline helped her heave the bags, then Willy, then herself, landing awkwardly on the heap of suitcases before the train departed. For months after that, she would have variations of a nightmare about a train pulling away with little Willy and all their bags on it, leaving her to scream alone on the platform.

It was a short ride to the central train station, and no one had asked for her ticket. At least there was that. Exhaustion and hunger dulled her usual resourcefulness. *One step at a time* was all she could allow herself to think. On top of it all, she felt a heaviness in her belly, an echo of the miscarriage that still haunted her.

The miscarriage. The images were sparse and scattered. Driving across Illinois, she saw a few spots of blood. Keep going, it'll be okay. A rest area on the interstate—cramps, gravity pulling on her insides. Hold on, don't let go. Can't lose this baby, not here. Make it to Indiana, friends along the way. The rest was a blur—arriving, quick hugs, race to the bathroom. Couldn't hold it, too much blood, pain, tiny creature in her hand. Clare didn't remember the ride to the hospital. She woke up hours later, baby gone, all traces of it scraped out of her. She tried to clear her mind of it as well. But at night she would lie awake in the dark with the aching emptiness, wondering what had gone wrong. The memory of miniature fingers and fragile ribs in the translucent torso hung like a painting on the back wall of her mind. Who might that little being have become?

These things happen, the doctor had said.

Then, somehow, there they were with the pile of suitcases in the middle of a huge train station.

"You stay right here with the bags, Willy. Okay?" He nodded, already half-asleep, and his fine blond hair slid down over his forehead. Clare started off to look for a ticket window, often turning to glance back at Willy. She noticed that he had flopped face first over one of the bags. Clare went back to join him on the heap. She had no gumption left.

"Kann ich dir helfen, mein Schatz?" a white-haired woman asked, seeming to appear out of nowhere. She reminded Clare of Elsa, a German woman who had been their neighbor when Clare was young, a grandmother figure of warm hugs and fresh cinnamon rolls. *"Kann ich dir helfen?"* the woman repeated. Clare nodded. Tears of frustration and relief streamed down her face as she let the grandmother-angel lead them to the Travelers Aid Center.

"First, you need to eat and drink and rest a bit, *mein Schatz*, and then we will figure everything out," the woman had said soothingly as she summoned a hearty young man named Hans, who threw all their heavy bags onto a cart and followed them silently. Clare signed over a traveler's check to Hans as they were finishing their sandwiches and tea. Soon he appeared with the train tickets and led them to the platform for Marburg. It had all seemed like a dream. As she hugged her angel goodbye, the woman asked once more, "Are you sure you don't want to stay in Frankfurt? We could help you find a place to live." It was almost tempting, but Clare had a job to do. Their year in Germany had begun.

June 2000

"Clare? Are you okay?" Stefan asked as he loaded their bags on a cart. "*Bitte? Oh, ja.*" It took a minute for Clare to come back to the present and follow her husband to the train. She thought about the mysterious young Hans as she walked. How old would he be now?

Here I am again. Clare noted the familiar hollowness inside her. This time the loss was not an unborn baby, but a father who had been part of her whole life: a miscarriage of all the future years she assumed she would have with him.

* * *

Clare awoke to the sound of a grandfather clock ticking through the dark. She was wide awake and hungry, but Stefan was snoring next to her, so she lay there awhile. *Where am I?* Then she remembered, hearing in her mind the voice on the train announcing, "Marburg!" She had dozed between images of towns and countryside streaming by and didn't remember much about the rest. It was still very light when they went to bed, their inner clocks completely at odds with German time.

They had been deeply disappointed a few weeks earlier when the apartment they hoped to rent for the year was no longer available, but at the last minute their old friends Jürgen and Christina had found a house that belonged to an acquaintance of theirs.

"The owner plans to be gone for a year but she didn't want the hassle of trying to find renters," Jürgen told them. "She was going to just shut the door and leave her life intact, paying a neighbor to look after things, but maybe it could work for you."

It was a serendipitous solution for all. Clare and Stefan would move into Hannah's life paying an affordable rent and taking care of her plants and the garden. They felt as though the place had found them and from then on, they referred to their new quarters as *Das Haus*. The House. Clare sensed right away the important role it would play in their second German adventure.

There were two bedrooms upstairs and they had chosen the smaller one across from what was clearly Hannah's room. They fell onto the double bed in the corner and sank into a deep sleep. Clare awoke some hours later and couldn't get back to sleep. She got up and tiptoed out of the room, feeling her way down the stairs. She didn't want to turn on a light, not sure she was ready to meet her new home yet. The numbness inside her was more comfortable in the darkness.

She sat in the kitchen, waiting in the timeless hour before dawn that should have been yesterday evening. Her mind seemed to be in sleep mode. Not entirely shut down, yet blank. She was aware of her heart beating with the ticking clock. At first it had seemed so dark that she had to blink to check if her eyes were open. But as her eyes adjusted, she realized that it wasn't entirely dark. The blackness softened and she could begin to see the shapes of things around her.

Am I asleep? Somewhere in between, I guess.

She had felt that way a lot in the nearly two months since her father's death: watching her life from a distance with her inner self on pause as the movie streamed by. Her usual busy work life had propelled her along. The sun rose each day, and everything looked the same. Yet it wasn't. Now the jet lag was another layer, a blanket on top of her sleeping self.

"Here I am," she whispered to the in between. "*Hier bin ich.*" What a strange thing it was to hop over the ocean into another world, losing time as you went.

Her father's death had felt like an accident of time, as though the world had shifted into a gear that landed her in a future where she didn't belong.

* * *

"You need to go ahead with your plans," her mother had insisted after the memorial service for her father.

"But I don't want to leave you alone."

"I'm not alone, Clare. I have plenty of support and friends who will check on me. And your sister will visit often as well."

"It just doesn't feel right."

"I have to get used to being on my own and I might as well start tomorrow."

"It's too soon and too far away. And I…"

Her mother smiled and held her gaze for a moment.

"Your father will find you, you know, wherever you are."

The comment hit home. Clare really did feel that she needed to stay near the place where her father had left them. What was she expecting? It was silly. But deep down, she wasn't convinced.

"And I don't plan on dying anytime soon," her mother added, with her characteristic pragmatism.

"Maybe you could come to visit us in Germany?"

Their son Will would be busy with work, and he had his girlfriend, Yolanda. It was hard to leave their daughter, Anja, but she had her summer job at camp and then would be starting her second year of college. They'll be alright. But what about Mom?

* * *

Clare was startled when Stefan came shuffling into the kitchen, bringing some normalcy to her liminal state. His sandy colored hair looked as displaced as she felt. He went straight for the coffee maker.

"Bless you, Hannah," he mumbled as he found a bag of coffee next to it. It wasn't the French press he liked to use at home, but it would have to do for now. Stefan was a coffee snob. He was very particular about how he made it. But in a pinch, it was caffeine before high culinary culture. Stefan was one of those people who could not begin the day until after coffee. Clare noted that the day had begun anyway, and the kitchen was regaining its form. The smell of coffee awakened her as well. She took a deep breath and looked around.

After sitting in the kitchen for a while, she got up to explore. Stefan had already rushed off to get some supplies. Jürgen and Christina had met them at the train station and had also found a car they could rent for the year at a reasonable price. Stefan had been busy making all the arrangements in the weeks before they left home. He had tried consulting her, but she was in her "whatever" state, not even sure she would go with him. Now she was beginning to appreciate his efforts.

Clare wandered through the house as the rays of the sun tapped the different areas of Hannah's life that she would soon inhabit. There were moments when the newness awakened a flicker of her old love of adventure despite her somnambular state. A large, framed photo of two trees caught her attention. The two trunks had intertwined in an intimate embrace. Or maybe it was one tree that had divided itself from the beginning. Clare had always loved trees. Her childhood was full of them. In her view, they were impressive beings that didn't get the respect they deserved from humans. There was such tenderness in the photo, the way the two trees leaned into each other. Her eyes filled with tears.

August 1980

"I'm tired, Mommy."

"I know, Willy, I'm tired, too."

"When will we get to our new house?"

"Well, we need to look for one. It will take a while."

"Where's Daddy? I thought you said he was in Germany."

"Yes, well, he is, but in another part. He needs to go to school for a while before he comes to live with us."

"Why does he have to go to school? He knows too much already."

"He does know a lot, but he's trying to learn more German so he can talk to people better. Lots and lots of new words."

"Oh. Let's go find our new house today."

"We'll try. And maybe this afternoon we can go down to the river."

"Will there be ducks?"

"I hope so."

Those first days in Marburg were both exciting and stressful. As she and Willy walked the streets and learned to ride the buses, Clare concentrated on keeping her calm and confident mother's face outward while the other one, anxious and exhausted, faced only inward. Willy was at times his exuberant and innocent six-year-old self, and at others, he was whiny and fretful. Thank God there were ducks on the river. It became a special ritual to take breadcrumbs to throw on the water and entice them to come quacking towards the shore.

15

Willy had a small notebook where he kept his words. Clare had made it a game. Each time he learned a new word in German, he got five *Pfennig*. Once a word was written down in his large wobbly writing, he owned it and the words became attached to his new life and experiences. The ducks soon became "*die Enten*" and were among the early inhabitants of that notebook. "When can we go feed *die Enten*?" became a daily refrain and Clare realized that the urgency she felt to get them settled needed to alternate with such moments of joy and escape.

They spent the afternoons walking the streets of the town to begin to map their new life.

"I like that one. What do you think?" Clare pointed to a small house with bright red flowers blooming on the balcony. "I love balconies."

"How about this one?" Willy countered with the house next to it. "It has a nice tree to climb." He giggled, getting into the spirit of their pretend house hunting.

"Let's see who can find the first blue house," Clare proposed to keep up his interest. "We need to keep walking to learn our way around and watch for opportunities."

"Here's a 'portunity," Willy declared, stopping in front of a sign that said *Eis*.

"Hmmm. You'd like to live here?"

"No, silly! I want some ice cream." He pointed to a picture of an ice cream cone on the window.

"Ah, we'd better check it out and see if German ice cream is any good."

"Another word for my notebook." He wrote *Eis* carefully on the first page, which was already beginning to fill up with words. Clare handed him five Pfennig.

"It sounds just like the English "ice.""

"How do you say ice cream cone?"

"*Eistüte*. Can you say that?"

"*Eistüte.*"

"Okay, let's go buy one."

For their first time in Germany, they had hoped that they would be able to live in the university apartments that were for visiting professors or research fellows. But since Stefan was not directly connected with the university, it was not an option for them. All his efforts to find housing before they left home had failed.

"I can't let you handle all that alone," he had said, his eyes full of doubt and concern. "Should we even be doing this?"

"Don't worry, it'll be fine," Clare had answered with genuine confidence. She was proud of her adventurous spirit. After all, she had taken students to Mexico, where nothing was certain. No matter how much you planned things, you always had to improvise. She thrived on the challenge. But that was before.

"Are you sure you are ready for this?" her brother had asked as he drove her and Willy to the airport. "I mean, so soon after the miscarriage."

"I'm used to jumping off a cliff without a parachute," Clare answered her brother, trying to convince herself as well. "I always land on my feet." She was counting on her ability to make the best of difficult situations. Besides, their plan was already in motion and she needed to go forward.

Germany was turning out to be harder than she expected. Who would have thought it would be more challenging than Mexico? In Germany, there was a well-ordered formality that was difficult to penetrate. At least you could drink the water.

By the third day of searching the newspapers and the streets, she felt a growing desperation. The little hotel where they were staying was expensive and the proprietor was getting nervous. He had grilled her when she arrived with her many suitcases and a little boy. It was as if he didn't believe that she had a husband or any plan at all. She decided to go to the university housing office and make a plea. The worst that could happen was that they would just say no again.

"*Guten Tag, Frau Holzer,*" Clare began in her best German. The grammar of polite German was challenging. "I hope you are having a wonderful day." That sounded dumb. "I… I would like to talk to you about our situation and see if maybe you could make a little exception…"

The woman had not even looked up when Clare knocked on the open door. Now, raising her eyebrows, she peered at them over her glasses.

"*Entschuldigung,*" Clare began again. "Excuse me, I'm sorry to bother you, but…"

Willy stood silently next to her, staring at the woman with his blue eyes under long dark lashes and willing her to listen with his best Obi Wan Kenobi imitation.

"Well, I don't know. This is a bit unusual."

"Could we maybe just stay there for a while until we can find something more permanent?" Clare could feel her inner face beginning to take over as her voice wavered. Every rental place she had seen in the paper required at least a two-year commitment. And some even said, "No children." Willy tightened his grip on her hand.

"Hmm. I can let you stay there for six weeks. No more."

"*Vielen Dank*! Thank you so much!" Clare squeaked through her relief. At least they would have somewhere to land while she figured things out.

"Come back tomorrow morning at nine and we'll make the arrangements."

On the way out the door, Willy turned to thank her. "*Danke schön*", he said, feeling the power of the words he had pulled from his list just above the ducks. A dimple winked on his cheek as he smiled.

They walked solemnly out of the office and the building. Once outside the door, they turned to each other with a precisely choreographed high five. Willy noted the relief and victory in his mother's eyes.

"Let's do 'Willy Nilly'," he suggested.

"I don't know, I'd feel kind of silly."

"Then we'll be Silly, Willy and Nilly!"

Clare chuckled, and off they went, arms out airplane style, as they careened down the sidewalk. It was their secret routine that had begun a couple of years earlier after a scary moment for Clare that had turned into a special bond between them. Four-year-old Willy had run off, just following his feet, as he liked to say. She and Stefan had searched frantically for him for almost three hours and were about to call the police, when they found him.

"Are you mad at me, Mommy?" Willy had asked after his parents had calmed down. Clare was still shaky from both the scare and her relief at finding him.

"No, sweetie, but don't *ever* do that again. You can't just run off willy-nilly without telling us. We were scared that something bad had happened to you." Her eyes filled with tears as she said aloud the unthinkable. Willy looked at his feet for a moment, his bottom lip quivering slightly.

"Who's Nilly?"

Clare burst out laughing and hugged him hard. She sometimes called him "Silly Willy" because he seemed to have such natural comic timing. After that, Silly, Willy and Nilly became their private mischievous trio.

June 2000

Memories of those first days, twenty years earlier, resonated with Clare's current state. At least this time they had a house. She and Stefan were both professors now, living their dream of academic careers. Their children were grown and the gift of this year together in their beloved Marburg was extraordinary. And yet…

"Maybe I should go feed the ducks," she said aloud to no one.

In the weeks before leaving home, after Clare had finally decided that she would go to Germany with Stefan, she had a recurring nightmare. She was wandering through a house, trying to find some clue about where she was and whose house it was. The echo of her footsteps off the walls of the empty rooms was a sad percussion to the soundtrack of her grief. She couldn't find a way out.

Hannah's house was the complete opposite. Clare knew nothing about the woman, but the rooms spoke of a life well lived and a house well loved. There were signs of inner exploration as well as mindful attention to the world outside. And pictures of joyful travel experiences. The nightmare house began to fade. Remembering their promise to take care of the plants, Clare soon discovered how many there were, both inside and out.

"Excuse me, Hannah, I'm just going to water the plants," she said as she entered Hannah's bedroom. The woman's presence was everywhere in the house, but the bedroom seemed especially intimate. It felt good to have an important task to establish their legitimacy as house guests, and to gain the confidence of the house, as though she were holding out her hand to an unfamiliar dog.

Clare spent the afternoon organizing the supplies that Stefan had bought, fitting them into the already full cupboards. It was great to have a kitchen stocked by someone who clearly loved to cook.

"You can tell so much about a person by their kitchen," she said to Stefan as they unpacked the bags. He paused and searched her eyes for a moment, feeling a momentary rush of hope from the energy in her voice.

"Look, I bought a French press!" Stefan had conquered the first big obstacle in their new adventure.

That evening they managed to stay awake a little later, though the sun still hadn't set. Clare awoke in the middle of the night, and she stayed in bed, hoping her exhaustion would bring more sleep. She did a mental toast to their good fortune at having such a comfortable house, something she certainly didn't take for granted. For the rest of the night, she floated between sleep and wakefulness, memories and reflections.

After coffee and breakfast the next morning, Stefan had to check in at the archive where he would be doing his research. Clare walked through the living room on her way upstairs and noticed a framed photo on a shelf. She picked it up and was met by the gaze of a woman resting her chin in both hands, and head tilted to the side in a gesture of affectionate familiarity. There were strands of gray in the woman's dark auburn hair, but an inner glow lit her face with youthful beauty. *Is that you, Hannah?*

Clare put the photo back on the shelf and walked away. Then she went back and looked again. The smile had seemed to follow her and she felt a connection. She picked up the photo and took it upstairs with her.

"I hope you don't mind, Hannah," she whispered, placing the photo on a desk in their bedroom.

Clare began unpacking suitcases, gently fitting their belongings into Hannah's world. She came across the writing journal that her father had given her the year before. It was a beautifully bound book of blank pages waiting to be filled. The cover was a deep brown Moroccan leather, with tiny gold foliage patterns around the edges, Renaissance style. It had a flap that folded over to protect the book when closed.

"A home for your writing," her dad had said. It was such a special gift. Even though she wrote mostly on her laptop, her creative projects always began with writing by hand in pencil. He had always encouraged her writing. That special bond between them had begun when Clare was a young teenager. She had discovered some of her father's writing in a library and it had impacted her deeply. She had always sensed something powerful in him, beyond his importance to her as a father. Clare was drawn to him, as were so many others, for his depth of soul and continual spiritual and intellectual seeking that opened hearts and minds. He was a wise and compassionate listener with the sensitivity of a poet.

Clare ran her fingers over the smooth surface of the cover and flipped through the blank pages. She hadn't yet been able to bring herself to mar their perfect whiteness with her scribblings. She had treasured the gift, even before her father's death, and now...now it felt like the closest connection she had with him, so it was the first thing she packed when she decided she would go to Germany with Stefan. After hugging the book for a moment, she placed it on the writing desk in the corner of their bedroom. The wood had been polished by many years of care and use. She didn't know if she would ever write in her journal, but it was the perfect spot to honor and admire it.

August 1980

"Can we go see the 'partment?" Willy asked after their silliness settled.

"I need to buy a few things first. Then let's find some lunch and after that we'll see if we can manage it. Remember, we can't move in there for a couple more days."

They walked around in town for a while, sightseeing as Clare checked out a few shops.

"Mommy, why do some people have white sticks?"

"White sticks?" She thought for a moment.

"Like that man over there," Willy said, pointing.

"It's not polite to point," Clare said, lowering his arm. "Oh, he is blind. That means he can't see."

"Why doesn't he open his eyes?" Clare was shocked that Willy hadn't yet learned about blindness. Kids could be so smart, but you could never be sure about their own blind spots. There was so much for them to learn.

"His stick helps him see."

"Is it magic?" That would have been the easiest explanation for him to understand. Willy understood magic.

"His eyes just don't work, so he needs a cane to help him feel where he is going. It's a different kind of seeing in a way. He has probably practiced that route many times, so he remembers each part of it."

"Are there lots of people like that? Blind, I mean."

"Well, yes, and especially in this town. There is a school here just for blind people. They use a white cane so other people will know they are blind."

"So they can help them?"

"Sometimes, but also so they are more careful not to get in their way or startle them."

"Maybe we could use those white sticks so people would always be nice to us."

* * *

"Those people look like Americans," Willy announced as they waited at a bus stop.

"Which people?" Clare asked without looking up from the map she was still studying.

"Over there," he answered in a loud whisper. "I think they're American."

"Why do you think that?"

"I don't know."

Clare looked up and had to agree with him, though she was not sure why. She approached them and said *"Entschuldigung*…do you speak English?" They were a young couple, maybe about her age, and Willy had been right. They were from California.

"Will this bus take us to the university housing?"

"Yes, indeed. The *Gästehaus*. That's where we live. We can show you around." They struck up an easy conversation. Clare was elated to be on the right route and to have met folks who would be their neighbors for a while.

June 2000

The next morning Clare decided to go for a walk and explore a little. She wandered along the narrow sidewalks that were bordered by the old *Fachwerk* style buildings; half-timbered dark wood sections framing white plaster. Window boxes of red geraniums added a dramatic splash of color. The warm sun and blue sky lightened her step and the haze of jet lag seemed to be lifting.

She followed the street as it curved and turned downhill, being careful to note landmarks so she could find her way back. She had never been great at orienting herself spatially and this part of town was new to her. A sign that read *Bäckerei* caught her attention. It brought back memories of her favorite dark breads and suddenly she had a mission. As Clare entered the bakery, a symphony of aromas surrounded her, and she was tempted to buy loaves of every sort. But one of the wonderful things about German bakeries was that you could buy a half loaf of anything, and it was freshly baked that day.

"Ich hätte gerne ein halbes Schwarzbrot und halbes Bauernbrot."

"Not bad, Clare!" she said to herself as she walked out with two half loaves of her favorite breads: a "black bread" and a "farmer's bread." She was surprised at the German that had come out of her mouth so easily. *Tomorrow there will be new fresh choices and I can come every day. I'm going to gain a lot of weight this year!*

She found her way home and took out her laptop to send some emails. Then she remembered. There was no internet connection at *Das Haus*. That afternoon Stefan drove her to an internet cafe in town.

"I need to write to the kids, let them know we are settling in here."

Stefan nodded as he drove.

* * *

Hey Will,

We're settling in. The house is great! It's amazing to be back in Marburg. How is work? How are you and Yolanda doing? Give her my love.

I went out walking today and bought some fresh bread. Remember Schwarzbrot? Yum! I keep seeing little Willy on the sidewalks. More later.

Miss you.

Love,
Nilly :-)

Dear Anja,

I hope you are enjoying being back at camp. Being a counselor is like being a mom, teacher, therapist, cheerleader, and older sister all in one. Take care of yourself.

The house is great and we're beginning to get over the jet lag. Marburg is beautiful and every baby I see reminds me of you. I can't wait until you come for Christmas. You'll finally get to see your birthplace!

Love you so much,
Mom

August 1980

"This is a cool bus. Look, Mommy, it's like two buses stuck together, with a 'cordian in the middle!"

"It looks like fun, doesn't it?"

They got on the "long bus," as they would call them. They sat in the front, across from Nick and Sharon, their new American friends. Clare was often wary of Americans abroad, finding that she sometimes had less in common with them than most "foreigners", who weren't, of course, foreigners in their own country. And when *she* was a foreigner, it was important to her to avoid the Ugly American syndrome. Her goal was to be admitted to the inner circle of the culture by embracing the language and habits of her new home. Fortunately, this couple was on the same page, and she had to admit it was comforting to share first impressions and challenges.

The bus took them very near to the housing campus. Nick and Sharon's apartment was cozy and pleasant. Clare felt an immediate connection to Sharon, whose voice had an inviting playful tone that sounded like she was just about to tell you a joke. Her long dark hair reached down below her waist in a thick braid. Willy noticed with glee the small playground in the central area.

"There's a community potluck tonight for the scientists with Humboldt fellowships. Why don't you stay and join us?" Nick suggested. "You could meet some other folks who live here."

"But we don't have anything to bring—and I'm not a scientist."

"Oh, don't worry about that; I'm sure you will be welcome and there will be plenty of food," Sharon added.

Wow, instant community. Clare wanted to jump up and down like Willy did when he was excited. "That would be nice, thank you so much."

They went outside and chatted, sharing brief bios of introduction while Willy played on the swings and jungle gym.

There was an uncomfortable silence when they walked into the apartment where the party was supposed to be. They didn't want to arrive too early but were late by German standards and the "potluck" turned out to be a rather formal sit-down dinner of only eight other adults. It was awkward as Nick tried to finesse the miscalculation. Sharon shrugged her shoulders and made a funny face but Clare was mortified. *This was a bad idea, not supposed to be here...typical American presumption...*She was working on how to make a graceful exit, when she noticed that Willy had already run off with a couple of kids about his age. Everyone relaxed as they saw the kids' easy welcome, and they settled into friendly conversation.

"This was lovely, and it was so nice to meet you." Clare said gratefully as she stood to take her leave. "We should go now."

"But the kids are having a great time. Stay a bit longer," someone responded. The evening had flown by, and it was getting dark.

"We really need to leave now to catch the last bus to our hotel." She was already feeling anxious about finding their way back in the dark.

"I can drive you there later," Thomas offered.

By the time the party wound down, the kids were all asleep on a big bed in the back, each in their own unique sprawl. It looked as though a spell had caught them in mid-flight as they fell onto the bed.

It was after ten when they arrived at the hotel and the door was locked. Clare got out the key she had been given. Willy had been loaded into the car still asleep, and he was limp as a rag doll when Thomas, her kind chauffeur, lifted him out of the back seat.

"Let me carry him up to your room so you don't have to wake him up," he offered.

"That's very kind of you." Clare thanked him gratefully. She was exhausted.

She had just gotten Willy settled into bed when there was a loud pounding on the door. She opened it to the angry face of the hotel proprietor. He was huffing and sputtering as he shouted at her in a German that she could barely follow.

"*...unverschämt...skandalös... ein fremder Mann... unanständig...*"

Clare caught a few of the words—enough to gather that he had completely misread her situation and was outraged.

"*Aber...*But please, sir, let me explain."

As she told the proprietor what had happened and he finally realized there was no strange man hiding in the room, Clare began to understand the assumptions he had made. His hotel was a decent, upstanding place and he would not tolerate any shameful activity. It had all seemed to confirm his suspicions that she was a loose woman, whose "husband" was just a convenient fiction. Willy slept on, unaware of the scandal swirling around him.

Clare was shaken by the proprietor's wrath. Despite her best efforts, she kept walking into difficult situations. It wasn't just her tired German. She felt unfairly judged and the man only saw her as a threat to his hotel's reputation. *People form opinions so quickly through their own myopic lenses,* she mused as she waited for sleep to overtake her. It was almost funny. Miscommunication and misunderstanding; the stuff of comedies.

Her night was restless. She dreamed that she was trying to find her way through a labyrinth of streets with an urgent need to get to some unknown place. At each turn, there was a gate. To pass through the first one, she had to answer questions that she couldn't understand. She took another street and tried again. At the second gate, she thought she understood the questions but her answers were all wrong. "Off with her head!" the Queen of Hearts yelled from a corner of her childhood.

3
Writing in Pencil

June 2000

Clare awoke to a sunny morning and the smell of fresh coffee wafting up the stairs. Stefan was already up. She was a bit disoriented from having slept through the Marburg night, even though her own clock was not yet reset, and she still carried the weight of darkness inside. She squinted at the bright light of morning in German time BC, Before Coffee, as Stefan would say. Although she was gradually moving into her new life during the day, at night the warmth of Hannah's world was invaded by scenes from Clare's past in the chaotic montage of her dreams. Since childhood, her dream life had always been intense, apparently more so for her than for most people she knew. Sometimes she woke up exhausted from them. Everything was fair game for those hasty scripts. Everything except the father she missed so terribly. He was conspicuously absent from her dreams.

"Hey, *Schlafmütze*." Stefan handed her a cup of hot coffee before she even sat down at the small round table in the kitchen. "Sleepyhead," he repeated in English, "how was your night?"

"It sure was busy. Everybody and their cousins were coming and going through my dreams. Everyone except Dad."

"Give it time," Stefan said as he massaged her tight shoulders.

"But it's been almost two months, and I usually dream about things soon after they happen. Why hasn't he visited yet? I miss him so much."

Stefan sat down next to her and looked at her with his steady blue eyes. "Well, maybe he's still moving in. You know, getting settled up there." He pointed towards the ceiling, the dimples in his cheeks betraying his almost smile. Stefan could always make her smile.

Dreams were fascinating to Clare, even the "bad" ones. She had done research on sleep and dreaming in her undergraduate days, finding an abundance of intriguing information. She had become obsessed with learning more about the other half of her life.

She knew a lot of folks who claimed that they didn't dream or at least didn't remember anything. For Clare, that would be like walking out of a large-screen theater with surround sound after a dramatic in-your-face thriller and not remembering anything you had seen. Impossible to imagine. She knew that scientific studies maintained that everyone dreams, that it is essential to neurological and emotional health. And of course, there was a long history of religious and psychoanalytic interpretations. For Clare, there were also many other dimensions: artistic, literary, philosophical, and metaphysical. Even the chaotic ones shed some light on the wild adventures of her brain while it was unsupervised at night.

"Are dreams real?" She asked her father once when she was a young child.

"What do *you* think?" he responded, wearing his listening face.

"I think they are real because I can see them."

"Hmmm..." He leaned back, puffing on his pipe.

"And I remember them. Like movies."

"Yes, that makes sense."

"Daddy, why do we dream?"

"That's a great question, my little dreamer."

In Clare's literature classes, discussions would often turn to fiction - its many layers and boundaries - while they tried to nail down a good definition of what it was and wasn't. Clare loved to follow with the question from her childhood. "Are dreams real?" After what always turned out to be a fruitful discussion, she would then ask her students. "What about fiction? Is it real?"

* * *

After a typical German breakfast of hard-boiled eggs and the rich dark bread she had bought with the cheesy, yoghurt-like *Quark* spread on it, Clare was ready for the day. She went upstairs to get dressed and nodded to the empty journal on the writing desk. A chorus of birds outside proclaimed that it was a beautiful June morning. There was a door from the bedroom that led to a small balcony covered in feathery vines with cascading blue-purple flowers.

Wisteria! Oh my god, how did I not notice that before?

28

Those vines were a familiar backdrop for many childhood memories. She picked up the journal and went out to sit on a bench in the dappled shadows of the balcony. It was a private retreat, hidden from both inside and outside the house. The birds fluttered around, coming and going with their cheerful commentary.

"Oh, Hannah, this is perfect." It felt like a place where she could find respite from the flood of memories in her head. She took a deep breath and patted the journal on her lap as she let out a long slow sigh.

"Clare? I'm heading out for a while," Stefan yelled up the stairs. "Hope your day goes well."

"Thanks, you, too. See you later."

She didn't know how long she had been sitting there, but the day was in motion, and she was still in her pajamas. She set the journal down on the desk and went to get dressed. On her way back to the stairs she stopped and sat down at the desk, with no particular purpose in mind. She looked up at the photo of the woman smiling at her. Waves of thick auburn hair fell gently over one shoulder and the soft light in her eyes suggested love for the object of her gaze. Clare felt it. It must be Hannah.

A sudden urge to write something made her search the small drawers of the desk for a pencil. It had to be in pencil. She remembered conversations with her father about the freedom of writing in pencil. It was the residue of a process, one that didn't make any claims to permanence.

"Thank you, Hannah," she said when she found one. She opened the journal and ran her hand over the first page, taking a deep breath. At the top, she wrote in large letters:

Marburger Tagebuch

This would be her Marburg journal. She watched her hand write a few lines that came to her from long ago.

> *He who binds to himself a joy*
> *does the winged life destroy.*
> *But he who kisses the joy as it flies*
> *lives in eternity's sunrise.*

Poetry by William Blake that her father had once shared with her. The verses had occasionally popped up in her past as a kind of mantra, but they had been buried for a long time.

The spell had been broken and the page was no longer virgin. *Jetzt geht's los*...Here goes. She began to write.

June 8
Gestern habe ich ein frisches Brot von der Bäckerei gekauft...

She wrote about the fresh bread from the bakery and her first venture out of the house.

Der Morgen war so frisch....The morning was as fresh as
the bread, and everything glowed in the sunlight. After a
few days in your house, Hannah, I feel as though I already
know you. It's like living in a novel.

The writing flowed from her hand as if the journal itself were controlling the pencil. She heard the clock ticking downstairs and stopped to catch her breath. She looked at the page half filled with her own handwriting and realized she had been writing in German. It was as though that part of her brain had been folded, compressed, and then stuffed away into a tiny compartment. When she opened that compartment years later, it had all sprung back to life, a bit wrinkled but usable. And each of those packed away words was tied to many memories.

Das Haus spricht viel von dir....The house says so much about
you. I could feel it right away. Please forgive me for using the
familiar form with you, Hannah, when I haven't even met you.
Aber du..., but you are here everywhere. "Du, du..." What a
tender word.

It seemed she was writing to Hannah. But, no, not really; she never imagined Hannah reading her journal. It was the house that she addressed and the narrative it contained of its owner's life. And the gift that she, Clare, had received of inhabiting that life for a while.

She looked up. The woman in the photo was still smiling.

August 1980

Willy came running in from the *Spielplatz,* the playground that was the center of friendship among the kids. Clare was impressed with how quickly children could establish a bond if the adults left them alone. There was a kind of parallel play that soon created a natural space for friendship. Willy was breathless from the play and the urgency of his mission.

"Can I go to the *Bäckerei?*"

"I'm a bit busy right now. How about we go after lunch?"

"I can go by myself. I know how, you know." He fished in his pocket for some coins to show her the handful of German words that he now owned. Each five Pfennig coin represented a new German word that Willy had mastered and entered in his notebook. Clare had started the game and Willy now felt rich with both the words and the coins.

"Do you promise to go straight there and come back right away?" Clare asked taking hold of Willy's face with both hands to get him to look her in the eyes.

"I promise. I'm just gonna buy one chocolate cream."

"Okay," she said, hoping she wouldn't regret it. Willy was easily led astray by his curiosity.

It had been a week since they moved into their new apartment, and it began to feel like a life. Willy was the first to notice the bakery near their bus stop and he pulled Clare by the hand to check it out. She had decided to make it a teachable moment and let him ask for what he wanted and pay for it with his own Pfennig. He was shy at first, but with one hand full of coins, he pointed with the other to a pastry behind the glass and said, *"Das bitte."* "That please." Then he held his hand high above his head to the height of the countertop. The woman behind the counter reached out and chose some coins from his palm.

"She gave me some back!" he exclaimed.

"Wow, you got your pastry *and* some change, sounds like a deal to me."

As they walked to their apartment, just a short block away, Willy was silent except for smacking his lips and sucking the frosting off his fingers. The cost of the pastry was minimal and the look on Willy's face was priceless. Clare wasn't sure which was more satisfying to him; the pastry or the act of buying it. After a few times with her supervising, it was time to let him go by himself.

Solo trips to the Bäckerei became a foundation for building Willy's confidence and vocabulary. The notebook was filling faster now as each new word became clearly grounded as the name of a thing or an activity. *Spielplatz, Freunde…*some words quickly leapt out of the notebook to live and breathe on their own. The language of play fluctuated, depending on who was there.

The Spielplatz became the birthplace of a new pidgin of languages. The families in the university housing came from many different countries: Some kids knew English, but a simple form of German often became the *lingua franca*. Clare was known to Willy's friends as *"Frau Willy."* Mrs. Willy seemed like an appropriate name since Willy was her constant companion.

It was good that they had come to Marburg when they did. The school would start soon for Willy, and it helped that they had a couple of weeks to settle in first.

"Willy! Time to come in," she shouted. "WIL-ly!!"

He pretended not to hear her.

Clare remembered with a smile the day that Willy's kindergarten class had had hearing tests. When she picked him up after school, the teacher said to her with mock gravity, "Of course, there *is* some hearing loss." When Clare looked alarmed the teacher laughed and added, "But only for parental voices. All kids have it."

"You need to come when I call you," Clare said, trying to control the annoyance in her voice as she pulled him by the arm.

"But I wasn't finished yet."

"Finished with what?"

"With spielen."

"How do you know when you are finished?"

"When all the kids go inside."

As they were eating lunch, Willy looked up and said in his best six-year-old parental voice imitation.

"Mommy, could you please call me Willy?"

"Isn't that what I always call you?"

"No, I mean, say it like 'Villy', so it will sound German. The kids call me that."

"Ja wohl, Herr Villy, Clare answered with a salute. She was impressed.

* * *

"Willy, time to get dressed. We need to go to town and buy some things for school. Remember, it will start soon. Tomorrow we can go visit and see what it's like."

"Can I buy some more Legos, too?"

"More Legos? But you already have so many!"

When they were packing for the year, Clare had told him that he could fill his daypack with whatever toys or books he wanted to take with him.

"But that's all, you hear? Just what can fit in your pack."

She imagined him sitting and sorting for days, trying to make difficult choices. But no, it was a clear and instant decision. He had filled his pack with Legos and a few small Star Wars figures.

"But Mommy, these are all plain Legos."

"Plain? What do you mean?"

"I need some fancy ones to make things. You know, more complicated stuff."

They ended up buying him a *Schulrucksack*, a special school backpack, and all the writing tools and notebooks that the school had prescribed. And they added one small but more sophisticated Lego set.

"How about a hamburger for lunch?" Clare asked as they passed an outdoor place that advertised "McMarburgers."

"Yeah, I already miss hambagers."

They sat down at a wooden picnic table to unwrap their lunch. The burgers were covered in an unfamiliar sweet and sour sauce and as soon as they unwrapped them, wasps began to zoom in for their own lunch. They gave up and rewrapped the burgers to take home with them.

"These don't even taste like real hambagers," Willy said after taking a bite when they got home. They had already picked a few dead wasps, *Wespe,* off before eating. After that they referred to them as *Wespeburgers.*

* * *

"We need to walk faster, Willy. We don't want to be late for the school orientation." She could tell he was nervous and was not sure he wanted to take on the next challenge.

"I don't know how to be in first grade," Willy said, looking down at his feet as they walked.

"You don't need to know before you get there. They will teach you."

"Will it be in German?"

"Yes, it will." Clare felt the weight of that even as she said it. It was a lot to expect of a young child.

"But I won't understand. They'll 'spect me to know all the words." He had brought his notebook along and was pressing it hard to his side as he walked.

"No, sweetie, they will understand. It will take some time. You just need to be there and let it soak in."

As they waited outside the school, Clare noticed another mother having what she guessed was a similar conversation with her own daughter. Clare recognized them from the Gästehaus, but they hadn't met yet. Willy waved shyly to the girl with long blond hair and blue eyes. She smiled at him.

"She doesn't speak English," Willy told Clare. They had met at the Spielplatz, but couldn't really talk to each other beyond the few German words they shared.

At that moment, the mother approached them, saying "*Guten Tag.*" They introduced themselves and recognized their common bond.

"My name is Julia," the mother said, switching to English when they realized that her English was better than either of their German. "And this is Zofia. We call her Zosia."

To Clare, it sounded like *Zasha*.

"We are from Poland. My husband, Aleksander, is a physicist and is working at the university lab." Clare could see the resemblance of mother and daughter: high cheekbones, blue eyes, straight blond hair—though Julia's was short, curving in just under her jawbone.

Willy and Zosia would both be in first grade, learning together as they built a friendship in German; one word and one Lego at a time.

June 2000

The days began to mold themselves around a comforting routine as Clare's inner gyroscope resettled in German time: morning appreciation of coffee and a new day, followed by quiet time on the balcony to, as a friend liked to say, "just be being." Then a walk in the neighborhood with a stop at the Bäckerei. Clare loved to walk in the door and breathe the delicious smells of so many different breads. It was even better than coffee to awaken her senses. She could picture the dance of tiny yeast cells getting drunk on the starch and sugar in the dough and creating an explosion of carbon dioxide— a magical process of fermentation that gave life to the bread and raised her own spirits. And they looked so attractive, those handcrafted loaves, to make you want to buy more than you could eat. She eventually learned to restrain herself and leave with just a half loaf for the day.

When she got back to Das Haus, Clare couldn't resist having a slice of fresh bread and a quiet moment in the kitchen. The bread was still warm as was the gentle touch of the morning sun through the window. She studied again a large poster on the wall for *Projecto Água Limpa*, a scene of clean air and mountains that reminded her of many summers hiking in Colorado. A clean water project, that sounded good. Must be Brazil, she thought, judging from the language and the scene. She wondered if Hannah had traveled there.

34

She took a cup of tea upstairs to sit at the writing desk. It was a ritual that sometimes produced a stream of writing, but other times she just sat and waited. The journal was patient and the book she was supposed to be writing was too big to take on yet.

June 11

This morning I noticed the crystal hanging in the kitchen window. The sun shone through it as it turned gently, leaving tiny rainbows dancing on the floor, on the wall, and on the 'Água Limpa' of the poster. When time pauses for these small moments, I feel the simple joy of being alive. But it's complicated, Hannah. Maybe I should say it's crowded. I am still filled with a great emptiness. How can emptiness hurt so much? It seems there is no quiet corner where joy can settle. Maybe joy is always fleeting. The winged life, I suppose.

June 12

I feel like I'm losing my father more each day, Hannah, as he slips farther away into the past. Why can't I even dream about him? After he died, I filled the void with my busy life. Now, I am alone in your wonderful house full of photos, memories, family, friends, herbs, and magical little figures that must have their own stories. And books, so many beautiful books. It's clear that you love trees as I do. It is hard to feel lonely here, and yet, I do. I have dared to open the door to the basement and the absence that was hiding there sometimes fills the whole house.

* * *

Stefan left for the archive and Clare took a moment to check the garden. It had rained lightly in the night and the flowers looked bright and fresh. She tended them lovingly, as she did the indoor plants. They were all children of the house left under her care.

June 14

Die Blumen sahen heute morgen hell und fröhlich aus…

Clare reported to the landlady of her journal about the garden. The cheerful brightness of the flowers quieted the sharp pain in her chest that greeted her each morning.

> *They are so farbenfreudig! That is my new favorite word: farbenfreudig. It just means colorful, But it is an example of the kind of word building that I love about German. Farben =colors + freudig=joyful. The poetic sensibility of a child with the efficiency of a language that doesn't want to borrow from Latin. It can get crazy though, like, for instance: "Ausländereinwohnungbestätigungsform"—foreign-resident-confirmation-form.*

Clare chuckled as she remembered how she had practiced saying that word many times outside the government office where she had gone to ask for the form twenty years earlier. She had taken a deep breath, squared her shoulders and released the mouthful all in one breath. There had been no applause, no notice of her great achievement, but they did hand her the paper that allowed them to stay in Germany legally. She hadn't thought of that moment for years.

* * *

Clare went out for her morning walk, greeting the memories that she passed along the way. But instead of curving down the hill to the bakery, she kept walking. A small boy danced along the sidewalk, pulling at his mother's hand as she tried to keep him from straying too far.

"Let's do Willy and Nilly," she heard from the past. Clare lifted her arms and did a little dance step. She smiled as she walked, missing her little guy. Where had he gone? Will was now a wonderful young man, tall and strong, with the gentle smile and grace of his father. She wouldn't trade him for anything. Yet here in Germany, she sometimes felt the loss of her little companion. *Ich vermisse dich, mein süßer kleiner Junge,* she thought. "I miss you, my sweet little boy. Villy," she said aloud, with the German pronunciation he had asked her to use long ago.

Clare soon found herself in the streets of the Oberstadt, literally the "upper-city," the old part that wound up the hill towards the 9th-12th century castle. She loved the way Marburg was a fairytale town with an archeological inversion: The oldest part was at the top. The half-timbered houses got older as she climbed. She kept walking, thinking of the Brothers Grimm, who had lived there for some years in the early 19th century, studying and collecting fairy tales. Graduates of Phillips University in Marburg, they became, in a sense, the founding fathers of folklore studies.

The sound of a harmonica pulled Clare back through many happy scenes of her life, leaving her with the sweet ache of nostalgia. She looked around for the source of the memories and saw her father sitting on a bench, his hands cupped around a harmonica and a far-off look in his eyes as he played. Clare blinked. Of course, it was not her father. The man didn't even look like him, apart from the white hair. But the gentle hands, the tilt of the head and that penetrating sound...

Clare felt a balloon expand inside her and thought she might explode. She looked around frantically. "I have to get home," she said aloud with urgency. She wanted to run but was afraid of losing control if she gave in to her panic. An overfilled emotional bladder that threatened to let loose any minute. With each brisk step, it already leaked out her eyes and streamed down her cheeks like rain running down a windowpane. Her desperate determination increased. She needed to get back to *Das Haus*.

Her hand was shaking as she put the key in the lock of the bright blue door to *Das Haus*. It all burst just inside the door as she fell to the floor clutching her chest. The deep sobs that came out of her now-unfamiliar body rose and fell in waves that left her helpless. She crawled toward the kitchen, hoping to make a cup of calming tea, but was overtaken by another wave that was so strong she thought she might vomit. The front door opened.

"Clare?" She felt arms around her and Stefan's voice saying, "I'm here, it's alright. Let it out, I've got you." He sat her on a chair and gave her a paper bag to breathe into. "In...out...in...out," he said, breathing with her. "Take it slow. Just breathe."

The house was respectfully silent, except for the comforting sound of the ticking clock that hadn't missed a beat during her whole drama. She drank the warm *Kamilentee* that Stefan gave her after her breathing became more regular.

"How do you feel?"

"A...bit...better." she said between slight aftershocks in her chest. "I feel so...so...empty. But better, I think."

August 1980

"I don't want to go to school, Mommy. It's too hard."

"I know, sweetie. I know it's hard, but it will get better, I promise. It just takes time."

"But I don't understand anything, and I can't talk to anybody. I don't have enough words." He threw his notebook on the floor in frustration. Clare picked it up and placed it gently on the table, patting down the rumpled pages.

"It's okay to be frustrated," she said, remembering when Willy had first learned the word as a two-year-old. He had used it often after that with his own endearing pronunciation. It was not only a good way to explain feelings he didn't know how to articulate; he learned that it was also useful to diffuse any tension he sensed in Clare.

"Are you *fwustwated*, Mommy?" would immediately take the air out of her anger, impatience, or exasperation.

Clare wiped the tears from his cheeks and kissed the top of his head. Even at six, there were still sometimes traces of that intoxicating smell that babies' heads had, that would give an extra dose of oxytocin to even the most exhausted new mothers. Clare felt like one of those new mothers. She wasn't sleeping well, and Willy was cranky and obstinate.

* * *

One night Clare woke up with a sinus headache. She rummaged around in the bathroom and then through her purse looking for some Tylenol. As she tiptoed back to her bed, she noticed that Willy's bed was empty. An alarm went off in her gut. He was usually such a sound sleeper. "Willy?" she whispered, quickly searching the small apartment. "Willy!!" Trying not to panic, she searched the whole place again. Should she go outside? Check the Spielplatz? Ask a neighbor? It was two a.m. She wouldn't even know how to call the police. *Polizei? Okay Clare, stay calm. Think.* She sat down on her bed and then she saw the fingertips of a small hand peeking from under

38

the comforter that hung to the floor over Willy's bed. She jumped down on her knees and lifted it to find him sound asleep underneath.

"Oh Willy." Clare sat back and watched him sleeping there for a few minutes to convince her brain, her whole body, that he was safe and sound. It took a while for the runaway adrenaline to calm down. Eventually, she extracted him gently from his under-the-bed cave and settled him back in his bed. She went to wash her face and cried into the washcloth. Then she took the Tylenol that she still held in her hand and slipped into her own bed. That night and for many after that, she awoke often and listened in the dark for Willy's soft breathing. A couple of times, she even got up to peer down at him, just to be sure.

Clare awoke each morning tired and shaky, recognizing the washed-out feeling of a sinus infection. It had been one of her graduate school companions. It seemed too hard to deal with going to a doctor, so she held frozen juice cans on her forehead and drank lots of herbal teas. She managed to get Willy to school each day, resorting to bribery and anything she could think of to motivate him. *I'm such a terrible mother.* The weather had turned gray and rainy. Some days she would go back to bed when she got home.

What if I can't find a place to live? What if Willy hates school all year?

"You are ruining my life," he had told her one morning that first week. His teacher was kind and she told Clare that Willy cried a little the first few mornings, but things seemed to be getting better and he and Zosia had formed a special bond in their misery.

"Give it time," she told Clare.

"Try again today, Willy, and after school we'll go buy another *Schlumpf.* He had been thrilled to see that they had Smurfs in Germany.

"And go feed die Enten after that."

"Right."

"AND, if you can make it through the whole week, we'll buy another Lego set," she added. *I know, it's bribery.* These were desperate times.

They made it through that week. The ducks were well-fed, and the Smurf family grew.

* * *

Some afternoons Zosia came over to their apartment and she and Willy played with Legos; silently at first and then occasionally Clare heard a *"Guck mal!"* "Look!" *"Mein Lego,"* *"Flugzeug"*, as they built their first sentences.

39

Flugzeug was a perfect Lego word, built from two simple words "flight" + "thing" = "airplane." Then they flew it around with their hands so there was no doubt what it was. *"Dein Lego hier,"* one told the other as they began to work together. The sun finally came out and the Spielplatz buzzed again. Clare went back to being Frau Willy.

June 2000

For the next couple days, Clare spent more time on the balcony to just "be being." She also bought more bread than usual. The third day she woke up feeling rested and stayed in bed for another half hour, enjoying the quiet.

Then she remembered her dream and laughed aloud. She couldn't wait to tell Stefan about it and ran downstairs to find a note on the kitchen table.

> *Left for work. You were sound asleep.*
> *Hope you had a good night.*
> *See you this afternoon. Love, S.*

"Why do Germans start the day so early?" she grumbled. She grabbed a slice of yesterday's bread with Quark on it and the thermos of hot coffee that Stefan had left next to the note. She went upstairs to get dressed but then sat down at the writing desk instead and opened the journal.

> *June 17*
>
> *It's been a strange few days. I haven't felt like writing. Some things are hard to put on paper. A kind of crisis. I saw*

Clare cursed at the eraser that wouldn't erase.

> *I saw a man playing the harmonica and I just lost it. I guess he reminded me of my father, and something grew inside me that I couldn't control. I hadn't really cried much since his death.*
> *The day he died, I had been teaching a class and someone came and said there was an urgent message for me. I was annoyed at being interrupted—it was a great class. They said my father had*

died, and it just wouldn't register. He wasn't young anymore, but he wasn't very old. And there was no warning. I guess I still had the childish notion that he would always be there. He was my rock. I called my mom and went into action in what seemed like someone else's life. I was busy. There wasn't time to cry. I think I cried three months' worth of tears the other day. Pretty intense.

Clare put the pencil down and sat back in the chair, shaking her writing hand. She had written fast, barely keeping up with the stream of images and memories. After a few sips of coffee with the slice of bread, she picked up the pencil again.

I had a great dream last night, Hannah. It was about my father. I have missed him so much. I can't tell you how great it was to see him! We, my mom and my sister and I, were visiting the community in Pennsylvania where I grew up, and we went to eat in the community dining room.

We walked in and there he was, sitting at a table in animated conversation with others. We were stunned. He was supposed to be dead! How could he be there enjoying himself like nothing had happened? It was so real. I can still see him leaning forward, gesturing with his hands. After a while, he looked up and saw our joy and confusion and said, "What? I may be dead, but I'm not deceased." And he went back to his conversation. He always loved deep conversations.

August 1980

"*Es ist so kompliziert, die Luft ist gut, das Geld...*It's so complicated, the air is good, the money, the bus comes, the letters, you have to turn it on and off..." The woman kept talking to Clare, seeming to change topics in mid-sentence at lightning speed. Clare tried hard to follow, nodding occasionally even though she didn't have a clue what they were talking about.

I understand the words but nothing she is saying makes any sense. Clare felt her head spin as she struggled to keep up. Sometimes, when she missed just one important clue, a whole conversation could derail rather quickly. But this was different. Word salad.

Clare remembered when she had interpreted once for a Spanish speaker in a court hearing. It was a young man from El Salvador, whose family had him admitted to a psychiatric hospital. He kept escaping, so there was a hearing to study the case. Clare prided herself on being a good interpreter and she had worked hard to translate exactly what he was saying. But after a while she stopped. "I'm sorry, Your Honor, it's hard to remember everything because it is so incoherent."

"Word salad?" the judge had asked, and she nodded sadly.

Clare realized she was lost in her own thoughts and had disconnected from the woman's fluid babble. They were seated on a bench waiting for the bus to arrive. The bus stop had become part of a familiar routine and at least she didn't have to wonder if it was the right one for her destination. She was learning to get a few things done while Willy was at school.

When she refocused, Clare noticed that her bench neighbor was gesturing wildly with her arms as she talked. Dressed in a black suit with a derby hat, the air of formality seemed out of place with the chaotic energy of her body. The woman had turned toward an old man on her other side without interrupting her incoherent stream.

The old man sat with his left hand on his knee and his right hand resting on a cane. His gaze was fixed straight ahead, his body seemingly frozen in place. He didn't acknowledge the presence of the woman next to him.

Is he deaf? Am I crazy? It was a scene from an absurdist play, and she was an innocent member of the audience who had been thrown on stage in the middle of it.

The bus pulled up and the strange woman jumped to her feet and began shaking her fist, yelling at the driver as the doors opened. The driver tried to reason with her quietly. Clare glanced at the man to her right, still carved in stone. Without changing his expression, he turned slowly towards her and tapped his index finger at his temple. Then he returned to his statue mode. She heard the woman's voice rise to an operatic pitch and then return to her scolding tone as she walked away.

Clare boarded the bus and looked out the window. The old man hadn't moved from the bench and sat stone still.

"What was that?" she said with a half laugh to the man seated next to her on the bus.

42

"Oh, don't worry about her. She's a little crazy but harmless. Everyone knows her. They call her *"Die Nachtigall von Marburg."*

"Nachtigall…The Nightingale?"

"The way she sings sometimes. Must be Tourette's or something like that."

"Oh. Poor woman. Does she live on her own?"

"I don't know, but I never see anyone with her. She always wears that black suit. People recognize her and kind of watch out for her, I guess."

"Or just ignore her."

"Yes, I suppose so. She makes some people uncomfortable."

"I can understand why. It makes you feel crazy yourself to listen to her."

"I know what you mean!" The man laughed.

"I wonder if the world seems crazy to her?"

The man shrugged his shoulders and smiled. They rode in silence as the bus climbed the hill towards her new temporary home.

June 2000

Clare set off towards town and the internet café. It was time to catch up on emails again and she felt like walking.

The air was pleasant in the early morning with the bloom of late spring meeting the lush green of early summer. She let her mind open to the breeze and the scents and sounds around her.

As she approached the block where the big Ahrens department store was, Clare noticed some new construction on a storefront that blocked the sidewalk. Lumber and other materials were scattered on the ground, looking like they had been hastily dropped for a morning break.

A young man just ahead of her was tapping his way along with a white cane. Clare wasn't sure what to do. Blind people in Marburg prided themselves on their independence and self-reliance. She didn't want to offend him, but this was not part of the normal route and the construction had been left unattended.

She ran up alongside him saying, "Excuse me, I wonder if you could help me." She took his arm and stopped to invent a question. "I'm new here. Do you know where to get good pizza?"

He laughed and said, "Well, yes, there's a pizza place in the next block. It sounds urgent."

"Actually, I was worried that you would run into the construction mess up ahead," she confessed. "I didn't know if you knew it was there."

"That's very kind of you. I didn't know about it, so I probably would have made a fool of myself running into it. Usually, they put up a warning."

"I think it's new and it looks dangerous," she said, embarrassed by her clumsy improvisation, "but I didn't want to assume that you needed rescuing." He bowed slightly and let her steer him around the construction and back onto the sidewalk.

"Now you are in front of Ahrens, and it looks like smooth sailing from here."

"Thanks. I've got it now." He turned towards her and smiled. "Oh—and enjoy the pizza."

August 1980

Clare awoke in the night to the sound of water. She had been dreaming about camping in the mountains next to a rushing stream and it took her a moment to realize where she was. It was a soothing sound and she let it wash over her. A steady rain beat against the windows and the small balcony.

Suddenly the sky ripped open with a blinding flash and a clash of giant cymbals in the same instant, telling her that it was right overhead. The air crackled with the electrical charge.

"Mommy, I'm scared." Willy's pajama-clad figure was at her bedside only seconds later.

"It's okay, sweetie," she said, pulling back the covers to invite him in with her. They snuggled down under the blankets as another strike hit.

"The sky is crashing!" Willy cried, pulling the blankets over his head, and trying to tuck his body even closer to hers. "Can it fall down?"

"No. I know it sounds like it sometimes. At least we're not in a tent. Do you remember last summer when we were backpacking in Colorado?"

"Yeah, when the tent almost fell down? That was scary!"

"It was quite a storm, wasn't it?" Clare admitted to herself that she had been afraid then, too. It was a family trip. The three of them were camped at

12,000 feet next to a lake and they felt very vulnerable as the lightning and thunder crashed all around them.

"Remember when we got up to pee later, after the storm had blown over?" Clare shivered with the memory. The cold had been a shock on her bare feet.

"The moon was so bright like daytime, but it looked funny, like a dream." Willy snuggled in closer.

"The water from the storm had frozen and coated everything with ice that glowed in the moonlight."

"Our dishrag was frozen in the morning and the grass sparkled," he said, giggling with delight.

"It was magical, wasn't it? You have a good memory, Mr. Willy." She hugged him tighter as the storm calmed and they drifted off to sleep.

June 2000

"Hey, how about going out for pizza tonight? Like we used to. I hear there's good pizza on *Universitätstraße*." Clare smiled to herself as she remembered her conversation with the young man. Somehow it seemed like going out for pizza now would redeem her awkward improvisation with him.

"Mmm. I wonder if that Turkish pizza place is still around. You know, the one with sauerkraut and bacon pizza. Or the one with tuna fish." Those were still Stefan's favorites.

"Yuk, that sounds awful to me. It *was* awful if I remember correctly," Clare retorted, going along with their usual repartee about pizza.

"What are you talking about? It was great. Everything to do with food sounded awful to you in those days. Have you forgotten?"

"Oh yeah, how could I forget? Potato chips and pickles were always good though."

"It's a wonder how babies can survive all that."

"And mothers, too, for that matter. So, pizza tonight?"

"Sure, why not?"

August 1980

"Why do we have to go shopping today if the stores are closed?" Willy complained, dragging his feet. "How about we just go down to the river and feed the ducks?"

"We can do that after I find the Phillips Apotheke. It's the only pharmacy open today, and I really need to get a few things."

"What kind of things?"

"Oh, just some more Tylenol and some Mommy things."

Clare had thought it would be easy. They had taken the bus to Wilhelmsplatz where there was a pharmacy right next to the bus stop. She had forgotten about stores being closed on Sunday. There was a note on the door about which pharmacy would be open for emergencies. Phillips Apotheke was in the Oberstadt, so they would have to climb.

"Let's see if we can find some secret stairs," she challenged Willy to try to make it fun.

"Secret stairs? Whaddya mean?"

"Well, there are some stairs hidden between buildings, so people can sneak up on the castle." She was making it up as she went along, but she did know where the nearest staircase was.

Willy took the bait and checked between all the buildings they passed.

"I found them!! Look, right here and nobody else is around so we can keep it secret."

"Good job! That's a lot of steps. Do you think we can count how many there are?"

They started up the narrow stone steps, counting first in German. *"Eins, zwei, drei...sechs und zwanzig, sieben und zwanzig..."* Willy soon ran out of numbers, so they switched to English. "...forty-eight, forty-nine...

"Can we stop counting now? My head is tired."

Their legs were also tired by the time they got to the Oberstadt. As they stepped out onto the cobblestone street, they heard music and headed towards it. A young man was playing a violin with a young woman next to him on a flute. First, they played the tune in unison and then staggered as a round. A few folks had stopped to listen.

Clare recognized the tune and wanted to sing. It was a simple folk song that she had learned in her high school German class. She looked around and met the eyes of an older woman. They started to sing together.

"Wenn unsere Flöten und Geigen erklingen... When our flutes and violins ring, the heart rejoices, and the mouth wants to sing..." The older man next to her chimed in after them, as a round.

"Hai dum, dideldi-dum, hai dum, dideldi-dum..." went the chorus and Willy soon joined in on the "dideldi-dum" response.

A few more people added their voices, and the song went around a couple more times. Gathered as strangers who were drawn to the music, they had quickly become a small chorus. They all applauded and clapped each other on the shoulder as they turned to go on with their Sunday afternoon.

"Hai dum..." Clare sang.

"Dideldi-dum," Willy responded as they walked down the street, buoyed by the music. They held hands and swung their arms to the rhythm of their new walking song.

In the weeks that followed, sometimes Clare would find herself humming the tune, and a six-year-old voice from the next room would echo "dideldi-dum." It became a special code between them when they needed a "cheer-up" moment.

4

The Seeds of Memory

July 2000

"I hope it's not too soon," Clare said, feeling a rush of her own grief. "It's been barely two months since her mother died."

"But I think it's better to reach out than to hold back too much," Stefan answered. "It must be very lonely right now for that family. And they did say they want us to come."

"Dear, dear Emma. She was so close to her mother. It still seems impossible that she is gone. It was so sudden, and Emma is only nineteen years old."

Emma had been an exchange student with a friend and neighbor a couple of years before, and Clare and Stefan had practically adopted her as well. Now, on the train en route to Münster, Clare was feeling nervous about the visit. Would it be awkward? Would it be too painful for them? And for her?

They had to change trains in Dortmund, but it wasn't clear where to find the right track. Clare asked the first person she saw.

"*Entschuldigung*. Excuse me, could you tell me...." The woman quickly apologized, saying that she was a foreigner (Japanese?) and couldn't help. Then she asked a man, who had the same answer. She couldn't place the accent. There seemed to be a lot more foreigners in Germany than before. She had noticed that already in Marburg.

"I think it's a good thing," Clare had said to Stefan one day. "The international additions will be good for Germany. New colors and cultures. Things feel more open and welcoming."

There had been many Turks in Germany since the *Gastarbeiter* program of the 1960s, the "guest workers" that Germany had invited to alleviate a labor shortage. But Clare had thought they were rather invisible in 1980. They had lived and worked in isolated areas. But now the growing diversity was notable.

* * *

Emma's father picked them up at the train station in Münster. They hadn't met any of Emma's family before, but there was an instant bond between them.

"It's good of you to come," Karl said, holding out both hands to them. He was gracious and kind and Clare felt the depth of his loss when they hugged.

The house was beautiful, full of love. The mother's presence was still very strong in the house, as was her absence. The garden in the back was a paradise of colors, with winding paths and artful structures.

"The garden was Ingrid's great love," Karl said quietly.

Clare felt conflicting emotions. The joyful colors of the flowers dancing against the bluest blue of the sky were a tribute to all she had meant to them. At the same time, its beauty seemed to mock their grief.

"Emma!" Clare exclaimed when they ran to embrace each other. They hugged for a long moment, both holding back the tears that threatened to drown them. Clare recognized the numbness that Emma still wore to protect her from the loss she couldn't yet face.

The visit was full of sadness punctuated by moments of laughter and happy memories. After a few hours and a delicious meal, Karl took them to the train station, and they were on their way back to Marburg.

"It was such a short visit," Clare said with a sigh. "But it felt long."

"Yes, and yes. But it's important that we went."

"It's so hard to be present in someone else's pain when you feel like you are watching from a distant shore. Grief is such a lonely place." They rode in silence for a while, as the scenes from the morning rewound outside the windows of the train.

"The greater the love, the deeper the hole it leaves," Stefan added after a long pause.

September 1980

Clare kissed Willy goodbye and watched as he approached the front door of the school without looking back. He looked like a regular German schoolboy now, with his little backpack and the small, insulated bag that held his *Zweites Frühstück*, a mid-morning snack they called "second breakfast." The second week of school had started better. Clare was feeling stronger, and she hadn't needed to up the bribes. She hurried back to the apartment. Michael was already waiting there for her.

"You must be Clare," a young man said.

"Yes, I assume you are Michael," she said, shaking his extended hand." It's nice to finally meet you."

Michael was another American Fulbright scholar in Marburg that year. He had been there for six months already and had written Stefan a friendly letter offering to help them if he could when they arrived. Stefan had written back with details, and it turned out that Michael would be gone for a few weeks in August when Clare and Willy arrived. Clare had called him and left her phone number, wondering if he would call her back.

"Thanks so much for coming by. I really appreciate your help. This housing business is so difficult!"

"Yes, I know. I have a few ideas."

She invited him into the apartment, and they sat down at the table where Michael spread out a few copies of the local paper.

"We'll check the classified sections. That's how I found my place. But it took a while."

"I tried that when we first arrived, but it was so discouraging. I couldn't find anything." Clare sighed with the full weight of her disappointment.

They pored over all the ads and circled a few that might work. Then they started calling. One was already gone, another didn't want children, and a third expected both members of the couple to have full-time jobs with good incomes and a two-year commitment.

"The same old story!" Clare said fighting the despair she had postponed for a few weeks.

"Okay, on to plan B," Michael said with energy.

"What is plan B?" she asked, trying to hide her skepticism.

"We'll place your own ad in the paper."

They worked for a while crafting a brief but clear ad that included her phone number.

"Ehepaar (30 J) mit Kind (6J) …Couple (30 yr.) with a child (6 yr.) seeks an apartment for one year. Contact Clare Muller…"

Then they took the bus to the newspaper office and placed the ad. Clare crossed her fingers and thanked Michael as he took a different bus home. For a week after that she waited. No response, except from her curious neighbors.

"Was that your husband?" she heard several times.

"No, that was Michael who is helping us look for housing," she answered, smiling awkwardly. *My husband is far away doing the fun stuff.*

"Ah."

"Stefan is coming for a visit next weekend, though. He'll want to meet you."

July 2000

"*Guten Morgen, Trauer,*" Clare said as she climbed out of bed. In the days following her dramatic catharsis, she had begun to accept her grief and give it a name. '*Trauer*' was the German word for grief. The outburst had released the internal pressure that had been building and had brought her some relief from the heaviness of her pain. Sadness was still her constant companion, but it helped to externalize it.

"Good morning, Trauer, how did you sleep?" was her regular morning greeting, though she always knew the answer to her question. When Trauer slept well, her dreams were lighter, and her father often visited. When Trauer was restless, things could get stormy, and her father knew to stay out of the way.

"How is Trauer this morning?" Stefan asked as he handed her a cup of coffee.

"She slept well last night, thank you." Clare had shared her strategy with him, and it became their private code.

"And how's your dad? Did he visit?"

"I saw him sitting on a park bench smoking his pipe."

* * *

51

July 5

*I keep thinking about dreams and how amazing they are, Hannah.
Scientists have shown that during REM sleep, when we dream,
our brains are even more active than when we are awake.
Billions of neurons fire to create unscripted movies that try to
make sense of our lives. Our own private one-time screenings
in technical perfection.*

*How do those billions of neurons know just what my dad would
say? Did he sign up for this night shift? What does he do during
the day? Where does he go?*

September 1980

"*Muller, Guten Tag*," Clare said as she picked up the ringing telephone. She was getting used to the German style of answering.

"*Guten Tag, Frau Muller*," came the answer. She didn't recognize the voice.

"*Ist Herr Muller da?*"

"*Nein*. I'm sorry, he's not here. Could I take a message?" Clare said, finding her best polite German.

"Please tell him that his photos are ready. When will he be back?"

"He is in Bavaria and won't be back for a few weeks." She still didn't know who it was on the phone. *Photos? It's probably the Fulbright people. Maybe they took some official photos.*

"May I ask how old you are?"

"... Excuse me?"

"Have you had children?"

"What?" *Did he really just ask me that? Did I misunderstand? Why would the Fulbright office want to know that?*

"I mean, are you still attractive?"

"Who ARE you? You have no right to ask me that!" Clare exclaimed, stumbling over the German.

"I just wanted to know if...*ob du schon gefickt worden bist.*"

Clare hung up. She wasn't sure if she had fully understood the complex use of the passive voice, but she knew it was obscene.

Oh my god, and I told him that my husband would be gone for a few weeks. Who is this guy? Am I in danger? And I was being so polite. I'm such an idiot!

Clare ran down to Julia's apartment. Aleksander opened the door to her urgent knocking and invited her in. Her knees were shaking, and it took her a minute to be coherent enough for them to understand her.

"I think I just got an obscene phone call. I was so stupid. I gave him too much information. Do you think we're in danger? Is he a stalker or is it just some dumb prank?"

"I've heard a few other women report obscene phone calls," Julia said, giving Clare a hug. "Nothing else has happened. He must know that there are many international couples living here and he strikes when he thinks he can talk to a woman while her husband is gone."

The next day he called again at the same time. Clare recognized his voice and slammed the phone down immediately. And again the following day. *It must be his break time.* She imagined him working somewhere nearby. Some pathetic guy whose only entertainment was to harass women. She resolved that if he called again, she would answer in Spanish, just to confuse him.

The phone rang the next day at the same time, and she picked it up saying,

"*¡Buenos días, pinche cabrón!*" She was angry and without planning it, she had repeated an obscenity that was common in Mexico.

"*Frau Muller?*" A woman's voice asked hesitantly. Clare was confused.

"*Frau Muller, ich bin Christina Hofmann*…My name is Christina Hofmann. I am calling regarding your ad looking for housing."

"*Ach, Entschuldigung!* Clare blurted out, trying to shift gears, languages, and the image she'd had of the horrible man at the other end of the line. "I thought…"

"We saw your ad in the paper. We have an apartment that might interest you. My husband and I have two boys, ages six and four. We are looking for compatible neighbors to live upstairs from us. We hope to find people who like children and would want to interact with us and…"

"Yes, yes, yes!!!" Clare said without hearing the rest.

"We have some other folks coming to look at the place this evening. My husband Jürgen will be home tomorrow. Could you call at 7:00 tomorrow and make arrangements with him?"

"Of course, thank you so much, Frau Hofmann!" She wrote down the number with a trembling hand.

Clare could hardly sleep that night. It sounded so perfect, even before seeing the place. *What if the other folks get it first? What if they don't like us? Christina sounded so nice on the phone. How can I wait until tomorrow evening?*

The phone rang the next morning at 7:30.

"*Frau Muller?*" It was a man's voice and Clare tensed up.

"*Ja,*" she said cautiously.

"This is Jürgen Hofmann. I expected your call at 7:00 this morning."

"Oh my god, I thought she meant 7:00 p.m. I didn't think anyone would want a call so early. I'm so sorry." *I'm such an idiot!* She didn't say out loud what he probably thought of her.

"*Kein Problem,*" he answered, then shifted to perfect English. "Here we usually use the 24-hour clock. We would say 19:00 for 7:00 p.m."

"Of course, I had forgotten that."

"I need to go to work this morning but later this afternoon could work. Let's say around 5:00 p.m., 17:00 as we would say. If you want to come by then."

"Yes, I'll be there. Could I bring my son along?"

* * *

The upstairs apartment was perfect. Small and cozy, with a balcony looking out over the city. Willy was quiet and polite and even managed to respond in German when Jürgen asked him his name.

"*Ich bin Willy*" he said proudly, pronouncing his name the German way.

Clare assured them that Stefan was a wonderful and patient man with German family roots. He hadn't grown up speaking German, but his father had. She explained a bit about his work and hers.

She had a good feeling about the people and the place, and after an agonizing day of waiting, she got the news that they could have the apartment. She couldn't know then how much the new friendship would change their lives, but she already felt the fullness of possibility.

July 2000

Clare awoke and stayed in bed a moment, trying to shake off the weight of dreams. The last one was still with her and was as real as the morning light that crept along the wall. She had dreamed about a flood and her father and little Willy had both been swept away by strong currents. She swam hard, trying to grab a hand or a leg to rescue them, to pull them back with her to solid ground. She could almost touch them. But the current was strong, and her struggles were in vain. The father of her childhood and the childhood of her son were both so close, yet forever out of reach.

"Okay, Trauer, it's time to get up," Clare said with resolve. After washing her face, she looked at herself in the bathroom mirror and plucked a few new gray hairs that seemed to have sprouted overnight. Stefan assured her that they were nice highlights to her dark hair. He had some, too, but they were mostly lost in his own sandy colored mop. She had always thought she would welcome gray hairs and wrinkles as a sign of her hard-earned status as a wise woman. But now they seemed more like markers of time lost, the ticking clock that left so much behind. She had been born exactly at mid-century and now, at the beginning of another, she was half a century old herself. Gray hairs and hot flashes were a constant reminder of that.

Though Trauer was still her daily companion, she had faded into the background of Clare's days. At night, she would sometimes whip up stormy nightmares, but there were nice dreams as well.

"Good night, Dad," Clare would sometimes whisper as she got in bed. "Hope to see you tonight."

* * *

July 7

Have you ever noticed, Hannah, how many strange contra-dictions there are in life? Like how the loss of someone you love leaves such a hole of emptiness, a nothing that fills your being with a painful something. I guess it's called grief. Trauer. I think we hold on to that inflated pain as our last contact with the person we lost. It's hard to let it go, but when we hold on to it, it makes it hard to breathe sometimes.

I just wrote a poem about it.

Grief

Emptiness
that hangs within,
a deep postpartum
vacuum.
Time turns back,
memories rewind
in rapid jerky motion.
The womb refills
with tender sorrow,
protruding only
inward.
Long, slow leak,
reluctant birth,
a gentle
un-gestation.

September 1980

"*Guten MOR-gen!*" Stefan heard a small voice whisper in his ear. He still had his arm around Clare in the twin bed they had shared for the night. "Ummm…"

"C'mon, Daddy, it's time to get up. I have some bread so we can go feed the ducks." Stefan had finally been able to get away for a few days to come visit them. Willy had many things to show him. As did Clare.

"Okay, little guy, give me a moment," he said, trying to disentangle gently from his sleeping wife.

"How about I make you some pancakes?"

"With lots of syrup?"

"You got it."

While they were eating breakfast, Clare wandered into the small living room rubbing her eyes. She was not a morning person. She ran her fingers through her thick dark hair, brushing it back from her face. It was smooth and straight enough that it immediately slid back to frame her face and neck.

"*Guten Morgen, schöne Frau,*" Stefan said, grabbing his wife by the waist. He had called her "beautiful woman," but she was still too groggy to notice. She had slept soundly, not getting up once to check on Willy.

"We have the day all planned," Willy said, smiling up at his mother.

"I bet you do." she said covering a yawn with her hand. "And we need to introduce your Dad to our new friends, so they can finally meet my real husband."

"Oh? Have you been parading false husbands around while I was gone?"

"Well, you know, it's nice to keep people guessing. Something to entertain them."

"Well, I'm glad I'm the *real* one," Stefan said, kissing his wife on the cheek.

"We can go by the house where we're going to live," Clare said, still feeling the excitement and disbelief that it had worked out. "You can't see the inside yet. The current tenants will move out in a few more weeks, soon after you finish with the Goethe Institute. Then we can all move in together."

"Yay!" Willy said, bouncing on his toes.

They decided to take the path through the woods down to the river.

"Can I ride on your shoulders, Daddy?"

Stefan hoisted Willy up and off they went, happy to be a threesome again.

"Hey, my little man, I think you've grown a lot in the last month," Stefan said, setting Willy on the ground. "You're getting too big for my shoulders. Besides, I need you to show me the way. I'm new here, you know."

Clare nodded. "Lead on, Herr Villy." Stefan took her hand and smiled as Willy scampered ahead.

When they neared the river, Willy ran to the grassy bank.

"But where are the ducks?"

"You have to quack to call them," Stefan said, winking at Clare. "You know, speak their language."

Willy quacked a few times and threw some breadcrumbs into the water. Sure enough, a pair of ducks appeared from the shadows of overhanging trees and quacked back to him.

"It worked!" Willy shouted, throwing some more crumbs.

"You have a smart Dad," Clare said, giving her real husband a kiss.

July 2000

*I think about you, Hannah, and wonder how your trip is going.
It's strange to remember that you exist outside your house and my
journal. I hope you are doing well. Are you familiar with the word
'saudade'? It is a Portuguese word that is difficult to translate.
Kind of like a mixture of German 'vermissen' "to miss" and
'Wehmut' a melancholy nostalgia, but with a gentle sweetness to
it. I imagine my Trauer walking down the street holding the hand
of a young Saudade, who sometimes looks like little Willy. Why
does the past seem sad sometimes, even when it is filled with happy
memories? Do those past moments still exist if we remember them?*

*Sometimes I see my father or little Willy as I walk around town.
It's strange how memories that are many years apart can inhabit
the same space and time. I wonder if they might meet someday.*

Clare made the rounds with her watering can, greeting each plant in the house as she went. "How are you today? Do you need a drink?" It was silly, if you thought about it, but she appreciated the company of those living beings in the house.

She heard a soft cry as she opened the back door. A gray cat sat on the doorstep and looked up at her with large hazel eyes.

"Well, good morning. Where did you come from?"

The cat answered with a sad lament and kept its gaze fixed on Clare.

"You know I can't feed you. Who do you belong to?" She bent down to pet the silky fur, noting the white bib under its chin and four white paws. "You are a pretty one, but you need to go home. Go on now. Go away! I can't give you anything or you will stay forever. I can't have a cat. This isn't my house."

The cat rubbed against her legs, repeating its story. Clare felt the lumpiness of its bulging belly brush her skin, weakening her resolve.

"Oh my, you are full of babies! But you look barely older than a kitten yourself."

Clare went to get a bowl of milk and some tuna salad from yesterday's lunch.

"Here you go, *mein Kätzchen*. I hope I don't regret this." Uh oh, I already called her *my* little kitten.

September 1980

After Stefan left and they settled back into their routine, Clare started to think about the logistics of their move. The new apartment would be *leer*, that is, completely empty. And in Germany, that usually meant not even a fridge or a stove. In this case, the stove would stay. Jürgen explained to her that *"leer"* often meant bare of even light fixtures. You couldn't assume anything. The challenge seemed insurmountable: they didn't have a car, they had very limited funds, and she didn't really know where to start. They had at least brought some sheets, blankets, silverware, and other odds and ends with them; hence the eight suitcases.

Michael told her about *Sperrmüll* and lent her a calendar of when it happened in each neighborhood. It was a scheduled time when people could put out on the curb anything they no longer needed and there was a window of a few days when anyone could come by and take what they wanted before the city came to haul the rest away. She would ask a friend with a car to take her around and see what she could find. But she was sure it wouldn't be enough to furnish the apartment, even as small as it was. She decided to go back to see Frau Holzer.

"Frau Muller, you are back. How are things at the Gästehaus?"

"Fine. Thank you so much for giving us this opportunity." Clare was surprised at the friendlier reception this time, even without Willy channeling The Force. "We have finally found an apartment and I am trying to figure out how to furnish it for a year. We don't have—"

"I was just going to call you," Frau Holzer interrupted her, "to tell you that something has opened up and you can stay at the Gästehaus for the whole year." She seemed pleased with the generosity of her news.

Clare nearly collapsed in an onslaught of conflicting emotions. All the stress and uncertainty along with the joy and relief of the Gästehaus apartment. She had even felt shame for practically begging to be allowed to stay there. There were advantages to staying in the little international community that they had found; the nearness of the school, the rent would be reasonable…

"But, but, I mean, thank you, Frau Holzer. I don't know what to say. I think it's too late. We have already committed to this new place and..." Clare realized at that moment that even with the unknown about the move, something told her it was worth the gamble. It felt right.

"I see. Are you sure?"

Claire nodded, now sure of herself. She was pretty sure that Stefan would agree, but she was uncertain about Willy.

"Is the place furnished?"

"Well, not exactly..."

"I could probably dig up some stuff from storage that you could use. Tell me what you need, and we'll see what we can find."

Well, hello Serendipity, my new best friend! Clare wrote a list of what she could think of and gave it to Frau Holzer: beds, sofa, table and chairs, night tables, maybe a small desk, a small fridge, a few lamps...

"*Vielen Dank, Frau Holzer.* I am very grateful for your generosity."

She was astonished at how easy it had been. Maybe Willy's charm was still working. She would call Stefan that evening and tell him of their victories.

July 2000

"*Muller, guten Tag,*" Claire said easily when she answered the phone.

"*Frau Muller? Guten Tag.*" A voice she didn't recognize. "*Ich bin Hannah Baumgartner.*"

It took Clare a minute to process—the name sounded familiar... "Hannah!! *Entschuldigung, Frau Baumgartner.* I shouldn't be so familiar. I haven't even met you. But I feel like I know you."

"Please call me Hannah."

"And I'm Clare." You are real! She thought, glad she hadn't said that out loud.

"I'm just calling to see if everything is okay with the house. It's not easy for me to call from Bali but I had a chance today to connect. How are things?"

"Your house is wonderful. It is helping me find my way. I mean, well, to settle into my new life." Clare didn't want to share too much.

"I'm glad. I'm sure the house is happy as well." The gentle warmth of Hannah's voice seemed to match her picture.

"Could I ask you a question?"

"Of course, but I will need to hang up soon."

"Um..." Clare's mind went blank for a moment. "Trees—do you have a special relationship with trees?"

"Oh yes, I think they are very wise beings who have a lot to offer us. I am fascinated with old trees."

"Yes, yes. I know what you mean! I love the books you have and the picture on the wall." There was so much Clare wanted to ask her, but there wasn't time. Bali! So that's where she had gone.

"It's so nice to talk to you and I'm taking good care of your plants," was all she managed to say.

"Lovely to talk to you as well. I'll try to check in occasionally."

Clare hung up and went out to the garden. A gentle breeze carried a message from the deep red roses by the door. It spoke of merlot and summer romance. She decided to cut a few for the table. As she turned to go inside for some garden shears, she heard a muted cry from somewhere in the yard. She stopped to listen and thought maybe she had imagined it.

"There it is again. Is that you Kätzchen?" The cat had not returned for food and Clare had assumed she had gone home. "Where are you?" She heard another soft cry and followed the sound. It seemed to come from deep under a bush. Clare crawled under and found the gray cat lying on her side, panting hard. "There you are you poor thing." She placed her hand on the cat's belly and stroked softly. "You can do this, Mama Kitty, don't worry. Your body will know how."

The labor progressed quickly and soon a small bundle packaged in an opaque sack was delivered. The young mother jumped up and tried to run away from the strange creature that had come from her body, but it followed her, still attached by a cord.

"Hey, it's okay." Clare pushed her down gently. "I know it seems strange, but this is your baby, and you need to deal with it." The cat lay down again and started to lick the bag with her rough tongue until it dissolved and revealed the wet black fur of a kitten. Its tiny squeak spoke of new life as the mother chewed the cord between them. There was barely time to finish the job when new contractions laid her flat again. Clare stayed with her until all four babies were clean and had found their way blindly to their first meal.

September 1980

Willy bounced in the door with a half-eaten pastry in his hand. He stopped by the Bäckerei often now on the way home from school. Clare and Julia took turns walking the kids to and from school, and it was Julia's turn today.

Willy had stopped writing in his notebook recently.

"There are too many words now, Mommy, I can't write them all."

It was true, he was starting to speak in sentences without even realizing it. And he could understand so much more. Clare decided to give him a regular allowance to buy a few things. She was still responsible for an occasional *Schlumpf* or Lego set.

"I can read." Willy announced when he finished the last bite of his *Shockoladencremegebäck*. The chocolate cream pastry was his favorite, and he was proud to ask for it by name. He also knew how much it cost and could put the right coins on the counter.

"Read? Well, yes, I know. In English." She looked at his intensely blue eyes and the chocolate icing around his mouth. It was good that he didn't understand yet how charming he could be.

"I can read," he repeated. "In German."

Clare was taken aback. Of course, he could write some words and recognize some things, but he hadn't studied sentence structure or spelling.

"Here, I'll show you." He picked up the little pocket-sized children's book Clare had just bought for him. She had planned to read it to him that evening. *Jacob und Julia Spielen Verstecken,* it was called. "Jacob and Julia Play Hide and Seek," she translated for him. "Except the name in German is just about the hiding part: *Verstecken,*" she added.

Willy began to read haltingly at first and then more fluidly as he went.

"How did you do that?" The story was simple, but not *that* simple.

"It's easy. You just learn how the letters sound. It's not like English."

"Could you understand all those words?" Clare couldn't imagine how he could.

"No, but I could read them." And he ran out to the Spielplatz to join his Freunde.

Both Willy and Zosia already had a strong background in reading their own languages. They discovered along the way that some of the German kids spoke a dialect of German at home that was different from what they were learning at school. So those kids had their own challenges. In some ways, it was easier for Willy and Zosia. German was a completely new language for them, and they swallowed it whole.

August 2000

Clare got on the bus with her shopping bags heavy and full. She was glad there were seats open near the front and she fell into one with a sigh. She watched a young woman come staggering up the steps, also loaded with shopping bags and leading a young boy by the hand. The boy's face was blotchy red, and a frown scrunched his forehead onto his nose.

"*Kein Jammern mehr, Emil,*" the mother said. "No more whining. Emil, please just sit down." Clare glanced at the mother's face as she recognized the mix of exasperation and exhaustion in her voice. A few tears glistened on her lower lashes and then rolled down the woman's pale cheeks. Her son slid in to sit by the window and the mother sank into her seat, jostling the bags in her hands. A carton of eggs on top of one of her bags teetered for a moment on the edge. As the young woman leaned forward to steady it, her motion flipped the carton out of the bag. It landed hard in the central aisle, upside down and open.

"*Ach nein…,*" she moaned, her hands still full of the bags. "Oh no…"

"Here, let me help you." Clare jumped up to take one of the bags from the woman's hand and set it on the seat next to her. She kneeled in the aisle and began to pick up the broken eggshells dripping with egg white. The woman set her bags down and joined her as the bus began to pull into traffic. They both tried to scoop the mess into the carton using the shells that kept cracking.

"*Zerbrechlich.* Too fragile," the young mother said, as tears streamed down her face. She sat back on her feet and wiped her cheek with the back of her hand.

The more Clare tried to pick up the eggs, the runnier they became, yellow and clear dripping through her fingers. She held up her hands and started to laugh. The other woman joined her and soon they were bent over holding their stomachs.

"Please take your seats, ladies," the driver said.

The young mother grabbed the edge of her seat to pull herself up. As she stood, Clare noticed the classic bulge on her slim frame. *About five to six months*, she guessed.

"My name is Clare." She reached out across the aisle to shake the woman's hand and then withdrew it as she remembered how sticky it was. They both chuckled. She wiped her hand with Kleenex and then offered her companion some.

"*Danke schön.* I'm Charlotte." They shook hands.

"When are you due?" Clare asked, taking a chance.

"End of December." Charlotte smiled gratefully. "Thanks for your help."

"Well, I wasn't much help, but it was fun playing together in the scrambled eggs."

"You did help. It felt good to laugh. They're just eggs."

"This is my stop." Clare grabbed her bag and left Charlotte's extra one on her seat. "Take care of yourself and good luck with everything," she said patting Charlotte's shoulder as she left. "You'll get through it."

October 1980

Just as Clare stepped out the door to call Willy in from the Spielplatz, she saw him fall. He had been balancing on the top of the jungle gym and his foot slipped, throwing him backwards in a slow-motion free fall as Clare watched in horror. By the time he landed hard on his back, she was already running. His head bounced against the ground and then he lay still.

"Mommy, mommy!" She ran past Willy's voice and turned in confusion.

"Willy? Oh my god, you're okay!?"

The boy on the ground wasn't her son, but he was someone else's Willy. She didn't stop until she knelt by the small boy lying spread-eagled as though he had just made an angel pattern in the snow. His face was pale and his eyes were closed.

"Willy, do you know him? Do you know where he lives?"

"No. I just sorta met him yesterday. He doesn't speak English."

"Willy, I need you to help. Run get Julia and tell her to call an ambulance."

"Hurry!!" she yelled after him as she saw blood spreading on the dirt next to the boy's head.

Okay Clare, stay calm. You need to stop the bleeding, but do not move him. Her first aid training came back to her as she went into action. She had nothing to work with and there was no time to lose.

The buttons flew as Clare ripped off her blouse, keeping her eyes on the boy. She wadded up the blouse and slipped her hand carefully under the back of his head, trying not to move his neck, in case it was broken. *Don't think about that now.* She placed her other hand gently on his forehead, leaned an ear towards his face and listened. He was still breathing. The boy's eyes fluttered a moment, and he looked up at her in confusion.

"It's okay, it's okay," she murmured softly. "Stay still, sweetie, don't be afraid." She remembered that Willy had said he didn't speak English. *"Ruhig, mein Schatz, keine Angst."*

Willy ran as hard as he could, pretending it was a race. As he reached the building where Zosia lived, he met a woman coming out the door.

"Kind fallen!" he panted. "Kid fell!" He pointed in the direction of the Spielplatz and then ran to find Julia.

"Don't go to sleep, sweetie," Clare said to the boy, trying to smile. *"Nicht schlafen."* She had no idea if he understood German either.

Just then a woman rushed up and fell to her knees next to them. Clare could see in her eyes that she was the boy's mother. She looked at Clare and spoke urgently. Clare couldn't understand or even guess what language it was.

"Mein Sohn!" the woman repeated in German. "My son!"

Clare nodded. She took the woman's hand and showed her how to hold the compress under the boy's head. Then she took her other hand and placed it on his forehead.

"Sehr still. Very still. Don't let him move. *Nicht bewegen."*

She ran her hands gently down the boy's whole body and didn't find anything broken but she didn't dare turn him over to check his back. His pulse seemed weak and slow, but it was steady.

Willy, Julia and Zosia came running.

"I called an ambulance," Julia said, catching her breath. "They'll be here soon."

"Talk to him," Clare told the mother. "We can't let him sleep. *Sprechen mit ihm, muß nicht schafen,*" she repeated in simple German as she opened her eyes wide and rubbed the boy's arm.

Clare sat back and took a deep breath. Then she remembered that she was wearing only a bra on top. Willy and Zosia ran to bring her a shirt as the sound of the two-tone sirens approached.

5
Nausea and Nostalgia

August 2000

"I've got to run," Stefan said, giving Clare a kiss on the forehead.

"So soon? It seems like your days at work are getting longer. I don't see much of you."

Stefan stopped and looked at his wife. "Well, things are really rolling and I'm trying to take advantage of this time I have for research. It will be over before we know it."

"I suppose," she said, frowning. Clare felt grouchy and resentful. Her long days alone were beginning to lose their charm. And her nights were not very restful lately. Too hot, then too cold. Fits of racing pulse and bouts of sadness.

"You know, your year will go by quickly, too. Have you started writing yet?"

"Some in my journal, but I'm not ready to face the book yet."

"Maybe you should start reading some of those heavy books you brought with you and jot down some notes as you go. You need to get on with your life, Clare. You can't keep living in the past."

"Isn't that what you historians do?" she snapped back, stung by his patronizing judgment of her. "I'm not sure I even *want* to write the damn book. But go, just go, and do what you do."

Clare sat glowering at the door that Stefan had slammed behind him. *I'm dealing with a lot of stuff right now. I need time*, she reassured herself. But the truth was, she was beginning to lose patience with herself as well.

* * *

August 10

I don't know what's wrong with me, Hannah. We all lose our parents eventually. Our children grow up and life moves on. This

67

should be the most productive time of my life and I should enjoy my freedom. But it's hard to let go of being fertile and in the prime of life. Although when I stop to think about it, in earlier years I was so busy with work and school and kids, I'm not sure I really appreciated where I was then. Why are we always running from where we are?

I am surprised at my own vanity and vulnerability in this transition to menopause. There should be a rite of passage for it. Instead, it feels like a kind of demotion, a secret loss of status and power. I could counter any other woman who said this with all kinds of feminist critiques of the world we live in, that she should be proud to be a strong and independent woman, ready to fulfill her greatest intellectual and artistic potential. I'm ashamed of my own doubts. This sabbatical from being 'The Professor' has opened room for many of them. When you step off the stage, you wonder who you really are.

Clare took a deep breath. It felt good to write. She put her pencil down and closed the journal, the secret confessional that made room in her days for new experiences. She felt the brush of soft fur on her leg and reached down to pet her new housemate. "How are you today, *Kleine Mutti*?" Clare called the cat "Little Mama." She wasn't ready to give her a name, which would imply more commitment than she could promise. The cat's purring idled like a well-tuned engine, making her whole thin body vibrate in contentment. "I should learn to purr like you, my little friend. Let's go get you some food."

She filled the cat's bowls with food and water and sat on the floor next to the cardboard box that was home for the kittens. Two gray ones that looked like their mother and two black ones suggesting the father. Their eyes were fully open, but still blue, and they staggered on wobbly legs. Clare was surprised how much joy it gave her to watch them develop. Her early childhood experience with litters of kittens had helped her to understand more about the beginnings of life.

Clare watched the cat eat. "What will Hannah say? How will we find homes for these kittens? Don't worry, Kleine Mutti. We'll figure it out."

68

October 1980

The phone rang.

"Clare, it's Julia. I just talked to Azadeh, the mother of the boy who was injured. She said he is doing well. No broken bones. He will be in the hospital a couple more days. It was a nasty gash on his head, and a very serious concussion."

Clare relived the scene when the paramedics had lifted the boy onto the stretcher. The sharp rock where his head had landed had told a grim story.

"Thanks for the report. I'm so relieved. I've been really worried about him. And so has Willy."

"Yes, same here. They are from Iran. Azadeh's German is limited so I didn't get much detail. Her son's name is Armin. Aleks met her husband, Hassan. Azadeh wanted me to tell you that you saved her son's life, and she will be forever grateful. They want you all to come visit later after Armin comes home."

"I would like that."

"Oh, and she also said she was sorry about your blouse."

That evening Clare gave Willy the good news. "His name is Armin and he is going to be okay."

"Yay!" Willy looked serious for a moment. "Mommy, did he almost die?"

"Well, he could have. It was a serious fall."

"But you saved him."

"*We* saved him, Willy. You were a big help." She held up her hand for a high five.

* * *

A big truck arrived full of furniture for their new apartment. It wasn't anything special to look at, but it seemed like a treasure. Stefan was back to stay, and they had fun putting their new home together; their *Dachgeshoß*— "roof apartment," as it was described in German. Willy had been sad to leave the Spielplatz and his group of friends, but Clare assured him that he could visit often or invite them over.

"This is Jonas," Christina said, introducing Willy to her son. Jonas said something they didn't understand, and he danced and sang a little tune. *Da da da da da da da...*

"This is Lucas," she said, drawing a younger boy from behind her back. He smiled shyly. "Willy will be our new upstairs neighbor," she explained to her sons. "You can all play together."

"Let's go play outside," Jonas said, grabbing Willy's arm and singing the little tune. *Da da da da da da da...* He danced while he sang it.

"*Der Ententanz!*" Willy exclaimed. "We learned that at school. The Duck Dance," he said to Clare. He put his hands under his armpits and started to dance like a duck with Jonas.

"You can play later," Clare said. "We need to get settled in first. It's so nice to meet you all."

Both boys gave her a pleading look. She could feel the urgency of their need like a full bladder in the night. "Okay, okay, go play for a while."

"Stay in the yard!" Christina called after them as they ran out the door.

"I already have a new friend!" Willy exclaimed, bounding up the stairs.

"I know. Isn't that great? Look, Willy, this will be your room."

"Really? I get to have my own room!" There was plenty of floor space to spread out his Legos. Clare and Stefan would sleep in the living room.

* * *

"I'd be happy to help you get started on your baby project again," Stefan had said on the second night of his visit in September to their old apartment at the Gästehaus. Willy had slept in the living room.

"*Our* project," she corrected him, though it was clear that she would be the one more intensely engaged in it. They didn't have a lot of time if this baby was to be born in Germany.

"It's a bit scary," she had whispered to him.

"I know."

August 2000

The morning after her fight with Stefan, things were still cool between them. Clare wanted to make it right, but she didn't know how to begin, at least not Before Coffee. And she still had one foot in a weird dream.

"I dreamed about my dad again."

"Oh?"

"I was sitting in a large room with rows of chairs and a group of people waiting for something to begin. A show? A program? There was a TV set in front of us, one of those old black and white ones. Then someone explained that if you took one of those old sets and tuned it to a certain channel that had only static, you could communicate with the dead, with your loved ones. I thought it sounded hokey, but I was still curious to see what would happen.

"A man's voice to my right said, 'It'll be interesting to see how this works.' I was shocked to see that it was Dad, sitting there right next to me!! He was younger, about my age now, and so vividly real. I hugged him and kissed his cheek. I still remember exactly how it felt with his rough whiskers and the faint aroma of a pipe, the sound of his voice, the hug. Then we both settled down to see what would happen. Isn't that strange? How could my brain come up with such a crazy thing? Like a sci-fi movie."

Stefan stood up and walked over to her, lifting her to her feet. "Clare Aisling Roney, do you realize how beautiful you are?" He tucked her dark hair behind her ears and kissed her on the mouth. "You are as stormy as the Irish Sea and as striking as the hills of Clare." Stefan had always liked the sound of her full name and the Irishness of her character. But he used it sparingly. "Your father told me once that *Aisling* is Gaelic for "dream" or "vision" and *Clare* means "bright, gentle or warm."

"What a perfect name for you, my big dreamer," Stefan told her.

"Well, maybe not the gentle part," she said sheepishly, giving Stefan a warm kiss. Damn, why did he have to be so perfect? It was hard to stay mad at him, even when she needed to.

Stefan hadn't always seemed so perfect. When she first met him, several decades earlier, she was turned off by what she thought was reserve or arrogance, or maybe he was just not very interesting. Since she was such an expressive and emotive person, it was hard to interpret his character. She had picked up some interest on his part, but it wasn't very convincing. "No use jumping into a lukewarm relationship," she had told herself. "A waste of time." But somehow over the months as she got to know him, his quiet manner reached inside and tickled her heart. She fell hard. Willy loved to hear Stefan's version of the story, told in terms of a great conquest. She let that one go.

Stefan was still that steady, gentle person, but it wasn't charming her much at the moment. Something was bothering her, and she wanted to fight. She needed something dramatic, passionate, to bring her back to life.

October 1980

The next day they rode the bus together, the one that Willy would need to take to school. He would have to walk down the alley from their back yard and catch a city bus that would drop him off near the school.

Clare began to feel queasy on the ride. At first, she welcomed the discomfort to confirm what she already suspected. "The sicker the better!" she had said to Stefan, hoping that would ensure a strong pregnancy. The test a week before had been negative, but she trusted the feeling in her lower belly.

The first week Clare rode the bus with Willy every morning, getting up in the dark and nibbling on some saltine crackers to settle her stomach. The nausea was getting worse, and it was clear she couldn't keep up that morning routine. Meanwhile, Stefan had hurt his back playing basketball with some colleagues and could barely get out of bed himself. The next week Willy would have to try it on his own. That's just what kids in Germany did. She had gotten him a renewable monthly pass to wear around his neck.

They walked down to the bus stop and waited for the #6 bus. Willy knew the routine and where to get off. *Aussteigen* was the word in German. They had practiced saying it a few times. Clare waved and smiled as he boarded the bus, swallowing her worry and her nausea. What could go wrong?

That afternoon Clare met Willy as he got off the bus and she applauded his victory. But he frowned and was silent as they walked up the hill.

"I'm not going back. I can't do it."

"Why not? It seems you did just fine."

"After I got on the bus this morning, a bunch of bigger kids got on and pushed me back. I couldn't get through," he said sniffling as tears wet his

72

cheeks. "I kept trying to tell them I needed to get off and they wouldn't listen."

He had remembered the word *aussteigen*, "to get off," but it wasn't enough. Clare's heart went out to him, and she could hear his little voice trying to get through the pandemonium.

"And then what happened?"

"We passed my stop, and I didin know what to do. The big kids got off at the next stop, but I didin know where I was. I was the only one left on the bus. I went up to the driver and told him."

"What did you say?" She imagined him trying to explain a complex situation with simple words.

"Ich muß Gerhard Hauptmann Schule."

I must Gerhard Hauptmann School, Clare translated in her head, impressed with what he had managed.

"He was nice, and he showed me all the cool buttons and switches to drive the bus. Then he turned the bus around and drove me back to my school."

Clare was touched by the driver's kindness and her son's courage. "You were brave and smart and I'm proud of you."

"Yeah, but I'm not going back."

"We'll talk about that later."

The next morning Clare accompanied Willy again, who insisted the whole way that he would not take the bus anymore. The #6 bus drove up and the door opened. Willy pulled back in protest but then he saw his friend. The bus driver gave him a big smile and told all the kids who were standing to move back.

"Make room for my special friend," he said with great authority. "Willy, you just stand here next to me and hold on to this pole. I'll make sure you get off at the right stop."

For the next month Willy's friend drove that route with Willy at his side in the place of honor.

The alarm clock rang at 6:30 every morning.

"Time to get up, Willy!" Clare would call from her bed, already nibbling on her crackers. Willy would get up, get dressed and then go make scrambled eggs for the two of them. That was his specialty, and he was proud to bring a plate to Clare in bed. If she got up too quickly, the nausea would overtake her in a rush. Stefan made Willy's snack for school, double checked his school bag, and then the two of them headed off down the alley toward the bus.

"I'm proud of you buddy," Clare heard Stefan say as they went down the stairs one morning.

"I'm getting bigger," he answered. She smiled at the confidence in her son's voice. "I know how to do things."

From then on, Willy went off to the bus on his own through the early morning darkness and came sauntering home in the afternoon with stories of his day at school. Sometimes he needed help figuring out something that he had understood only partially, but he seemed to have gained the confidence to struggle through. He and Zosia laughed together a lot, comparing their confusion in their own pidgin German. When it got too hard to communicate, they would go back to the Legos.

The new pregnancy seemed very solid, if Clare's discomfort was indeed an indication. Stefan had the idea that it meant strong hormones, which could protect the embryo.

"It's probably a girl and you're getting a double dose of hormones right now."

Clare wished she could retract her statement about "the sicker the better."

* * *

"How's it going with setting up the apartment? Do you have everything you need?" Jürgen asked as Clare came in the door with a few bags from their shopping trip. "I would be happy to drive you somewhere if that would help. Feel free to ask."

"Thanks, Jürgen. That's very kind." She didn't want to be too dependent on their new landlords. "We're doing well so far. Except when I wanted to buy some *Beleuchtungskörper*. They looked at me funny, like I was speaking another language."

"You were!" Jürgen laughed. "That sounds like *Amtsdeutsch*. It's a kind of official, bureaucratic German that nobody speaks. Something like 'Illumination bodies.'"

"I looked it up in the dictionary," Clare said, feeling embarrassed about making the kind of error her students often made. She called it Dictionary Dialect. You had to be so careful. There were lots of traps.

74

"Did you mean *Glühbirne?*" he asked, recovering from his laughter.

"Glow pear?" she asked, translating literally.

Jürgen mimed the shape of a pear and then pointed to a ceiling light. "I believe you call it a lightbulb in English."

Clare had to laugh. Jürgen was such a good language teacher. While honoring their wish to speak only German together, he recognized those few moments when it was better not to push too far. He enjoyed the humor of it with good natured sympathy.

"Why don't you come in for a cup of tea? You look like you could use a break. Christina will be home with the kids in a moment."

Clare accepted gladly. Stefan had run back to the archive for something.

"Do I remember correctly that you teach at the School for the Blind?" Clare asked.

"*Ja*, I teach English in the high school there."

"Wow, that must be challenging. I'd love to hear about it."

"There are some logistical challenges, but it is basically teaching language, just as you do, am I correct?"

"Yes, and it does have its challenges," she said, nodding as she spoke.

"With my students I just need to remember not to count on visual cues. The students type all their assignments on *Punkt* typewriters. I believe it is called 'Braille' in English. Class time is mostly speaking and listening. We do have some Braille texts as well."

"Did you already know *Punktschrift?* Clare dissected the descriptive word as she often did for her new words in German: *Punkt=point, Schrift=writing*, remembering the raised dots of Braille she had seen. Clare couldn't imagine adding that challenge to her teaching.

"No, but I taught myself to read it by sight. I learned the alphabet and then could decipher my student's work. When I first started, I had to create a new curriculum. The materials they had were so outdated and boring. I record personal cassettes to give my students feedback on their work."

"Wow. That sounds like a lot of work. Let me know if I can ever be of help."

August 2000

"I brought you some *Kräuter* from the garden," Jürgen said as he and Christina walked in the door.

"Fresh herbs! Danke schön."

"And some pastries," Christina added.

"Yum. I'll put on water for tea. It's so nice you stopped by. It makes this house really feel like our home when friends visit." She gave them each a hug. "Especially old friends." It had been wonderful to come back to their friendship of more than twenty years.

"We're not *that* old," Jürgen teased her.

"How are the kittens?" Christina asked.

"They are at that adorable stage, where you want to keep them all." They walked into the living room, where four little balls of fur were walking around on shaky legs. One bumped into another, and they both rolled over. Another approached and all three landed together in a tangle of soft paws and floppy ears. It was entertaining to watch.

"So how are *you* doing?" Christina had a way of zooming in gently to Clare's inner world. Their dark shoulder length hair made them look like sisters, though Christina was shorter and had a deep dimple in her cheek that gave an air of mischief to her smile. Like the men in Clare's life.

"Some days are kind of long and I'm not sure what to do with myself," Clare confessed. "I know I should be reading and working on my book, but I'm just not ready yet."

"You're still getting settled and grief is a long journey. Come by sometime and let me do some of my acupressure and massage treatment. It might help to balance and reset your energy."

"That sounds great. Let's make an appointment."

"I know what else you need," Jürgen said. "You should come with us on a *FKK* outing."

"*FKK?*"

"*Frei Körper Kultur,*" he explained. "Nothing like a little time in the fresh air as free as you were born."

Free Body Culture, Clare translated for herself, puzzling over what that meant.

"He means naked," Christina clarified. "We go to a nudist beach sometimes, on a big lake. You are welcome to come with us tomorrow if you like. It's very relaxed, nobody pays any attention, and it all feels natural."

"Sure, why not?"

The next day they arrived at the lake. The awkward part was undressing on the beach, but then she got used to the "Free Body Culture." There were people of all ages, sizes and shapes and everyone seemed very comfortable. It was nice to swim and feel the water caress her whole body. *I could get used to this, but only in the right company.*

"It seems like clothing is the problem," she said to her companions, then immediately thinking that was a strange thing to say. "I mean, like it's all about the imagination or the suggestion of what is under the clothes that makes the body sexy or taboo. When it's all out there, it just is what it is. Does that make any sense?"

"Perfect sense."

* * *

"So, do you feel freer?" Stefan asked Clare when she got home.

"Maybe a bit. Lighter or something. Too bad you missed it."

"I've never been to a nudist beach, but I did go with Jürgen once to a Swedish sauna. It was naked all the way—in the sauna, at the bar, walking through the bar to the pool. Everyone was naked, no towels even."

"Co-ed, I assume."

"Yup, we all just sat there talking to each other as though nothing was different. It was fine for me until we went to sit at the bar. That was weird."

"I can imagine."

"But I'd do it again."

November 1980

The weeks went by, and the weather got colder. Jürgen and Christina were wonderful neighbors and landlords. They were renting the house and subletting the upstairs to them, so officially Jürgen and Christina were the *Obermieter,* literally "over-renters," and Stefan and Clare were the *Untermieter,* "under-renters." They all laughed at the irony that the Obermieters lived downstairs and the Untermieters lived upstairs. They began to form a solid friendship rather quickly, which still seemed miraculous to Clare, after those early desperate weeks. Jürgen and Christina were both teachers, so they all had a lot in common.

"Do you want to speak in German or English?" Jürgen had asked her that first day.

"It would be great if we could always speak in German," she answered timidly, knowing it would be harder. "As a language teacher, I know that is the only way we can become fluent. Maybe English sometimes, so you can practice, too," she added realizing her perspective sounded selfish.

Jürgen had a great sense of humor and was good at helping them laugh at their mistakes or unexpected puns. Christina had a sweet and lilting voice that belied the stereotypes about German being a harsh and rough-edged language. Clare loved to hear her talk. It had the soothing sound of German Lieder, those beautiful semi-classical songs that could touch even the most resistant skeptics.

And Willy had a playmate who was his partner in many adventures and occasional mischief. Jonas was a kid with lots of energy and momentum and verbal expression to match. It was overwhelming for Willy at first, but soon he was swept along on an intensive language immersion course. He managed to keep his head above water most of the time, and he eventually forgot that their play was always in German. Lucas sometimes tagged along. He was a quiet little boy who smiled most of the time, a calming presence to the frenetic energy of his older brother. Willy was somewhere in between, and Clare thought they made a good trio, though Lucas sometimes got left behind.

Nick and Sharon stopped by occasionally. They had often shared dinners together during those first weeks at the Gästehaus. One day as they were drinking tea, Sharon told Clare that she was pregnant.

"We're on the same German baby plan!" Clare exclaimed, hugging her friend. A few weeks later Clare got the same news. There was a sense of solidarity and they got together regularly to compare their misery and excitement. Once they tried going out for tea and pastry. It seemed like a great way to celebrate. They ordered what sounded good and then sat there looking at what they couldn't bring themselves to eat. They laughed together.

"We're pathetic, aren't we?" Sharon said. Clare nodded and they laughed some more.

"Pregancy is supposed to be a happy and fulfilling time that completes you as a woman. At least that's a popular—shall we say— 'misconception.' I mean, it certainly fills you up, literally and metaphorically, but for me there is also a kind of existential nausea that goes with it. Like, who am I to create a being who will be thrown into such a mixed-up world? In fact, who am I at all? What arrogance to assume such a god-like responsibility. I sure don't feel very god-like."

Sharon nodded. They sipped their tea in silence.

* * *

Clare took on more of the shopping, trying to regain a sense of self-worth and competence. Sometimes Willy went with her, helping to carry the bags back up the hill. The nausea was still strong and more than once she said to Willy:

"We need to get off the bus. Now."

"But I thought we were going to Ahrens to buy food. And maybe another Lego set?" he added hopefully.

"Now!" she said urgently. She had to find somewhere that didn't move.

"Is it the pregnasy?" Willy asked, looking worried. "We can look for a bathroom if you need to have a miscarriage." He put his hand on her arm.

"What would I do without you to take care of me?" she said, feeling genuinely grateful for his company. After a few deep breaths she was ready to try again. It was a matter of will. They got to Ahrens. And along with the groceries they bought a Lego set that day.

As things got a little better, Clare went off on her own, trying to take as few buses as possible. She often shopped at the smaller store nearby, at the bottom of the hill. When she needed to go downtown, she would walk there and then take the bus home with her purchases.

One time she was about to pay for some groceries and had to ask the clerk to hold her cart while she ran outside. She sat down on a bench outside the store and took out a piece of stale bread to nibble on in hopes of calming the churning waters of her stomach. The bread was awful, but it was just what she needed.

"*Schmeckt's?*" she heard from a slurred voice nearby. An old man sitting on the next bench was leaning towards her, swaying unsteadily.

"*Schhmmeeckt's*? he asked again, this time with breathy effort, making it clear what he had in his small brown bag. The heavy smell of alcohol and bad breath nearly knocked her over. Clare realized that he was asking if her pathetic piece of bread was tasty. He looked hungry, and she felt like she should share it with him, but she wasn't sure she could get home if she did.

"*Wooo...sind wir*? Wheeere are we?" the man asked." She tried not to look straight at him as she gagged internally. "I mean...what city is this?"

"It's, uh, Marburg. We're in Marburg. Germany"

"Ahhh."

This is too weird. She made an extreme effort to go back inside and pay for her groceries.

* * *

I sure hope this kid is worth it, she thought, as she trudged up the hill with her bags. It was hard for her to even imagine not always feeling queasy. Stefan and Willy were excited about the baby. Stefan would pat her belly and Willy would put his ear close to listen and say, "Hello, baby! Are you in there?" Clare had checked out a book about pregnancy from the library and she and Willy read it together. It had colorful illustrations of each stage of development. By now the baby looked less like a tadpole and almost human, though it was still very small. Willy was sure it could hear him.

"I waited a long time to be a big brother," he said seriously. He had been campaigning for a couple years. He had wanted a little brother, promising that he would take care of him. This came soon after the four-year-old facts of life conversation.

"Why don't you do that thing now and make a little brother for me?" He had responded immediately with the simple clarity of a child's reasoning. His parents explained that it wasn't a good time for them. Maybe later.

"Could I plant one of those little seeds and grow one myself? I could put it in a pot like our tomatoes. I would take care of him all by myself." They had noted that though he hadn't quite gotten the concepts straight, it was probably good enough for the time being. But then, the next day they discovered a drawing of two stick figures, clearly a man and a woman, lying next to each other. There was a hole cut out in the middle between the two figures. It was taped to the headboard of their bed.

"I just wanted to remind you," Willy explained later.

"Why is there a hole in the middle?" Clare asked.

"That's for the *baby*," he answered, with a tone of impatience for her missing the obvious. Clare had loved the organic simplicity of his image. If only it were so easy.

She knew that he, too, had been disappointed by the miscarriage, but now he seemed to be genuinely concerned about her.

"You still have *me*," he had said over the phone as she was recovering in the hospital. They had put her in a maternity ward with new mothers and their babies. She wondered if they realized how cruel that was.

"Yes, and I am so lucky to have you," she had answered, fighting back tears.

They had packed up their whole house to rent it and were on their way to Pennsylvania to visit family before Stefan would leave for Germany. The first day out she lost the baby. She had packed lots of maternity clothes since she would need them for most of the year. She wore them tucked in or with a belt for the first months until she began to fill them out with new hope. And the baby clothes sat in a suitcase under a bed, out of sight but not forgotten.

Now that they were growing a baby again, they had to keep reminding Willy that it might be a girl. In fact, Stefan was sure of it.

"I guess that would be okay," Willy said, after considering it for a moment.

August 2000

"I think I'll walk downtown this morning," Clare said as Stefan was heading off to work. "I need to go to the internet cafe and want to explore some old haunts as well."

"Have fun. Don't forget to come back from the past."

Clare loved the walk to the center of town. It was varied and peaceful and full of memories. Sometimes she wished they had internet at Das Haus, but most of the time she was glad to be free of it. She did need to stay in touch with family and emails were the easiest way.

"Remember all those letters I wrote before?" she said to Stefan one day. In 1980 she had tried to report every week to both her parents and his parents, a kind of pre-internet blog on those thin blue airmail letter forms.

One day some years later Stefan's mother had presented her with a large envelope.

"I saved these for you," she said smiling.

Clare opened the envelope to find all the letters she had written them from Germany, full of news and stories of their adventures. She read them all, reliving that first year they had spent in Marburg.

"That was such a nice thing to do," she told her mother-in-law later. I had forgotten some of those experiences. I didn't write them down for myself at the time."

"Now you have the stories to preserve your memories."

* * *

Some things had changed along the old streets; a few new stores, a few old ones gone, but the old buildings looked the same. And Elvert Bookstore, that was her favorite place. She went in to browse for a while, remembering how she loved the smell of books and the beauty of shelves packed tight with their colorful bindings.

"Now Clare, you don't need any more books right now," she said aloud to herself, thinking of that heavy suitcase she had brought with the books still mostly untouched since she had arrived. "I'll get to them soon," she whispered to the academic voice that haunted her. "Give me time."

Oh my God, I forgot about the elevator! She noticed it still there right next to the bookstore. She got in with a flutter of excitement, remembering her discovery twenty years earlier. It was just a simple outdoor elevator to the upper floor of the bookstore. But that upper floor was in the Oberstadt, in the old part of the city. You just walked out of the elevator and went back in time.

Clare exited and looked around. Everything was pretty much the same as she remembered. She walked a few steps and then turned the corner to the Marktplatz, with its cobblestone streets and the stone Rathaus, a sixteenth century town hall right in front of her. Just then the large clock near the top of the building tolled the hour. A metal rooster, perched above the clock, raised its wings and crowed. Clare laughed, still charmed by the absurdity of the ritual and delighted that she had timed it right. She'd forgotten about that old guy.

November 1980

Stefan was at the archive and Willy was at school. Clare felt restless. *I'm not sure what my life is supposed to be right now, besides maybe being pregnant.*

"But that's not who I am!" she said aloud to the empty backyard. "I'm not just a mom, a wife and a baby vessel." Sometimes she felt lost and detached from her life. But she had to admit that the break from the intensity of graduate school, teaching, and trying to be a good mother was welcome. She had often felt overwhelmed in recent years by juggling all of that and never quite measuring up to her own standards in any category.

It was hard to be an excellent teacher when she could barely keep up with her own studies as a student, and to expect her son to clean his room when she couldn't manage the house herself. Of course, Stefan helped with everything, but even together it always seemed like they were trying to establish order and routine on quicksand. There was never enough money, never enough time. Yet, she reveled in it all because she felt alive, challenged, and productive. It was good to have time to remember that.

"Guten Tag, Frau...Frau Muller?" She looked up to see an older woman waving from the yard next door. Clare walked over to greet her.

"Guten Tag, she said, reaching out to shake her hand. "Clare Muller."

"Adele Schröder, the woman said as she shook Clare's hand. "It's nice to have a new neighbor."

"So nice to meet you," Clare agreed. "I was just feeling a bit lonely. I'm used to working and here everyone else is off at work except me." She was glad to unburden herself but wondered if she was sharing too much for reserved German society.

"I can relate to that!" Adele answered rather forcefully. "I lived in Peru for forty years and it was such a different world. You could go out in the street every day and talk to people. There was always movement and noise and color - the bustle of life."

"I know what you mean. I've spent a lot of time in Mexico, and I often feel subdued, even depressed when I return."

"Do you speak Spanish, then?" Her new neighbor asked, barely containing her enthusiasm.

"Claro que sí! Of course!" Clare was equally excited to find someone to speak Spanish with her. *"No lo puedo creer!* I can't believe it!"

"*Mi esposo...*" the woman continued in Spanish. "My husband retired last year. He worked for a bank in Peru. We came back to Germany, though I really didn't want to. We've been back for a year now, and it's been hard to readjust. I can't seem to reconnect with what used to be my own culture."

"Oh, I so look forward to many future conversations with you," Clare responded, first in German and then remembering she said, "*en español.*" She held Adele's hands in hers and studied her neighbor's face for a moment. It was a face that had clearly seen lots of sun and wore the curved lines of many years of stories.

"Yes, so do I! And *por favor,* call me Adelita. That's what everyone called me in Peru, and I got so used to it, it feels like my true name, though people here don't know that."

That was the beginning of many regular meetings in the backyard or for tea and pastries at one house or the other. Clare was thrilled to have a new friend and to hear many stories of her life in Peru. And all of it in Spanish, which was Clare's first language-love. It brought her sunshine, energy, and passionate colors whenever she spoke it.

6
Spiderwebs

September 1

I haven't written for a while, but I haven't forgotten you, Hannah. My head feels kind of scrambled and it's hard to sit down and write. There is a scent of fall in the air, though the flowers in the garden are still bright and happy.

Every few days I do some cleaning and notice that the Spinnweben are back. It's funny, I never seem to see the spiders, die Spinne. I think they do their work at night. Even after I sweep away their webs, they go right back to spinning new ones. I've begun to appreciate the beauty of their creations and am going to leave them for a while. Sometimes I feel like there are spiders in my brain, spinning new stories every night, even after the daylight erases them. I also think that those webs somehow become part of my neural network. I used to think that "spinnen" in German just meant to spin, but apparently it also means to be crazy.
I guess all writers are crazy.

Sept 5

I have been reading some of the books I brought. Lots of ideas, too many—they seem to take me farther and farther away from being able to write. Don't tell Stefan. (As if you could!)

The kittens are doing well. Their eyes are no longer blue, and their noses have popped out. They have been practicing in the kitty litter and seem to understand what it is for.

November 1980

"Hey, why don't you join me for lunch at the Mensa today?"

"Sure, I've been curious about that place. I can't promise I'll eat much, though."

Stefan had talked about meeting interesting people at the university cafeteria that everyone called *Die Mensa*. There was good food for a reasonable price and an interesting international mix of students.

Clare put more on her plate than usual, hoping it might inspire her to eat. The cafeteria was already quite full, and they stood with their trays in hand looking around for a place to sit.

"*Dürfen wir?* May we?" Stefan asked a young couple at the nearest table. It was common to try more than one language in that international space.

"Of course," they both answered in German. "Please join us." Clare was already intrigued. They were a beautiful couple; both tall, dark skinned and graceful.

"*Ich bin Clare.*" She extended her hand to the young woman, whose eyes were warm and deep. Her thick black hair was tied back loosely with a green scarf.

"Nice to meet you, Clare. *Ich bin Samira.* This is my husband, Omar." They shook hands all around and jumped into a lively conversation. Omar's German was fluent, but Samira's was somewhat hesitant. She explained that they were from Somalia.

"I've only been here for a year, and I spend too much time with other Somalis. Omar's family moved here when he was twelve, so he has become German in many ways." They soon switched to English, which Samira spoke with an elegant almost British accent.

"I went back to Somalia in 1978," Omar explained, "to take some courses at the University of Mogadishu. I was studying medicine and wanted to get some perspective on public health issues in Africa. And I also wanted to visit relatives I hadn't seen for ten years. That's when I met Samira." He turned to smile at his wife.

"I was studying public health at the university as well. We noticed each other in a class and a year later we were married," Samira added. "Omar wanted to come back to Germany, and I was ready for something new."

Clare's enthusiasm for eating had faded and she laid her fork down with a sigh. Samira noticed, raising her eyebrows in a question as she looked down at her own half full plate. They didn't say anything, but Clare felt a secret connection.

September 2000

Clare sat in the internet café and looked out the window to watch people going by. She had finished reading her emails and had a sudden urge to write to Julia and Sharon. How long had it been? *Why have we lost touch?* But they were the kind of friendships that could survive long dormant periods, she was sure of that.

Sept. 10

Dear Julia,

It has been so long since we've been in touch. I think of you often, even more now that we are living in Marburg again. I don't think I told you about that plan. Or that my dad died suddenly, and the bottom fell out of my world for a while. It's great being here and memories bloom everywhere I look. I can see little Willy and Zosia skipping down the streets or playing with Legos together. But especially I remember many long conversations with you about everything.

It was such a miracle that you ended up moving to Iowa and that we could see each other now and then. But it seems strange that you are there now since you do still live here in my memories. Anyway, we should talk sometime and catch up on our current lives. Where do the years go? Being here makes time double back and meet itself twenty years ago!

Love to Aleksander, Zosia, and Jan,
And to you, Julia, my dear friend.

Clare

Sept 10

Dear Sharon,

How are you? I don't know how the years go by so fast! We are
in Marburg again, and here, you are still a young woman with a
long, dark braid and a new baby. I often feel the urge to stop by the
Gästehaus to see you, since I still picture you living there.

We'll be here for a year. Stefan and I both have sabbaticals and
we're each supposed to be writing a book. Stefan is well into his
work, but I'm having trouble getting started. My dad died recently,
and I haven't quite gotten past that yet. Good thing I have a year.

How is Laura? And you have a son I've never met! I keep running
into so many memories and they remind me of friendships I don't
want to lose. I hope things are going well for you and your family.
We should get together again sometime when we get back.

Love to you, dear friend and fellow traveler on our baby
journey here in Marburg, twenty years ago.

Clare

Clare lifted her gaze from the computer screen to rest her eyes and return
to the world of the moment. She looked around the internet cafe and
wondered who each person was. *Why are they here? What connections are
they making at this moment? What inner thoughts and memories are they
sharing? The internet is a strange world that creates the illusion of intimacy
with others far away, while you completely ignore a stranger breathing right
next to you. A room full of bodies that are not fully there.*

A woman across the room seemed to be staring at her. Or maybe at
someone else. Clare checked behind her to see who else it might be. Too
many times in her life she had waved back to someone only to discover that
she was just an obstacle in their path, awkwardly lowering her hand as they
passed. But no, she seemed to be the person of interest. The woman stood

up and was walking towards her. The dark elegance of her face and the graceful confidence in her walk felt familiar to Clare, but who…

"Samira?" She shouted in a whisper. "Oh my God, is that you? *Salaan, sidee tahay?*" The words came out of her mouth before she had even thought them. Everyone turned to watch the two women embrace. "How *are* you, my friend?" she repeated in English.

"Clare, I knew it was you! You haven't changed."

"Neither have you. Well, maybe more beautiful. I have so often wondered where life has taken you. I even found your old phone number in my address book, but it didn't work. I thought maybe you had gone back to Somalia."

They each paid for their time on the internet and moved outside, talking as they walked.

"We did go back for a while to work in public health, but things were getting worse there and we couldn't stay. We are German citizens now and this is our home. Our kids are becoming more German than Somali. We try to speak Somali at home, but their lives are so much in German."

"Kids? How many do you have now?"

"Two. Bashir and Casho. A boy and a girl, just like you."

"Bashir would be nineteen now, like Anja."

"Yes, and Casho is sixteen. How is Stefan? And Willy must be all grown up. Do you have any more kids?"

"No, just the two. Stefan and I came here alone this time. Will is working and Anja is at the university. We're both on sabbatical with writing projects. Well, I'm supposed to be writing. It's hard to get started. It's a long story."

"We'll have to get together to catch up more. Give my regards to Stefan. Here's my phone number."

"And here's mine. Give my best to Omar."

"It's so great to see you!" Clare said, giving Samira another hug. "*Is arag danbe.*"

"I can't believe you remember that. *Is arag danbe, saaxiibkay.* See you later, my friend."

November 1980

"Julia! I'm so glad you could come to see our new place," Clare said as she opened the door to her Polish friend.

"I love it already! It's a sweet house from the outside, tucked away on this quiet little street." Julia was also charmed by the apartment upstairs. It was small, but not compared to the Gästehaus apartments. "The balcony, look at this view! I think you can see The Gästehaus from here. Oh, and here are some papers that Aleksander said to leave with you."

"Ah yes, I offered to check his English on a couple of articles he wrote. It will be interesting to read them."

"Good luck with that. It's about physics, which is kind of its own language, you know."

"Thanks, I am forewarned." Clare laughed.

"*Komm rauf,* Christina!" Clare yelled to the knock on the door at the bottom of the stairs. "Come on up!"

"I invited Christina to tea as well, Julia. I want you to meet each other. I think you have a lot in common, besides both being my dear friends."

"I brought some pastries from your favorite bakery." Julia said, setting a bag on the table."

"*Perfekt!*" Clare said as she went to greet Christina. She felt a swelling of joy as she introduced her two new friends to each other. It formed a circle for her as the women shook hands and began to chat while Clare went to fix the tea. She thought about whether to tell her friends what she suspected about being pregnant. But no, better to wait until she knew for sure. She hoped she could eat some of the pastry.

"Clare tells me you are from Poland. How long have you been in Germany Julia?"

"Not very long. We arrived in June, just a couple months before Clare. My husband is a physicist and is doing post-doctoral research at the University lab. And I, well, I'm taking German classes and being a mother. Have you always lived in Marburg, Christina?"

"No, I was born in the *Erzgebirge*, a mountain region in Czechoslovakia, and spent my childhood there. It was a small area on the border of East Germany. My parents were German and there had been Germans living in that region for hundreds of years."

"The Sudetenland, right?"

"Yes."

"What brought you here?"

"It's a crazy and complicated story. My family decided to leave. After my father died, we moved to West Germany to be near my mother's relatives who had been exiled here. I always considered myself German, but I had never lived in Germany. I went to school in Czech and heard it all around me. My homeland went from being Czech to part of Germany and then back again.

"I can relate to that. Poles have always lived in the middle, in constant fear of our neighbors invading our country, taking our freedom, and treating us as subhuman. That fear was the backdrop of my childhood."

"Yes, it was hard for me, too, growing up," Christina answered, her voice catching on the word "hard." "First, I was proud to be German, then people were mean to me for it. For a long time, I felt ashamed and tried to hide my identity."

"In Poland we were proud of our heritage but it was always under attack. Even after we gained some illusion of freedom, thanks to the Solidarity movement, the Soviets crushed it. We loved our homeland, but any hope of a better life was destroyed."

"That's the way *we* felt. We were poor, but the land was beautiful, and we were attached to it. The name changed, but it was the same land. Before I was born, much of my family had been forced out of their homes into exile, hauled away in cattle wagons. That image haunted my childhood, which ended abruptly when my father died. When we finally moved to what was supposed to be our homeland..." Christina paused and shrugged her shoulders. "...it wasn't home."

"And now *my* family and I are finding a home in the land of one of our enemies, while the other enemy takes over Poland again. What a world we live in." Julia sighed and reached out to squeeze Christina's hand as they sat in silence together.

Clare came back with a pot of tea and the pastries to see her two friends leaning towards each other. "I hope you two have been getting acquainted."

"Oh yes, just making small talk," Julia said, winking at Christina. They both laughed.

"We have a lot in common," Christina added, smiling back at Julia.

September 2000

Clare was dreaming about her father so often, that she didn't bother reporting to Stefan in the morning. Some of the dreams didn't make sense, but she still appreciated his presence. She wrote most of them down in her journal. It felt good to remember him each time.

September 16

He was just there, watching, listening, all night.

September 20

I had gone to visit Mom. I went into her bedroom to kiss her goodnight. I stopped in the doorway and was suddenly overwhelmed by something that filled me. I was dizzy and I couldn't move. I felt empty, yet filled, in a momentary trance. It was like I was dreaming. (!) From deep down inside me came a voice. Not really a voice, but a breathy distant whisper speaking through me. In barely formed words it said, "I love you." I knew it was Dad, but it wasn't really his voice. It wasn't clear if he was talking to me or to Mom through me. Maybe both. I felt Dad's fleeting presence as I awoke, as though he had just left the room.

Clare heard a high-pitched mewing sound on the stairs. One of the kittens had tried to climb up and got its tiny claws caught on the rim of a step. It wasn't strong enough to pull itself up and was left hanging there by its front paws.

"Hey, kleines Kätzchen, what do you think you are doing?" She picked up the little black kitten that fit easily in one hand and cradled it against her chest. "How about joining me on the balcony for a bit, little kitty?" She sat in silence, enjoying the fresh air and the company of the tiny being that purred in her lap.

"Do you know how lucky you are to live in this house?" she whispered, stroking its soft little ears.

November 1980

"Willy!" Remember we're going to go see the castle this afternoon. You need to get all your Legos picked up and clean your room before we go. Don't forget to take the broom to sweep the cobwebs out of the corners."

"But Mommy, they're so pretty. Look at this one." The morning light through the window had the spider's artwork glowing. "Does each spider have its own design? How does it decide which one to make? I think it's so cool that they can pull silk thread out of their butts like that."

"Okay, you can leave the spider webs, but get the floor clean and take the sheets off your bed."

It was Saturday, so the street market would be open on their way. They had long talked about walking up to the castle.

"The castle is from the 13th century, built on older castle remains from the 9th and 10th centuries!" Stefan shared enthusiastically with his son. "That's a very long time ago, kiddo."

"Like a hundred years?" Willy asked, his eyes wide.

"More like seven hundred years."

"Wow."

"Pretty cool, huh?" Willy nodded and they did a high five.

"I'm going to turn seven soon."

"You better get your room clean first." Stefan grabbed Willy around the middle and wrestled him onto the bed with a tickle attack.

"Okay, okay!" Willy wriggled and laughed.

The Marktplatz in the Oberstadt was full of the usual Saturday market street vendors. There were many kinds of foods: fresh breads, special cheeses, sausages, fruits and vegetables. Buckets of water held bouquets of colorful flowers next to tables of small crafts and toys. Clare loved the quiet bustle of people shopping and chatting, admiring the freshness of the fruit, and choosing items for their bags. Tourists took pictures of the old buildings around the marketplace.

It was a warm day for November, with big puffy clouds hanging over the rooftops, suggesting rain for the evening. They crossed the market square and climbed the steps towards the castle that watched over the whole town. It wasn't quite the Disney style castle that Willy had pictured, but up close it did seem full of mystery and fantasy. He imagined a royal family living there and maybe someone locked in a dungeon. There was a large garden behind the castle that was fun to run around in, but it seemed too normal for his royal fantasies.

Clare enjoyed trying to imagine life 700 years earlier right there in the same place. All those years since with many lives and stories woven around the structures that were still standing. Clare could picture a time lapse photo full of the colorful trails of human activity through the centuries.

On their way back they stopped for lunch at the Ratschänke, their favorite restaurant in an old building in the town square.

"Why is it called 'The rat...present'?" Willy asked. Stefan and Clare laughed, thinking he had made a joke. His face was serious, and he looked perplexed.

"It means 'Council Tavern' in German," Stefan explained, still chuckling. See the big house over there? That's the Rathaus," he said, pointing to the large stone building across the square. "The word means the Town Hall. It was the government office."

"You mean like the mayor?"

"Yes, *Rat* means 'advice,' so it applied to the leaders of the town. And the word sounds like *schenken*, which does mean to give a gift, but in this case it's spelled differently. So, this restaurant is where the town leaders would come to eat."

"There aren't any rats?"

"Nope, no rats in this story. Not on the menu either."

"*Ich will Schnitzel und Pommes Frites,*" Willy announced, without even looking at the menu. Schnitzel and French fries were his favorite meal, tasty and dependable. Clare had tried to get him to say "*Ich möchte...*" "I would like," ...a more polite way to ask instead of *Ich will*, "I want," but he owned that word and wouldn't be dissuaded.

"Will-he want Schnitzel or Will-he not? Willy will order what he will." Stefan said, savoring the word play.

"Silly Willy really will!!" Willy added, giggling hysterically at their private joke.

"I think I'll order "*Handkäse mit Musik,*" Stefan said, winking at Clare.

"Don't you dare!" she said, already wanting to gag. They had tried the stinky cheese dish before and just thinking about it made her wrinkle her nose. It was a soft cheese-like specialty of the region, based on curdled sour milk with a raw onion vinaigrette topping. The "hand cheese" was traditionally formed by hand and became quite pungent in odor and flavor when "ripe." The "music" referred to the ensuing flatulence that was part of the experience.

It was so very German to include that in the name, Clare thought.

"Seriously, you can order it all you want after we get past this morning sickness phase."

"We?" Stefan said, feigning innocence.

"You better believe it, Bud. We're in this together."

September 2000

Sept 26

It's been twenty years since I was last in Germany, and the memories (and my German) had drifted ever farther away. I could hardly put a sentence together when we got here in June. It's strange how fully they awaken, the language and the memories, when I'm here again. By now, I feel as though I never left. Every day I meet another old friend, a word I used to know that pops up in my mind in some context. It feels good in my mouth and lights up some small corner of my brain. It's like exploring the house of my subconscious and finding a secret forgotten room that has been closed for a long time. I clear away the cobwebs and there it is—a familiar word full of memories. I dust it off and it's good as new. German is not a Fremdsprache, a "foreign" language, for me, but rather an old Freundsprache.

When you carefully and tenderly peel away the layers (Schichten) of time, language, and memory, you find a whole Geschichte; a great word in German that, like the Spanish "historia", means both history and story. Our lives and their stories are layered in a time that is not linear or uniform. I feel like my life has curved around in a circle to meet our last stay in Germany twenty years ago, and the experiences are all connected by silken threads. In some ways, these two times are closer to each other than to all the twenty years in between.

A cat meow wandered through the house. Clare recognized the voice of a mother calling to her children, which was different than the sounds of hunger, pain or loneliness. Or the murmurs of contentment while nursing, the brief commentaries as she gave each kitten its bath. The kittens were growing up and straying farther from their mother and she expected them to check in regularly.

"You're a good mother, Kleine Mutti," Clare said as she reached down to pet her little housemate, who had just brushed against her leg and greeted her with a soft rising trill that sounded like a question. Clare answered with something similar in a falling tone.

"I'm learning your language, Little Mama, though who knows what I actually just said."

November 1980

They walked together in silence, letting the quiet of the Friedhof, the large cemetery nearby, settle over them. Even Clare's ever-present nausea had subsided for a moment. She looked at Christina, who walked next to her but was far away in her own thoughts. Clare had stopped to talk with her in their back yard and was surprised when Christina agreed to accompany her. Her new friend and downstairs neighbor seemed to be ever busy.

"I feel drawn to that peaceful space just over the fence from us," Clare had said. "Too bad we have to walk all the way down to the street and around to get to it."

"Yes, I know what you mean. I love that it is always there," Christina replied. Maybe it's a good thing we have that long walk first. It helps me unwind before I get there."

Christina stopped to look at a few grave sites that were nearly overgrown with ivy.

"It's interesting how complex our identities are during our lives, but after we die, we are reduced to such a simple story. This person, for example, died in 1953, the year I was born. We assume he was a typical German who lived in Marburg, but who knows what his life really was?"

Clare nodded and looked at her friend.

"I keep thinking about my conversation with Julia and how many layers our real stories have. I have lived most of my life in Marburg and have always felt German, and yet my family's history is complicated. I grew up bilingual, speaking both German and Czech. We were required to speak Czech in school. A few years before I was born, during the war and shortly after, the national boundaries shifted and shattered around my homeland, and many of my relatives were scattered, exiled far from our home."

"How old were you when your father died?"

"I was twelve. That was a sudden end to my childhood. About a year later we moved to West Germany, where my mother's relatives were. We lived in a refugee camp for a while. It was a long time ago, but I remember so clearly the feeling of chaos and uncertainty. And we were the lucky ones. Countless people had died on the Death March twenty years earlier, right after the war, when most Germans were forced out of the Sudetenland. It was a time of arbitrariness and cruelty. Some were shot for trivial reasons. Others died of illness, exhaustion, or starvation."

Clare hooked her arm around Christina's, and they walked on together in silence through the peace of the Friedhof.

September 2000

Clare awoke with new energy. It was a bright sunny morning that pulled her outside even before breakfast. Just a short walk to stretch her legs. She was feeling adventurous and decided to explore a little. She followed a small road, led by her curiosity. Soon *Hohlweg*, "Hollow Way," divided in two. Should she take the *Die Helle Hohle*—The Bright Hollow, or the *Die Dunkele Hohle*—The Dark Hollow?

She was intrigued by the bright one, so she started down the path. A chill washed over her under the large leafy trees that darkened the way. "I thought this was the Bright Hollow," she muttered. As the trees gave way to open fields, she welcomed the warmth of full sun with a shiver. But the "goose skin," as Germans called it, did not subside in the sunlight. She noticed the small bumps on her arms that made each hair stand on end. Then she saw a sign that said *Totenweg*. "Way of the Dead," she whispered. What is that about? Maybe she was already on it. "Okay, time to turn around."

Clare walked into the kitchen and immediately started answering the question in Stefan's eyes.

"I went for a walk, and I found this road, more of a path, really, called *Totenweg*. That was after following The Bright Hollow that didn't feel very bright. It was strange. I felt a dark energy even before I saw the sign. Do you know anything about why it's called Way of the Dead?"

"Good morning to you, too. You're up early." He zoomed in for a kiss.

"Oh, good morning. Sorry, I meant to leave a note." She sat down and took a sip of the coffee he offered. "I just woke up feeling like a walk and kept going. So, do you know anything about Totenweg?"

"Well, Marburg was part of the parish of Oberweimar until maybe the 12th century or so. The village of Oberweimar was the official religious center of the parish and I think folks had to take their dead there to bury them. Ockershausen was an independent village until the 16th century, so they would have continued taking their dead to Oberweimar until then."

"That's a long trek."

"Yeah. That's just the way it was, I guess. It must have seemed normal to them."

November 1980

It was a Sunday morning and Clare and Stefan stood on the little balcony looking out over the quiet city. Everything was closed on Sundays. They had learned to shop for the weekend on Saturday morning. Since they didn't have a car, they shopped almost daily. Sundays were a nice day off from that.

"Listen," Stefan said. The church bells were ringing, filling the air with overlapping tones of reverent invitation.

"I love that sound," she said, "the way it echoes around the city."

Thanksgiving was approaching and Clare wanted to have a big dinner with friends. Of course, it was not a German holiday, but everyone seemed on board. Even if she couldn't enjoy eating much, she welcomed the celebration of community.

"We need to find *eine schöne Pute*," Jürgen announced.

"*Eine schöne Puta?*" Clare couldn't contain her surprise and laughter. Jürgen looked perplexed.

"A beautiful whore?" she repeated in English.

He was usually quick on the uptake, but he couldn't understand where she was coming from.

Then she realized the translingual trick that her brain had played on her. The word *"Pute"* meant a turkey hen in German, but it sounded exactly like the word *"puta"* in Spanish, which meant "whore."

Like so many of the mistakes and misunderstandings throughout the year, this was added to their collection of jokes of the house.

It was a great Thanksgiving gathering. They had decided to have it at the house that their friend Michael shared with a few graduate students. Jürgen and Christina were there, as well as Nick and Sharon, Julia and Aleks, and Michael's friends. Willy, Jonas and Zosia sat together.

Clare was the last to arrive. She had come straight from an appointment with an obstetrician. Stefan looked up when she walked in. She smiled and nodded, and he crossed the room with his arms wide, ready to fold her into them.

"Can we announce?" he whispered through the wide grin on his face.

"Why not?"

They all sat down and held hands through a moment of silence. Clare's heart was pounding.

Stefan tapped his fork on a glass and stood up. "May I have your attention please? We have an announcement." He waited a moment as everyone turned towards him. With a hand on Clare's shoulder he said, "We are expecting a baby!"

"And I'm expecting a baby brother!" Willy piped up. "Or maybe a sister," he added, remembering what his parents had said.

Everyone applauded.

Nick glanced at Sharon, and she nodded. He stood up and looked around.

"I guess we should announce that we are also expecting a baby. It must be contagious."

More applause and laughter and the meal got off to a joyful start. Clare thought it was a perfect Thanksgiving meal, where each person brought their own favorite dish. It was an international feast, ending with the requisite pumpkin pie.

Clare patted her belly and said, "I feel so full." People looked at her in surprise, for they had noticed that she had only picked at her food. She laughed and said, "Nothing to see yet, but she's in there, believe me!" She had already adopted Stefan's certainty that it would be a girl.

Sharon gave her a knowing look. They, too, were expecting a girl. Even though they were both scientists, they had the same "gut" feeling.

September 2000

Sept. 30

I had the strangest dream last night, Hannah. I dreamed that your whole house was filled with giant spiderwebs. They hung down from the ceiling to the floor. They were so strong I could climb on them. In fact, that was the only way to get through the living room. You had to swing on them like vines. The patterns were beautiful and fascinating, but it was very inconvenient, and it was getting hard to live there. Stefan kept suggesting that we should clear them out, but I wouldn't let him. "They are art," I said, "and they belong to the house."

I woke up in the night and lay there for a while. What kind of spider could weave such a huge web? I got up, my heart racing, and tiptoed down the stairs, just to check. I felt silly, but it had seemed so real. The house was clear—no giant webs—so I went back to bed.

* * *

Clare liked walking to town to do errands. She knew that it would be more efficient to drive to a supermarket somewhere and stock up on food and other essentials. But shopping almost daily gave structure to her routine and got her out walking. Besides, it seemed like the German thing to do.

She picked up her pace, swinging the shopping bags as she went. The old folk song about flutes and violins kept running through her head and she found herself humming the tune. *"Hai dum diddledy dum..."* She sang the chorus aloud and could hear little Willy's voice echo in her memory on the *diddledy dum* part. A young woman approached on the sidewalk with her dog pulling hard on the leash. Clare smiled at the woman and bent slightly forward to reach out to the dog. She loved dogs and often found them to be a conversation opener between strangers.

The dog wagged its tail and thrust its nose towards her hand. The friendly gesture suddenly turned to bared teeth and a snarl that sent Clare stumbling backwards. She heard a growl behind her as she went down, her legs tangled in a confusion of leashes and dog wrestling. She hit the pavement hard and felt the scrape of bare skin against rough ground. The owners were shouting over what sounded to Clare like a fight to the death between the dogs. Dazed and immobilized by the leashes wrapped around her legs, she had a momentary vision of the two dogs turning on her and...*Move Clare! Get up! You have to get up!*

The din settled and she felt the straps loosen around her legs. The dog owners had managed to unhook the leashes and drag their pets apart, pulling hard on their collars.

"*Ach, mein Gott*, I am so sorry! Are you hurt?" she heard above her. The owners were each holding their dog with one hand and trying to untangle the leashes with the other hand. They finally managed to help her up.

"Are you alright?"

"I...I think so." Clare moved her legs and arms. Nothing broken.

"Oh no, look at your arm!"

The numbness of her forearm was just beginning to turn to sharp pain associated with a raw scrape that went from her wrist almost to her elbow. Her right knee began to throb as she watched blood drip from her arm onto her pants. The man behind her stepped up and handed her a cloth, which she wrapped around the scrape.

"I don't think it's serious," Clare said, still trying to orient herself to the shock of the whole incident. "I just need to get home and clean up."

The two dog owners consulted and by that time it seemed that maybe even their dogs were focused on helping her. The woman sat her down on a low stone wall, while the man went to hail a taxi, pulling his dog with him. The woman tied her dog to a small tree and then knelt to check Clare's leg, asking her to extend and bend it. "I'm so sorry," she kept repeating.

"Really, I'm okay. It was just a freak accident."

"We'll send you home in a taxi. Here's my phone number. Please call me later to let me know how you are."

Soon a taxi pulled up and the man helped her in the back seat. He handed her a business card with his contact information and gave the driver some money.

"Are you sure you'll be alright ma'am?" The driver asked as he walked her to her front door.

"I'll be fine, thank you. My husband will be home soon."

She heard the front door open as she sat drinking some tea and surveying her injuries. The cloth around her arm was spotted with red.

"Clare? I'm home. Thought I'd take an early lunch break, since I…good grief, what happened to you?!" Stefan stood with his mouth open as Clare shrugged her sore shoulders.

"Oh, I just got in a fight. You should see the other guy."

"Seriously, are you okay? What happened?"

"Well, I did get in a fight, or at least in the middle of one—between two dogs. It happened so fast; I'm still trying to understand it."

"Didn't anyone tell you that you shouldn't intervene in dog fights? It's very dangerous."

"I didn't intervene. I was just in the wrong place at the wrong time, in their way when they wanted to kill each other."

"Oh, well that's different. I assume they didn't actually manage to kill each other."

"No, they calmed down and looked at me like they wondered what I was doing there."

November 1980

"Come in, come in." Julia met Clare, Stefan and Willy at the door. "I'm glad you could come. We've missed you at the Gästehaus." The women hugged and the men shook hands. Willy ran to find Zosia.

"Thanks for inviting us. It's good to be back. And it's nice to see you both again, Marya and Noam." Clare went over to greet another couple that she had known from the early days at the Gästehaus. "Stefan, did you meet…"

"Yes, I believe we did," Stefan answered as he and Noam shook hands.

Noam and Marya Thalheim were from Israel and their son Yaniv was the same age as Willy and Zosia. The three kids ran out to play at the Spielplatz while the adults chatted, switching between German and English.

Clare had asked the Thalheims when they first met what had brought them to Marburg.

"Mainly Noam's work," Marya had answered. "He is an Old Testament scholar doing research at the university here."

"But we were also uncomfortable with the growing militarization and political extremism in Israel," Noam added. "It's ironic, in a way. We are Israeli Jews but we are more at home here in Germany."

"How long have you been here?" Clare had asked.

"Almost ten years. Yaniv was born here."

"Please sit down," Julia said as she brought the food to the table. Clare went out to the balcony to call the kids.

"I made you some Polish specialties," Julia announced when they were all seated. "These are *pierogi* with sauerkraut and mushrooms. Those are *golabki*, ground beef, mushrooms and onions wrapped in cabbage leaves. And of course, *gotowane ziemniake*, boiled potatoes."

"It all looks delicious," Stefan said.

Clare nodded, hoping she would be able to enjoy eating. The food looked wonderful. Julia patted her head as she walked by to sit down.

They shared bits about their lives and their work. Clare was surprised to learn that Julia had been a lawyer in Poland.

"We really struggled with the decision to leave," Aleks shared. "Julia would have to leave her work and to be honest, it was hard to come to Germany with the history between our two countries."

"My grandparents lost their home to the Germans, and they were evacuated on cargo trains," Julia added. But things have changed, and this was an incredible opportunity for Aleks. It was a professional dream for him. He could have access to computers, high quality lasers and other equipment."

"Tell us about your work, Noam," Julia invited.

Noam began to talk about his research. He fit Clare's stereotype of a dry and dusty academic and she struggled to keep her focus on what he was saying. As a scholar of ancient Hebrew and Greek, Noam's special interest was the many mistranslations of original biblical texts. *Oh, language and translation—that could be interesting.*

"It's not just about poor word choice. There were key contexts in which the translations egregiously, possibly intentionally, changed the significance of the whole message."

"Can you give us an example?" Clare's interest was awakened, despite her fading energy.

"For example," he offered, "the Hebrew word *chayil* used in the Old Testament originally meant 'strength,' 'force,' or 'liberty' and appears as such in many translations when referring to men. But when the same word refers to women, it is translated as 'virtue,' or 'chastity.'"

"Wow, that's crazy!" Clare blurted out.

"The biggest one is in Isaiah of the Old Testament—the story of a young woman who gives birth to a child who will be called Emmanuel. The pregnant woman is never called a 'virgin' in the original Hebrew. The word that is used just means 'young woman.' The Septuagint, the early Greek translation of the Hebrew Bible, includes a mistranslation. The Gospel of Matthew in the New Testament describes the 'Virgin birth of Jesus' by quoting that mistaken Greek translation."

"Oh my God, that's huge!" Julia said.

"It's staggering how little twists of words can alter history, especially for women," Marya added. "The Virgin birth is such a central theme for Christianity and women's place in it ever since. The pure mother chosen by God. A mother who never had sex."

7
Words and Dreams

September 2000

Clare found new places that hurt when she got out of bed the next morning. A few more bruises and scrapes appeared, seeming to have bloomed in the night. Stefan had taken her to see a doctor about the large scrape on her arm, which was now wholly bandaged. She noticed the bloody cloth in the trash. It looked like an old-fashioned white handkerchief that the man had handed her to cover her wound.

"How does it feel this morning?" Stefan checked the bandage to make sure it was on securely.

"Well, I need some new vocabulary to describe the subtle changes in pain, but at least my arm lets me know it's still there and doing its thing. I feel old and stiff."

"I don't see any injuries on your face, so I guess I can kiss you, right?" Stefan leaned in for a kiss, not waiting for an answer from Clare. She smiled and kissed him back.

"Thanks for taking care of me." They ate breakfast in silence. Clare kept shifting her position to accommodate a hip bruise and Stefan tried to shoo away images in his mind as his thoughts wandered to how bad the scene could have been if the dogs had turned on her.

"So how is your research going?" Clare was determined to move on.

Stefan studied her face for a moment. It wasn't the first time she had asked, but this time she seemed more genuinely interested.

"It's going very well and getting more interesting since I got a hold of the *Kirchenbuch.*" Clare understood the word literally as "Church book".

"Tell me more. What kind of book is this?"

It was a parish register from the early 18th century. The pastor had recorded every birth, baptism, marriage, and death in the nine villages of the parish of Oberweimar from 1700 to 1749, with some description about the circumstance and the family. Stefan was a social historian and he worked from primary sources to reconstruct as much as possible a narrative about the life, practices, and attitudes of the time.

"This document is amazing because it's a kind of diary by this pastor who witnessed so much. It tells what he saw, but also how his own attitudes changed and indirectly how it all affected him. I hope to tease out more than meets the eye from this text. People's attitudes toward death reveal so much about their lives."

"It must have been a hard job, being the pastor of a whole parish. Especially the death part." Clare had often noticed in her own time how central religious leaders were in the business of the social management of dying and death. The usual biblical references of Christianity had never done much for her, but she wasn't sure there were alternatives that would be any better.

"His name was Busch, Pastor Georg Wilhelm Busch. He was a Lutheran pastor for rural peasants in the wake of the Reformation and the rise of Lutheranism. Basically, he had to find some meaning and consolation for people for whom life was a struggle and death was part of daily life."

"We have our own George W. Bush these days," Clare said with a laugh.

"Ha! Think they might be related?"

"Yeah, like I am to the Virgin Mary. But seriously, do you think they could be?"

"Well, maybe very distantly, in the way English and German are related."

"So, I assume people died young in your George W's time."

"Yes. In 1724, the mean age at death was around 40. That's because many children died in their first year of life. Sometimes as many as half of the babies a woman gave birth to."

"Wow, what a life. Guess we have it easy."

November 1980

Clare had offered to help Jürgen with reading students' writing in English. It wasn't that she thought he needed her help as far as the English, but she just wanted to do something for him. And she had to admit that she was curious. How would his students manage the intricacies of writing in another language? It was a process that seemed so visual to her. She found herself often "seeing" words in her mind as she wrote. Not quite literally seeing the letters, but the shape of things verbal seemed to have a visual echo on the mental screen of her thoughts. How would that work for blind people? Would their brains process things differently as they wrote?

Jürgen gave her some exams from his advanced students, printed pages of short essay responses to questions. He suggested that she just read through some of them to see if she would have any questions for him. She sat looking over the first page as she finished her morning coffee. Suddenly she stopped. Wait a minute, how did they do this? Clare realized that she had been processing the writing unconsciously as always, not even questioning that it was the way she always read. Why is this not in Braille? Did someone translate, or transcribe it into this print type in English? It was such an obvious oversight, she recognized, laughing at the irony of the word "oversight." She ran downstairs to ask Jürgen about it.

"Oh, my advanced students learn to type on regular typewriters. You know, touch typing. They memorize where the letters are. It's quite different on a Braille typewriter, which has six keys that correspond to each of the six dots of the Braille code, a space key, and a line return key. They learn to use those first and it is easier for them, since they 'visualize' the words in Braille."

"It's fascinating to imagine what 'visualizing' would be like for someone who has never had vision. I wonder if they have some sort of images in their mind's eye?"

"We don't know a lot about it, but they do have a spatial sense of things and what's stored in their brains might be somewhat like visual memory."

Clare caught herself already trying to visualize what that might look like.

"But the pages I gave you were typed by the students on regular manual typewriters. So, when you read, you'll need to try to distinguish what are just typos from other misspelling or grammatical and lexical errors."

Wow, Clare thought as she went back to reading. That is another dimension of language learning. Spelling in English was often far afield from the phonetic representation of sounds. That must be an extra challenge, on top of the difficulties of writing in general. She was impressed with the students' writing, even without all those considerations.

September 2000

Clare couldn't stop thinking about how many children died in their first year of life in the times that Stefan was studying. How did people move on and have more babies? She remembered the courage that she had needed after the miscarriage just to try again.

October 2

Loss is part of life. But how much do we lose just through our fear of loss? My miscarriage was a blessing, nature's way of preventing tragedy by aborting an unviable life. I grieved the loss at the time, but at least it was more the loss of a dream than of a beloved child whose life was in our hands. I imagine that people didn't have the luxury to grieve the deaths of their parents much in those days. They were too busy burying their babies.

October 3

I dreamed that Dad was singing to me. He was rather young, and it was a sweet moment that I wanted to remember. I kept wanting to write it down—the dream (in my dream.) The rest of the night I kept dreaming that I needed to write down the dream about his singing to me. I didn't want to lose it.

October 5

A strange dream. The pastor was standing over the grave as they lowered a small, shrouded body into it. The family huddled around with bowed heads. The sky was gray, and a cold drizzle chilled the bones. I was there, I saw and felt it all but was watching the scene from above. The pastor began to read from a text. It went something like this:

> *But the righteous, though they die early, will be at rest. For old age is not honored for length of time, and a blameless life is ripe old age...*

I must have read something like that in Stefan's notes. It was supposed to be comforting that God had taken the child because she was already "ripe" in His eyes, the perfection of innocence. Suddenly I felt myself zoom down and I became

that mother standing there in helpless submission. "NOOO!!!
I shouted, lifting my face to a misguided God. "It wasn't her
time; she hadn't even begun to 'ripen'." When I woke up, I felt
bad for the pastor. He was probably trying to give them the only
consolation he could. Imagine the poor man having to do that
year after year. I would not have been a good Lutheran
in those days.

December 1980

"Happy birthday dear Willy, happy birthday to you..." they all sang, followed by "*Zum Geburtstag viel Glück...*" to the same tune. And then a song that Stefan had learned as a kid: "*Wir kommen all' und gratulieren zum Geburtstag unseren Willy heut'.*" "We all come to congratulate our Willy on his birthday today," Stefan translated for him. Then they sang it again as a round.

Willy was beaming at first but by the third rendition he was getting restless.

"Can we eat cake now?" he asked with an edge to his voice.

They had invited his best friends: Jonas, Zosia, Yaniv and a few others from school and the Gästehaus community. He had been excited planning the party, but today he seemed tired.

Clare looked at him for a moment with concern. He had dark circles under his eyes, accentuated by an unusual pallor. That morning she had asked him if he felt okay.

"I'm just 'cited 'bout the party," he answered with flushed cheeks against his pale face.

The kids played some games and then he opened his presents: a new Lego set from Zosia, a "really cool" metal tractor and dump truck from Jonas to play with in the dirt of their little cave under the bush in the backyard, a few other toys, and a colorfully illustrated book of fairy tales in German.

Parents arrived to pick up their kids and after brief visits, all were gone.

"Happy birthday, Willy," Clare said, giving him a hug. "Are you okay?" He didn't look well. His appetite had been subdued recently and she noticed he hadn't even finished his cake.

"Let's get you to bed and maybe check with the doctor if you don't seem better tomorrow." He didn't resist when she tucked him in early.

"Mommy, can you sing '*Gut Nabend*?'"

Clare sat on the edge of his bed and began singing "*Guten Abend, gute Nacht, mit Rosen bedacht, mit Näglein besteckt, schlupf unter die Deck'*..." Halfway through the first verse of *Wiegenlied*, Brahms Lullaby, he was already asleep. She tiptoed out of his room and stopped in the doorway to look back at him once more. Something was clearly not right. Looking at Willy's pale face made her stomach tighten.

"*Schlaf süß, mein Liebchen*," she said as she closed the door. "Sweet dreams, my dear little one."

The rest of the verse kept singing in Clare's mind as she drank a cup of tea. *Morgen früh, wenn Gott will, wirst du wieder geweckt*..."Tomorrow morning, if God wills, you'll awaken again..." She shuddered and went to bed. What kind of lullaby suggests to a kid that he might not wake up the next day, or only if God wills it? It wasn't as bad as Rockabye Baby, where the branch breaks and the cradle crashes to the ground. *What's wrong with people? Kind of like most of the fairy tales, I guess.* Clare knew that the Brothers Grimm didn't write those tales, they had just collected them. Still, their last name seemed apt for most of the stories.

The next morning Clare let Willy stay home from school and sleep late. She hoped that the extra sleep might perk him up. Stefan had gone off to work but he promised to come home early that afternoon. After he got up, Willy played quietly in his room with his new Lego set. He looked a bit better, but she decided they should visit the doctor anyway.

"Mommy?"

"Yes Willy," she answered absently, expecting to be called in to see a new Lego creation.

"Mommy?" he said, now standing next to her.

"What is it, Willy?" She looked at him carefully.

"I was playing with my Legos, and I felt something funny. It was...it was tickling my butt and I didn't know what it was. So, I reached into my pants and..."

Clare's mind froze and couldn't imagine what would follow.

"...and I pulled out a snake."

"What? A what?!" For a second, she wondered if this was one of his Silly Willy jokes.

She put her hands on his shoulders. His blue eyes looked as earnest as ever.

"Okay, tell me again."

"I grabbed something that was tickling me and pulled and pulled and out came a snake." Clare felt queasy. Snakes were on her short list of things she could not deal with.

"Want to see it? It's in my room."

She followed him on shaky legs and there on the floor in the corner of his room was a snakelike something with its head sticking up above a coil. *Is this some sick joke between Stefan and Willy - one of those rubber snakes to tease people like me?* Then she saw it move.

"Mommy?"

"Mommy?" What's wrong? Why don't you say something? Are you okay?"

Clare pulled herself back from the urge to faint and snapped into action. She took Willy into the living room and closed his door. "You wait here. I'm going downstairs to see if Jürgen and Christina are home."

"I'll be right back…" she called from halfway down the stairs.

Jürgen opened the door to her urgent knocking. She was so glad he was there. He knew a lot about natural remedies. Sometimes he gave her some fresh herbs for her nausea. He seemed to have a cure for everything. They affectionately called him *Herr Hexe,* "Mr. Witch."

"Willy pulled something out of his butt…a snake? I don't know…could you please come upstairs?"

Jürgen went to the kitchen and calmly got a jar with a lid and a paper bag and followed her upstairs. He picked up the "snake" and examined it before putting it in the jar. *"Ein Spulwurm, ja,* that's a nice *Spulwurm,"* he said, looking at Clare. When he saw her face, as pale as Willy's, he sat her down in a chair.

"Don't worry, it's just a roundworm. They're quite common. This is an impressive one, though." He put the jar in a paper bag and handed it to Clare. "Take it and Willy to the doctor and they'll give you some medicine to clean him out."

The doctor took the jar out of the bag and whistled. *"Das ist ein schöner Spulwurm!"* You could go fishing with that." He showed it to the nurses, and they laughed and were impressed as well. Clare didn't think it was the least bit cool or funny.

"Don't worry." the doctor told her. "There's no shame in it. Anyone can get them."

Did he realize that was not reassuring?

"Does he play outside a lot? In the dirt or a sandbox?"

"Oh yes, all the time."

"Has he seemed tired and rundown lately?"

Clare nodded.

"This creature has been stealing nutrients from him for quite a while."

Kind of like being pregnant, Clare thought, and then she was horrified by the image.

"I'll give you some medicine and vitamins to give him," the doctor went on. "You need to clean his room, wash the sheets and his clothes well to make sure there are no eggs around. Also scrub under his fingernails. He could pick it up again or someone else could."

"Could…could I get it? I'm pregnant and…" She could already imagine a tickling feeling…

"Possibly, but you couldn't take the medicine until your third trimester, so…just wash your hands well."

It took months to erase from her mind the image of the worm-snake inhabiting her little boy, stealing his food as it grew. And the other unthinkable one of that thing growing inside her, curling around her womb next to her baby, taking nourishment from both of them. She washed her hands a lot.

October 2000

"I can't believe we're sitting here together again, twenty years later in the same place. Some things don't change." Clare squeezed Samira's hand and studied her face. The same high cheekbones and smooth, dark skin. And the fire in her eyes.

There they were at their favorite meeting spot, Café Barfuß, at the same corner table where they used to sit. The sounds of life on the street drifted in through the open door. Clare thought it was crazy how time went by, seemingly slowly at the time, but then, looking back, it just collapsed into a blurry streak.

"It's so good to see you again, Clare."

"So…," they both started, and then laughed together.

"You first," Clare said. "Give me the short version of those twenty years."

"Well…, let's see. Omar and I both finished graduate school. Omar is a doctor now, a pediatrician, and I got a degree in public health. I focus on women's health and related social issues. We thought we would go back to Somalia, where that kind of work is sorely needed."

"And you did go back, right?"

"Yes, after Casho was born. I had really wanted to see my parents and for them to meet their grandchildren. We decided to go for a year to see if we might consider moving back permanently. It was great to be with family and reconnect with our culture. For a while we thought it could work long term, but the government was becoming oppressive, and we worried for our kids. Especially Casho. I couldn't imagine raising a daughter in a society where women's rights were becoming more and more restricted.

"We had been in Somalia for about a year when Omar was offered a job in Marburg. It was too good to pass up, so we came back. I've been working in public health with refugees here at the immigrant center, focusing on women's health and social needs. There have been a lot of Somali refugees, even outnumbering the Turks recently. I deal especially with issues around female sexuality, health, pregnancy, and childbirth."

"How do refugee women react to you as an independent Muslim woman?"

"It's a challenge. Sometimes they can't accept me and my modern ways, but since I speak their language and understand their culture, they at least let me help them. So, what about you, Clare? Tell me about your life."

"That's a long story as well, but not nearly as interesting as yours," Clare began. "I went back to finish a PhD in Spanish language and literature and have been a professor ever since. It's a very busy life that is sometimes stressful, but I love it. This sabbatical certainly came at a good time for me to regroup."

"Sounds like it is well deserved," Samira commented.

"Well, certainly much needed. My father died recently, and I am still struggling with the grief."

"I'm so sorry. Was it unexpected?"

"Yes, it was quite a shock. I hadn't really processed it until I got here. But I'm doing better now."

"Samira…"

113

"Yes?"

"Would you like a kitten?"

December 1980

Willy regained his healthy color and energy and continued playing in the dirt outside. There was no point in making him anxious about things. He seemed to shrug off the Spulwurm episode as one more adventure. He'd always been fascinated by worms and other creatures around the creek near their house back in Iowa. Clare had had a hard time keeping him out of that creek, and he would deny that his muddy shoes were from there. So now, in Marburg, she just let it go. But she often checked his face for signs of fatigue.

He was comfortable in school and would sometimes read aloud to her in German. One day Clare was in the back yard when he came striding up the hill from the bus. She waved and he walked with her to the house.

"Those bushes have some kind of sour stuff on them," he announced with authority.

"Sour stuff?" Clare repeated, puzzled by the idea.

"Yeah, plants do that. They put it out in the air and people need it. I learned it at school today."

"Hmm..." Clare didn't want to challenge what he was learning at school, but... "Ah, she said thoughtfully. How did they say it in German?"

"*Sauerstoff*. Just like I told you. Sour Stuff." Clare stifled a chuckle before explaining.

"Remember how I told you that German often puts words together to make new ones? Kind of like describing the thing. Do you know what oxygen is?

"Something in the air?"

"Yes, we need it to breathe. In German they call oxygen *Sauerstoff* because...well, scientists used to think that oxygen had something to do with acids, which are sour. The word 'oxygen' kind of means that from its Greek roots..." Clare stopped because her explanation seemed to be getting more confusing, even to her.

"Well, it doesn't smell sour to me," he said. "But I think it's cool that plants help us breathe."

"It sure is. And, by the way, good job at school."

Stefan came up the stairs right after them, singing as he climbed. Clare joined in the round, as a voice echoing from above.

"Froh zu sein bedarf es wenig, und wer froh ist, der ist König."
"Froh zu sein bedarf es wenig...

Stefan had taught it to her years before and they hadn't sung it together for a long time. Pretty soon Willy was picking up on it.

"Did you understand the words?" Stefan asked him.

"Something about being happy and a king?"

"Yes. It says that it doesn't take much to be happy, and whoever is happy is a king."

"Or a queen." He smiled conspiratorially at Clare. "It sounds happy. Let's do it again!"

October 2000

Oct. 15

I've been thinking about writing. I mean in the theoretical sense. Poetry is a radical form of writing - a radical act. Why is that? I think it's because it puts together things that "aren't supposed to" go together. Who says they aren't? Life is poetry. Narrative is our way of trying to make sense out of the fragments we are given. Dreams do that, too, but they are more honest about the chaos.

I have been reading a lot. I need to get busy on my book. Don't even have a title yet. Something about fiction and time?

* * *

Clare sat in front of the computer at the internet café, rereading the brief email from the chair of her department. She had been dreading the question that she knew would come.

Oct 14

Hi Clare,

I hope you and the family are well. We miss you here! The new assessment stuff is driving us crazy. I hate to ask, but could you respond to the attached questions? We need your input.

How's the book going?

Cheers,
Nancy

Oct 15

Hi Nancy,

We are doing fine, thanks. I hope you are well and surviving being department chair. It's a tough and thankless job and I appreciate your being willing to do it. I don't look forward to my next turn!

It has taken a while for me to get back into academic mode. I'm still in kind of a slump that way but life is full and challenging here. I am learning so much and my German has come back strong. I have written many letters of recommendation for my students. I promised I wouldn't abandon them this year. I've also been reading. Lots of ideas, but I haven't had the courage to start writing yet. I'll be happy to answer the assessment questions and will get to it soon.

All the best,
Clare

December 1980

I've been thinking a lot about the slipperiness of words, Clare wrote in a letter to her parents. She had learned her love of language from them.

We use them, and we know what they mean to us and hope that they will arrive intact to others. But most of the time we don't know their origin or even the nuances contained within them. A word is just a collection of sounds that we associate with objects, actions, qualities... often an intersection of multiple meanings and contexts.

Clare's contemplations had arisen out of frustration trying to sort out the latest slang words that appeared everywhere, which made it hard to pin down their meaning.

One word in German that everyone seems to love to use is 'toll.' I know it is a positive reaction to a situation or experience, something like 'cool' or 'great' or 'wonderful' in English, but I'm still not entirely sure when to use it. I looked it up in my dictionary and that just made matters worse!

Toll: adj. mad, crazy, raging, wild, furious, boisterous, great, marvelous, terrible...The list went on and on. It seems to be a word that could fill any hole, a kind of expressive glue. Or maybe a seasoning. At least now I understand my own confusion!

October 2000

It was a soft day, as Clare's Irish relatives would say when the sky was gray, and a mist brushed your skin with an almost rain. Christina had stopped by and invited her to go for a walk. They followed the street down the hill, stopping for a moment to admire the view of the castle. Christina suggested that they walk in the Friedhof, the large cemetery next door to the house where they had lived together twenty years earlier. Clare agreed eagerly since it was one of her favorite places to walk. The still green grass glowed under the overcast sky and the leaves above them were beginning to turn colors.

Clare paused and took a deep breath. "It's so peaceful here."

"*Ja*," Christina agreed.

"How's the kitten doing?"

"She seems fine, though she cries occasionally. I think she's looking for her mother."

"Thanks so much for taking her."

117

"Hey, we've already fallen in love with her."

The clean paths and occasional benches made it feel like a park; an inviting place to stroll and chat or sit and listen to the sounds of life around. Clumps of rhododendron bushes reminded Clare of her Pennsylvania childhood. Christina paused to read the names on a few grave sites, cryptic stories of the lives of families or occasionally a lone child.

"I want to show you something," Christina said, taking Clare's arm and leading her up the path. They stopped in front of a newer grave.

"*Adele Irene Schröder*," Clare read, her voice slowing on the last name, as she realized who it was.

"She died last spring. It was peaceful. I went to see her a few times in the nursing home. Then her daughter called me one day and urged me to come quickly. I hurried over, but Adele was already gone. She was still lying in her bed with that same kind face we had grown to love. I was glad I could be there for her daughter and honor the passing of a sweet and gentle woman."

"*Adelita*," Clare whispered, "*te voy a extrañar, mi amiga*. I'm going to miss you, my friend," she said in German for Christina's sake. "I hope they speak Spanish in Heaven."

***

Oct 22

Dear Clare,

Thanks for doing the assessment stuff. I know how much fun it is! :-)

As for the book, don't worry. It will happen. You surely have a case of burn out fatigue. It's so common in our profession, especially for women. The same thing happened to me on my last sabbatical. I had a great project and thought I would jump into it. But as soon as I let go of things I crashed for a while—a long while. I eventually got going when I was ready and then it went quickly. (That's why I always advise folks to take a yearlong sabbatical, even though you lose some income.) So be patient and don't beat yourself up about it.

I recently read an article about women in academics and how they often put so much into their work, their students, the institution, that they burn out. A kind of motherly sense of responsibility makes it hard to set limits on the endless needs before them. And then there is the sense that we need to work harder than the men to prove ourselves in academia. Not to mention the grieving process you are going through, which they say takes about a year.

Enjoy the Germany experience to the fullest and the writing will come!

Best,
Nancy

December 1980

Die Weihnachtszeit, the Christmas season, was approaching, and Willy was excited. Clare's relationship with food was improving and a little baby bump was beginning to show.

Christina and Jürgen helped them stay on top of German traditions for a child's Christmas. On the night of Dec. 5, Willy had put his yellow rainboots outside the door to his room so that *Sankt Nikolaus* could fill them with nuts, candy, and a few small gifts. It was usually just one boot that got filled, but Willy thought his were too small, so just in case he put out both.

Jonas told him about a guy named *Knecht Ruprecht*, who would sometimes come with St. Nikolaus to decide which mischievous children needed to be taught a lesson. Sometimes they would just get coal or a switch in their boots, but in extreme cases he would capture children in his sack and take them to the dark woods to scare them. When Willy told his parents about that, they assured him that it was an old story that wasn't real. And anyway, he was a good boy. They wouldn't even let that guy in the house. Still, he had trouble falling asleep that night.

The next morning, Willy got up very early to see if he could catch sight of St. Nikolaus. His boots were already filled with goodies, and he ran to wake up his parents to show them. They tried to act surprised and excited and told him he could open the gifts, before settling back into their interrupted sleep. Willy sat on the floor by their bed sorting the nuts and candy into piles and lining up the small gifts, wanting to wait to open them when his parents could watch.

As soon as Stefan opened an eye, Willy bounced on the bed and told them it was time to get up. He was pleased with the gifts, even though there weren't any Legos. Maybe *Sankt Nikolaus* didn't know about Legos. He loved the matchbox cars, though, and he started creating a little racetrack for them with his old Legos.

Every morning Willy got to open a window on the *Adventskalender*. There was a small chocolate candy under each window as well as a colorful picture of the season. He was counting down the days until Christmas, though he wasn't sure what it would be like since St. Nick had already come. But then maybe that was the German *Sankt Nikolaus*, and the real Santa Claus could still come. He didn't want to seem greedy, so he didn't ask. He would just wait and see.

They went with Jürgen, Christina, Jonas, and Lucas to a couple of the *Weihnachtsmärkte* in town. These were colorful, joyous outdoor Christmas markets, with lights and all kinds of special treats, crafts, and small handmade figures you could buy. It was hard for the boys to keep their hands off the many tempting things laid out right within their reach. They were each allowed to choose two things to buy. What a torture to make those choices! There was also *Glühwein* and *heißes Shokolade* to warm them up before they headed home. Clare bought a couple of angels for their small Christmas tree and Stefan bought some *Stollen*. Of course, he and Jürgen had to joke about having stolen it. *"Wir haben den Stollen gestohlen."* Willy laughed hard at the joke, proud that he got it.

Nick and Sharon came over for a Christmas Eve dinner together. Nick and Stefan prepared a special meal, while the two women rested on the big bed, trying to will their stomachs to enjoy the food. At one point Clare and Sharon turned their heads to look at each other and then said *"Übelkeit!"* in unison. They laughed at their favorite German word for the nausea they shared, loving the way it sounded like what it was. It had the feel and the sound of the English expression "Eew," so a literal translation of *Übelkeit* would be something like "eew-ness."

"But you know, the smells from the kitchen are making me hungry. I feel like I could eat a real meal."

"Yeah, me too. A Christmas dinner almost sounds appealing. That's exciting, isn't it?"

"Look!" Willy shouted as he pointed at the windows. "It's snowing!" They all went out to the balcony and let the large flakes fall on them. No one had expected to see snow and it was extra special for their first Marburg Christmas.

Santa Claus did arrive somehow on Christmas Eve with a few presents, though Jonas told him the next day that it was the *Christ Kind* who brought the gifts. The Christ Child. They argued about it for a while and then decided there was probably room for both. Willy thought it was kind of dumb to expect Baby Jesus or any baby, for that matter, to handle such a job. But he didn't say anything about that. Stefan told Clare later that Martin Luther kind of invented the idea of the *Christ Kind* in the 16th century, but they stayed out of the boys' argument.

Willy had made a couple of presents for his parents and they were thrilled by them. He was getting good at *basteln,* the making of small crafts out of whatever one could find. He had snatched some corks left from wine bottles and asked his mom for toothpicks. Then he made reindeer out of them and painted faces on them with his markers. He made a sleigh out of a small box and a Santa with red paper and cotton. He glued everything onto a piece of cardboard. His parents were surprised even though they had seen parts of it along the way. He also made a Christmas painting with his watercolors.

Willy thought it was the best Christmas. He even got some more Legos.

November 2000

"Morgen, Schatzi. Ich hoffe, du hast von Engeln geträumt," Stefan said as he looked up from his notes. They were now speaking German with each other most of the time. He often greeted her that way in the morning, hoping that she had dreamed of angels.

"Ja, Liebling, sehr hübsche Engel, muß ich sagen," Clare teased him, saying she had and that they were very handsome angels indeed, even though she knew it was just an expression to ask someone if they had slept well.

"Are you still obsessed with death today?" She kissed the top of his head.

"Yes, definitely. It's a bit tedious sorting through so many entries in the register and deciphering Busch's handwriting and his 18th century German.

Quite a guy. All those births, baptisms, marriages, and deaths - giving blessings, sermons, Bible verses, and recording it all by hand."

"It was good of him to be so thoughtful for you nosy historians a couple hundred years later." Clare thought of her own journal and who might read it in some distant future. Something to think about.

"He even buried his own wife along the way."

They lingered for a while after breakfast, chatting about home.

"Did I tell you I got an email from Anja? It seems like her classes are going well. She loves the theater class. I think that might be a serious direction."

"Well, whatever calls to her is a good thing, as long as she also takes a variety of classes," Stefan replied, leaning back in his chair. "I think that's built into the general requirements."

"Did you see anything new about the election yesterday when you were on the internet?"

"No, just the same questions and speculation. And tempers are rising on both sides. I feel sorry for Gore. First, he graciously conceded, then he had to call back that night to take it back. And now, it's just wait until they sort it out, I guess."

Clare and Stefan had mailed their vote-from-abroad ballots as early as possible and then followed the results on Jürgen and Christina's television. It was very close, but undecided.

"It's crazy, here we are the supposed leader of the free world, and we can't get our shit together." Stefan said. "At the moment we still don't even know who the next president will be."

"The recount in Florida may decide things. I think Gore will win. People are finally beginning to realize how important it is to pay attention to the environment."

"I hope you're right. But people also don't like to hear bad news."

* * *

Nov. 11

How could Pastor Busch bear to watch so many small bodies being lowered into that cold ground? Did he ever get angry with God? I'm not sure if I even believe in God, but I still get angry with Him. Really? Why did I say "Him"? I guess I still have an image of some old man in the sky, which is so childish. We seem to need a face, even one to not believe in. Guess we don't have anything better to replace it with.

Nov. 12

Hannah, I started reading one of your books about the history of Fachwerkhäuser, those beautiful half-timbered houses I love. It's fascinating and has great pictures. I read that they have been around since the early Middle Ages. I keep wondering how old your house is. I feel the presence of many, many years of stories in its walls. Layers and layers of Geschichte. I think the construction of those houses is clever and attractive.

Clare opened her laptop to write. She clicked on a file titled "Notes for Book" and sat for a while contemplating the fragments of ideas of the first pages. There was a section of loose phrases and possible titles.

Notes for Book

Layers of Fiction? The Fictions of Fiction? The Truth of Fiction?

She had begun to jot down anything that came to her, thoughts that had sprouted during the summer and fall, no matter how wild and disjointed they seemed. She, who had taught literature and even creative writing, and had coached, evoked, and evaluated her students' writing for years, had found herself helpless in the face of a monolithic nothingness when it came to her own book project. It seemed too big, too distant, too theoretical from outside the walls of academia.

"Just write," she had often told her students. "Write anything. It may be a beginning, middle or end. You may weed it out later, or it could be the seed of a whole thesis. Just start."

As she gradually shed the layers of responsibility, stress and grief, Clare had felt she was drifting ever farther away from such a huge undertaking. It reminded her of what she called "The Moo Factor," a concept she had read about twenty years earlier during their first stay in Germany. It explained, in a rather humorous manner, how even the most intelligent and professional women would feel their minds being affected during pregnancy and nursing by a bovine-like retreat into their bodies as they built and then nurtured a new being.

"Well, it's a start," she told herself. She patted her belly, like old times during pregnancy, as she felt a "quickening," a flutter of life in her new writing project that had already been gestating quietly inside for several months.

December 1980

"*Prost Neujahr!*" They all shouted as they clinked their glasses of *Sekt* or whatever else they were drinking. The kids and Clare and Sharon had some non-alcoholic sparkling juice. Clare and Stefan had invited their friends to celebrate *Silvester* with them, the German name for New Year's Eve. Jürgen and Christina were there, with a few of their own friends, as well as Aleksander and Julia, Nick and Sharon, Noam and Marya, their neighbor Adele, and Michael. Willy, Jonas, Lucas, Zosia, Yaniv and two other kids were in constant motion, weaving through the adults, chattering in fluent German.

Right at midnight the sky filled with fireworks, illuminating the fairy tale city with multicolored flower-like explosions. Church bells all over town rang in joyful accompaniment. The adults toasted to the new year and the babies-to-come. Clare and Sharon celebrated the end of the Age of Nausea as they patted their growing bumps. From their balcony, the view twinkled with the lights and wishes of houses across the dark nightscape. The castle was lit up at the top of the hill as always, bathed in the golden glow of the imagination. Stefan made a toast to new friends and new experiences, and they all clinked to that as well.

"Happy New Year!" Willy echoed one more time in his solo voice, raising his glass high over his head.

8
Inside the Walls

November 2000

Clare sat at the usual table in Café Barfuß, sipping her coffee as she watched shoppers and casual strollers go by on the street. She still marveled at the relaxed pace of most people in the streets of the Oberstadt. Maybe it was the cobblestones that slowed people down. Or possibly the atmosphere of old buildings, watched over by a castle, that cast a spell on them.

"*Hallo* Clare. Sorry I'm late." Samira leaned down to give her a kiss on the cheek.

"Samira, hi! No problem. I was far away in my thoughts."

"I brought a friend, hope you don't mind," *Ich habe eine Freundin mitgebracht,* Samira said, switching to German as a young woman stepped forward. "We met at the immigrant support center."

"*Na sicher, kein Problem,*" Clare answered, continuing in German. "Of course! No problem. It's nice to meet you," she said, taking in the short dark hair and broad smile of Samira's companion. A slight gap between her front teeth added a charming, almost impish warmth to her smile. Long eyelashes drew attention to her dark, deep-set eyes under gracefully arched black eyebrows that suggested an ever-present question.

"Clare Muller," she said, holding out her hand.

"Isra Baris, nice to meet you."

"Isra just moved here from Berlin, with her partner Esin. She is originally from Turkey," Samira added.

They settled into coffee, cake, and light conversation.

"What brings you to Marburg?" Clare asked, looking for a way to wade in deeper.

"Esin, my partner, was offered a job here in microbiology research. The job was too good to pass up."

"And you…"

"Yes, well I haven't found anything yet. I'm still trying to figure out what my life here will be. Esin got to Berlin a few years before I did, and she was already well along in her career. I didn't want to leave Berlin, but I also didn't want to hold Esin back. So here we are."

"It's hard to uproot and start again," Clare said sympathetically. "I've heard that Berlin has become a dynamic and diverse city. It sounds like you had settled in well there."

"Yes, we had."

They sat for a while, sipping their coffee.

Clare looked directly at Isra, who was staring into the coffee cup she held firmly in both hands. She sensed that Isra had more to share but it wasn't easy.

"I hope this works out for both of you. It's good that you found the Immigrant Center. Samira has helped a lot of people find connections and opportunities here."

Clare was proud of her friend, who had not only made a good life for herself but had also offered a hand to many others along the way.

"It's hard when who you are doesn't fit anywhere," Isra said, breaking the silence. She hesitated and looked at Samira, who encouraged her with a nod. Clare had the feeling that Samira already knew much of Isra's story. "My family in Turkey is strict Muslim, so the idea of even an independent woman is hard for them. When I took off my head covering and cut my hair, that was the first step that was not acceptable. For them it was an extreme act of betrayal. I believe that head covering does not make you Muslim and taking it off does not make you non-Muslim. It's a multi-layered symbol, but many people do not see that."

"Well said. I had a similar experience." Samira ran her hands over her own long hair, as though still surprised to find it uncovered.

"After that, there was no way that I could admit to being attracted to women as well. Even though women spend much of their lives in the company of other women, the notion of intimate relations is unthinkable. I don't know why it needs to be such a huge political-religious thing. We just love who we love. My parents wanted to arrange a marriage for me, just to 'get me on the right path' quickly. That's when I knew I had to leave. You know, my name, *Isra*, means 'Freedom' in Turkish. Kind of ironic, huh? My parents should have thought about that when they named me."

Clare smiled and nodded.

"Anyway, here I am, a bit lost in my freedom," Isra said with a sigh. "With this bundle of contradictions that I am, it's hard to find a place in a world that likes neat categories."

"I know what you mean." Clare often felt that way, even though by all outward appearances she seemed to fit the norms.

"I think identity is like a buffet." Isra paused and looked at each of her new friends. "You start with what you are given and choose the parts that work for you. You fill your own plate and create your own unique self. Why is that so threatening to people? I hope I can find a community here like the one we had in Berlin, where people like me can find a home."

"I think you will find your community here. It will take some time, but I have a few ideas," Samira reassured her. "Hey, how about we meet here again next week."

"Sure. Same time?" Clare smiled at her new friend. "You are welcome, Isra, if you are free."

Clare replayed Isra's story in her mind as she walked home. Why did Isra have to give up so much just to be herself? Why does anyone? No one fits easily in one box. I sure don't. It makes me angry to be rejected because the boxes are too small. How hard it must be to be Isra!

* * *

Nov. 15

I think we are all migrants in search of a meaningful life as we flee the prisons that confine us. It's about freedom and belonging. We look for webs of connection that bind us to our ourselves. We are not just one thing or the simple negation of something else.

January 1981

The kids had a few more days off from school and they even got some snow to celebrate the new year. Willy, Jonas, and Lucas made a small snowman that began to droop as the day warmed up. The kids never ran out of things to entertain themselves. One day they decided to dress like *Schlümpfe*. They wore blue shirts and pants with their white thermal underwear on their heads to imitate the classic Smurf image. They painted their faces blue and bounced around together singing *"Wir sind die Schlümpfe, wir sind die Schlümpfe! We are the Smurfs!"* It was quite comical, and Clare took pictures. Getting the blue color off was much less fun than putting it on. That's pretty much always true of cleaning up, Clare mused, as she helped Willy scrub his face clean.

* * *

"Warum gibt es Jahre?" Willy asked a few days into the New Year.

"Why are there years?" he repeated in English when no one answered.

"So we can have birthdays," Stefan responded, distracted by his reading.

"Coward," Clare whispered to him, thinking he took the easy way out.

"But who made them up?" Willy insisted.

"Well…" Clare began, thinking that maybe Stefan's approach was better after all.

"History." Stefan answered.

"But who made history?"

"Okay, *Herr Fragen*, I think you have swallowed too many questions and it's time to tickle them out of your tummy." Stefan jumped up, already wiggling his fingers. Willy shrieked and laughed as his Dad chased him around the table.

"The answer is a very long story, kiddo," Stefan said as they both collapsed on the couch to catch their breath. "Maybe you'll be able to explain it to me someday when you grow up."

After that, *Herr Fragen*, "Mr. Questions," became one more of Willy's nicknames.

Fortunately for all, school would start again soon.

November 2000

Nov. 23

I cried a lot in my dreams last night. It wasn't clear why. Dad put his arms around me and just let me cry. Then I composed myself and said, "I need to let you go now." He looked at me a moment. "I don't have much else to do these days," he told me. Then he put his hands on my shoulders and added, "but I know you need to move on. You are ready now." As I was walking away, he called after me: "You can still come see me whenever you want."

You know, Hannah, I think dreams ARE real. They are as true as any of our memories and stories. They tell us things about ourselves that we can't see through our waking minds. At night the brain tries to defragment itself and clean up the debris of the day – all those many things that we let fall as we stumble through our experience. Just as historians take fragments and texts of the past and try to reconstruct a rational narrative out of them, our dream writers sweep up the detritus of our experience and try to construct emotionally coherent stories.

I'm really getting into reading these days and I feel like my brain is waking up.

* * *

Notes for Book

Writing to understand

Writing arises out of the multiple experiences of life. Everything we see and feel and hear filters into our thinking and the way we read, the trails we follow in our research. The intellectual life is not abstract (literally "drawn away from" life) but rather centered in it. It is an attempt to understand deeply what we think we know experientially, a kind of "self-conscious" excavation to which we bring our whole selves.

A sharp tapping sound startled Clare from her journal writing. Where was it coming from? She looked out the bedroom window onto the street. No one at the front door. The tapping had stopped. She sat down at the desk and resumed writing.

We can't completely compartmentalize our writing any more than we can our brains. We are...

The tapping again, persistent and regular. She got up and followed the sound to a window near the balcony. A small bird on the windowsill pecked at the glass. Clare knocked from the inside and the little bird flew off. She shrugged her shoulders and went to shut her laptop. *I'll come back to you later.*

January 1981

Clare decided to sit in on some classes at the university. She had just completed a masters in Spanish language and literature before leaving for Germany. It was nice to not have the stress of deadlines and the impossible juggling act of being a mother, a student, and a teacher. The income she and Stefan got from teaching basic classes at the University of Iowa was barely enough to live on, but essential. And she loved teaching. In fact, she loved it all, but she struggled with feeling spread so thin and never quite living up to her own standards. It was hard to hold standards to her students that she couldn't live up to in her own studies. Not to mention the compromises she made as a mother.

"That's a great idea," Stefan had said when she floated it to him.

"I think I'll visit the *Romanistik* department and see what graduate classes they have in Spanish. At least that way I can keep up my Spanish and meet some new people."

The first day of class, Clare was excited to immerse herself in Spanish again and read some great books, undoubtedly with new perspectives. What she hadn't prepared herself for was switching back and forth between Spanish and German. Both languages fought for the same space in her brain—the foreign language track, she called it. Spanish had been dominant for years and had forced German or any other aspiring language to the back. Now she was finally becoming quite comfortable with German, and it had managed to elbow Spanish out of the way.

At one point, the class was working through a difficult passage in the novel they had begun, and a student said she had trouble understanding the

Spanish in one paragraph. The professor asked if anyone would like to translate it and Clare raised her hand with confidence. Just as the professor pointed at her, she realized that of course he meant to translate it into German. She lowered her hand and shook her head. "Translate" automatically meant for her into English, or English to Spanish, and she was very good at it. But there was no direct track connecting German to Spanish in her brain.

With time, she got used to such mental gymnastics and began to enjoy it. There were times when a kind of Span-German came out of her mouth, without her even realizing it. Like the time she asked a classmate in Spanish what her plans were for after class, using German syntax translated literally into Spanish. As soon as she said it, she knew it sounded wrong but was puzzled for a moment about why. They both laughed when they realized what had happened. As they walked to a nearby cafe, her new friend asked her.

"Kriegst du ein Baby?"

"Bitte?" Clare was caught off guard by the verb *kriegen*, "to get," though she understood the gist. Am I getting a baby?"

Her new friend looked at her small roundness and Clare laughed, patting her baby bump.

"Sí! I mean, *Ja!* In June. My husband says it will be a girl. We have a seven-year-old son who can't wait to be the big brother."

November 2000

Jürgen and Christina invited them over for dinner with a couple of their other friends. Clare was fond of Milo and Emilia, whom they had known in 1980. They still lived in a village outside of town. Originally from Poland, they had both grown up German and their kids knew no other life.

"It's amazing how fast the years went by! How did we get so much older? It feels like just yesterday we were going for walks together." Clare said to Emilia.

"And you were very pregnant!" Emilia remembered.

"Yes, I was more than ready to be done with it by that time."

"Speaking of babies…would you folks like to take a kitten home with you?"

Emilia looked at Milo. "Gee, I don't think we can. We already have a dog and a cat."

"Oh well, it was worth a try. The neighbors are taking one, so now there's only one left. A gray one just like its mother."

"I would like to make a toast," Stefan declared, raising his wine glass. "To old friends!"

"*Prost!*" they all said together, clinking their glasses.

"Tomorrow will be Thanksgiving in America," Clare said. "There is a lot to be thankful for, but I didn't feel like trying to do the traditional Thanksgiving dinner this year."

"No *schöne Pute?*" Jürgen asked with a wink to Clare.

Clare laughed. "No, it doesn't seem appealing this time. Things are so crazy politically at home. It's a bit scary to have the election hanging for so long."

"Like the hanging chads?" Stefan said.

"What are hanging chads?" several asked at once.

"When a ballot choice is not punched all the way through, leaving it possibly ambiguous," Stefan clarified.

"So, there may be another recount, or maybe not. It's a mess," Clare added.

"We think the world needs Gore to be president. For the environment." Jürgen said. "I think he would win in Germany right now. That is, if anyone asked *us* to vote."

"Well, I'm glad to be in Germany. I hope we all win this time," Clare added emphatically.

January 1981

Clare went to the Ahrens department store in search of a few things she needed. She had been missing her hairdryer as the weather got colder, and she wanted to find a small, travel-size one.

"I'm looking for a *Fön*," she said to the store clerk who had offered to help. The woman looked at her blankly. "A *Fön*," Clare repeated. She had been proud to know the German word for it. "You know, *ein Apparat um dein Haar zu trocknen...* a machine to dry your hair."

132

"Ah, ein Haartrockner," the woman said, with a look of why didn't you say so? *Duh! One more page for my feeling foolish in German collection.* Clare found out later that the word *Fön* was originally a brand name that became the name for a hand-held blow dryer. *Fön* sounded like the word for a warm wind (*Föhn*), though with a different spelling. As with the word "kleenex" in English, the brand name eventually became the common name for the item. *So, I wasn't wrong. Did I pronounce it wrong? Or maybe I was just more with it than that store clerk.*

She was also supposed to get some dandruff shampoo for Stefan. She hadn't bothered to look up that word but figured it would be easy by the description on the bottles. It wasn't. There were too many complex descriptions and claims about what each miracle shampoo could do for you and Clare was more confused than ever. She finally resorted to asking the same clerk. *Here we go again...*

"Ich suche..." she began. "I'm looking for some shampoo for, I mean against, those little white things in your hair... from the... from the...*Kopfhaut!* She finally remembered the word for "scalp," your "head skin." That same perplexed look made Clare want to give up, but instead she did a scratching motion on her head. She could hear Jürgen's voice saying, "Just enjoy the humor of it all."

"Ah!" The woman looked as relieved as Clare felt. *"Schuppen-Shampoo!* Here you go," and she handed Clare one of the bottles she had looked at many times. Somehow the word *"Schuppen"* just didn't seem to fit the image for dandruff.

"Danke schön," she said to the woman coolly as they headed to the checkout counter. While her two hard-won successes were being rung up, she heard a voice behind her.

"Clare?" She turned around to see a face that was familiar, but for a second the name and context were blank. *"Ich bin Samira,* remember...?"

"Samira, of course! It's great to see you again." Clare didn't try to explain how exhausted her brain was from two such simple shopping errands. "Would you like to go get some tea and a snack upstairs?" she asked, feeling a sudden blood sugar drop.

"Perfect," Samira answered, patting her slightly rounded belly.

"Oh my God, *du bist* — you are pregnant, too!" Clare patted her own belly and they grinned at each other.

"I had a feeling when we met that we both were…that we shared a problematic relationship with food, shall we say." Samira winked at her.

Clare laughed and said, "That's for sure. At least I can finally eat. Now I *need* to eat often."

"Same here. Let's go do it."

They went upstairs to the cafeteria above the department store, where a wall of large windows gave a panoramic view of the town winding its way up to the castle. They chatted about their pregnancies and discovered that they were due just a couple weeks apart.

"We have signed up for a prenatal class that starts in May. I'll check and let you know more if you're interested."

"Thanks. I'll talk to Omar about it."

"Samira, your English is so good. How many languages do you speak?"

"Well, my native language is Somali. But we use Arabic quite a lot. Also, English and Italian."

"Really? I didn't know that."

"There is a long history of British and Italian colonialism in my country. I went to an Italian school for most of my childhood. And I have an Italian grandfather."

Clare studied her face more closely and thought she could see some trace of Italian in it.

Samira went on about the complex and turbulent history of her country. It had gone from sultanates to republics, revolutions, guerilla warfare, continued colonization. Mogadishu had been the capital of Italian Somaliland for over sixty years.

"Life was not easy, especially for women, though it improved during the 1970s. Women gained rights to education, participation in public life, even politics. But there are still lots of arranged marriages, FGM, social restrictions."

"FGM?"

"Female genital mutilation. It's very common. Supposedly to control a woman's sexuality, initiate girls into womanhood. It is still expected in some areas as a requirement for marriage. Some even claim it is more hygienic. And attractive."

Clare had trouble imagining that.

"Fortunately for me, my parents did not believe in it, despite tremendous social pressure. That's one of the reasons I studied medicine and public

134

health. Then I met Omar. He wanted to return to Germany and things were feeling less stable in Somalia, so I agreed. I hope to go back someday if things settle down."

They chatted like old friends until their watches reminded them that they needed to move on.

"Thanks so much for sharing your story with me. I admire you." Clare hugged Samira as they stood in the street outside the store. She had seen pictures of Somali women and had met a few. Such beautiful people, it was hard to imagine that they carried those painful hidden scars.

"Someday I want to hear more about *your* story, Clare."

"And I'd love to share it with you. Let's do this again, soon."

"*Ciao.*"

Clare walked back to the house, swinging her little bag of shopping successes.

"I kind of envy her," she would later confess to Stefan. "She seems so heroic to me, with such a sense of purpose to make a difference in the world."

"Ah, the burden of privilege," Stefan commented. "Do you feel deprived of oppression and sacrifice to give your life meaning?"

"Ouch!" Clare responded, wounded by his comment that hit the mark.

November 2000

Nov. 27

A little bird, a sparrow I think, keeps tapping at my window. I wonder what it is trying to tell me.

Have you ever dreamed about dreaming, Hannah? I think they call it lucid dreaming. I seem to spend a lot of time questioning reality in my dreams, the very place where "reality" has different rules. But what is reality? I looked it up: "the world or the state of things as they actually exist." But where do they have to exist? We usually require evidence to corroborate the reality of things. Dreaming is real but not in the same world that we demand for our waking life. That's why we label people with certain neuro-logical differences 'crazy.' Their perceptions threaten the stability of the rules the rest of us count on. So do religions, social practices, gender identities, even languages other than our own. It seems like a slippery slope to me.

Nov. 30

I am becoming more patient with myself. My night job keeps me busy. Dreams are the place where we can freely do the work we need without fear of embarrassment or misinterpretation. It's kind of the inverse of our daytime self. At night, the "shoulds" get put in the closet while we open all the windows and doors and air out the basement.

Dreams are like fiction. We can try anything on in our own private dressing rooms.

"Real liberation comes not from glossing over or repressing painful states of feeling, but only from experiencing them to the full." (Carl Jung)

Clare heard a knock on the door and looked out the bedroom window to see who it was. "Come in, Christina, I'll be right down!" she yelled, hurrying to finish dressing. They had a weekly morning walk together that Clare had come to treasure.

"Sorry to keep you waiting," Clare said as she ran down the stairs. "I lost track of time writing in my journal."

"That sounds like a good thing."

They headed toward the Totenweg trail, which Clare had avoided for a while after her first exploration. But it was close by and had become their favorite place to walk together.

"How was your week, Christina?"

"Busy. But good. I got a call from the Red Cross. They need volunteers again."

"More Russian immigrants?"

"Yes. Some are ethnic Germans who lived in Russia for many generations. But most of them only speak Russian, so I volunteer to help with translating."

"I had forgotten that you speak Russian!"

"I heard Russian a lot as a child. My degree was in English and Russian, but I never really had a chance to use it. There were hardly any jobs around here.

"Are any of the current immigrants ethnic Russians?"

"Yes, and some Ashkenazi Jews. Most of the members of the synagogue here in Marburg are from the former Soviet Union and Eastern Europe. The new immigrants not only need to learn German, but also about their own heritage."

"What do you mean?"

"They say it wasn't possible for Jews to practice their religion in the communist countries. The synagogue offers classes in religion and modern Hebrew as well as a welcoming community. And they promote Christian-Jewish dialogue, which helps to integrate their members into the whole town."

"It must be rewarding to use your Russian again and to be able to help people."

They picked up the pace and walked in silence for a while, enjoying the brisk December air and the sunlight filtering through the bare branches of the trees along the path.

January 1981

"It's a strange experience to know you are inhabited by another being, before you can really feel it," Clare said to Stefan as they stood on the balcony looking out at the moon rising over the evening sky. "I mean, in spite of the nausea, tender breasts, and overall different feeling of my body, the baby won't seem real until I can feel it move."

"Well, there is that little bump." Stefan said, rubbing his hand over her slightly bigger belly.

"Yeah, this is the stage when no one says anything, because you might just be putting on a little weight and people don't want to risk offending you."

"Hmm. I think it's sexy."

"I've been thinking a lot about my new roommate. Or maybe I should say tenant? Am I the Obermieter? Or maybe the Außermieter? The outer renter, I guess you could say, subletting to this little creature within."

Stefan laughed. "Well, this tenant of yours certainly gets a good deal. Free room and board and full benefits."

"She's more like a 'body mate'. We share this body that we both inhabit. Though I'm not sure if I *inhabit* my body or if I *am* the body. I don't know why I'm thinking about this stuff so much this time," she said, shaking her head. I guess with Willy, I was too busy with work, and it was all so new."

Stefan draped his arm over her shoulder as they watched the colors of the sky deepen into night.

* * *

Clare opened her eyes and lay in the dark. She had pretended she was sleeping for a while, but it hadn't convinced her brain. As soon as she opened her eyes her brain said "Aha! I knew you weren't asleep." And then it was a free-for-all that let out all the leftovers of the day that were meant for her dreams, to frolic in the night.

She couldn't stop the existential thoughts that were swirling around her. She often joked to herself that her brain had a mind of its own and wouldn't obey her wishes. And yet where did her wishes come from in the first place? She had read about that once, that we designate the brain as an organ in the head but that it is inextricably linked to the intricate network of the nervous system that resides in the entire body. Like the heart, she thought. We assign our emotions to that small muscle in the chest, which is equally absurd.

"Why are we thinking about this now?" she whispered to the committee inside her skin. "Can we please adjourn for the night?"

"What does all this feel like to you, my little body mate?" she said as she got up with a sigh. After a drink of water and half a banana, she wandered to the back room and sat down at the little table. She could feel a poem coming on. Clare had never considered herself a poet, though she did occasionally write poems. She didn't feel like a writer because they just came out of her when needed, inspired by an involuntary internal pressure. She grabbed paper and pencil and waited to catch the words as they fell. They came in Spanish first, as they often did, already formed before they were visible to her.

Querido bultito, te tengo unas preguntas,
Como ¿en qué momento te hiciste persona?

Dear little bump, I have some questions for you,
like at what moment did you become a person?

She sat for a moment. It was peaceful and the night wrapped her in a muffled silence. She knew there was more. It was like a stomach bug in the brain, which meant there would be another wave.

What is it like in your nocturnal sea
without words, schedules, or days?

Clare waited, listening to her breathing, and feeling the soft beat of her heart under her ribs. The pencil in her hand vibrated with the coming tide of images.

You, who swim in the wee hours of becoming,
don't forget the marvel of your existence.

She relaxed in the chair, while the darkness held its breath.

We forget so much, the adults of this world,
and we are afraid of mystery and darkness.

Clare didn't feel finished, but a sleepiness washed over her, so she padded back to bed. After a few hours of deep sleep and dreaming, she awoke to the first light. A restless stirring within kept her from going back to sleep. The rhythmic accompaniment to the poem was still playing, as though she had just taken a breath between phrases of a song. The pictures formed in her mind as the words took shape. The painter had paused as well while she slept, and waited now, brush in hand, for the next frame.

Some day when you grow and go out into the light,
and things are all dressed in their names,
I will tickle the secrets from your dear little fist
and you'll say "Yes, mommy, I remember."

We'll laugh and sing of all that is possible,
in the freshness of the morning, you and I.
We'll talk about your belly button, the moon, the stars
and the gift from the dark night sky.

That was it. Clare felt empty and relieved, as though her brain had finally cleared itself. She would come back to her scribblings later in the day to see if they made any sense.

December 2000

Dec 1

Will's birthday today.

Clare looked up from her writing. "*Guten morgen, kleine Haussperling.*" The bird had become a regular companion to her writing. It was what they called a "house sparrow" in German.

"Are you trying to tell me something?" She got up and went to the window. Some said that sparrows brought news of a transition in your life or a message from someone in heaven. Clare wasn't particularly superstitious, but she liked both of those images.

The tapping rhythm that had at first been startling to her, even disturbing, had become part of a sense of momentum in her writing, almost like the clicking sound of old typewriter keys that used to make her feel so productive.

I can't believe Will is twenty-seven years old! A little bird agrees with me. I need to go to the internet café and write to him.

* * *

Dec. 1, 2000

Dear Will,

Today is a special day. Twenty years ago today is as present in my mind as is this moment that I write to you. What a wild and crazy year that was! Every year on this date there is a big party in my heart, a convention of Willys and Wills who get together to remember their dreams and adventures over the years. We all celebrate together the miracle of you. Happy Birthday!!!

I love you so much.

Mom

Dec. 1, 2000

Dear Anja,

I'm glad to hear you got the money we sent and we're very happy that you have your plane ticket for Christmas. I really miss you and I'm so excited to share this experience with you. We will meet you at the airport in Frankfurt.

Good luck with exams. We're so proud of you and love you tons. Can't wait to see you!!!

Love,

Mom

* * *

Clare, Samira and Isra continued to meet at Cafe Barfuß most weeks. They shared pieces of their lives, weaving an ever-stronger fabric of friendship with each new story. The more intimate and vulnerable the revelations, the stronger the bonds among them grew.

"I think our understanding of love changes as we grow," Isra began. It was her turn to talk about her first love. She put her fork down and looked at her plate as she struggled against the deep undertow of painful memory. The patient silence of her friends drew her back to the moment.

"I...I haven't really talked about this. There was someone, a girl. We were part of a group of young women, and we didn't know each other well. We only spoke with our eyes, but each time she looked at me I felt my heart race. A smile made my legs go weak. One day we held hands—as girls often do—but for us it was electric. We became obsessed with each other and tried to find ways to be alone together, if only briefly. We managed to keep our relationship secret for over a year. As our passion for each other increased, it became harder to hide."

"What was her name?" Clare asked.

"Aisha. Her name was Aisha. I haven't said it aloud since..." The undertow again, the feeling of drowning. Isra took a breath and looked at Samira, who tilted her head sympathetically. "One night she...Aisha snuck out of her house and climbed through the window of my bedroom. We knew it was reckless, but there was a force between us stronger than our judgement. My parents found us locked in naked embrace in my bed."

"Ooh." Samira released a sigh.

"That's when my parents began their arranged marriage plan."

"How did Aisha's parents react?" Clare touched her friend's shoulder.

"Worse. They went berserk. She wasn't allowed to leave the house or communicate with me. I never heard from her again. I thought maybe she had just let it go and I tried to move on. My parents had an acquaintance, an older man, who was looking for a young wife, and they thought he could manage me and give me a good proper life."

"Oh." Samira sighed, shaking her head.

"I had a couple friends who had plans to move to Berlin, so I joined them. I had been working part time and had saved enough money. So that's how I ended up in Germany."

February 1981

"I don't wanna go on a trip. I wanna stay here and play with my friends."

142

"But Willy, we're going to meet your great uncle Peter," Clare said, trying to avoid a standoff.

"I have another uncle?"

"Yes, he's my father's brother, which makes him my uncle, and your great uncle." Stefan added. "We'll take the train to Frankfurt. It's near there."

"The train? When can we leave?" Can I sit by the window? Will there be a little room like last time?"

The first time Willy and Clare had taken the train down to Bavaria to visit Stefan for a weekend, Willy had declared, "We have our own little room!" Clare had thought it would be a nice getaway from the stresses of school and looking for a place to live. And she also needed to show Willy that Germany was a big place and that his dad was indeed in the country.

"Yes, I like those compartments, too." Clare agreed. Two small benches facing each other gave it a cozy feeling.

When they got to Kronberg, where the relatives lived, Willy rallied for the introductions, after at first hiding behind Clare. She reached back and drew him forward.

"And this is..." she began when Willy interrupted her.

"*Ich bin Villy*", he announced, emphasizing the German pronunciation of his name, as he stuck out his hand.

"*Ich bin Peter, dein Großonkel.*" Peter said bending over as they shook hands solemnly.

"Your great uncle," Stefan translated.

"I know that!" Willy responded impatiently. "I used to have a great grandma, but she died." he informed Peter. "*Ich gehe in die Schule.*" he added proudly. "I go to school."

It was a lovely visit. Peter drove them to the train and they said their goodbyes. He bent down to shake hands with Willy.

"It was nice to meet you Willy, my grandnephew," he said. "Did you know that my father, who is also your grandfather's father, was named Wilhelm? That's like William in German. So you have the same name."

Willy smiled up at the tall man with white hair, who had suddenly become part of his family. He felt proud to be related to him.

"Auf wiedersehen, Großonkel Peter!" Willy called as he waved from the train. "See you soon!"

December 2000

Clare scanned some of the pages that Stefan had painstakingly transcribed and translated from Pastor Busch's Death Register. It was a bureaucratic accounting by a public official, but one section caught Clare's attention—an epidemic of dysentery that had taken many babies and young children. Even through the cryptic descriptions, Clare felt the stories jump out at her. Seeing the names, ages and circumstances of each child made it all more real, and even poignant.

In the year 1711

Anna Elisabetha, Johann Adam Rupp's daughter from Hadamshausen attacked unexpectedly by bloody dysentery, died peacefully on the 7th day of January in the evening about 7 o'clock and was buried on the 9th day of the same, at age 2 years less 12. weeks.

Andreas, Hans Jacob Becker's (past shepherd) son from Allna, born in Hermershausen and passed away there from red dysentery on the 13th day of January was buried the 16th day of that month, at age 17 weeks less 2 days.

Anna Margretha, Johannes Ammenhauser the younger's daughter from Hadamshausen, was afflicted by currently horrifying red dysentery and after a 9 day weakness, blissfully released on the 18th day of January, and brought to the grave on the 20th day of the same month, at age 21 weeks and 3 days.

Johann Peter, Johann Adam Rupp's (blacksmith), youngest son from Hadamshausen, had red dysentery 4 weeks, whereupon he passed away on the 20th day of January in the night about 12 o'clock and was buried on the 22nd day of the same month, at age 3 ½. years 7 weeks.

The list went on and on. At one point Pastor Busch's own voice intervened in a lament that went beyond the usual restraint of his duties.

The number of deaths we suffer presently, striking particularly children we were entrusted with and love, of which we have sung the last death song for and accompanied to the grave in the current month…

In the earlier years of Busch's death register, the notes were brief, often referring to being "returned to the earth," "ripe before their time," "escape from an evil world to sleep in the earth."

"What a terrible job to have," Clare said with a sigh as she handed the papers back to Stefan. "Can you imagine having to bury so many children?"

"Maybe there was some reward for him in trying to console the families. Death was such a part of their lives during those times."

"Remember when Willy was confused about his grandmother?" The references to being returned to the earth had sparked a memory that made her smile. When her own grandmother died, she had tried to explain death to Willy in simple but real terms. Not an easy task.

"Your great grandmother has died…" she began. His four-year-old face looked sad and a bit confused, but he nodded when she asked if he understood. He had never met her, and she lived far away, so Clare imagined that it didn't seem very real to him.

A few months later she told him one day that his grandparents—her parents—were coming to visit and they would go to the airport to pick them up. Willy looked confused for a moment and then asked.

"Did she grow back?"

"Who?"

"Grandma. You said she died and went into the ground to go to heaven."

Clare almost cried when she realized that all that time Willy had thought that her mother was gone, his "great" grandma.

He was excited when they got to the airport, and he gave his grandma an extra-long hug.

"I'm glad you didn't die," he said to her.

"Why don't we go see them more?" Willy had asked on the way to the airport.

"Well, it's a tiring trip for them and flying in an airplane is expensive."

Willy thought for a moment. "But why can't we just go get them and bring them back. It's easy."

"They don't live at the airport, kiddo." Stefan turned to smile at Clare. "It's a long trip for them to get there."

"Oh. Will they be there this time?" They had always been there waiting for them whenever they went to the airport.

"Sure, unless their plane is late."

February 1981

"We have to do *Kopfrechnen* tonight," Willy said after supper. The teacher says you're spose to test me."

"*Kopfrechnen...*" Clare stopped to decode the word she hadn't heard before. "*Kopf* = Head + *rechnen* = to calculate..."

"It means you have to make up 'rithmetic problems for me to do in my head."

"Ah. Like two plus two?"

"Yeah, but not like that. That's too easy. Like 3 + 5 - 2 + 4. You have to say "*drei plus fünf minus zwei plus vier.* Say it."

"Okay. *Drei plus fünf minus zwei plus vier*"

"*Zehn!*" Willy shouted almost before she finished saying it.

Clare did the math in her mind. Yes, ten was correct.

"You can make them harder."

Clare wrote the numbers down so she could remember what they were while Willy calculated in his head. He got so good at it that she had to keep making them longer and harder. It seemed to her like a tough thing for a first grader to do, but he loved it.

* * *

Stefan would often make up stories for Willy that soon became collaborative and open-ended. They would sit on the balcony and create episodes together with their favorite characters.

"So, they were on the raft floating down the river and Tommy's paddle was swept away by the strong current. 'What will we do with only one paddle?' he cried."

"They were scared and didn't know what to do," Willy continued. "But then Cory grabbed a branch hanging over the water..."

Clare stopped to watch the shapes of the two guys she loved, dark against the sunlight as they leaned towards each other. She couldn't make out all the words, but the murmur of their voices danced on the cadence of storytelling.

One day Willy asked Clare to put some paper in the old typewriter they had acquired. She showed him how to punch the keys. The German keyboard didn't bother him since he had never used a typewriter before.

Clare had trouble getting used to the "y" and the "z" having changed places, along with a few other differences. She left him pecking away slowly, one finger at a time, seated at the small wooden table they had put in the tiny back room of the apartment.

"What are you writing?" she asked him when she came back to check. He had almost half a page of painstaking typing and creative spelling.

"I'm writing a novel," he said seriously.

"What's it about?"

"It's about two kids in a boat on an adventure. Lots of things happen to them and it's really 'citing." Though it never got past that first page, Clare treasured it and kept it for years.

* * *

While Willy was at school and Stefan at the archive, Clare continued attending classes and gradually got better at the direct German to Spanish track. She also started taking a water aerobics class for pregnant women. Sharon joined her. It was impressive how much emphasis German culture put on wellness and proactive healthy practices. She really appreciated the regular exercise and being in the water made her forget the growing heaviness of her body.

At first, she felt self-conscious undressing in the locker room, especially with her new distorted shape. In the United States, maternity clothes were all about disguising the roundness with roomy, flowing clothes. But the German women were comfortable in their bodies. They would undress at their lockers and walk naked to the showers. Clare soon joined in the fun of comparing shapes and sizes of their protuberances: high, low, round, basketball, football, five months, seven months. The women rubbed and patted their bellies like they were old friends. Occasionally the babies would get in on the action and stick out an elbow, a knee, or a foot to the applause of all. They all shared the challenges of pregnancy with laughter and camaraderie.

Some of them had temporary names for their babies, besides just *Das Baby*. Since Stefan was so sure they would have a girl, Clare chose a name that she knew she would never give to a real daughter: *Gertrude* (an echo of 'protrude', pronounced with an exaggerated gagging-on-peanut-butter-in-

147

the-back-of-your-throat-sound that German offered. "Ger-troooo-duh."
Gertrude didn't seem to mind.

December 2000

Clare sat down at a computer in the internet café. She hadn't checked her
email in almost a week, and she knew there would be a backlog of messages.
She had written to Julia the week before and scanned through the list to see
if there was a response from her.

Dec. 4, 2000

Dear Julia,

Thanks for your last email. I do remember the Thalheims, and I
have often thought of them since I heard their sad story years ago.
Have you ever managed to track down Yaniv to see how his life
has gone? I remember you told me that Noam and Marya were
killed in a car crash in 1985 and Yaniv was adopted by a German
family with a son around his age. Do you have any more news of
him?

Will wonders about him sometimes and so do I.

Love,
Clare

Dec. 6, 2000

Dear Clare,

In answer to your question, I have not been able to track Yaniv
down directly, but I have heard news from a family that was
friends with his adoptive family, who no longer live in Marburg.
The family that adopted Yaniv was very kind, and their decision
was immediate when they heard about the accident. Since there

weren't any close relatives in Israel, the German family took him to live with them right away.

The family had two older daughters who were already university age. They both took classes in Hebrew so they could honor Yaniv's Israeli Jewish identity and support him in it if that was what he wanted. Isn't that a touching story? I hope he is doing well, wherever he is. Yes, Zosia also wonders about Yaniv. We all do. Hope you are well.

Love,
Julia

Dec. 2, 2000

Dear Mom,

Thanks for the birthday thoughts. I often think of that year in Marburg. I used to say it was both the hardest and the best year of my life. I have lots of memories, images of people and moments that have stayed with me. It's funny how the learning extended long after we went back home—a timed release experience that I continued to process for many years. Sometimes German phrases come back to me even now alongside my memories. (By the way, say hi to Die Enten for me!)

Thanks to you and Dad for the gift of that experience. It's fun to think of you there now.

Love you both so much!
Will (Herr Villy)

P.S. Have you found out anything about Yaniv? I think about him sometimes.

Dec. 2, 2000

Dear Mom,

I can't wait to see you! It won't be long!! Will offered to drive me to the airport. I'm going to visit Grandma with him and Yolanda for a few days soon.

I'm excited to finally see Marburg. I have all these pictures in my head from stories you and Dad have told me. It will be strange to meet the reality.

Give Dad a hug for me.

Love, love, love,
Anja

February 1981

"What are you going to be for *Fasching*?" Zosia asked Willy.
"What's that?"
"There's a parade and everyone wears a costume."
"You mean Halloween?"
"What's that?"
When Willy asked his parents, Stefan explained that Halloween wasn't really a thing in Germany. Willy had been disappointed when it passed unnoticed in the fall. Stefan told them that *Fasching* had originated in medieval times, an old tradition, when the common people would dress up in costumes and masks to mock the pomp and flaunting of wealth by their overlords. Much like Carnival and Mardi Gras in other countries.

"In Germany the *Karneval* season starts officially on November 11th, and it starts at exactly 11:11 am," Stefan added. "But the parades are in February. It's coming up soon. it's a fun and colorful holiday that kids enjoy. We'll check out what's happening here and where it will be. They usually throw candy for the kids from the parade."

Willy had tried to follow his father's answer to his question, and as was often the case he couldn't quite take in all of it. But he did like the sound of the parade and the candy.

"Ich will ein Cowboy sein," Jonas announced, and Willy immediately decided he would be *"ein Indianer."*

Clare was surprised to find that many Germans were obsessed with the American Old West. She learned that it was a direct influence from the works of the German writer Karl May, who wrote many novels in the late 1800s and early 1900s about the American West. It was an imagined one, much like in Hollywood. More than 100 million copies of his books sold to German readers.

It wasn't hard to find the costume Willy wanted, the classic fringed imitation buckskin get-up, complete with a wig of straight black hair. Clare and Stefan looked at each other.

"We could be back in the 1950s," Stefan remarked.

"I always wanted to be an Indian when I was a little kid," Clare agreed. "I imagined a romantic and noble life in the forest. But later I read stories about the real history of Native Americans at the hands of white people and I began to ask questions. The fantasy became tinged with shame."

"Yeah, myths are important foundations to cultural identity, but they leave out the messy and shameful reality around them."

"At what age do children learn about shame? How do we teach them about the heavy fortresses around those myths without destroying their childhood fairy tales?"

"I think Fasching is even better than Halloween!" Willy exclaimed, on the way back from the parade. He was swinging a bag of sweets that he had collected in the scramble on the street as the parade went by, and his shiny black hair swished as he walked.

December 2000

Clare had noticed all through the summer heat that Das Haus stayed rather cool and comfortable. It had also weathered the fall rains and now the early winter cold.

"The Fachwerk construction is ingenious," she commented to Stefan. She had read that it had been used for many centuries. Ancient Germans would start with a deep hole for each of the heavy wooden poles that created the main supportive structure. Then they would weave wicker rods into the gaps and fill in with a mixture of straw and clay that was called *Lehm*.

In the 11th century there was a significant climate change and as it got colder, they began to build the houses higher with stone foundations. Later they added beams and struts to create sturdier and more elaborate structures. But the concept of the Lehm that filled in the spaces had continued into modern times. It was much like the adobe used in many cultures in the southern hemisphere.

"Lehm is very adaptive," Stefan commented. "It absorbs moisture in times of high humidity and then releases it when the air is dry."

"I think maybe it does that with stories, too," Clare mentioned.

"What do you mean?"

"It absorbs and preserves all the stories that have lived in the house over the years, and then releases them when we need them."

"Hmmm." Stefan looked at her and smiled. "The words of a writer."

* * *

Dec. 12

Hannah, I've been thinking about your house a lot recently. I feel like it hears all that we say and think and holds it for us discreetly. Even the secrets we keep from ourselves. Every time I come home from whatever wandering or errand that takes me out, I see the little plaque hanging inside your front door. I feel the wisdom and safe protection of the walls around me.

Abends kehr ich	*In the evenings*
Gern mit Freude	*I come back*
In mein liebes	*with joy to*
Heim zurück.	*my loving home.*
Hier vergeß' ich	*Here I forget*
Müh und Sorgen	*worries and troubles.*
Hier blüht Liebe	*Love and happiness*
Mir und Glück	*bloom for me here.*

152

Dec. 13

*Sometimes I feel oddly pregnant. It's strange how emptiness
can take form and fill you as you learn to live with grief. At first,
you are filled with the loss, but then something else starts to grow
in its place. Like the more I let go, the bigger the new life inside
me becomes. I'm not sure what that new life is, but it seems to
have room for my father to live with me, as well as many lives
from a past that I never knew. My brain is tingling with ideas.*

* * *

Notes for Book

Even real people are turned into literary characters when they
become part of a story or a dream.

Fiction isn't much different than the 'reality' of our lives. Our
sense of self is an ongoing narrative construction based on images,
memories, experiences, and the reinforcement of the construction
itself.

Fiction as a mental theater, analogous to memory and dreams

The Fachwerk house is a model for writing. The poles and beams
are the cultural/historical premises of our understanding and
perceptions. We weave our narratives (the wicker) to give body
and boundaries to the story and then fill in with the clay (*Lehm)*

February 1981

"Nick told me about a choir that I'm thinking of checking out," Sharon
told Clare one day after their water aerobics class. "He's been playing oboe
for the musical director of a church, part of some services, I guess. The same
guy directs a choir. Want to try it out?"

"Umm…I suppose that two women with round bellies would add some
class to the group," Clare teased. "I do love to sing."

"I used to sing alto in a college group, but it sounds kind of intimidating,
in German and all," Sharon responded.

"Yeah, I know. But what do we have to lose? No one knows us, so if we don't like it, we can just not go back. So, yeah, why not? I'm in."

The rehearsals were in the Oberstadt, and to Clare's delight they gathered in an early 13th century stone chapel. It was small with a short tunnel-like entrance. Inside, the ceiling was a perfect round arch that had good acoustics, but still felt cozy. It was as if they had stepped into another dimension, a timeless space of music.

Clare sang soprano and was placed next to an older woman, who welcomed her warmly. She was glad to know it was only the second rehearsal, so she wouldn't be too far behind. She opened the folder she had been handed and took out the sheet music for the first piece. It was in Latin. Thank you, Professor Johnson. That semester of intensive Latin had been challenging, and surprisingly useful in many ways.

As they began, Clare could hear the strong voice of the woman next to her, who seemed to know the music very well. She glanced at her briefly and was surprised to see that she wasn't reading the music. In fact, she didn't even have a folder on the stand in front of her. Clare was impressed and astonished. How can she know all the music already? With another glance she understood. The woman's fixed gaze told the story. She was blind!

Clare began to look forward to those Thursday evening rehearsals. It would be once a week for a while and then more often as they neared the performance. At night, the Oberstadt was lit with yellowish streetlamps that imitated the gas lamps of past centuries. The soft light on stone streets and ancient buildings gave a magical intimacy to the experience, even before she entered the chapel. She worked on the soprano parts at home and reminded herself to belly breathe to sustain her voice, occasionally apologizing to Gertrude for invading her space.

Most of the songs were in German, but the two in Latin were her favorites. The Latin syllables were so open to the resonance of the human voice, and they easily filled the little chapel with beautiful sounds. One evening, one of her fellow sopranos made some gentle corrections to her pronunciation of some of the Latin words. She felt defensive and indignant until she realized that she had studied classical Latin and these songs were in church Latin, a medieval version that had reigned in the Catholic church for centuries and applied to any related music. She thanked the woman and quickly adapted her pronunciation.

That evening after the rehearsal, she and Sharon were invited to follow the director of the choir to the back of the chapel. They went through a small, dark passageway to a door. It was kind of spooky. Clare wasn't sure what the pastor's intentions were. At least Sharon was with her. Another door revealed a very narrow winding stairway that led to a second floor above the chapel. It was all rather mysterious, but then the director opened a door to a small apartment where he lived with his wife.

"*Erfreut, Sie kennenzulernen, Frau Klein.*" Clare managed to find her formal German as she shook hands with a short, gray-haired woman who resembled Herr Klein in stature and roundness. "Delighted to meet you." It was all she could do to keep her polite smile from turning into a giggle. Mr. and Mrs. Klein (*Small*) lived in that little apartment at the top of narrow stairs above the ancient, diminutive chapel. Another fairy tale.

December 2000

"I think the little bird is right," Clare commented to Stefan over coffee. It had continued to accompany her writing with its percussive rhythm.

"What do you mean?"

"I don't know, but I feel a gathering of momentum. They say that a bird tapping on your window can signal a transition in your life. Even if you don't believe the myth behind it, there seems to be a correlation."

* * *

Notes for Book

Challenge structuralist dichotomies, where everything is defined as either one thing or the other. Reality doesn't fit in those models. The lines between opposites are often blurry, messy, or even non-existent.

So much of our sense of reality is based on human conventions. Sleep is not a shut-off of being awake. The human brain spends half of the night working harder than during active awake times. Day/night, present/past, fiction/reality; these are hypothetical poles that we use to understand our existence, and to be able to talk about it, but they are not as clear as they sound. We are limited by language and language is limited by those limitations.

Opposites are defined by each other. But most of reality lives in between in a kind of twilight that we spend our whole lives trying to name. Cultures and religions have different definitions for when life begins and ends, how time works, the form of the universe. And different languages that reflect and shape all of that.

The sparrow flew off with a chirping flutter of wings. Clare looked up and smiled.

"Thanks, little one. See you soon."

February 1981

Stefan finished pasting the most recent labels into his beer and wine scrapbook. "This one was especially good," he said to Clare, pointing to the dark beer he had enjoyed the night before.

"I'm sorry I can't join you in immersing yourself in that important aspect of German culture," Clare said with a slightly curdled irony. She did like good beer and wine, but they were off limits while she was pregnant. And Stefan's enthusiasm seemed over the top to her. She resented his freedom and clueless abandon.

"Hey, I'm a social historian and this will be history someday. I'm obligated to collect the data. Can you believe how inexpensive good beer and wine are here? I need take advantage of that. Besides, it's stressful being pregnant." He grinned at her.

"Yes, well you're keeping up with me so far in the growth around the middle project. I hope you don't plan on that for the whole nine months. You won't shed the weight as suddenly as I will, you know."

"Don't be so judgmental. I'm working hard and enjoying myself. What's wrong with that? And it's not my fault that I have to drink it all myself."

"What? You can't be serious. And by the way, I've noticed that your clothes smell like smoke sometimes. I thought you quit."

"I did, several times."

"You know what I mean. Why would you start smoking again with a baby on the way?"

"Just a few here and there. It's too expensive to smoke like I used to."

"I can't believe you. Why are you being such a jerk?"

"I only smoke outside and I promise I'll stop when the baby arrives. Don't get so worked up about it. It's not good for the baby."

Aargh!! "I just want to make sure that you are around for a while. I don't want to raise these kids by myself." She glared at Stefan and then stomped off to the kitchen in search of a snack. She could feel her blood sugar falling as her blood pressure rose.

9
Russian Dolls

December 2000

"There she is!" Clare shouted as she saw her daughter through the glass separating them from the passengers in the Customs area. They ran to the front of the sliding doors, joining the crowd that was held back by thick ropes attached to metal stanchions.

When Anja walked through the doors, Stefan elbowed his way through the crowd and put his arm around her shoulder, guiding her towards Clare as he grabbed her suitcase.

"Anja, I'm so happy to see you!" Clare said as they locked in a tight embrace, rocking back and forth. "I can't believe you're here!" She pulled back and smiled through tears.

"Oh, Mom." Anja hugged her again and said, "You're not supposed to cry when I arrive."

"You know me. I cry at everything."

They didn't stop talking the whole time as Stefan steered them towards the train. Soon after they got settled in their seats, Anja closed her eyes in mid-sentence and was out. Clare tucked her jacket around her sleeping daughter, moving the long dark hair that fell over her face gently back over her shoulder. She couldn't take her eyes off the beautiful young woman who had been her baby. *Has she grown up so much in the almost seven months since we left for Germany, or am I just noticing it now?* It was jarring to have her there in the country of their past.

Clare blinked away visions of train rides with a tiny baby. When they arrived at the airport that morning, she had remembered the feel of her four-month-old baby girl strapped to her chest, while balancing a large carry-on bag in one hand and leading Willy with the other. The trip home in 1981 had been the reverse of her arrival since Stefan had needed to stay longer to finish up. But instead of arriving in Frankfurt carrying the loss of a baby, she had stepped off the plane in New York with big brother Willy and his baby sister. Exhausted but full of a future.

* * *

Anja would sleep in Hannah's room. It seemed fitting since their names were related. "Hannah" from Hebrew and the Latin "Anna" meant "grace." Anja was a variation of both names. Clare and Stefan had felt her grace, as the gift of her birth in Germany and as the person she had grown into. They had considered the Irish name *Aine* for her, but then opted for the German spelling with almost the same pronunciation. Some claimed that the name was Russian. It didn't matter, for it seemed to have found a home in many countries and it felt just right to them.

"I know a girl in school named Anja. I think it's pretty and I'd like to have a sister with that name," Willy had announced one day during their discussions. That had decided it.

Clare gave Anja a couple days to rest and settle in. Between naps and meals, they sat in the kitchen and sipped their tea. They also spent some private moments on the balcony. The blossoms and leaves were gone but in late afternoon the sun would shine through and warm them as they talked. There was much to catch up on.

They walked to the bakery and Anja delighted in the choices. She, too, was a big fan of fresh bread. She had stopped in the doorway, just as Clare liked to do, to breathe in the weaving of yeasty smells that floated in the air.

"I love the way they make real bread here. With some substance," Anja commented as they left with a couple half loaves of her choice.

"Not like the *Schlabberbrot* we have at home," Clare responded.

"The...what?"

"That's what they call it here. It means something like "floppy bread.""

"That's it. That's what I'd call it. How do you say it again?"

"*Schlabberbrot.*"

"I'm going to remember that one. It sounds like a cross between slobber and flabby," Anja said with a laugh.

On the way home Clare took a longer loop to show Anja more of the neighborhood. She felt like a little kid in an amusement park dragging a parent to one favorite ride after another. Anja was quiet and patient, but her eyes sparkled as she took it all in.

A whirlwind of Christmas markets, strolls through the Oberstadt, favorite cafes and shops filled their days. They took a bus to the Gästehaus

159

and Clare told her stories of the early days with Willy. There was so much that she hadn't shared with her daughter before, things she hadn't even remembered until returning to Germany.

"Willy and I had many adventures. Wonderful times with the three of us, as well as difficult ones. But that year was also about you. You know, I grew to feel grateful for that miscarriage. If it hadn't happened, we never would have had you. You were already there in our hearts, and we were waiting for you, through the months of nausea and then as you grew visibly inside me, swimming and stretching your way into your own life."

* * *

"Fröhliche Weihnachten!" Stefan said, as he put the angel on the top of their small tree. They had bought it at the Christmas market, along with the traditional *Glühwein* and *Stollen*. Stefan made the old pun about having "stollen" it. Anja and Clare rolled their eyes at the same time and then burst into laughter. There were a few small gifts under the tree. They had all agreed to keep it simple and focus on being together. Their big treat would be eating out at a gourmet restaurant in one of the centuries-old buildings in the Oberstadt. The specialty there was a variety of *Wildfleisch*, exquisitely roasted selections of wild game and fresh vegetables.

Clare had found a special gift for Anja in her favorite little shop of international crafts. Anja opened it to find an oval shaped wooden doll. She ran her fingers over the smooth surface with delicately painted features and designs.

"Open it," Clare said, and Anja looked at her quizzically. "There's another one inside." Anja pulled it apart in the middle and there was an identical one, just slightly smaller.

"Russian dolls!" Anja said, remembering a story she had read that featured them. She opened the second one, and then the third. There were five in all, the last one being a tiny solid one.

"I saw them, and they made me think of you."

"They did?" Anja lifted her gaze with a puzzled expression.

"The smallest one is the baby that was born here in Marburg. As you grew, you added new layers and experiences, as we all do, but that precious baby is still there inside. I think we carry all our different selves with us throughout our lives, even though they may be hidden from others, and even from us. I'm just so happy you can be here to meet that little German baby."

Stefan gave her a colorfully illustrated book of The Brothers Grimm fairy tales. It included an English translation on the facing pages and stunning photos of Marburg streets that still looked much the same as they had in the times when the Brothers Grimm collected the stories.

"I would love to show you some of those streets," he offered.

"Sure, Dad. I'd like that."

February 1981

"This is fun. It's nice to get out. I've been studying so hard and working extra," Samira said, after giving Clare a hug.

"Yes, it's great to see you again. How are you feeling these days?" Clare responded, patting her own round belly.

"Much better. I'm hungry all the time! I do miss my family now, especially my mother." Clare saw the longing in her friend's eyes. Those dark eyes seemed able to hold so much emotion, while her own green ones spilled over easily.

"It feels strange to go through it all without their support," Samira went on. In Somalia I would have a community of women to help me throughout the pregnancy as well as during and after the birth."

"It must be very lonely for you," Clare said as she laid her hand on top of Samira's. "I am hoping my own mother will come over for the birth. We are such a mobile society in the U.S. that most of us don't have those communities anymore, but our mothers are very important to us."

"I don't know what my parents will do. There is a military dictatorship in Somalia now and it's getting worse. My parents are both teachers and they don't want to leave. They are dedicated to trying to keep education alive there. I really worry about them."

"I can imagine." Clare sometimes worried about her own parents as they got older. But at least they were getting older in relative safety.

They talked on about the challenges of pregnancy and adjusting to life in Germany. Samira shared more of her experiences while Clare pondered the differences in their lives. She was only a temporary visitor, but Samira was an immigrant. That could mean forever.

"There is a small group of Somalis in Marburg and I like talking to them, hearing their stories. But it's not easy. They think I'm too independent. Most women my age would already have several children and follow more of the traditional ways. I consider myself Muslim and I still pray to Allah, but I can't accept that women are second class and that men should have all the authority over them."

"Does Omar accept your views?"

"Yes, thankfully, he is with me on that. We both want to maintain our cultural identity, our faith and our language, but we also believe in education and expanding our horizons. It's a delicate balance."

"I am impressed with both of you and wish you the best in your balancing act."

"It's sad, you know. Women's status and equality have been improving a lot in Somalia in the last ten years or so: the right to education, to own property and participate in public life. But now, things are swinging the other way again, becoming more authoritarian, even totalitarian. I love my homeland, but I hate where it's going. And I feel guilty that I was privileged enough to be able to escape."

They talked for a long time about culture, family, and art. Along the way they discovered that they both wrote poetry.

Clare's poems were spontaneous responses to personal experience.

"I can feel one coming on, almost like an illness. A pain, a tickle, an itch, that won't leave me alone until I let it out. Then I feel restless and distracted until the words settle into their final form. After that, they're on their own."

Samira's poems came out of a long history of Somali women's poetry. They had a structured format, tied to oral tradition, a kind of storytelling in verse that was performed.

"Poetry has been an important part of our culture for thousands of years," Samira explained, "a journalistic commentary on life. It is recited publicly and shared with other communities, by traveling...how do you call them?"

"Bards? Troubadours?"

"Yes. Something like that. Women didn't used to be allowed to recite in public, except maybe for other women or family. Khadija Abdullahi Delays was the first woman to sing on the radio and record her music. She was my hero. She sang about the strength of women and their potential, and she encouraged Africans to love their blackness."

They sat for a while in comfortable silence.

"Samira, would you teach me a few phrases in Somali?" Clare asked tentatively. "I'm kind of a language nerd. Do you understand that expression? It means that I am very interested in languages, intensely interested."

"Maybe I am one of those nerds as well, though my culture has always had many languages. Each one has its own flavor, a unique music and way of expressing things. So, in Somali you could say: *'Assalaamu calaykum,'* which is a greeting. It means 'May peace be upon you.' A more informal greeting is *'Setahay,'* 'how are you?'" Clare repeated them several times. *"'Nabad gelyo'* is 'good-bye' and *'Is arag danbe' is* 'See you later.'"

They hugged. Each one felt the intimate touch of their shared motherhood as they embraced.

"Is arag danbe," Clare said as she turned to wave.

December 2000

Stefan and Anja walked along through the middle of town, stopping to look at an old building or to check a new view of the castle. Clare had stayed home to read and give the two of them time alone together.

"It's beautiful," Anja exclaimed, "this whole area!"

"Ockershausen used to be a village, but now it is part of Marburg," Stefan said. "That's true for other parts of the city as well. Many of the spaces have filled in to make it one city, but it's surprising to me how little new building goes on in this town. They work hard to protect the old buildings and the green spaces within and around the town."

"I love that," Anja said. "I wonder how they manage it. The population must not be growing very fast."

"That's true for Germany in general."

They crossed a stone bridge to the other side of the river that flowed gently through the town.

"Now this part of Marburg used to be the village of Weidenhausen. It is said to be the second oldest settlement in the city, after the Oberstadt, the area around the castle. The Oberstadt was the earliest settlement, starting around the 9th century or so, and became a town in 1140. Weidenhausen was outside the walls of the original town, and it was where families from the town had garden plots. *Weide* means "pasture," so the village was originally in pastureland by the river. The first version of that bridge that we just crossed, over the Lahn River, was built in the year 1200, and it was the only connection to the town of Marburg. People often stopped to buy leather from the tanners who worked along the river, and then crossed into Marburg."

Anja pictured groups of men scraping and beating animal skins at the water's edge along the pasture, eight hundred years earlier. It was hard to overlay that image on the modern city that had since subsumed the river and all the small villages around it.

She followed Stefan down a narrow curving cobblestone street lined with very old Fachwerk houses. Even the design of the cobblestones was artful and beckoned them into that world of long ago. A few small stores and cafes were nestled among family homes, some of them dating back to the 1500s. The houses were a variety of colors, both the exposed half-timber framings and the *Lehm* plaster that filled in the squares and triangles inside them. Intricate designs and carvings gave each one a unique character. Red geraniums in a window box or pink roses climbing up a wall added extra accents of color. One building had a red rose bush on each side of the door. The branches had grown up the wall to frame the door and meet high above it, spreading out in the shape of a heart.

"They look so romantic and picturesque."

"Yes, but they probably have sloping floors and tiny bathrooms," Stefan countered. "Less romantic on the inside, not to mention the centuries of ghosts you might have to live with." Anja realized he was teasing her and shrugged her shoulders with a smile.

They walked along Pilgrimstein Street to the stately gothic cathedral of Saint Elizabeth. The church had been built starting in 1235 by the Knights of the Teutonic Order in honor of Elizabeth of Hungary. She was a princess who married the Landgrave of Thuringen in central Germany at age fourteen and became known as an advocate for the poor and unfortunate. Widowed by twenty and left with three children, she refused to remarry and was cast out by her husband's family. Elizabeth went to live in Marburg, where she built a hospital for the poor with money from her dowry and stayed to care for the patients. She died at the age of twenty-four and was canonized for her many charitable works and a handful of miracles ascribed to her.

Anja wasn't particularly into gothic architecture or old churches, but the story of this one fascinated her. She read more of the information provided in the brochures and was struck by the contrast of the simple humanity of the young woman and the cold grandeur of the building. Elizabeth's acts of independence and generosity had been criticized and even punished during her life. But after she died her image became an icon of the Catholic Church and the cult of St. Elizabeth that extended to many lands for centuries thereafter.

Standing in the middle of the cathedral, Anja leaned her head back to look up at the ceiling where the graceful arches came together in a gesture of exaltation. The morning sun streamed through the stained-glass windows, warming the walls with shafts of soft colors. She could imagine glorious music filling that place of reverence and pilgrimage as she paused to take in its beauty.

"It's beautiful, but I can't shake the irony of the story," she said to Stefan as they left the cathedral.

"What do you mean?"

"Well, it's a memorial to an independent and rebellious young woman built by a militaristic and often violent order of men. It seems that the only real paths open to women in that time were motherhood or sainthood; imprisoned in the house or cast in stone in a church."

"Pretty much," Stefan agreed as he put his arm around her shoulder.

They walked on to explore an old building of stone and Fachwerk that stood behind the church. A plaque on the front of the building told a brief history. *Das Deutsche Haus,* "The German House" as it came to be called, was originally the living quarters of the Order of Brothers of the German House of St. Mary, established in Jerusalem in 1190. Also known as the Knights of the Teutonic Order, they were famous for founding hospitals and providing mercenary armies during the Crusades. The well-preserved building was currently occupied by the Geography Department of the university.

"Such strange and fascinating layers of history here," Anja commented. It says that in the nineteenth century the building was an *Accouchieranstalt.* Do you know what that is?"

"I think it was what they called a 'lying in hospital'—for childbirth back then."

"Weird. And now it's the Geography Department!"

"Thanks for the tour, Dad" Anja said as they walked along the river towards the university. "It was amazing."

"You are very welcome." Stefan had delighted in filling in his own knowledge of the early history of Marburg and sharing it with his daughter.

"Did you notice the painting in the church of the Virgin Mary as midwife?" Anja had been puzzled by that image.

"Yes, I've seen it before and wondered what it was supposed to signify. Is it about the sanctity of birth in general or does it reinforce the image of Mary as the mother of mothers?"

"A kind of patron saint maybe," Anja suggested.

"There is one more important historical site to show you along the way." Stefan led her to a grassy bank along the river where they stopped to watch some ducks swim by.

"This is where your mother used to come with little Willy to feed the ducks. Apparently, it was very important to the early history of this family in Marburg." Anja grinned and took her father's arm as they approached the university where they would meet up with Clare and some friends for lunch.

They arrived at the Mensa, the university cafeteria where students and others ate and socialized. Anja gave her mother a hug and said, "We met the ducks."

Clare laughed and answered, "Well, maybe not THE ducks, but clearly their descendants. Anja, I want you to meet our friends from back in the early days of the Duck Dynasty. This is Samira, her husband Omar…and Bashir and Casho, whom I've just now met," she added smiling at the two young people who had clearly inherited the beauty and grace of their parents.

"This is our daughter, Anja," she said to all as she took Anja's hand. They shook hands around and then Samira hugged Anja.

"You are as beautiful as I imagined," Samira whispered. "We have already met, you know, some years ago. Did your mother tell you that we were in the hospital together when you and Bashir were born just one day apart?" Anja and Bashir both nodded, looking at each other in awkward silence. It was a bit much to take in, but it clearly meant a lot to the mothers.

"We wanted to eat together at the Mensa, for old time's sake," Clare explained. This is where we first met, the four of us," she said, taking Stefan's arm and gesturing to Samira and Omar. They all smiled in appreciation and headed for the cafeteria buffet.

February 1981

Christina invited Clare to go with her once a week to an indoor swimming pool. With the water aerobics classes and lots of walking, Clare was feeling fit, even with her new front pack. Swimming was like a vacation from pregnancy. The buoyancy took the strain off her back, and she imagined little Gertrude doing synchronized swimming with her. The rest of the time, the baby did her own thing; sleeping when she wanted, dancing and partying whenever, sometimes even in the middle of the night.

Once, when Clare was singing in choir practice, Gertrude decided to kick a soccer goal right underneath her heart. Fortunately, it was timed just as her soprano part hit a high note. The note came out with such force that a few around her turned to look.

The middle months of pregnancy had awakened a new energy in Clare. Maybe it was just in comparison to the first trimester that was a blur of nausea and tiredness. She had read a theory once that the morning sickness—a misnomer she thought, since it lasted all day—was an evolutionary adaptation to keep the mother from eating or drinking something that might be detrimental to the embryo in its most vulnerable stage. Clare didn't lose weight, but she had the feeling of her own body wasting away as the little parasite took all it needed, even though she was hardly eating. But by the fourth month she was suddenly hungry all the time. She and Gertrude were gaining weight fast.

"Ooh." Clare stopped as she climbed up the ladder to exit the pool. Her body was suddenly heavy again. Then she felt it. A little flutter in her middle, like sometimes happened when she stood in front of students on the first day of a new class.

"Are you okay?" Christina asked with concern.

"Yes, I'm fine. I think Gertrude is still swimming. I felt something." She grinned, imagining those tiny legs kicking in the private pool where her baby lived.

"Did it just now move?" Christina asked with a smile.

Clare nodded, a grin spreading on her face.

"For the first time? *Oh, wie schön.* What a special moment."

These days her whole body was alive and glowing, and more sensitive to everything, including Stefan. Instead of gently pushing his hand away at night as she had done in the early days, she opened to his touch and enjoyed the sensuality of her new body and the freedom from contraception. She sometimes felt like it was a kind of deception for those poor little guys with tails, swimming their hearts out with no hope of conception. A whole army sent off on a futile mission. Only one of them would make it into that giant egg at the end of the long dark tunnels and even that was doomed to fail.

It was all a bit strange, knowing that there was another little person nearby on the other side of a thin wall. But Gertrude was discreetly quiet during those times. She surely didn't know any better yet than to accept all the vitality of life around her.

* * *

Julia and Aleksander invited them on a trip to Mainz the next Sunday. They gladly accepted, deciding to take advantage of the good timing. Clare and Gertrude were still portable, but she knew that she would become more rooted in the final stages of pregnancy.

Willy had become an enthusiastic traveler. It didn't matter much to where, as long as they got to ride the trains. It was only a couple hours to Mainz and he and Zosia had lots to talk about. They were settled in school by then and their German flowed easily. Clare never ceased to marvel at the apparent ease with which children adjusted to a new language. Of course, she hadn't forgotten those early weeks that had been hard for Willy. But kids didn't seem to agonize as much about losing themselves for a while. Adults often felt reduced to a young child's inarticulate state, as though robbed of their whole intellect, status, and identity. It was a precarious and humiliating process for many.

"Language is so central to our sense of self," she would explain to her students on the first day of a beginning Spanish class. "Remember to celebrate what you learn and not worry about what you don't yet know. It's a process, so let go and trust it."

With Julia and Aleks, they alternated freely between English and German. Although Clare and Stefan were comfortably fluent in German, Stefan with a very convincing German accent, they most often reverted to English. Like so many Europeans, Julia and Aleks were very proficient in English.

They walked around the old town part of Mainz, with its half-timbered houses and medieval market squares. The Marktbrunnen, a Renaissance fountain with red columns, the Mainz Cathedral made of red sandstone and the Gutenberg Museum were high points.

Clare walked arm in arm with Stefan and enjoyed seeing Julia and Aleks do the same. Aleks was tall and slim, with straight dark hair—a contrast to Julia's shorter stature and light blond hair. Somehow, he didn't fit Clare's image of a Polish man; a silly stereotype, she acknowledged.

It was a glorious sunny day and Clare didn't want it to end. But the kids had school the next day and Aleks and Stefan had to get back to work. By the time they settled on the train, Clare realized how tired she was, and her back was grateful for the comfortable seat.

January 2001

The Christkind and Santa Claus had come and gone, and *Silvester* was upon them too quickly. Clare and Stefan had a party with their friends to bring in the new year and to celebrate Anja's visit. Samira and her family were there, as well as Isra and Esin. Jürgen and Christina had known Anja as Gertrude and as a new baby. They had invited their friends, Milo and Emilia, who had only known her as Gertrude. Some commented on how much Anja looked like Clare. Her long, thick hair was almost as dark as Clare's but with some lighter highlights and a touch of Stefan's free-spirited waves. Emotionally as well, she had some of Clare's intensity tempered with Stefan's calm.

"People like to focus on similarities, but Anja is clearly her own self," Clare responded, glancing with a smile at her grown up daughter.

* * *

There was still much to fit into the few days left of Anja's visit. Clare suggested they go for a long walk and see how far they might get. The two of them started with a stroll through the large cemetery that was not far from Das Haus.

"This is beautiful," Anja said as they climbed up the paved paths through the terraced lawns and trees of the cemetery. "It's so peaceful."

"Yes, another of my favorite words. *Friedhof* literally means a 'peace yard.' In 1980 we lived right on the edge of it. I'll show you the house later. Some people think cemeteries are creepy or scary, but I have always found this one to be the opposite. I remember walking through here with friends in the last days of waiting for your arrival."

"Mom..."

Clare turned all her attention to Anja and waited. That tone usually led to a serious discussion. New boyfriend? Drop out of school? Pregnant? Her mind started racing. They had discussed the possibility of Anja coming with them to attend the university in Marburg. But she wanted to do a semester program in France her junior year and was worried about getting behind.

"Mom..." Anja repeated. "I don't know what to major in. I don't know who I am or what I want to be."

"Oh, sweetheart, that's exactly what the first years of college are supposed to be about. You open your mind to everything, explore, try things on—"

"Yeah, but I have to declare a major soon and figure out my future career and get a job after I graduate and decide who I want to be in this world."

Clare took a breath and looked up at the trees whose bare branches arched above them, leaving intricate shadow patterns on the path under their feet. She had always sensed wisdom and patience in such old trees.

"You know, everything you learn will be useful in your life. You can't know how or when, but it all will be. It doesn't really matter what you major in. It won't be your identity and it may or may not even become your vocation. The idea is to study something in depth. Pick something you love that brings you joy, challenge and excitement. Explore the connections between things, how they touch the world and how they connect to you. We are never one thing, Anja. We keep adding layers and—"

"Theater. I love theater, but who gets a job in theater? I'm not sure how relevant it is."

"Well, remember what Shakespeare said, that "All the world's—"

"a stage and the men and women merely players." Anja finished the quote impatiently. "I know, I know. I just...I also love science and linguistics and psychology and..."

"Just pick one or two areas and take a few more courses for now. Sometimes a particular professor will turn the tide." Clare couldn't count the times she'd had students in her office agonizing over their majors. One

170

young man changed majors nearly every week. It became their private joke. But he did eventually settle on something, and it turned out fine.

Clare stopped and pointed to a house on the other side of a fence bordering the Friedhof. "Upstairs, where the small balcony is. That's where we lived when you were born."

"Wow." Anja looked for a few long minutes and Clare tried to imagine what she was thinking. "I wish I could remember it," she said. "I do remember seeing pictures."

They walked back to the street and then headed up a hill and onto a stone street towards the Oberstadt.

They decided on *Kaffee und Kuchen* at Cafe Vetter and stayed until their conversations dwindled.

"Would you like to walk up to the *Schloß*?" Clare asked, pointing toward the castle perched at the top of the hill.

"Sure, let's do it. The exercise feels good and how many times in my life will I have the chance to be in a castle? No princes on the horizon, as far as I can tell."

Anja stopped for a moment and looked all around her, imagining life five hundred, even seven hundred years earlier in that very place with many of the same buildings. The past was so much more present on those streets than in the United States. It was as though all the years had accumulated there, all that time up to right then with them standing there.

"It's like all the past moments exist together in this spot," Anja thought aloud. She stood still, fast-forwarding in her mind a movie of people and events over the centuries passing through the streets they had just walked.

Clare had often felt something like that. The notion of linear time didn't seem to fit human experience. She recalled the vision of her father playing harmonica on the bench in front of them. That image would be forever present for her.

"I sometimes picture the moments of our lives nesting inside each other through time, like your Russian dolls."

"Well, we humans do seem to be time-challenged. Even our computers were threatened by the new millennium. But they have survived the supposed Y2K collapse of the universe."

Clare laughed, remembering how everyone had waited with bated breath as the calendar turned to 2000. It was only about predicted glitches in the formatting and storage of computer data, but the big scare was that the

171

"bugs" would have huge global financial repercussions. People were awed by the beginning of the next thousand years. Yet, it was only one more day, like birthdays—completely insignificant in the grand scheme of things.

March 1981

Life was full and busy for Clare. In addition to the water aerobics, swimming, classes, choir and the daily shopping, there was also Willy's Kopfrechnen and reading and writing homework in the evening. Willy had become more self-sufficient in many ways, but there was the need to navigate and negotiate his social life and explorations. He still played in the dirt and Clare was vigilant. No more parasites so far.

In the pockets of time that were left, she had managed to finish a linguistics article she had been working on, going back and forth with her advisor through the mail with drafts typed on the clunky old German typewriter. When her thoughts started to flow, she would still often confuse the "y" and "z," which were reversed. "Many" would come out "Manz" and "type" would be "tzpe." "It's driving me crayz!" she wrote in a P.S. to her professor. There was no deadline to finish the article, but she felt some urgency to prove that her mind had not been taken over entirely by the "moo factor."

The regular appointments with the obstetrician were going well. Clare was enchanted yet again with the descriptive word building of German. Her doctor was a *Geburtshelfer*, literally a "birth helper," which sounded more like a partner in the process than the all-knowing and all-powerful obstetrician.

She had gotten over the awkwardness of her first visit with him. A few weeks after her initial negative pregnancy home test, she had decided to go straight to a doctor for confirmation of what she already knew. The nausea, tender breasts and generally strange feeling in her whole body were familiar to her. After filling out the paperwork, she had been told by the nurse to undress completely and leave her clothes behind the curtain. When she was ready, she should open the door and then sit on the examining table.

So, there she was, completely naked, with no sheet or cover in sight. Had she misunderstood? Was she really supposed to undress completely? Shit! What would the doctor think to find her sitting there *splitternackt*?

"Splinter naked," as they would say in German. She was just about to jump off the table and run for her clothes, when the doctor walked in. He was fully dressed in a suit and a white lab coat, looking very doctorlike and imposing.

"*Guten Tag, Frau Muller,*" he said, shaking her hand and looking only at her face.

"*Guten Tag, Herr Doktor.*" She wasn't sure how formal you were supposed to be in such situations.

"*Wie fühlen Sie sich?* How do you feel?" he asked her.

"*Schwanger,*" she answered. "Pregnant." She listed the symptoms that confirmed her suspicions of being pregnant. She left out the part about feeling embarrassed and awkward, remembering with amusement how Willy used to say "I'm 'barrassed" about something, which sounded like "bare-assed." And there was the common mistake her Spanish students made, translating "I am embarrassed" with "*Estoy embarazada*", which meant "I am pregnant," a very false cognate that did often lead to embarrassment in those cases. That all ran through her mind as the doctor gave her a pelvic exam, chatting all the while as though they were meeting over coffee.

"*Nun, Frau Muller, Sie sind tatsächlich schwanger.*" the doctor said with conviction. "Mrs. Muller, you are definitely pregnant. About six weeks along," he estimated.

Clare left the office elated as the nausea rushed in, as though the pregnancy now had official permission to honor her "the sicker the better" statement.

At each visit she would hand them her *Mutterpaß*, a "mother passport," to be stamped and updated. At one later visit they needed to draw blood to do some routine tests. Clare wasn't a fan of needles in her arm, but she had learned to relax and get through it. The doctor came in and said:

"I hope you don't mind, but we have a new intern with us. You are her very first official patient."

Oh shit. "Of course, no problem," she answered, giving a friendly smile to the girl, who looked nervous.

"I hope I don't hurt you," the girl said, her hands shaking visibly. Clare went into teacher mode and talked calmly, assuring her she could do it and telling her to take a deep breath and relax. She was reminding herself as well. They got through it and the girl grinned at her victory, while Clare recovered from the most painful blood draw she had ever had.

I guess that's what they mean by practicing medicine.

At six months it was time for the second ultrasound check on the baby. The first one had revealed the shape of a miniature being, cradled in a dark cave with a giant floating cable attached to its belly. It already had a face and tiny fingers and toes. Its chest was transparent enough that they could see the little heart beating. That was when Gertrude became a real baby in her mind, though Clare had already felt movement for a while. This time it was impossible to see the whole body at once. The medical technician ran the device with cool gel on it over her whole belly, revealing parts of the baby as she went. They were asked if they wanted to know the sex of the baby yet. Clare and Stefan answered *"Ja!"* in unison! If Stefan was wrong about it being a girl, they would need some time to adjust and think of a name for a boy.

As the technician hovered over the buttocks and nudged the baby a bit to get her to turn over, she said dramatically,

"I see...I see...nothing!"

Clare pondered that for a moment as Stefan immediately shouted.

"A girl! I told you."

The technician said it was probably 80% reliable. The lack of a visible penis made it more than likely a girl, but it could be the angle, or that the tiny appendage was hidden, covered up by the cord or something.

Clare contemplated for a moment that quintessential definition of female identity. The lack of a penis. A woman's sexuality was hidden, defined by what it was not. Psychoanalysis was full of talk about the lack of the phallus and the unconscious castration complex and all... Clare quickly pushed all that aside and celebrated their healthy baby who was probably 80% female. That sounds about right, she chuckled to herself. They had said they would be happy with a boy or girl—just a healthy baby. But secretly, she had thought it would be great to have a girl, so they would have one of each.

January 2001

Anja had gone back to her college life, having decided to take another theater class and try out for a play. She also signed up for philosophy and science classes to fulfill basic requirements as well as a class in linguistics, to test her interest there. Clare and Stefan felt a big hole after she left, but they gradually fell back into their routines. Clare had hoped that her mother would also come for Christmas, but she hadn't wanted to travel in winter.

"Maybe in the spring," her mother had responded to Clare's disappointment. Will had promised that he and Yolanda would spend some time with his grandmother over the holidays. Clare missed her mother and worried about her, but she also realized that her own new life in Germany had a momentum she needed to ride. She had promised herself that she would focus hard on her book after Anja left.

* * *

Notes for Book

The postmodern era is so named for what it is not, as much as what it is. (We are all named for what and whom we follow.) Fragmentation, rejecting the master narrative, embracing the meta-everything. A self-conscious awareness of the fictions that create our realities, fictions that comment on themselves: meta-commentary.

The metaphor. What is the meta for? Ha ha. And where do things like irony, Murphy's Law and serendipity fit in? And sarcasm, the bitterly ironic questioning of the fictions and follies that govern our certainties.

Clare took a deep breath and let it out slowly as she closed her laptop. She was on a roll with her writing and sometimes forgot to take breaks. The sparrow hadn't been back for a few days.

"I miss you, my little friend, but I'm on my way now. You can go tap on someone else's window."

* * *

Jan 10

I dreamed that I had become a professor of Sarcastology, a cutting-edge field of study that had become popular in academia.

175

Professors playfully called themselves 'anti-fessors,' 'inter-fessors' or sometimes 'meta-fessors.' It was all about deconstructing everything with a mocking irony that left every-one confused about the analysis of anything. It was crazy!

I was so glad to wake up in your house, Hannah, where the walls breathe and adapt to the stories we tell and the structures of our thinking. So many different times have lived here—still live here. How many centuries? I really want to know when the house was built. I can feel the layers of years past float freely in the present when we turn off the lights.

Jan. 15

My dear Hannah, I dreamed that I was writing my book by hand on the outside of your house! I had white paint and a small brush to write the titles and main ideas on the dark timbers of the frames. On the white plaster sections I had to use bigger brushes and colored paint. As I wrote, I could feel the house breathing and I couldn't concentrate. I tried to sort my thoughts into clear, analytical prose, but the colors would run together, dissolving the words. I kept painting over what I had written since I could not erase anything. It was a mess. I worried about what you would think when you came home.

March 1981

"How about we sit for a while in this nice grassy spot?" Clare suggested. "My back is getting tired."

She and Julia sat on a bench under the shade of a maple tree. The sunlight danced through the leaves. Julia offered some nuts and dried fruit and Clare accepted gratefully. As they chatted, a woman approached them, singing and talking to herself cheerfully. She was dressed in a black suit with a black derby hat to match, dark curls bouncing under the brim.

"I think I know her," Clare whispered to Julia. "I've seen her before. Wait, I know, it's Die Nachtigall!" The woman began to sing for them, arms outstretched and smiling at her appreciative audience. They clapped when she finished singing and then stood up to continue their walk. Die Nachtigall saw Clare's protruding belly and had lots to say about it.

"You need to sing to your child. And talk to her. Tell her lots of stories. Stories every day, lots of stories. Stories, stories. And songs. Singing is good, you know. Never enough songs. And stories. Songs and stories. She's listening, you know. She will hear you and you need to talk to her now so she will know you when she's born. She will remember."

"How do you know it's a girl?" Clare asked with a laugh when the woman paused for a breath.

"Of course it's a girl. She just is. She needs your stories. And songs. Now don't forget."

Clare thanked her and they waved as they walked away, leaving Die Nachtigall singing with the birds in the trees around her.

"A strange woman," Julia said, shaking her head, "but rather charming."

"She is in a better mood today than the first time I saw her. Delightful, really."

"Now don't forget to tell Gertrude stories, lots of stories," Julia repeated, patting Gertrude on the back or butt or whatever part had just moved. "And songs."

"I think Gertrude agrees with her," Clare said laughing.

January 2001

Life was good. Stefan had found many stories in the Archive and layers of historical and metaphorical complexity. He often talked about his research as a form of archeology of the lives and minds of people in the past. He was now deep into the writing and construction of his book. Clare was writing as well, and they enjoyed their parallel activity in the house—Stefan at a table in the living room, and Clare upstairs at the writing desk in their bedroom. They could both be lost for hours in their individual rabbit holes, but they remembered to take breaks and resurface to the time and space they shared.

"Time is such a complex concept, though we treat it as the most mundane theme of our lives," Stefan shared over a second cup of coffee. "Hannah Arendt wrote about how our limited life span as humans transforms the continuously flowing stream of change into time as we know it."

Clare had been running into more questions of time herself. The circular time of life cycles, memory, writing. She remembered that when she was writing her dissertation it had become clear to her early on that she couldn't write the beginning or the end until she had written the body of the work. She had jumped in and started in the middle, wrote all the internal chapters and then after she had finally written the conclusion, she knew how to write the introduction. It was all connected and the book found its form in the process of writing.

"The end defines the beginning, and the rest is not linear," she said, taking a deep breath and then a long exhale.

"As death defines our lives."

"Hey, how about a walk?"

"Great idea." And off they went, enjoying the room in their lives for spontaneity. "And maybe a stop for…"

"*Kaffee und Kuchen*," they said in unison. German cakes were as good as German bread.

"None of that fluffy sugary stuff with no flavor," Stefan had said once.

"No *Schlabberkuchen* for us," Clare responded, remembering the word she had learned about flabby bread.

"Is that even a word?" Stefan wondered.

"It is now!"

It was a chocolate lover's heaven. Their favorite cake was *Sachertorte*, of rich chocolate layers with apricot preserves in the middle. Or the *Schwarzwälder Kirschtorte*, another chocolate delight with cherry and cream filling.

"I think the only reason that Germans aren't all fat, is that they walk before and after the indulgence." Clare commented as they walked out the door.

* * *

Jan 29

We're eating too much cake and bread these days, Hannah. Pure, delicious sin. I think we're going to need to do more walking, like the long hikes we used to take through the woods and fields to nearby villages. But Stefan and I are both consumed by our writing.

178

* * *

"Isra, did you ever hear from Aisha again?"

The three of them were sitting in Café Barfuß in their usual spot. Clare and Samira waited quietly for Isra's response to Samira's question.

"No. I was heartbroken but eventually I managed to move on. After I had been in Berlin for a couple years and I had moved in with Esin, I got an email from an old friend I had kept in touch with. She told me she had heard news about Aisha. Many from our group had wondered about her since no one had ever seen her again. There were theories about her being sent away somewhere."

Isra paused and rested her forehead on her hands.

"She's dead. It was an honor killing."

"*Ilaahayow!* My God!" Samira turned to Clare to explain. "It's when a male family member kills a woman or girl who has dishonored the family. It happens in Somalia, too."

"So, all that time that you didn't hear from her, she was…" Clare caught herself as she began to state the obvious.

"I have lived with that for a couple years now and it still haunts me daily. I feel partly responsible for her death. It's a horrible burden."

"You shouldn't have to carry that," Samira said with a mixture of sadness and anger. "It's not your fault. Centuries of tradition have kept alive that despicable cultural practice. I don't believe it ever was or will be Allah's will."

"Thanks. I don't either." Isra sighed. "Life moves on and I try to forgive those men—and myself. I am so grateful to have Esin, who is the love of my life and helps me cope with it all. I don't know what I would do without her."

March 1981

"I heard about a couple lectures at the university next Tuesday. I'd like to check them out." Clare said one morning. "Can you be here when Willy comes home from school?"

"Sure. What's the topic?"

"José Ortega y Gasset's philosophy and his relationship with the university here in Marburg and the neo-Kantians of that time. A professor

179

from the university will give a talk in German and then a visiting professor from Spain will give one in Spanish.

"That sounds intense."

"It could be." Clare was not a philosopher, but she was intrigued by some aspects of the field. She had done an independent study project on Ortega y Gasset's philosophy the year before in her graduate program and had found it fascinating and reasonably accessible. It was worth checking out.

"So, how did it go?" Stefan asked when she got home.

"Well, the first talk in German gave me a headache. It was so convoluted, and I kept waiting for the verbs at the end of long sentences. I don't know, I began to think that I didn't understand Ortega's philosophy at all. But I stuck around for the one in Spanish. It was totally different! I mean, it was essentially the same topic, but it was all so clear. Sure, my Spanish is still better than my German, but the lecture seemed so different in Spanish. '*Yo soy yo y mi circunstancia.*' That pretty much sums up a big part of Ortega's philosophy. 'I am I and my surroundings.' His major writings were all about the idea of life as the dynamic dialogue between the individual and the world."

"That didn't come across in German?"

"Maybe it was me, but it just seemed so complex and overly structured, it didn't match Ortega's style or thought. But who am I to say?"

"Well, you know, some German scholars of philosophy say that they prefer to read Hegel in English translation rather than deal with the original in German."

"That makes sense. I heard a funny story about when Ortega y Gasset met Martin Heidegger at a conference in Darmstadt. They apparently had a friendly tension where their philosophical works overlapped and differed. At one point, Heidegger said to Ortega 'So what do you really think of my work?' Ortega answered, "Dance, Mr. Heidigger, dance'."

Stefan laughed. "Ha ha, that's a good story."

"I'm not sure how to interpret it, though," Clare confessed.

"He was probably just telling the guy to lighten up," Stefan added, as Clare looked down to watch the interpretive dance moves that distorted her belly. "You know how those German philosophers could get pretty weighed down with their theories, as though they didn't want regular people to be able to understand them."

February 2001

Feb. 5

I had a strange dream last night. Well, I guess all dreams are strange, by our waking standards. I was asleep in my bed, and someone was touching me gently with their fingertips moving slowly all over my body. Each touch left a charge that was almost electrical as I floated in a timeless semi-conscious state. The arousal awakened me (in my dream) and I watched as the seduction continued. With each touch a small green shoot sprouted there. Pretty soon, I was covered with them. My body became a garden of greens, with some blossoms beginning to form. It was so intense that I woke up (for real) in bed next to Stefan. We made love as fiercely and passionately as in the early days of our romance.

* * *

When Clare awoke the next morning, Stefan was leaning on his elbow staring at her.

"Have you been watching me sleep?" She hated the idea of someone observing all the inadvertent and unflattering habits of the unconscious body.

"I was just noticing how beautiful you are when you're asleep. Your face is relaxed, and your skin seems to be glowing with health."

"I do seem to remember a special Swedish massage in the night. Or was it a German one?"

"Specialty of the house." Stefan smiled and began to trace his fingers over her face.

"I think we need to get on with our day," Clare said with a laugh in her voice.

"That's just what I was doing…"

181

She was already on her way to the bathroom, appreciating the European custom of bidets. She also loved the big deep tub in Hannah's bathroom. She planned a luxurious soaking bath, even before coffee. A new day in the prime of her life.

As she sat watching the tub fill and bubbles from her bath oil beginning to foam up, she noticed something she hadn't seen before. On the inside of the tub wall near the top was some writing in small gold letters. She stepped into the bath and as she slid her body into the silky warmth, leaving only her head above water, she saw it again. *Bamberger.* It was probably the name of the company that made the bathtub.

But wait, Bamberger...Bamberger...why does that sound so familiar? Oh my god, it's my great grandmother's family name. Or was it my great-great grandmother? Bamberger... yes, that's the German root of my family tree! Clare remembered seeing an old picture of a white-haired woman with a bun and a little cloth cap with strings tied under her chin and a long dark dress with a white apron.

"I think she was my mom's great grandmother." Clare added, after telling Stefan the story. "I don't even remember her first name. I don't think my mom ever knew her. I need to ask her sometime. It's not like it really matters, but the connection just struck me."

April 1981

"I'm really 'cited 'bout my first *Fußball* practice." Willy bounced around the apartment in his new soccer shoes. He was already experienced with the sport and looked forward to playing again.

"It may be a bit different than what you're used to," Stefan warned. In kindergarten Willy had been part of The Dinosaur League for little kids. They played what Stefan and Clare called Swarm Ball. The kids would all run after the ball in a clump and every parent just hoped their kid could get a foot on the ball at least once.

"Whadya mean?" Willy asked, his enthusiasm fading.

"Well, some kids start kicking the ball around at a very young age here and..."

"Never mind, let's get going. It'll be fun, you'll see," Clare added, giving Stefan a "What are you doing?" look.

They came home after practice and Willy flopped on his bed.

"How about a snack?" Clare offered.

"I don't wanna eat."

She sat on the edge of his bed. "Don't be discouraged. You'll catch up and learn some new skills. And just think, when you go back home, you'll be ahead of the other kids."

"I don't wanna catch up."

"Okay, but right now you need to come eat and drink something." Clare recognized the signs of low blood sugar feeding his disappointment. "We'll talk about it later."

Willy decided to give it another chance, mainly because he'd made a new friend. Till had smiled at him and passed him the ball on the field. As they were leaving, he waved to Willy and said *"Bis nächste Woche!* See you next week!"

"I guess I wanna go back and try again." Willy announced after his snack. "Till is 'specting me to be there."

Stefan bought him a small soccer ball and some days after school they practiced dribbling and passing. They talked a bit about the structure of the game. In Germany it was clearly *not* Swarm Ball.

* * *

Willy and Jonas had a spring project. The weather was warm and the rains had stopped so they returned with renewed enthusiasm to their little cave—a dirt hollow sheltered by the thick tent-like covering of a large bush. The branches reached nearly to the ground in a tight weave of twigs and leaves that created a perfect hideaway from the world of adults. They called it *Die Höhle.* The Cave.

"We need to make it bigger," Jonas declared one day. They had some new toy trucks and tractors to play with and plans for excavation and construction.

"We could dig it out and make it deeper," Willy suggested.

But there was one problem. A large stickery plant had grown up right in the middle of their little house.

"Don't touch it, it will burn you," Jonas advised. He spoke from experience.

"How can a plant burn you?" Willy was skeptical.

They tried digging it out with a toy "dig-up tractor," but the clay dirt was packed hard around the strong roots. Finally they gave up, discouraged by the insurmountable obstacle.

"We have to ask my dad." Jonas sighed in defeat.

Jürgen arrived with thick gloves and a trowel and studied the situation with respectful seriousness.

"*Das ist eine schöne Brennnessel.* A nice burning nettle," he explained to Willy. "It stings you if you touch it." He soon held the offending intruder in his hands. "This will make a delicious soup," he told them. "It's also used to treat lots of ailments." The boys looked at each other as Jürgen went off whistling with the treasure in his hands.

They all gathered that evening for the nettle soup. Willy was reluctant to taste it, but when he saw that nobody seemed to be suffering from a burning mouth, he gave it a try.

"It tastes good!" he exclaimed, then waited to see if he could feel the magic plant fixing any problems inside that he didn't know about. Willy looked at Jürgen with new respect. Jonas' dad was wise and he knew secret things.

February 2001

"How is Isra doing?" Clare asked Samira, as they walked along the main street in town. "I haven't seen her for a while."

"I saw her last week. I think she's doing okay; she's busier now. She found a part time job at the lab where Esin works. I didn't know that she already has a degree in Biology and some lab experience. She also volunteers at the immigrant center. Her German is pretty good, so she can be of help there."

"That's great. I was really moved by her story. I keep thinking about how we all have been outsiders in our lives in some way. Of course, for migrants that is intensified. You start as outsiders and give up so much to belong to your new home. When do migrants stop being migrants? How long does it take? How many generations?"

"I have often wondered that. I definitely feel like a hyphenated person myself, a Somali-German." Samira thought about it for a moment. She couldn't give up one side for the other, but they were each changed by the

184

presence of the other. Bashir and Casho identified as German. Their Somali heritage was important to them, but it came second.

"It's hardest for people like Isra," Samira continued, "who were already outsiders in their home of origin, having to deny a part of themselves to pretend to belong. But even with all the challenges and losses of the new life, it's a chance to start again, to find a home at the intersection of multiple communities and individual relationships."

"Maybe that intersection is a more honest picture of who we all are," Clare responded as they approached a crosswalk at a traffic light.

They stopped and waited for the light. A young woman came up behind them and asked, "Have you pushed the button yet?" Clare shook her head. "If not, it can take forever to cross," the woman said, walking towards the pole and feeling for the button. That's when Clare realized that the woman was blind. While she and Samira had walked casually along and not paid close attention to where they were or the specific intersection, their new companion knew exactly where she was.

"Traffic doesn't seem too heavy today," the young woman commented.

"No, I guess not," Samira answered, smiling at her.

Clare wondered if the woman could hear a smile. "It looks like it might rain," she added, to make small talk.

"Yes, it does." The young woman said, "I can feel it and smell it. There we go, we can cross now. Have a nice afternoon." She crossed the street with confidence and purpose before Clare and Samira even realized the light had changed.

"This town really is a city for the blind," Samira said. It's amazing how well set up it is. She could hear the beeping just as the light changed."

"Have you noticed that the bus stops talk?" Clare had heard them before, but she hadn't really paid attention. "I think it tells the routes and times of the buses that come through there. And maybe which one comes next. It makes me realize how we tune out so much that doesn't directly affect us."

Samira took Clare's arm as they crossed the busy street together. "I have also heard that there are ridges and bumps on the sidewalks to warn people of hazards or barriers coming up, or maybe even something like a bus stop. Some buildings have raised maps and floorplans and a few city landmarks have miniature bronze models that people can feel."

"Pretty amazing." They stopped on the other side. Clare turned to Samira. "You know, being here now, this year that we are spending in

185

Marburg...I...I feel like I'm learning to see in new ways. It's not just about becoming more aware of the obstacles and opportunities for people who are blind, though those are still mind-blowing for me. It's also about seeing through the lenses of different languages and cultures, the stories of my new friends, the great marvels and burdens of being a person in this world. We create routines and put on blinders to get us through the labyrinths of life, the overwhelming complexity of it all. Yet we miss so much that way. These days I notice little details: the way the bare branches of a tree carve up the sky, how drops of rain roll gently off a leaf, the shape of your mouth when you speak in Somali."

"That's poetry, my friend. That's why we write." Samira looked at Clare, her dark eyes melting a little in that tender moment. "And that's why I love you."

10
Gestation

April 1981

Clare sent off the final version of her article to be submitted for publication. It was a study of two words in Spanish, *saber* and *conocer,* that both meant "to know," one of those lexical pairs that were confusing to students of the language. Through her research, Clare had discovered that it wasn't just a vocabulary problem, but rather more of a philosophical one. What *can* we know and *how* do we know it? The semantic distinction in Spanish existed in English, but only through descriptive explanations. The British philosopher, Bertrand Russell, had written essays talking about "knowledge by description" and "knowledge by acquaintance." There were no words that could substitute satisfactorily for the Spanish ones. It was an interesting challenge for translation.

She had been pondering a strange question for a while. What is a word? she asked herself. What we call a "word" is just a collection of sounds that evolve in a living context, that come to mean something we think is collectively understood in the same way. But what about the deaf, for whom a word has only visual symbols? Or the blind, who have tactile symbols for the sounds they hear? It was one of those questions that should have a simple answer but that could uncover a complex network of ambiguity underneath.

Some words, perhaps most words, were an intersection of many meanings, like a three-dimensional object with multiple perspectives that gave it a solid life. Clare had read about an amazing new medical invention called magnetic resonance imagining, that relied on a series of single images to create a full picture that allowed doctors to see inside the body, even inside the internal organs. Linguists sometimes tried to do that with words by studying their origins, functions, changes over time, place, and current uses. But most people just flew by, trusting that what they said would be received by others as more or less what they meant.

"There is so much that we take for granted, " Clare thought aloud as she mailed the package.

"Oh, *Entschuldigung*," she said when the clerk looked up at her. "I was just thinking about something."

It was easy to get lost in the mystery of things. Like looking through a microscope, seeing a whole new world there and forgetting that you had to zoom back out to the level that human culture accepts as reality.

February 2001

Stefan had left early for the Archive. Clare went out walking, lost in her thoughts about time, memories, friendships. And language. Everything seemed to be connected through language. Just to be able to communicate at all implied a shared understanding, a trust that each word we utter will resonate in the same way in another's ear. Friendship and love were about building a common vocabulary connected to shared experience. Like Willy's Enten.

Writing was a way of creating experience, a friendship with each reader, anonymous but intimate; to build a kind of community; dispersed and unknown, but connected through the collective journey of a story. In the end it would be a different story for each reader.

Clare found herself back at Das Haus and went upstairs to write in her journal.

Feb 10

I've been thinking about language a lot lately, Hannah. When you learn another language, a new world opens—one that was always there but was invisible to you. Like the moon in its new moon phase. The shape of the moon doesn't ever change, just our relationship to it, our perspective. As our world turns, we see things differently.

In learning another language, we move into a foreign reality where most things are familiar, but they have other names. A kind of parallel universe. Only through experience can we learn to trust our old friends in strange new clothing, as well as meet new ones we have never imagined.

* * *

Notes for Book

Are dreams fiction? A construction of the subconscious? A ghost
screenwriter of censured experience?

Explore this more:

literal vs. figurative meaning
Do things happen literally (exactly, to the letter)?
Or do they happen literarily (as part of our narratives)?

Fiction vs. History

Fiction announces its false premises, its freedom from fact and
reason. From the outset. It says, "This is a novel, so no apologies
for our inventions and imaginings," but reality and truth are
housed safely within its walls.

History proceeds with a foundation of documents and reason,
analysis and analogy, though there may be fictions hiding within its walls. There are checks and balances on its assertions, but
we must often call on the imagination to fill in the cracks.

Writing is a pact with the reader about what to expect within its
house, though there may be deception and disguise in either
form of narrative, whether intentional or inadvertent.

History and fiction have cross-pollinated over the centuries, and
they have shared and exchanged conventions of form and content.

April 1981

They had met for lunch at the Ratschänke restaurant in the Oberstadt,
and afterwards Julia invited Clare to walk with her to the Physics
Department building of the University. Clare was glad for a little more
exercise, and they headed down the hill, chatting all the way. After

delivering some papers to Aleks, they continued walking through quiet neighborhoods, on the way down the hill to catch a bus home.

"I think we can cut through here to get down to the street," Julia said.

One of the things they both loved about the town was the way it was built on hills, nestled among forests and small mountain ridges. They kept discovering new little alleys or stairways up towards the castle or down to the lower part of the city. Sometimes they were narrow passages between tall Fachwerk buildings that seemed to lean in from both sides. Other times it would be a hidden path through old trees and tidy homes.

"How are Noam and Marya doing?" Clare asked as they walked. "I haven't heard anything about them for ages."

"I think they are fine, very involved in their work and Yaniv's cello lessons. They think he has a lot of talent and they're pushing him hard to develop it." Julia sighed. "It's a bit much for a seven-year-old, if you ask me."

They walked on for a moment, nodding to a man who was unloading bags from his car.

"Do you ever think about chance?" Clare wondered.

"In what sense?"

"Well, like about how all our little daily decisions create our lives. For example, if Frau Holzer hadn't let us stay at the Gästehaus, I never would have met you. Or maybe not even then, if our kids hadn't gone to the same school."

"Yes, I think about that, too. If we hadn't left Poland when we did, our lives would be so different now. Hey, let's try this way. 'Leckergäßchen,' what a great name!"

"*Leckergäßchen...* Delicious little alley?" A treelined path with mossy stone walls on either side sloped gently downward toward the main street. There *was* something delicious about walking through the greenness, the leafy shadows on the pavement amid spots of sunlight.

"Speaking of chance, I was just thinking about the little concert that Die Nachtigall gave us the other day. What are the chances that you would run into her twice in this city?" Julia commented.

"Yes, and...wait a minute, that looks like...Hey Samira, is that you?"

"*Hallo!*" Samira looked up and waved.

"We were just talking about chance meetings and the paths our lives take. How great to meet on this sweet little alley. Julia, this is my friend

Samira," Clare said, thinking of the easy sprouting of friendships and community she had found among women. "Samira is from Somalia. And this is Julia, one of my first friends here in Marburg. She is from Poland. We met each other through our children."

"So nice to meet you," they said in unison.

"I was just on my way to the Marktplatz. This is my favorite little shortcut," Samira shared.

The three women chatted for a while and then went on their ways, one up the path and two on down it.

"If we had stayed at lunch or the Physics Department a moment longer, I wouldn't have met her today," Julia mused.

"And if I hadn't had a miscarriage, I wouldn't have Gertrude now. Or if we had conceived a moment earlier or later, it wouldn't even be Gertrude."

February 2001

"I've been thinking..." Clare said softly into her first cup of coffee.

"Already? So early?" Stefan teased.

"I've been thinking that most societies throughout history have been structured around the enclosure of women."

"Well, there is some truth to that. Where—"

"Like breeding stock, you know? And they married so young, still children themselves, really. They didn't know any other life."

"Where are you going with this? Do you feel enclosed yourself? You did marry young, but so did I, for that matter." He reached for her hand. "We've done alright, haven't we?"

Clare looked up and smiled. "Yes, of course. I'm one of the lucky ones. But it does often seem like a man's world outside the home. Many men still feel that women are invading their space, running wild where they don't belong. I suppose your women married early."

"My women?"

"The ones you are studying."

"Oh. No, in fact they didn't. In the 18th century peasant women usually married later, due to inheritance questions or land availability. With each generation, there was less land to pass down. The mean age of marriage for women in 1724 was over 24."

191

"Wow, I didn't expect that. So did that mean they had fewer children?"

"Yes, exactly. The mean age of death for women was 40.78 years old. The number of children was 3.22, with only 1.92 surviving their mother. A hundred years earlier, those numbers were double that."

"How strange. Why would that be?"

"Well, for one, there was more mobility in later years. More exposure to the outside world meant more illness and poorer chances of survival for children. Not to mention plagues, poverty, wars, famine, harsh winters. Some families tried to have more children so enough would survive to take care of them in their old age. Pastor Busch talked about the hourglass whose sands varied in volume."

"Meaning…"

"That some people had shorter lifespans. And of course, he meant children."

"That sounds so dark and depressing. I guess people adjust to what they know, what they think they can expect. I'm glad we ended up with two whole children."

* * *

Feb. 17

I had an awful dream last night, Hannah. I lived in a small Fachwerk farmhouse with my husband and a couple children.

It wasn't really me, but I was there—it was like I was in the life of Stefan's 18th century stories. My husband kept saying we should have more children so we would end up with enough that would survive to take care of us when we were old. "No!!" I shouted. "There is not enough food now and my body is already worn out after five pregnancies. And God told me last night in a dream that I was only supposed to have 2.3 births." What a strange thing to dream. It's funny, that's kind of what I had in this life— two children and a miscarriage.

* * *

"I picture a God with white hair and beard," Clare told Stefan the next day. "You know, the standard patriarchal image of a guy sitting up there working out the odds for each woman. 'Now, this one gets 4.1 births but only 1.9 children survive'. Like Santa Claus doling out presents according to each kid's karma."

"You do know what a statistical mean is, right?"

"Yeah, I know. I was just being sarcastic. Like my dreaming brain."

"Ah. Watch out for that dreaming brain."

"Sometimes I dream that my dad says strange things to me. I'm there trying hard to make sense of it all and then I see the twinkle in his eyes, and I know that he's just teasing me. Maybe God is teasing us half the time."

April 1981

Easter arrived and so did the *Osterhase*. Willy didn't really believe in the Easter Bunny or the Tooth Fairy anymore, but he pretended that he did. His parents pretended that they thought he did. Sometimes those fictions were what sustained holiday rituals. They dyed eggs and planned an Easter dinner with their friends downstairs. It would be a traditional *Lammbraten* with *Salzkartoffeln, Grüner Soße* and an *Osterlammkuchen for dessert.*

"Lamb Roast, salt potatoes, green sauce, and Easter Lamb Cake?" Willy translated aloud. "What are salt potatoes?" he asked Christina.

"Peeled potatoes boiled in salty water, with a little *Petersilie* on top," she answered.

"*Petersilie?*"

"Um, I think it's par…"

"Parsley!" Willy shouted.

"What's the green sauce? It sounds yucky."

"It's a creamy sauce with lots of green herbs in it. It is a specialty of this region and it's quite delicious." Clare smiled at Jürgen, thinking he would surely provide the herbs.

"But lamb cake?" Willy was worried.

"It's just a cake made in the shape of a lamb. You like cake, don't you?" Willy nodded enthusiastically.

"Would you and Jonas like to help me make it?"

"*Ja!*" They answered in unison.

193

"Can we lick the pan?"

Easter morning Jürgen and Stefan got up very early and hid the dyed eggs and some candy in little nests around the yard. There were lots of good hiding places in the uneven terrain that sloped down the hill. The Osterhase had been generous and there was an impressive harvest of goodies. The meal was splendid, and they all ate too much.

"I like German Easter," Willy declared as they went upstairs. His parents agreed.

* * *

A few days later Willy's very loose tooth finally came out. Stefan had kept suggesting that they tie a string to the tooth and around the doorknob and—

"No!" Willy would shout, running off to his room. Clare gave Stefan a look. She knew he wasn't serious, but really? Why did he torture his son with that old myth? She remembered her father doing the same with her. It might have encouraged Willy to finally pull the tooth out himself. He came running into the living room with the tooth in his hand and victory on his face.

"Does the tooth fairy come to Germany?" he asked his parents.

"Absolutely," his father assured him. "But her name is '*Die Zahnfee.*' Go hide the tooth under your pillow and we'll see what happens."

Willy came out the next morning with a coin in his hand and a sad smile.

"Wow, that's a lot of money! A whole German Mark," Stefan said.

"But I wanted more coins like these." Willy opened his fist to reveal a handful of five- and ten-Pfennig coins.

"Let's count how much they are worth." Stefan offered.

"It's sixty-five." Willy announced after counting.

"One Mark is worth a hundred Pfennig. So which is more?"

"One Mark," Willy said reluctantly. "But I still like Pfennig more."

"Well, let's see if I can change that for you." Stefan pulled a handful of change out of his pocket, and they counted the different size coins together. Clare threw in some more and they managed to add it up to a hundred Pfennig total—one Mark. Willy sauntered off with his pockets jingling and feeling much richer than he had with just that one heavy coin.

February 2001

"I think I'll go for a walk," Clare declared, after their morning coffee break. "I need to clear my head. I have so many ideas and threads of things swirling around but I don't really know how I'm going to put it all together. I'll be back in an hour or so."

"Don't get lost."

Clare wasn't sure if Stefan was referring to her walk or her work. Maybe both. Sometimes she could go out walking and be so submerged in her thoughts that when she came up for air, she would not be sure where she was. It was like the automatic pilot she used to blame on her car when she was driving to the supermarket and would end up at the university. "What am I doing here?" she would ask herself and remember that she was supposed to go shopping. The horrifying part was that she was somewhere else in her head the whole time, though some part of her brain was clearly functioning to drive the car. "It's the curse of the intellectual," she used to say to herself. "We live in our heads too much."

This time she was determined to empty her mind and focus on the world around her. She decided to head to the little park a few blocks away. It was a sunny day, though still a bit chilly. The promise of spring was in the air.

Clare sat on a bench and listened to the birds, closing her eyes to the sounds and smells around her. She leaned her head back to turn her face toward the sky. The air was cold, but the sun felt warm on her skin, and she let her shoulders relax. She heard footsteps pass in front of her and a breathing sound, maybe the panting of a dog? She opened her eyes as an old man turned to greet her.

"*Schöner Tag heute.*"

"*Ja,* a lovely day it is. Spring can't be too far off. *Guten Tag, Herr....*"

"...Schmidt," he said, putting out his hand. "Johann Schmidt." She had seen him there several times before and they had nodded to each other and smiled as they passed.

"Clare Muller," she responded as she shook his hand.

"May I?" he asked, indicating the bench. His dog parked in front of her without asking permission.

"Yes, of course, please sit down."

Clare looked more closely at her new acquaintance. It was hard to tell how old he was. Deep wrinkles in his face and gnarled hands suggested he had several decades on her. But he had a full head of white hair, walked upright and his voice was steady. Over eighty, for sure.

They began to chat, and Clare found herself petting the dog as they talked.

"Where are you from?" It was obvious that she was a foreigner.

"*Ich bin Amerikanerin.* My husband and I are living here for a year, doing research and writing."

"*Ah. Sie sind hier willkommen,*' he answered with a smile that creased his face even deeper. "You are welcome here." Clare had often noted a social reserve in Germans, who didn't interact easily with strangers. But this man seemed very comfortable in his old age and open to the world.

"*Danke schön.* I love living in Ockershausen." She began to tell about their stay in Marburg twenty years earlier and her experience this time. "Have you lived here long, Herr Schmidt?"

"My whole life. I was born in Ockershausen, a few blocks from here." He pointed in the direction of her street.

"Do you still live in the same house?" Clare was confused but didn't want to pry too much.

"Yes, I do. But that's not where I was born. I was born at the midwife's house. Most of the locals were, back in the day."

"Hmmm, that's interesting." She decided to leave it at that. *I wonder...I'll ask Hannah about it someday.*

May 1981

"You look like you swallowed a big soccer ball, Mommy."

No kidding. Her 'soccer ball' had been practicing for a while already. Gertrude was sometimes a ball at rest and other times a very active player.

Clare's days were full of activities. Stefan's work was going well. They enjoyed occasional dinners and outings with Christina, Jürgen, Jonas, and Lucas. Clare still liked to take long walks, except that she had to pee more often. A tree or a bush would do just fine when they were outside of town. But in town, she had to keep in mind where the next bathroom might be. She was no longer worried about a miscarriage, she assured Willy.

Choir practice continued and she loved it. That ancient sacred space and the pure sound they could produce together there had a soothing and uplifting effect on her. Sometimes Gertrude slept through it or maybe just quietly enjoyed the music. But other times she played her own special organ, that is, kicking one organ or another in Clare's body to produce different sounds. That was a special challenge since those notes were not in the score. There was a concert coming up in a few weeks and Clare hoped that Gertrude would cooperate. Too bad she couldn't leave her with a babysitter yet.

Willy was happy in school. They were reading a lot and his cursive writing was developing nicely. German schools preferred to start kids off with cursive writing right away in first grade and the kids seemed to pick it up easily. They began with big letters, but as the year progressed the writing got smaller and began to flow more naturally. The German style of script was more ornate and complex than the American handwriting that Clare had learned in her childhood days.

Willy told her that in second grade they would learn to write with a fountain pen. He didn't need to practice Kopfrechnen anymore because he had it down. Clare was relieved because she had found it hard to keep up.

* * *

One afternoon Clare was busy reading for one of her classes. It was a novel by the Puerto Rican writer Rosario Ferré, one of her favorite authors. *La casa de la laguna,* The House on the Lagoon, was a family saga with the ongoing dramas of many generations. It was a story full of the history of Puerto Rico following the social and political changes in the country along with the parallel changes in the family's house over the years.

The novel also contained the story of its own writing. The female protagonist was writing a novel about the history of their families, and her husband, a historian, found her manuscript and secretly began writing in the margins, critiquing the falsehoods of the fiction. It raised fascinating questions. Clare had read the book before in a graduate class and she really enjoyed reading it again.

She was deep into a chapter and the images that the writing evoked, when suddenly she felt that something was wrong. Leaving behind early 20th Century Puerto Rico, she tuned in to her present time in Marburg. It was almost 3:00 and Willy should have been home by 2:30. She felt a nervous slither in her stomach that roused Gertrude as well, but they tried to keep calm.

Clare ran downstairs and phoned Julia to see if Willy had a playdate with Zosia that she might have forgotten about.

"He's not with us. Do you want me to come help you look for him? I saw him waiting for the bus."

"Thanks. We'll wait a while longer. Could you check the Spielplatz and the Bäckerei for me in the meantime, just to be sure? It's hard to imagine him going there without asking me. But sometimes he gets lost in his own world and just follows his curiosity."

Clare went out to the backyard to see if she could see Willy coming up the hill along the path. No sign of him. Did he miss the bus? Was the bus delayed? Had he stayed to play with a friend? He had never been late before. She went back to talk with Christina about what to do next and decided to give him until 3:30. If he didn't show up by then, they would start driving around and then maybe even call the police.

"What if the bus had an accident?" Clare suggested, her heart pounding.

"Could he have accepted a ride from someone he didn't know—"

"He wouldn't do that!" Clare said with such vehemence that Christina looked startled. Clare was trying to convince herself.

Just then they saw Willy zigzagging up the path, kicking a small stone and twirling around a couple times.

"Willy!" Clare shouted, running toward him.

"Hi Mommy," he said cheerfully, a bit surprised by her intensity.

"Are you alright? Where have you been? I was getting so worried!"

"I'm fine, Mommy," he said calmly. "Are *you* okay?"

"Why are you so late? It's almost 3:30!"

"Oh, yeah, well I just decided to try a different bus today."

"What are you talking about? A different bus?"

"It was getting boring coming home the same way every day, so I decided to take a #7 bus instead. It went to the Bahnhof and so I got off and then took a #3 home. It was fun."

"You went all the way to the train station? How did you know what buses to take?"

"I just got on to see where it would take me and then I would figure it out."

Clare hugged him hard. Things had surely changed since the fall when the bus ride had been so scary and overwhelming. She took a deep breath while fear, anger and pride wrestled it out inside her.

"Okay, I am proud of your resourcefulness, but don't EVER do that again. Do you hear me? This is a big city and it's not safe to do that."

"I wasn't worried. What does 'sorcefulness mean?"

"It means you are smart and brave to figure things out. But don't do that with the buses anymore. Okay?" He shrugged his shoulders.

"Okay. But can I still be 'sourceful?"

"Of course, that's one of the things I love about you." Clare put her arm around his shoulders as they walked up to the house. Christina waved and smiled, having understood the gist of the story from their body language.

That evening, Willy told his dad of his adventure, with all the pride of his "'sourcefulness." At the end, he looked at Clare and then added, "But I won't do it again 'cuz Mommy gets too worried."

March 2001

"Muller, Guten Tag."

"And a lovely good day to you, Clare. How are you?"

"Hannah! It's great to hear from you." Though they rarely talked more than a few minutes, they had become more informal along the way.

"How is everything at the house?"

"The house is fine as always. And we're both deep into writing."

"Prima! That's great."

"Hannah, did your house by chance once belong to a midwife?"

"Yes, it did! That's a long story. Sorry I can't talk long right now, but I'll tell you all about it when I come home."

Wow, I don't know if I can wait that long! Clare's mind was racing, and she was excited to tell Stefan about it. He was at the archive, so she went out to the balcony. As she sat down, her conversation with Anja came back to her, as clearly as though it had been just that morning. Their words, Anja's face, the sun warming the chilly air, were all right there with her. Clare realized she hadn't been out there since early January. It was partly the cold weather, but also that she had been swept along by her writing and the conversations with Stefan. And her grief, she noted, with almost a touch of sadness, had softened and faded quietly into the background.

"That's crazy!" she exclaimed to the vines heavy with buds. Do I actually miss the pain of grieving? I guess grieving is attached to the loss, which is the closest contact with the dad I loved. Death was the last one with him. And yet, the farther away we get from that day, the freer he is to spend time with me in all his forms.

Clare's father had become regular company in her dreams, appearing in his different father-ages throughout her life. One night he was the father of her five-year-old self, the next it could be the one who had just died or the father at her wedding. He was a versatile actor.

* * *

Notes for Book

Fiction is a form of art which presents its truths veiled, under the mask of pretending. Can we say that fiction pretends to tell the truth so that we will believe that it is in effect *pretending* to tell the truth, to hide the fact that deep down…it really *is* telling the truth?

Postmodern novels can be subversive by challenging traditional notions of plot, narrative, chronology, and character development. They are self-reflexive; that is, they contemplate the nature of fiction and their own creation and sometimes include other kinds of texts within the novelistic world. (*Don Quixote* was a "postmodern" novel four hundred years before its time!)

May 1981

"I think we should speak German when we're on the bus or in stores," Willy announced in a serious voice.

"Okay," said Clare. "Why do you think that?"

"So people won't look at us. I don't wanna always be American."

"Does that make you not be American anymore?"

"You know what I mean. I don't want people to only think that. I'm not *just* American."

"Well said. You are a wise little guy."

Some days Willy came home from school and started to tell Clare about his day in English and then he would look frustrated and switch to German. She realized that he was having to translate his experience, which had all been in German. She was also living much of her days in German, and she often contemplated how that shaped the nature of her own learning.

* * *

"Have a good day at school," Clare said one morning as she kissed Willy on the cheek. He already looked like a German kid, with his bookbag, the monthly bus pass hanging around his neck and the confidence in his routines. "And remember, take the bus straight home."

"Always every day you tell me that," Willy complained. "That I know already." Clare smiled to herself as she watched him march off. He had probably been thinking in German and had unconsciously mapped German syntax onto his English. That's a sign of true assimilation of a language, the linguist in her thought. The mother in her was proud.

"Seven-year-olds are both delightful and exhausting." Clare remembered her mother telling her once. "They are little judges. They remember everything you say and hold it against you when they need to."

Wise words, Clare thought. Willy was gaining confidence in himself and realizing that his parents didn't know everything. They could be challenged at every turn.

"You say it's good to talk to people, meet new people and be nice to everybody. How come you tell me I shouldn' talk to strangers? If you talk to them, they aren't strange anymore. Like my bus driver. On TV there are bad guys, and you know they are bad. How can you tell if someone is bad outside TV? At my school in Iowa, we saw a movie 'bout bad people and we shouldn' let them help us. I was walking home from school one time and I asked a lady if she was bad. She said no she was a mommy and she loved children. Can mommies be bad? We read a book in school 'bout people who were black and people thought they were bad, but they were just reg'lar people and people were mean to them. Why are people mean? Johnny was mean to me once but his mommy said he was just sad and confused 'cuz his parents were getting deforced."

"I think you mean divorced," Clare answered, going for the low hanging fruit. Where to even start with his questions?

"I was bad when I picked Mrs. Haskin's flowers. I didn't mean to be bad, I just wanted to bring you some flowers," Willy added, with a shaky voice.

"Don't worry, sweetie, we knew you were trying to do something nice. And you were only five then. Sometimes we make mistakes even with good intentions. It takes a long time to sort out these things." Like your whole life, she thought, but didn't want to say that to him.

"My 'tentions are always, I think mostly, sometimes good," Willy said thoughtfully before running off to play with Jonas. Clare took a deep breath. *I guess even seven-year-olds can get tired of their own inquisitions.*

March 2001

"*Guten Tag, Herr Schmidt.* How are you today?" Clare squatted down to pet his dog.

"*Frau Muller,* nice to see you. You could call me Johann, you know." He patted the bench next to him. "We've been meeting now for quite a while." He winked at her with his eyes sparkling.

"Of course, Johann. And please call me Clare," she said with a grin. She had already become quite fond of her companion in the park.

"How's the writing going?"

"It's going well, thank you. I have lots of notes and a structure is starting to take shape. I'm fascinated with the midwife's house. Could you tell me more? I believe that I am living in that house."

"I remember my mother used to visit her. Her name was Elizabetha. Sometimes she would take her a cake or some fresh bread. My mother was a wonderful baker. Elizabetha didn't just deliver babies. She treated the women during pregnancy and took care of the mother and baby at her house for a week after the birth. She knew lots of herbal remedies for things and people would consult her sometimes for milder maladies."

"Like *Spulwurm*?" Clare asked, with clear memories of what the awful creature looked like.

"Oh yes, that was common. I remember when my mother was pregnant with my younger brother and then my sister, I would go with her for her checkups. My father was off at the war—the first World War—so I went everywhere with her. There was a little balcony where I would sit to wait for her."

"I can picture that," Clare said with conviction. "Do your siblings still live here as well?"

"My sister does. I never knew my brother. He had serious problems and he only lived a few days. He died in that house."

"Oh my, how sad! Do you know what happened?"

"Not really. My mother never talked about it. She said that he wasn't meant to be in this world and God took him back to heaven. I just accepted it. That's the way it was."

"And your sister?"

"She is five years younger than I am and she lives nearby with her family."

"Do you have a family, Johann?" She asked tentatively.

"My wife died a few years ago. We could never have children of our own but we adopted a girl who lost her parents. Her name is Mia. She met an American when she was at university, and they moved to the States. I have three grandchildren and seven great grandchildren there."

"Do you see them often?"

"I used to go visit every year, but I don't travel much anymore. They come here to see me now and then. I have a niece and two nephews and their children who live in Germany. They come by sometimes."

"Well, I'd better get back to my writing, *Herr*...er, Johann. I'll see you tomorrow." She leaned over and planted a light kiss on his cheek. She was going to suggest to Stefan that they invite him for dinner sometime, when she felt ready. She was strangely hesitant to have him come to the house, as though being there in the actual building might break the spell of his memories. She had so many questions.

May 1981

"*Tief atmen. Unterschenkel anspannen und lockerlassen.* Breathe deeply, tense your lower legs and then release." Clare responded with her eyes closed as she listened to the woman's hypnotic voice. They were all lying on mats, their eyes closed, eight couples in a *Geburtsvorbereitungskurs,* a childbirth preparation class. Half of them had bulging bellies. They were guided through the whole body, tensing and releasing each area, to learn how to identify different muscles and command them to relax.

Clare wondered how Samira was doing with it all. She opened her eyes to sneak a look at her friend. Samira had her eyes closed and seemed to be following the exercise. She had shared with her that in Somalia, during labor and birth, a woman would pray to Allah for guidance. She would be surrounded by her community of women who would pray with her. Clare wondered if Samira was following the exercises or practicing her prayers. She chided herself for letting her mind wander.

"Now expand your breath deep into the lower abdomen, pushing your lower back muscles outward as you make space around the baby and give the uterus room to do its job." Clare loved that the womb was called *Gebärmutter* ('birthing mother') or *Mutterleib* ('mother body') in German. It made her feel a closer kinship to that part of her body, like she had a mother-partner in the pregnancy.

"When you feel contractions, you can expand your pelvis with them and ride the waves. Remember that your body knows what it is supposed to do." The men chuckled as they tried to imagine their bodies doing any of that. The coach had insisted that they go through the exercises with their wives so they could be helpful when the time came. Clare turned her head to smile at Samira and check how Omar was doing. She was glad they had decided to come to the class. It gave them another connection and she enjoyed being around them.

"You are all entering or are already at a viable stage in the pregnancy. That means that your baby could probably survive if born today. All the important parts are there, and it is just getting stronger and bigger."

"No kidding," Clare whispered to Stefan. This was her second time watching her body being taken over, impossibly stretched and misshapen by a beloved creature; yet she still found it amazing. The life that filled the center of her being and added many pounds to her body as it elbowed her own internal organs out of the way— it was *of* her, *in* her, yet it was not *her*. It was not even hers. Gertrude had already been her own person for quite a while in Clare's mind and body. And Clare was certainly already her mother, giving the baby everything she needed before her own body got what was left. In this case you didn't get to put your own oxygen mask on first, as the airlines always suggested.

"Imagine the contractions now. Observe the pain, but do not fear it," the coach continued. "Breathe deeply, expand your pelvis and picture the baby moving downward toward the birth canal."

"Yeah, that's the hard part," Clare said to Stefan later. "This huge soccer ball that I swallowed, as Willy says, is supposed to come out the narrowest part of my body. Sometimes I think the architect could have done better with that design."

"It's all about the breathing," Stefan said, shrugging his shoulders. They both took a deep breath.

"Hola, Carmen!" Clare stopped to talk with another new friend, a fellow round bellied woman and her husband José. They were from Spain, and Clare's language radar had sensed that they were Spanish speakers, even when they were speaking German. She found out that Carmen was also attending a class at the university, so they had arranged to meet for lunch or coffee a couple times. Carmen's baby was due about a month after Gertrude, so they often compared notes on their progress as well as their experience as foreigners in Germany.

"Hey, Samira." Clare gestured for her to come join them. Sharon had been there as well, but she was feeling tired and went straight home. "How about we three meet up for lunch or coffee sometime this week?"

"Maybe not coffee," Samira said. "My baby is too active already."

"I can identify with that." Clare nodded.

"Mine is a calm one," Carmen added. "A little wine with dinner and she settles in for the evening. It's at night that she wakes up. That could be a bad habit to start before she's even born."

"So, you know it's a girl already?" Samira asked. "We decided we didn't want to know yet. It will be a surprise." They parted ways with a plan to meet the next day for lunch.

"*Is arag danbe!*" Clare said, waving to Samira as she and Omar left. Samira turned and grinned at her. "*Is arag danbe,*" she replied. "See you later."

"Do you speak Somali?" Carmen asked.

"Only a couple phrases. *Is araq danbe* for *hasta luego*, and *Salaan ka waran* which means *¿Cómo estás?* Guess I'd better get going before Stefan leaves without me. *Adiós, Carmen. Hasta mañana.*"

March 2001

"More coffee?" Clare nodded as Stefan paused over her cup with the coffee pot.

"Tell me more about Pastor Busch's metaphors and sermons." As dark as Stefan's research sometimes seemed, Clare was fascinated with the fortitude and resilience of people whose lives were so much more difficult than hers.

"Well, the notion of eternity was hard for people to understand."

"Still is, I'd say."

Stefan nodded. "We think of our lives as a timeline. Busch used spatial metaphors to make it more easily accessible for his parishioners. He wrote of striving towards The House of Peace and Heaven as a paradise which is above us."

"A Sunday school image still dominant today. I can't remember a time before I learned that." Clare added.

"He also began to talk about their lives as a *Wanderschaft*, a pilgrimage. It was a metaphor but there was a physicality to it. Not only was God visible but paradise had a spatial location above."

"And how did he deal with women's lives?"

"Busch also had passages for women. He used them to mark female gender and to structure women's roles. A recurrent negative theme was the lustfulness and impurity of women. He also emphasized the ordeals of women, whose salvation could be underscored by work and childbearing."

"Of course. It's the old 'women are responsible for leading men astray' trope." That one had always rankled her. "I know, I know, it was the times. And I suppose he found biblical verses to support that. You can find almost anything in the Bible."

"Yeah, well, the guy was juggling a lot of stuff, trying to acknowledge his parishioners' difficult lives and console them in their suffering. There had to be some picture of hope to sustain them. His own ideas seemed to change over time, as Christian moral explanations began to cohabitate with more modern medical ideas of death. He spoke sometimes of how difficult the sudden, unexpected deaths were for people. It left them confused and in shock."

"I can relate to that." Clare sighed.

"I know." Stefan reached over and stroked her hand.

"When folks were old, very sick or slow in dying, it made more sense and was easier for the family. They had time to process the experience and prepare for what was coming."

"I don't think that has changed much."

"In some ways, I would agree, though for most of us now the medical view dominates. But there is often still an underlying metaphysical or moral confusion about 'Why me? Why now? Is it my fault? Am I being punished?' We are also taught to fight death and if we lose, it is a failure, or at least a tragedy. For much of Western culture, there isn't much support for facing death with courage and equanimity."

"Well, on that note, it's time for my walk and my rendezvous with Johann."

"Should I be jealous?"

"Absolutely," Clare murmured as she kissed the top of her husband's head.

May 1981

"Three very pregnant women walk into a cafe..." Clare thought it sounded like the beginning of a joke, but then left it hanging. They had considered eating at one of the tables on the street, in front of Café Barfuß, where they could enjoy the warm spring weather and watch people go by in the Oberstadt. But they looked at the straight-back chairs and opted for the comfortable sofa seating inside in a corner of the café, where they could talk. Clare was impressed by how open they could be with each other right away. They had emerged from three very different cultures as independent, outspoken women, who enjoyed each other's company. They toasted to their healthy pregnancies and complained about the challenges that they presented.

"I lost a baby early on, just before arriving in Germany," Clare began. "It was a miscarriage that was a blessing, I guess, because that baby wasn't going to make it. But it was still hard. It makes this time around seem like such a gift."

"I lost a baby five years ago," Carmen said. "An abortion." Clare and Samira looked at her in surprise.

"In Spain?" Samira asked. "That's hard to imagine. Was that after Franco?"

"It was shortly after his death, but it wasn't in Spain. I went to London." They waited in suspense for her to go on. "It was a tough time."

"Abortion is illegal in Somalia, though sometimes it is permitted to save a woman's life. Things have become somewhat more liberal in recent years, but for most Muslims there is still great shame associated with it. It is a very patriarchal society and women do not have much say over their bodies. Most families would consider abortion a sin."

"Carmen, what did your family think about your situation?" Clare asked.

"They didn't know. My family is conservative Catholic, and you can't talk about such things. I didn't even tell them I was pregnant. They would have been scandalized. I was single and it was…it was unwanted."

"And the father? What did the father think?" Samira added.

"I didn't see him again. I didn't know him. It was…., I was…" She closed her eyes and a few tears fell. "I was raped."

"Oh my God," Clare and Samira said in unison, reaching out to their friend. Clare's own loss suddenly shrank in her mind.

"That happens a lot in Somalia—to young girls even. Often, they are forced to marry the perpetrator."

"It happens in the U.S., too. But at least now we have a law that legalizes abortion. It is still very controversial socially, though."

"Even contraception is shunned in Somalia. Most people believe that if Allah gives us these babies, we should want them. Many women give birth every year. The only acceptable way to control that is to nurse each baby for two years."

"Does that work?"

"Sometimes, but women get worn-out giving birth and nursing so much of their adult lives. It's common to have at least five children, sometimes many more. You know, I do believe that children are a blessing from Allah, but I don't accept that it means we can have no say about it. It would be hard for me to choose to have an abortion, but I believe it should be my choice."

"The Catholic church in Spain is still totally opposed to contraception, but many Catholic women use it anyway. For centuries, midwives had helped women with all of that: childbirth, abortions, contraception. Then the male-led medical establishment saw midwives as a threat and worked to discredit them, sometimes accusing them of witchcraft.

"Our bodies are still not our own in many ways," Carmen went on. "I'm from Barcelona and just last year a group of women was arrested there for having abortions. It has become a big political deal. During the Franco era people were also punished for being homosexual. Lesbianism was considered a disease and they proposed medical treatments and psychotherapeutics to cure the problem. But that has been changing in recent years."

"Yeah, that notion still exists in the States," Clare said, shaking her head.

"In Somalia homosexuality is completely illegal, sometimes punishable by death."

"That's intense!" Clare exclaimed. "How do things get so extreme?"

"When the people in power are afraid of losing that power, they hold on tighter. It seems to be the same everywhere." Samira's voice was thick with anger.

"These days, our bodies are literally not our own," Clare said, patting her belly, in hopes that Gertrude would settle, "but at least we invited the intrusion."

"I wonder what it would be like if women ruled the world."

"Well, not perfect, but surely different."

"Anybody for dessert?"

"I wish. There's nowhere to put it."

March 2001

Mar 8

Some days I forget to write. I don't know why. It is really calm-ing for me, Hannah, to write in this journal. I just put down whatever comes to mind or pours out without me even thinking.

It is such a personal and intimate space. I guess that's why women's writing has traditionally centered around journals, letters, or private poetry. In times past that was the only acceptable outlet for most women. Yet from ancient times there have always been a few female poets, scientists, philosophers, physicians, who have written. I wonder what their lives were like.

209

There is a popular notion that there is a clear line between personal writing, creative writing, and formal academic writing. The first is assumed to be subjective, undisciplined, and informal, the second is the finished work of artists, and the third the product of disciplined abstract thought and argument. I have noticed more and more recently how these categories are oversimplified and there is much cross-fertilization and legitimacy in all of them. Just as dreaming is an important part of a healthy mind, so emotion and intuition are crucial to the intellect and vice versa. Living is a creative process.

* * *

Notes for Book

Why do we write? Is it to document? Explore? Educate? To vent, understand, analyze, entertain...? How does our writing begin? What will we call it? Can we really know when we start what it will be when it's finished?

Possible title for my book: *The House of Fiction*

11
The Flow of Time

March 2001

Clare sat in the kitchen, musing about her walk by the river the day before. She had stopped to sit on a grassy bank in the morning sun. It felt good to be alone. A slight breeze rippled the water that gurgled by like soft laughter. Her thoughts settled into a quiet place in her mind. She felt a deep awareness of self, a wordless presence that surrendered to the calm of the river.

"The river is an apt metaphor for human understanding," she said to Stefan as she watched the patterns of sunlight dance on the kitchen wall.

Stefan handed her a mug of hot coffee.

"Thanks," she said between sips.

"It's a powerful image; sometimes a positive, hopeful one, and sometimes the opposite. *Nuestras vidas son los ríos que van a dar en la mar, que es el morir.*"

Stefan looked up over his coffee mug, waiting for a translation and explanation.

"Jorge Manrique wrote that in 16th century Spain. 'Our lives are the rivers that flow into the sea, which is death.'"

Stefan nodded. "Ah yes, that would be the negative kind. Our lives as a path toward death. The notion that no matter what we do, we can't stop that journey."

"I found another quote in my notes—Marcus Aurelius, around second century A.D. I think."

> Time is like a river made up of the events which happen, and a violent stream; for as soon as a thing has been seen, it is carried away, and another comes in its place, and this will be carried away too.

"I think this one is more about change," Clare offered. "The present does not exist as a static moment, but rather floats on a current from past to future. As soon as we observe a moment, it has already become past. The problem

211

with that linear image is that it seems backwards. If time is a river that flows from the past toward the future, then the present is swept along towards the future, not the past."

"Hmm. Well, in a sense that is what happens," Stefan added. "Although our present moments constantly and instantly become part of the past, our new "present" is the next step forward towards a future. We're on a moving walkway."

"Ortega y Gasset said that life is a series of collisions with the future. But meanwhile that future that we just left behind gets farther and farther away from us as we move along. It's like each newly formed past moment falls off the walkway or becomes debris on the banks of the river. Or maybe the past does move with us, while it also stays behind? It makes me dizzy to think about it."

"Hence, the notion of time as the fourth dimension of the universe."

"Or as a human invention to try to understand our experience.

"And then there is the world of physics and quantum mechanics."

Clare snorted. "You'll lose me there!"

"Don't worry. I think the simple summary of all that, is that we can't really understand any of it."

May 1981

"*Guten Tag, Muller.*"

"Clare? It's Nick.

"Hey, what's up?"

"I just wanted to let you guys know that we have a baby girl!"

"What?! But..."

"Yeah, I know. Three weeks early. We certainly weren't expecting it yet and it all happened fast."

"Stefan! Nick and Sharon had their baby!! Nick, how's Sharon? How are *you*? Did everything go okay?"

"Yup, she's fine. They both are. We're still kind of in shock. Sharon was hoping to make it for the concert."

"Wow. Well, congratulations!! I can't wait to see the little one. Let us know if we can do anything to help."

* * *

"I'm nervous," Clare said as she dressed for the concert. They had been preparing for it for months and the day was upon them.

"But you said you felt really good about the music, both your part and the whole chorus."

"Oh, I do. The rehearsals have been going very well."

"Then why are you nervous?" Stefan put his hands on her shoulders and made her stop and look at him.

"It's just...well, I never know what Gertrude will do. What if she is playing soccer and tries to kick a goal just when I—"

"Maybe drink some chamomile tea before you go to calm her down a bit?"

"...or if my water breaks or..."

"It's too early for that. You'll be fine. I'm looking forward to hearing the music."

She drank some tea and rubbed the big soccer ball as they walked out the door.

"You gotta help me on this one, sweet baby. We can play soccer after the concert."

Clare wondered sometimes how long she could keep going to classes and shopping and just being out by herself on foot. It was early still, but Murphy didn't always respect what was supposed to happen. In fact, wasn't that the definition of Murphy's Law?

The concert went well. Clare forgot her worries and immersed herself in the joy and power of the music. She had loved the intimacy of the small chapel and the pure acoustics it offered, and the first time they rehearsed in the church, Clare had found the space intimidating under those sweeping high arches. But there was something glorious about filling the large nave of the church with their voices and by the time of the concert, their small choir had opened to its full potential. They sang as one voice that was a weaving of many voices. Having an audience to receive their offering stirred an energy that seemed to carry their music beyond their own reach and abilities. It was magical.

And Gertrude behaved. Clare imagined her singing along. After all, she had been at all the rehearsals.

Gertrude wasn't always as patient in classes and Clare occasionally made a funny noise or jumped in her seat. By now, the class was already in on the game, and someone would say *"Guten Tag, Gertrude!"* or "Gertrude one, home team zero." And everyone would laugh. Clare hadn't planned to share such intimate details, but it was hard to hide it. She appreciated the little community of support, and it made her feel less self-conscious. It was one thing to try to repress your own bodily functions in public, but this was beyond that. There was another person involved, who did not yet know the rules of polite company.

March 2001

Mar 12

Is time a continuum? Or maybe it's just a bunch of molecule-moments bouncing along to create the illusion of continuity. It seems to me that the future and the past are both imaginary: the future because it is unknowable, the past because our experience and our memories are only partial.

The moments of our past, that were once an unwritten future or a fleeting present, remain only as fragments from which we can construct our stories. We're not even sure if we remember them, or maybe we only remember our memories of them. Like photos in a family album or the shards unearthed at an archeological site, our memories seem strangely incomplete and out of place as we re-member them into our present narratives. Even the future that we imagine is a pastiche from the archives of our experience, which is the only real material we have, to create a sense of continuity in the river of our lives.

Clare closed her journal and opened her laptop. She sat for a moment, not sure how to begin. She had many loose ideas floating in her brain and scattered notes from her reading. How to pull it all together? It was overwhelming. A distant memory of her mother dumping the contents of a thousand-piece puzzle box on the table popped into her thoughts. Clare was four or five years old then and she had wanted to cry. There was no way to create a coherent picture out of that huge mass of gray pieces.

"Now, let's spread them out and turn them right side up, her mother suggested. As they flipped the pieces, a chaotic world of color began to emerge. "You sort them by color and I will look for straight edges that could be part of the frame. One step at a time. We don't worry about the big picture yet."

Soon Clare was focused on collecting pieces with green in them that might fit together somehow. That was manageable.

* * *

Notes for Book
The House of Fiction
(A Half-Timbered Tale)

Chapter 1: The Foundation

Premise: Fiction, Non-Fiction, History, Philosophy, Science, are all defined by the ground they are built on, claims to truth, a contract with the reader.

History of writing history and fiction, how their forms influenced each other and changed places.

History of fiction / fictions of history

Narrative and human culture

Fischer narrative paradigm: humans tell stories to understand their world.

Oliver Sacks: We each have a continuous inner narrative, that is our life, our identity. We need such a narrative to maintain a sense of self.

Etymology of word 'narrate': Lat. 'narrare' to tell, relate, recount, from 'gnarus' PIE (proto-Indo-European) 'gno-'= to know.

215

We narrate not so much to express what we know, or think we know, but to make our world more knowable.

The foundation of the Fachwerk House was made of stones that were gathered locally. The stones are symbolic of the cultural paradigms and contexts on which our stories are built: the stories (floors of the house) and the layers of our lives and understanding.

* * *

"*Hallo.*"

"Hi Samira. *Setahay*? How are you?"

"I'm fine. But busy! How have you been?"

"Busy, too, but good. I just called to say 'hi.' I miss you, Samira. Time is going by too quickly and I don't want to lose touch."

"Yes, let's get together soon."

"I met an interesting guy I want to tell you about."

"Oh? A guy?"

"No, not like that. An older gentleman named Johann. I'll tell you about him when we meet."

"Now you have me curious. How about lunch tomorrow?"

May 1981

"How come I always have to clean my room?" Willy was in a whiny, stubborn mood.

"It's about responsibility and it will make you feel better. It's like washing the dishes so you can start with clean ones when you eat." That sounded lame even to Clare, but it was the best she could do at the time. She didn't feel much like doing her own cleaning chores either.

"It's my room and I like it messy."

"But I don't like to see the mess."

"Then close the door."

"Just do it because I asked you to, okay?"

"Sometimes you don't do what I want. Why do I always have to do what you want? Can you 'splain that?"

"The word is **ex**plain, Willy."

Willy paused for a moment; eyes turned upward as though seeking an answer from the ceiling.

"Heather's mom use ta talk 'bout her 'x'. Heather told me that was her dad, who wasn't her mom's husband anymore. Does x-plain mean it use ta be plain?"

Clare laughed. Willy laughed with her, but his expression was still earnest. She worried sometimes that his hearing was compromised, the way he dropped syllables and shortened words. But tests had shown that his hearing was sharp.

"It must just be his personal shorthand," Stefan had said once. "His mind races ahead and he doesn't want to waste any time on unnecessary syllables. He just goes for the essence of the word."

"And he thinks about words a lot." Clare said. "Our little philosopher-linguist."

March 2001

Mar 20

I had a dream last night, or maybe I should say "I watched a dream." The woman was already exhausted, and the labor was not progressing well. Elizabetha helped her up to walk around some more. "I shouldn't have come to you so soon," the woman said. She was worried about her little boy staying with the neighbor for too long. They went downstairs and Elizabetha handed her a small cup. "Drink this," she said. It was a tincture of blue cohosh, to help move the labor along. They walked around in the garden for a while, pausing for the waves of pain. It was dark and peaceful, and the contractions began to come faster and stronger. Elizabetha led her back upstairs and told her to rest between the contractions. "Breathe deeply and let your pelvis open to the pain."

It's so strange, Hannah. I dreamed that scene like I was watching a movie. But I was there, and I felt everything that the woman did.

217

I was her, but I was also outside watching her. When Elizabetha said to her / me "Don't worry, your baby will be fine," I woke up in the dark in our bed. Stefan was sleeping next to me, and Elizabetha was gone. Yet I still felt her presence.

I've been reading about the medicinal herbs that midwives used to use, and still do, I believe. It's fascinating. Stinging nettle, comfrey, oat straw, red clover blossom, blue cohosh, and many others.

* * *

"I've been thinking about time again," Clare said as they settled into their morning writing break. Stefan handed her a slice of still warm dark bread. She spread some *Quark* and *Preiselbeermarmelade* on it and took a bite. "God, this is heavenly! This bread with sour Quark and sweet lingonberry jam just makes my day. How will I live without it when we go back home?"

Stefan smiled and nodded as he ate his own slice and washed it down with his favorite dark roast coffee.

"You know, I don't think Germans drink as much coffee as we do."

"Yeah, but it's such good coffee. And it's part of writing, a better addiction than smoking, I'd say."

"Yes, I'm glad you left that one behind."

"So, what were you saying about time?" he asked, picking up the topic that had been suspended in their culinary delight.

"Oh yeah. Well, time is complex in literary narrative. I used to think of the variety of structures used by writers as just literary techniques. But in many ways, they represent our reality. We think of time as linear and yet our experience with it is rarely that. Our current moments constantly interact with memories of the past and future projections. It seems like time is defined and redefined for us by our own lives."

"Heidegger's *Sein und Zeit*, Being and Time. Now there's a headache for you!"

Clare laughed. "Yes, I suppose I should read that, but I've always been intimidated by German philosophy. I know that he was important in the

218

school of philosophy at the University in Marburg. Did you know that Hannah Arendt was his student?"

"Yup. And his lover."

"Tell me more about Heidegger." European intellectual history was one of Stefan's specialties.

"Well, he believed that death is what gives time meaning. We can only understand it because of our own mortality. He talks about *"Dasein"* as literally 'being there;' being in the world."

"I can see how Ortega's philosophy relates to that. And didn't you say that Hannah Arendt talked about how the presence of humans, with their consciousness of a limited life span, created the concept of time as linear?"

"Yes, we need a spatial metaphor to understand it, so we think of the past as behind us and the future ahead of us on the path of life."

"And we invented clocks to measure time and try to control it."

"And how's that working out, do you think?"

"Well, personally I never seem to have enough time, no matter how I plan it. Sometimes it feels like it speeds up and slows down on me."

"That's just your wild Irish nature."

"But seriously, my years of exposure to Mexican culture changed my allegiance to the linear notion of time. In many indigenous cultures their cosmology is based on a circular concept of time that is both cyclical on Earth and formed of concentric spheres of origin, life, and the afterlife. You can see it in modern daily life. In Mexico City, for example, they uncovered ancient temples right in the middle of the city, which was originally built on a lake so the foundations of the past are shaky. They even named stops on the Metro for some of those Aztec structures."

"And then there's Elena Garro. Wasn't she a Mexican writer?"

"Yes, and the queen of writing about that tangle of timelines! Remember when I went to see her?" Clare felt a wave of sadness as she recalled the image of the frail and depressed old woman she had met, once recognized as one of the great Mexican writers of her time. Yet the world in which the woman lived was one of loneliness and poverty.

"I think so. Wasn't there something strange about time?"

"Definitely. It was unreal. Unless, of course, you are familiar with Garro's writing. She often mixes past and present moments in creative ways. I went to see her because I wanted to give her a copy of my first book, which included a whole chapter about one of her novels. I found out where she lived and went to meet her.

"We spent several hours talking about her writing and narrative in general. I realized that it was getting late, and I needed to catch a bus back to Cuautla. I looked at my watch and thought it had stopped, but then I realized that it said it was earlier than the time I had arrived! I said goodbye to Garro and left feeling dazed, not only by the time confusion but also the intensity of meeting her. I had alternated between thinking she was brilliant and deciding she was crazy. When I checked my watch again, I noticed that it was running backwards. I mean, the second hand was literally going counterclockwise!"

"Doo doo doo doo..." Stefan imitated the eerie musical intro to the old *Twilight Zone* television series. "Creepy."

"But whenever I tell that story to people familiar with Garro's writing, they always just nod and say 'Of course.'"

May 1981

It was the last water aerobics session, and they were all quieter than usual in the shower. Two of the women had already had their babies, one right on time and the other, Sharon, unexpectedly early. They wished each other well, hugged the best they could and waved as they walked out the door.

"Do you have any idea how hard it is for two very pregnant women to hug each other?" Clare commented as she told Stefan about her day.

There were a couple more sessions at the childbirth class, but there, too, one more couple had already left. There was no news of them yet. The relaxation exercises had become easier and were a welcome respite for Clare. They also learned about how and when to push and how to stall that urge when needed. Clare appreciated the frank discussion of labor and birth, even though it wasn't new to her. There was a popular saying that women forget a lot about the details and the intensity of childbirth—nature's way of convincing them to go through it all again. She knew it would all come back in the moment, but not always in calm clarity.

"The vocabulary in German surrounding the birthing process is so full of mother imagery, it connects everything."

"It certainly gave me a new perspective," Stefan agreed.

"The uterus is the *Gebärmutter*, the birthing mother, the midwife is the *Hebamme,* originally the old woman who lifts, or the *Wehemutter,* the pain-contraction mother."

"Sounds like a couple of extra mothers already." Stefan laughed. "I believe the English word 'midwife' originally meant 'with woman'—the one who accompanies the mother in childbirth."

"The cervix is the *Muttermund* or 'mother mouth.' The placenta is the *Mutterkuchen,* the 'mother cake' and then you have *Muttermilch,* 'mother milk.' If a baby is born with a birthmark, it is called a *Muttermal,* a 'mother sign.' I looked that one up. Apparently, in the 16th century these marks were thought to be signs of the mother's cravings during pregnancy. I think Gertrude's would look like a potato chip. Meanwhile, you have a mother helping to pull the baby out and another one squeezing from the inside. It's like a whole team of mothers!"

"I wonder if there is any relationship between the word *Mut*, 'courage,' and *Mutter* '*mother,*'" Stefan said. "If not, I think there should be. Speaking of mothers, is your mother still planning to come?"

"Yes, she already has a ticket for a little before the due date. She's going to stay for a few weeks."

"That's great. She'll be a big help. Only a month to go!" He held out both hands with thumbs tucked under curved fingers. That was the German gesture they had learned to wish for good luck. They had also been told that crossing your fingers meant you were lying.

"I hope we don't get too much bigger. My back is already aching."

The next day was orientation at the hospital. They waited in the lobby for their guide to meet them. It was an attractive building with friendly greetings and peaceful photographs. This was one example where Clare preferred the Latin-based euphemistic word "hospital" from *hospes* meaning "guest," to the straightforward German word *Krankenhaus* or "sick house." She looked around and imagined coming back as a "guest." There was a beautiful poster of a mother nursing a baby with soft romantic lighting that was supposed to make you feel warm and safe. In large letters at the bottom, it said *Stillen ist gut für Mutter und Kind.* Breastfeeding is good for mother and child.

"I love the word *Stillen*," she whispered to Stefan. "It sounds so peaceful and calming. I like the way it focuses on an intimate moment of stillness between mother and baby, not just a hungry baby sucking on your breast."

"Please follow me, if you will," said an efficient young woman to the group. "I will be giving you a tour of the *Geburtshilfeflügel,* the 'birth-help wing', of the hospital. We want you to feel comfortable and know what to expect when your time comes."

"Please be seated," their guide said as she showed them into a small meeting room. "A midwife and a doctor will be here in a minute to talk to you about the procedures and options." They waited in silence for a few minutes until a woman and a man walked in. The woman addressed them in a relaxed and friendly manner.

"Hello, everyone. My name is Schwester Monika Wagner, and I am a nurse midwife. When you first arrive, we will check your vitals and the progress of labor. We'll also monitor the baby and make sure that everyone is ready for this great event. You will have some options along the way, depending on the stage of labor and how fast it is proceeding. We midwives direct the process right up to delivery and we will be your partner in decisions along the way."

"I am Doktor Fischer." The man had sat down on a desk behind Schwester Monika and stood up to introduce himself. The white coat and stethoscope around his neck had already made it clear who he was.

"A doctor will also check in with the midwife occasionally and be present for the delivery if needed, especially in case of an episiotomy or other surgical interventions. I want to emphasize here, with great respect, that this is one of the most, if not *the* most, athletic events a woman will experience in her life. For most women, this is very hard work, and you will be assisted by the Gebärmutter, a remarkable organ with the strongest muscles in your body.

"Now you can't know ahead of time how it will go, even if you have had a baby before. Sometimes it goes smoothly and sometimes not. But remember: your anatomy has to adjust to what would seem an impossible feat."

The talk was accompanied by slides on a large screen.

"The Muttermund is an amazingly adaptable part of the system that closes tight during pregnancy to hold the baby inside the Gebärmutter and protect it from microorganisms. It then gradually softens and becomes longer, forming a mucous plug in the center to keep it firmly closed as the baby develops. By late in the third trimester, it will start to soften more, thin out, stretch, and eventually dilate to prepare for the passage of the baby. The opening goes from about the size of a pea to ten centimeters, the size of a bagel, at full dilation."

Clare already knew this, but the image still impressed her.

After the presentation, they were shown the labor and delivery rooms and they learned more about possible options and outcomes.

"It was a lot to take in," Clare said when they got in the car they had borrowed from Jürgen and Christina. "But I feel better being able to visualize the place and the staff."

"I agree. I liked Schwester Monika. I wonder if she will be our midwife."

"I hope so."

April 2001

"*Guten Tag*, Johann. How are you today?"

"*Guten Tag,* Clare. I'm fine. I want you to meet my sister." He turned towards a white-haired woman sitting next to him on the bench.

"Erika Meyer. Nice to meet you, Clare." She moved over and made room for Clare to join them.

Clare looked at the two of them sitting there waiting for her and she felt tenderness in the place where her grief had lived. She wanted to fold them into her being and carry them with her, to add their stories to the growing fullness inside her. She had so many questions, especially about the midwife.

"I don't remember much." Erika began. "I am younger than Johann. But I did ask my mother in her later years what she remembered about those days. By that time, she was able to talk about things that we had never heard as children."

"My own daughter was born here in Marburg," Clare inserted, "and I had a midwife at the hospital. Schwester Monika. She also came to the house every day for a week after the birth, to check on me and the baby. It was wonderful."

"From the stories I heard, Elizabetha was great that way." Erika smiled at Clare as she went on. "When labor began to get serious, the mother would go to her house for the birth of the baby. She would also stay for a week after the birth to make sure everything was going well. Elizabetha took care of the mother and baby, giving the mother time to rest and get the milk flowing. And to make sure the baby was thriving."

"And that was allowed by the medical establishment in those days?"

"You know, I think there was some tension between hospitals and midwives, but it was still allowed, I guess. Elizabetha consulted with doctors at times, especially for difficult cases."

Clare knew there had been a long history of doctors trying to discredit midwives. Science versus folk medicine passed down through millennia. Although the training and certification programs for midwives had been rigorous for centuries, they were not always respected. She had heard about the *Geburtshaüser* in the 19th century; public birthing houses where poor or unmarried women would go to have their babies. The conditions were terrible and there was often a power struggle between the doctors and midwives. The birthing mothers served as practice cases for the young medical students and the mortality rate for mothers and babies was very high.

"Did your mother talk about your brother, the one who died soon after birth?"

"Yes, she did. I had wondered about that my whole life. She finally started telling me about it. I think all those years she had just wanted to forget that painful story." Erika stopped for a moment to listen to a contrapuntal chorus of birds perched in the trees around them. They seemed to compete in their joyful pronouncements, a call and response of comments on a spring day.

She smiled and went on with her mother's story.

"Her labor was very long and hard and she was getting weaker by the hour. Elizabetha kept giving her teas and herbal tinctures. Her baby had stopped moving and she was afraid it was dead so she lost the will to continue. He was finally born alive, but he only lived a couple of days after that. He was too weak to eat. My mother lost a lot of blood, and she was also very weak.

"'Poor Elizabetha had to take care of both of us,' she told me. 'All we could do was sleep.' My mother began to gain some strength just in time to see her baby die. Our neighbor took Johann to visit her, and she told me that was what gave her the courage to get better."

"Fortunately for all of us, you came along a few years later," Johann said, patting his sister's arm. "You were a healthy and happy child."

June 1981

"Which fairy tale do you want tonight, Willy?" Stefan asked as they settled on the big bed in the living room.

"Um, how about The Frog King? Mommy, are you coming?"

"I'll be right there!"

Soon the three of them were snuggled together for their nightly ritual of reading. Sometimes it was in English and sometimes in German.

Willy began to read.

"*In alten Zeiten, als es noch nützlich war, sich das zu wünschen, was man wollte, lebte ein König...* In olden times, when it was still of some use to wish for things, there lived a king..."

It was slow going, but he did well. After a couple of pages, he handed the book to Stefan.

"Here Dad, it's your turn. I'm tired."

Stefan continued the story about the beautiful princess and her golden ball that a frog retrieved for her. The details were a bit different than the Disney version they were familiar with, but the gist was the same. The frog returns her ball, exacting a promise that she is reluctant to keep. Instead of kissing the frog, she throws him against the wall and he turns into a handsome prince. But the story is also about the prince's faithful servant, Heinrich, who was so saddened by the spell that turned his master into a frog, that he placed three iron bands around his heart to keep it from bursting in grief. As the prince and princess get into the carriage to go off and live happily ever after, they hear loud cracking sounds. The prince thinks the carriage is breaking apart, but it is just the iron bands snapping with the newfound joy in Heinrich's heart.

"That's a funny ending," Willy said.

"The story is sometimes called *Eiserner Heinrich*, 'Iron Heinrich,' Stefan added after they finished. In English, it is usually The Frog Prince."

Sometimes they read from *Watership Down*, which Clare thought was a bit violent, or *Alice in Wonderland*, which was crazy in an ironic adult way.

"Stefan, I'm not sure any of these books are appropriate for a seven-year-old, but Willy seems to enjoy them. The fairy tales aren't quite like the ones I remember from my childhood."

"I know. They have been cleaned up in modern written versions, then even more by Disney. They weren't really meant for kids anyway, originally. They were oral folktales that often had a message for the public that heard them. They were performed before an audience that would respond and comment, creating shared meanings for their times. Many of them are from several hundred years ago."

"It's fun to imagine them being told in Marburg that long ago. I love oral storytelling. I guess we'll just trust Willy's judgment here."

April 2001

April 5

I was lying in bed, drifting in and out of consciousness. I remember Elizabetha trying to rouse me often. "Here, take this, dear, it will give you strength." I couldn't remember where I was and why I was there. "This will stop the bleeding...and this will help you sleep." "Where is my baby?" I asked groggily, remembering suddenly where I was. "He is resting now." She kept coming back and trying to get him to nurse. He didn't want to wake up. I just wanted to sleep. "She'll be okay," a man's voice said. "What about the baby, doctor?" Elizabetha asked. "I can't do anything for him. He's gone. Yes, that's it," the doctor said.
I heard it all, but I was too tired to react.

I woke up from a deep sleep, Hannah, and there I was in our bed in your house. I was heavy with the sorrow and exhaustion of that poor woman. I felt like I'd been asleep for a long time. I checked the bed, the same bed as in my dream. There was no blood and no baby, but I felt empty inside.

* * *

Notes for Book

Chapter 2 The Hormones of a Culture: Myths and Undercurrents

Jung's collective unconscious – cultural inheritance of ways of seeing and understanding, internalized stories about identity and reality, common (often unconscious) references.

The filter of language that shapes our understanding

Narration as a form of therapy

Sigmund Freud – The purpose of art is the veiled presentation of deeper truth under a mask of pretending.

* * *

The phone rang just as Clare closed her laptop. She ran downstairs to the kitchen to answer it.

"*Guten Tag...Muller.*" She said, trying to catch her breath.

"Mom? Hi, it's Will. How are you? Did I catch you at a bad time?"

"No, I was just upstairs. Is everything okay?" It was rare for them to talk on the phone.

"Yes, yes, we're fine. Great, in fact. We have some news to share, and I wanted to tell you directly. Is Dad around?"

"I think so. Stefan? Are you still here?" She yelled. "He's coming. So, what is this news? I can't stand the suspense."

"Well, Yolanda and I are getting married. Don't worry, it won't be until after you get back, but we just wanted you to know."

"Oh, that's so exciting!" Clare's voice rose to a high pitch as Stefan came running from the other room. "It's Will. They're getting married!"

"We're thinking maybe in October. Not a big formal production. We'll let you know more soon when we figure out the details. We just decided last night."

"Oh Will, I'm so happy for you. Yolanda is a treasure and I think you two are right for each other. Thanks for sharing the news. I'll let you talk to your dad."

Clare watched as Stefan and Will talked, and Stefan's face spread in a grin. After he hung up, they hugged and bounced around the living room.

June 1981

Clare waddled in from the yard, feeling like an old cow with unstable hips. She had spent an hour weeding the small garden plot she had planted with a few vegetables. It was wonderful to have that little project and enjoy the fresh air and spring weather.

The biggest challenge had been battling the slugs that liked to eat everything. Jürgen had explained to her that *Schnecke* was the word for both slug and snail. The difference was whether or not they carried a house. Slugs were *Schnecken ohne Haus,* without a house, and snails were *Schnecken mit Haus,* that is, with a house. The trick was to fill plastic cups with flat beer that would attract them. They would slip into the cup and drown in the beer. The first cups of beer full of drowned slugs were not very appealing, but it seemed to do the job.

She had sat cross-legged on the ground briefly and then kneeling for a while. It wasn't very comfortable, but she wanted to do something useful. When she finished, she wasn't sure she could get up. Her back hurt and her legs were stiff.

At the visit to the doctor the day before, Clare had complained that it hurt to turn over in bed. The doctor explained that her pelvic bones had separated and that's why she felt so unsteady. At night when she wanted to turn over, she would have to grab her belly and help roll it over to the other side. She discovered that now it also hurt to sit on the ground. The second trimester and into the third had been a respite. The last month was a real trial.

"I can't even see my feet or legs, much less tie my shoes," Clare complained to Stefan. "And I definitely have an outie now," she added, smoothing her loose dress over the huge protrusion to show how her belly button stuck out like a little kid's. I feel like the whole world can see inside me. My very private internal organ is exposed and looks like it's about to explode. I might as well be naked. Meanwhile, Gertrude likes to do push-ups on my bladder." At that moment, a foot stuck out above her navel, distorting her shape.

"Oh my god, do you have a kid trapped in there?" Stefan said, feigning shock. He grabbed the little foot for a moment. Clare giggled.

"I've been trying to keep it secret, but it's getting harder all the time. I'm glad Mom will be here in a couple of weeks. I think Gertrude is feeling crowded, too. Maybe she'll decide to come out early."

April 2001

Spring had finally come to stay. Buds were opening and the fields around the city were a patchwork quilt of bright greens. Clare came in from the yard and took off her gardening gloves.

"I finished cleaning up the garden beds and trimmed the rose bushes. There are already lots of green shoots coming up and some buds ready to open. I love the smell of the damp earth and the bursting of new life."

"How about a little road trip?" Stefan suggested. "Let's leave the books and get out of here."

"Sounds good to me. Where do you want to go?"

"How about we drive around to some of the villages in the area."

"I'll get the map. I love to look at maps." Stefan went to collect their jackets and a snack to take with them. He came back to find Clare poring over the map that she had spread on the table. There were small villages scattered all around the edges of Marburg. Many of them had been officially absorbed into the city of Marburg, even when they were still surrounded by open farmland.

"Hey, how come so many village names end in -*hausen*? Hadamshausen, Ockershausen, Hermershausen, Weiershausen... They seem endless. Were they family names, as in someone's houses?"

"I think -*hausen* meant 'homestead,' so I would guess that was attached to family names. It's an old Frankish word. The Franks were in this area from around the fifth to eighth centuries. Many villages have descriptive names from the Middle Ages, often ending with a geographical identification."

"Like -*berg*, meaning mountain or -*burg* meaning castle, right?"

"Yeah. And -*bach* is stream, -*tal* is valley, -*feld* is field."

"-*Brück* for 'bridge,' -*heim* for 'home.' Let's see, what else? I suppose -*hafen* is a harbor or port?"

It was a beautiful drive, curving roads through wooded hillsides, rolling green fields, and small villages. Each village was unique, yet many had a similar feel. There was a small central square with the traditional community houses around it. The town hall, church, and small stores. Each yard was carefully tended as was the whole village. Most were surrounded by farmland that was clearly still cultivated. It was as though time had stopped and preserved the past unchanged over the centuries.

"It looks like people take great pride in their town, their heritage. I wonder if it feels oppressive at times. Like living in a museum." Clare could imagine both.

"I think the rules are pretty strict in these villages. They depend on tourism for one, but I think it's also important to their identity."

"I admire it, but it wouldn't be the life for me." Clare was sure about that.

June 1981

"*Guten Tag, Frau Muller.* How are you today?"

"*Guten Tag,* Schwester Monika. I am tired of being an old cow and I'm counting the days."

"Well, the baby has dropped already, so we may be looking at an earlier delivery date. Just be ready. It won't be long now."

"My mother is arriving tomorrow, so I'm ready any time after that."

* * *

"Jürgen drove Stefan to the airport to meet her," Clare told Julia, who had called to ask about her mother. "They should be here soon. It will be great to have her around during these last days and after the delivery. Gertrude and I are getting impatient."

"Well, hang in there. You, I mean, not Gertrude. Tell her to get ready to move out."

"I'd better go. I think they just arrived."

In her mind, Clare ran to hug her mother when she stepped out of the car. In reality, it was a slow swaying motion.

"Oh my, look at you!" her mother said with a big smile.

"Meet Gertrude. Gertrude, this is your grandmother," Clare said, patting her belly.

"Gertrude?"

"Never mind, I'll explain later. Let's get you settled."

"Thank you so much for fetching me at the airport," her mother said, turning to Jürgen.

"My pleasure," Jürgen answered in perfect English. "It's lovely to meet you Mrs. Roney."

"Please call me Rosemary," she answered, smiling at Christina as well.

* * *

The room in the back was just big enough for a single bed, a dresser, and the little wooden table with the typewriter. There was a small window that looked down on the street. The house was at the end of a narrow cul de sac, so there was no traffic.

"I'm sorry it's so small, but it should be quiet. The neighbors on the right are all underground, so they won't disturb you."

"A cemetery," she added to her mother's quizzical expression.

"It's lovely and looks cozy and comfortable."

"I'm so glad you came, Mom." Clare and Gertrude hugged her hard. "It means a lot to me."

Her mother had given birth to four healthy babies and had some nurse's training as well. And she was Mom. It was comforting to have her there.

* * *

"Another one?" Her mother asked as they finished the third round of double solitaire.

"I need to get up and move," Clare answered, thinking she would go crazy if they played any more card games. "Let's take a walk and a bus ride."

"Are you sure you're up to it?"

"Let's find out."

They walked down the hill to the bus. Downhill was good.

"I want to show you the Gästehaus, where we lived the first weeks we were here." They went to the very back of the bus, where it would be the bounciest. Clare was ready to do almost anything to provoke labor. Her

231

mother had been there two weeks already and there was no sign of progress. The due date had come and gone. The light contractions were those Braxton Hicks warm-ups that didn't go anywhere.

"That's the bakery where Willy started speaking some German on his own. He loved to go there and spend his Pfennig to buy his favorite treats. And here is the Gästehaus. I promised my friends Julia and Sharon that we would stop by so they can meet you."

"This is my mother, Rosemary Roney, and Mom, this is my dear friend Julia—one of my very first friends in Marburg. She moved here from Poland with her husband Aleksander and their daughter Zosia. Zosia and Willy are good friends and in the same class at school."

"So nice to meet you," they said in unison as they shook hands and then hugged.

"Still waiting, I see," Julia said with sympathy.

Clare sighed. "We've tried riding in the back of the bus to jostle Gertrude, but she seems to be happily entrenched in her little home. I'll let you know if she ever decides to move out."

Then they went to visit Sharon and her new baby. Clare was wearing a loose maternity dress that Sharon had passed on to her.

"It looks good on you," Sharon commented. "At the end, it was the only thing I had that was comfortable. After that, I never wanted to see it again."

"Sorry," Clare grinned, "but it *is* comfortable, especially for this hot weather."

"Would you like to hold her? Her name is Laura."

Clare rocked the little baby in her arms for a few moments before handing her to Rosemary.

"They sure feel different on the outside," Sharon said. "It'll be your turn soon."

"You have lovely friends." Rosemary took her daughter's arm as they walked back to the bus stop.

"Yes, they are very dear. We lived at the Gästehaus for the first six weeks until after Stefan came back from Bavaria and we moved to the house where we live now."

"I remember the stories in your letters. It all sounded challenging."

"It was a tough time, but also full of discovery and small successes. I was very proud of Willy."

"Are you going to make it?" Her mother asked as Clare puffed her way back up the hill from the bus.

"I...think...so," she answered.

Christina met them at the front door. "Samira called. She thought you would have had your baby by now and she was worried. I told her you were still waiting."

"Thanks. Just waiting and waiting...Samira must be getting close to time as well." Clare went straight for her bed when they finally made it to the top of the stairs. It felt good to lie down for a moment—until Gertrude woke up.

An unusual heat wave had hit Germany early that summer. Air conditioning was rare and seldom needed. Their little upstairs apartment held the heat from the day, not to mention Clare's own crowded internal apartment. Sometimes the only respite was to lie down on the hard tile floor of the hallway or sit in a cool bath. The days dragged by, and she surrendered to more card games. One afternoon, when she was about to play a card, Gertrude shot the goal of a lifetime. Clare was launched out of her chair with an involuntary shriek. Her mother jumped up as well, wondering what had happened.

"She kicked...right...under...my heart." Clare gasped in spurts. "That's the hardest one yet. A super goal. I didn't even know what happened at first."

"Okay Gertrude, my little granddaughter. I think it's time for your debut. Past time, I would say."

April 2001

"*Es war einmal ein reicher Mann...*" Clare read from their book of Fairy Tales. It had been one of Willy's favorites. "*Aschenputtel*," "The Little Ash Girl," was one of the most famous of the stories gathered by the Brothers Grimm. The Disney version of Cinderella that Clare had grown up with was a rather drastic rewrite of the one in the Grimms' collection. In the original Grimm version, "the little ash girl's" wish is granted not by the magic of a fairy godmother's wand, but from a hazel tree that grew on her mother's grave, watered by the girl's own tears. The desperation of the stepsisters to make the glass slipper (here a golden one) fit their feet, leads one sister to cut off her big toe and the other to cut off part of her heel, both leaving blood in the shoe. A pair of doves chants like a Greek chorus, commenting on the outcome.

> Blood in the shoe:
> The shoe is too small,
> The true bride still waits at home.

The story was full of violent images, clearly not a Disney world. Clare had found a book in the library about the Grimms' collection and was fascinated by the long history of the folktales.

"Did you know that the story of Aschenputtel / Cinderella, was around in ancient China and Egypt?" she asked Stefan during their morning break the next day. "The details change, depending on the historical and cultural context of the storytelling. Meanwhile, the Grimms' collection has been translated into over 150 languages."

"That's amazing!"

"It was common in oral traditions of storytelling for the stories to go on for centuries, adapting to each new time and context."

"I read that the 'original versions' of Aschenputtel that we have were already edited and improved by the Grimms to make them more *kinderfreundlich* than the stories they had first documented." Clare added.

"More like pastor-friendly, actually. In many ways, the Grimms were pioneers in the study of folklore. The notion of collecting stories 'as faithfully as possible', in their words, was the beginning of a new branch of anthropology."

"I didn't know that."

"Yes, they were also part of a romantic nationalist movement to separate German culture from the Frenchified culture of the Enlightenment, to build pride in their own identity. You see this in the language as well."

"It's interesting that their storyteller informants were women."

Clare knew she had opened the door to one of the main rooms of Stefan's research. Sometimes it was annoying to her how easy it was to elicit a mini-lecture from him in their conversations, especially when the mansplaining kicked in. But in this case, she was genuinely interested. And to be fair, it went both ways. Her own passions were always there under the surface and could be released by a simple comment or question. She sometimes wondered if she should post a sign. "Caution. Beware of geysers of overexuberance."

And now, here they were right in the middle of that history that seemed to live all around them. She could see Stefan sorting through his mental library to synthesize a short version for her. He began to tell of the cultural settings for the stories. One of the main arenas for the performance of folk tales in the eighteenth century had been the *Spinnstuben.*

"These were spinning rooms, usually in the home of a wealthier family, where women would gather to spin together in a *Lichtstube,* a room lit by candles. Not only would that save on tallow for the candles, but it also became an enjoyable social occasion to do the tedious work together."

"Why did so many of the stories involve women sacrificing something?"

"Well, that's a long story, central to some of my research, as you know. But the short answer is that these stories are full of symbolism that often involves magical transformations arising out of family conflict, anger, fear, and deprivation."

"Sounds like an early modern form of magical realism."

"Yeah, in a way. At least as far as the literalization of metaphors in the context of traditional society clashing with modernity. The stories I study reflect especially the disconnectedness and marginalization that drafted Hessian soldiers faced. It was brutal, and their sisters sometimes sacrificed their dowries to save their brothers from it. It is all tangled up in military structures and family inheritance practices."

"A far cry from simple entertainment for children."

June 1981

The morning after Gertrude's super goal, the warmup contractions became stronger and closer together. Clare asked Stefan to stay home that day, since it might turn out to be "The Day." *Dar a luz, dar a luz,* she kept thinking. To give birth in Spanish was "to give to the light." The proverbial light at the end of the tunnel.

"How close are they now?" Stefan asked again.

"I'm not sure. But they do seem stronger." He started timing the contractions and they were every five minutes. They decided to head for the hospital.

"I'll wait here for Willy," her mother offered.

"Keep in touch," Jürgen said as he dropped them off at the hospital. Clare was grateful for the orientation they'd had as they headed straight for the birthing wing.

Schwester Monika examined Clare right away.

"The Muttermund is definitely dilated, and things are moving along, but it could still be a while." They strapped a machine to her belly to monitor the baby's heartbeat. Schwester Monika left the room for a moment and soon came running back to Clare's call for help. She was clutching the monitor as it dangled over the edge of the examining table.

"What happened?" Schwester Monika asked.

"Gertrude didn't like the monitor, so she kicked it off."

"What? Gertrude?"

"The baby. That's our nickname for the baby."

"Well, that's a first," Schwester Monika exclaimed, shaking her head. "I think your baby is doing just fine."

"Yes, with a strong will it seems."

A woman in a white coat stopped by to say hello. "I am Doktor Schäfer. Dr. Fischer is on vacation this week. I will be taking his patients."

"Nice to meet you. I'm sure he expected to be done with me by now. By the way, what is the longest human gestation can last?"

"Um...well, let me look at your chart. I see, your due date was two weeks ago. There have been cases that go a few weeks past 40, but it's often hard to pinpoint the actual date of conception."

"Not in my case," Clare said with confidence, remembering Stefan's visit in September.

"Be glad you're not an elephant. They are pregnant for 18-22 months," Schwester Monika added playfully.

"I've been feeling like an elephant lately."

After a couple of hours, the contractions slowed down and the dilation hadn't progressed.

"Why don't you go home and rest? We want to see you again tomorrow."

"I feel so silly, like we rushed in too soon," Clare said as they rode home in a taxi."

"Not at all. It's much better to be cautious and check in, especially—"

"—with a stubborn tenant who doesn't want to leave."

* * *

"We learned about families today at school," Willy announced at supper.

"What did you learn?"

"About *Verwandten* and all the different kinds we have."

"Relatives," Stefan translated for Rosemary.

"Andreas said that he has an *Uroma*, a great-grandma," Willy went on. 'Or an *Urgroßmutter*,' the teacher said. 'Like your grandmother's mother.'

"Then I said that my *Urgroßmutter* died. But I have *eine tolle Großmutter*—a "great" grandmother. Like a cool one. The teacher laughed 'cuz she knows English, but the other kids didn't get it."

Rosemary put her arm around Willy's shoulders and said, "Well *I* get it and I love it!"

Willy grinned up at her.

"And you are my "great" grandson," Rosemary added, giving him a full hug.

April 2001

Notes for Book

Chapter 3   Framing the House: Time and Place

Time frames, timelines, time span, poles and trusses

The skeleton: In postmodern writing, like the half-timbered house, the structure of the story is often exposed on the outside. With the Fachwerk House, the varied sections of its construction and content serve as the unifying concept that holds it together.

Setting: spatial mapping, intentions, sections created by time and topic: chapters. Not only where the story is located geographically with respect to the world, but also in what cultural world—how do ethnicity, language, class, race, gender, circumstance, etc. define the setting? Emotional and psychological space are also part of that setting.

How is time defined by place and vice-versa?

* * *

"Mmm, this coffee hits the spot." The warm liquid was already waking her up, even before the caffeine hit her system. "Only one slice of bread this morning. I'm carrying a few extra pounds these days."

"How is the writing going?"

"Pretty well. I'm working on rough drafts of each chapter from the notes I already have. I'm on Chapter 3 right now. It seems overwhelming at times, but I just need to keep going and get something to start with. How about you?"

"Similar. Lots of data to look at still, but I'm working on rough writing as I go."

"Well, I'd better get going." Clare wiped her mouth and stood up.

"Are you off for your walk? Say hi to Johann."

* * *

"*Hallo, Johann,*" Clare said, giving him a kiss on the cheek. She sat down on the bench in front of his dog, who waited patiently for her attention. "I dreamed about the midwife last night."

"Oh? How was she?"

"Well, she was doing her job. It was intense and it seemed so real."

"Hmm. There are many stories in that house."

They sat in silence, enjoying the warm sun.

"Clare…" Johann began after a long pause. "I have something I want to show you. I haven't shared this with anyone for a very long time." He leaned over and picked up a violin out of an old, battered case on the ground next to him. Clare held her breath as he plucked the strings to check the tuning.

Then he closed his eyes and drew the bow across notes so sweet that she could almost taste them. It was a soulful tune that filled her with hope and sorrow at the same time. She closed her eyes and surrendered her whole body to the sounds. When the music stopped, they sat for a minute in the silence that framed it.

Oh Johann, that was so beautiful!" she said with tears in her voice. "Thank you for sharing it with me. What a gift. Have you played all your life?"

"Yes, well, no. I started at a young age. My uncle gave me a child-size violin and taught me the basics. Eventually I was lucky to study with a great teacher. I used to play every day, even when I was in the army. But then I stopped for many years."

"Why did you stop?" She couldn't imagine giving up such a relationship to music.

"It's a long story." Johann sighed and put the violin away.

"I have time."

"Well, I had dreams of going to the university and even had someone to sponsor me, but then my father died suddenly, and I had to work to help my mother and my sister. By then, the university wasn't a great place to be anyway. As the Nazis took over, everything became rigid and ideologically strict. Teaching and learning were stifled, and many people left. I worked whatever jobs I could find until I got drafted."

"Oh no!" Clare said, remembering how many of her generation had been sent to Vietnam.

"I had thought I wouldn't be drafted because I had a Jewish grandmother. That could disqualify you from the army. My grandmother lived with us until she died in 1935. Shortly before she died, she called my mother and me to her bedside. 'I need to tell you something,' she said. 'The new law requires every German to produce documented proof of their German roots—parents and grandparents. With even one Jewish grandparent they consider you Jewish. It's going to get very ugly. But you don't need to worry. You need to know that you are both fully German.'

"'But how...' my mother began. We couldn't imagine where she was going with that. 'I am your mother,' she said to my mother, 'but I did not give birth to you. Your birth mother died in childbirth and your poor father was beside himself. I was their friend and neighbor, already widowed myself at a young age. I moved in to help take care of you and soon we were married. We never told you because I became your mother and loved you as much as anyone could. But now you need to know.'

"She handed us a document from a Lutheran parish register that had recorded my mother's birth. We hugged her and cried together. I have often thought since then that I would rather have taken my chances as a Jew than the road I was forced to follow. I have missed her so much—my very real grandmother—all these years.

"So, I had the *privilege* of serving in the German army." He emphasized the word with bitter irony. "I hated it. We were sent here and there and all I had to console myself was my violin. I played for my comrades in the barracks and the wounded in the infirmary and soon the officers started asking me to play for them. It saved my life a few times, when they had me travel with them instead of with my unit. More than once, many of my buddies didn't return. I felt so guilty. My violin was my best friend."

"That must have been very hard." Clare folded her hands in her lap.

"The worst was when we went into Russia and they made us round up Jews. They told us they were communists, but it wasn't true. I had never told anyone that my mother's family was Jewish on her mother's side. My mother had memories of the synagogue from when she was a child, and she held on to a few holidays. I remember her telling us about Rosh Hashana and Yom Kippur and we would light a menorah for Hannukah. But they were just holidays. We didn't have much sense of a religious tradition. I never understood why it was such a crime to be Jewish, why it was such a threat to others.

"I wasn't prepared for the brutality of that war, of any war, I suppose. You had two choices: either you hardened yourself to it, or you let it destroy you. Music kept my soul alive."

"How long were you in the army?"

"Too long. I was no saint. I did some things for which I will never forgive myself. I let the music save me when possible, and I tried to help others when I could. I hoped that the music might soften the hearts of the officers. Maybe it did. A few of the younger ones seemed terrified at finding themselves in the center of such madness. Sometimes they would do small acts of kindness, but then they would be harsher the next moment, fearing punishment themselves.

"I eventually got wounded and was sent home to Marburg. For years, I couldn't play the violin, because it reminded me of the war and my cowardice. But it wasn't all sad. When I met Klara, the sun came out again."

"Your wife's name was Klara?"

"*Ja,*" he said, smiling at her. "Sometimes you remind me of her."

"And later you had Mia as well."

"Yes, she was indeed a blessing. I told you that we adopted her after she lost her parents. What I didn't tell you is that they were Jewish and they were taken away one day. We hid Mia for a while and then just acted like she was our daughter. It's a miracle that the Nazis didn't find her."

"I can't imagine the fear and stress you all suffered."

"We just went on with our lives as normally as we could. We didn't want Mia to grow up in fear. And we didn't want it to look like we were hiding something. She was always with other kids, and no one ever betrayed her. At first, I think the kids consciously protected her and then they eventually forgot that it was ever necessary."

"What happened to her parents?"

"We never found them. We searched for them after the war. It took years to find out that they had died at Auschwitz. I wish they could have known that their daughter was okay. We gave her all the love we could, and she became our daughter. It was very hard for her, but she has had a good life. She is a wonderful mother and now a grandmother. I think she replaced her loss with her own new family."

"My dear friend," Clare said, pressing both hands to her chest. "I hope you will keep giving your music to the world as long as you can. And remember this Clara, who will always love you."

241

12
Into the Light

July 1981

The night was stormy. Wild winds, rain and intense humidity added to Clare's restlessness. She couldn't get comfortable in bed and her nightgown twisted around her as she tried to turn over. She threw it off in frustration and paced the hallway in her misshapen nakedness, parting the darkness with her bare skin. Lights from the distant hills blinked through the blinds in the living room.

The contractions were stronger and then she noticed a little blood. The plug! She woke up Stefan and they waited and paced together until morning. Stefan went to get Jürgen, who had made them promise to call at any hour if needed.

"I think this is it this time," Clare said, as she settled into the back seat of the car. "I sure hope so!"

They had called the hospital and were met with a wheelchair at the door of the emergency entrance. Schwester Monika was waiting for them in the birthing wing.

"Definite progress, but not quite urgent yet. Let me show you to the garden where you can walk around a bit. That often helps to get things moving faster. How is the pain?"

"It's manageable, I guess, but frustrating. It seems to all be in my lower back."

"Okay, well, remember your breathing and come back in when you need to."

"Thanks, Schwester Monika."

It was a peaceful garden in full bloom with a bench every few yards. The air was still heavy and close, and Clare could feel sweat trailing down her sides. They managed a half hour of slow walking, then sitting, then walking again, with Clare leaning on Stefan during each contraction. She was grateful for the childbirth classes. "Learn to breathe into your back," the teacher had said. "You might find it useful."

When they got back to the birthing center, Schwester Monika led them to a room with a small round table and two chairs. "Sit here and relax for a minute. I'll be right back." She returned with two cups of herbal tea and some cookies.

"That's so nice of you," Stefan said. "I feel like I'm having a baby, too."

"You are." Schwester Monika smiled at him. She turned to Clare. "I'll come back in a moment to take you to the bath. Would you like a nice bubble bath to help you relax?"

"Do I get one, too?" Stefan asked playfully.

"Sorry, this one is just for the mother."

"This is all so different than my experience with Willy," Clare said when Schwester Monika left. "I expected German hospitals to be bureaucratic and overly efficient. You know the stereotype. Yet things are stricter in the U.S. You're not supposed to eat or drink anything before the birth, and a bath would be unthinkable."

"There is too much amniotic fluid so the baby's head can't engage," Schwester Monika said, examining her after the bath. "We have a couple of decisions to make. We can take the slow route and wait to see what happens. It would be more gradual but could be quite long. Or I can give you some oxytocin to make the contractions stronger and speed things up a bit. Probably more painful. It's your choice."

"Faster is better, for sure. I'm ready to be done with this. Do whatever it takes."

"I'm also going to break the sack."

With the gush of fluid and the drug, things moved along quickly. Soon she was in the delivery room and reminded of her options there. There was even an old birthing chair there if she wanted to try it. Clare opted for standing, no longer even noticing that she was completely naked. It was an athletic event, with her team cheering her on. A young man came into the room to ask politely if he could attend as well.

"I'm an intern, but more importantly, my wife and I will be having our first baby very soon and I want to learn as much as I can. Is that okay?"

"Why not?" Clare shrugged her shoulders. Modesty and privacy had already moved to the back of the stadium.

"What if it's a boy?" she panted to Stefan at one point.

243

"Don't worry about that now," he reassured her. "It doesn't matter." They had come up with a couple of names for a boy, just in case. But she hadn't really imagined the possibility.

Finally on the table, she realized it was the home stretch. *"Nicht pressen! Nicht pressen!* Schwester Monika said with urgency. Don't push! Clare told herself, trying to breathe against the opposite message that her body was giving her. The doctor had arrived and she and the midwife were busy with their end of things. "Okay, now you can push," they told her. "Go for it!" Clare gave it all she had. I don't care if I all my insides go with her, I'm getting this baby out! A flash of fear that she might split open like an overripe watermelon, but there was no time to dwell on it.

"Push, push!" She could hear Stefan cheering her on. "Go girl! My wild Irish rose. You can do this, Clare Aisling Roney!" The rest was a blur until Gertrude burst into the light in a rush of victory. Amidst the clamor she heard Schwester Monika say: *"Mädchen, es ist ein Mädchen."*

A girl. Good-bye Gertrude, hello Anja! They laid the baby on her chest, still connected to her. Everyone cheered and clapped. The young intern smiled at her with tears in his eyes. "Thank you," he mouthed.

"We need you to rub her back," they told her, "to stimulate the circulation." Clare watched as Anja's skin turned to a healthy pink color. She would never forget how soft it was and how sweet the face that lay on her chest, blinking at the light. Stefan leaned over and kissed them both.

"I'm going to go call and let folks know the news. I'll be right back," he said.

"Make sure Mom calls Dad right away." She could picture him waiting alone by the phone.

"Of course."

Clare heard the words *Mutterkuchen* and *Nabelschnur* as the midwife and doctor continued to work on finishing the process, but she was completely absorbed with the feeling of the baby on top of her, on the outside, skin to skin, as they lay on the table together.

"My daughter," she said, trying out the words for the first time as she marveled at the tiny pink fingers with perfect little fingernails. *"Meine kleine Tochter."*

May 2001

May 3

There was a knock on the door early in the morning and I went to answer it. A young woman, a girl really, begged me to let her in. She was pale and distraught, so I brought her in and fixed her some Kamilentee to calm her. "Now, tell me what your problem is," I said, laying a hand on her shoulder. The thing is, Hannah, this was another dream that was like a movie that I watched but I was also in it. I was Elizabetha, sort of. It's hard to explain – to be both inside and outside of the story. The girl said that she was from a neighboring village, and she knew she was pregnant. "I have to end this pregnancy," she said and began sobbing. "Why?" I asked, though I already had an idea. At her age, an unwanted pregnancy was often the result of unwanted sex. "I just have to," she said, trying to compose herself. I always try to question further (I? Elizabetha? Who was that "I"?) to make sure the patient has thought through her decision.

Finally, the girl was willing to tell me her story. She had gone to the priest for confession one day and he took her into a back room—for "private consultation and consolation," he had told her. It was God's will, he assured her, as he undressed her and initiated her to womanhood. I was furious but kept it to myself. "Okay," I told her. Let's check and see if you really are pregnant." The girl was indeed pregnant, and it was a dilemma for us. I felt sorry for her and knew that her life would be a misery. She was poor and could never reveal who the father was. "I will help you, but you must never tell anyone about this," I / Elizabetha said.

I woke up in a panic, Hannah, afraid of the risk we were both taking. I was so relieved to find myself in my own bed in your house; in the present, that is. I couldn't shake the anxiety of that scenario all day, and I can't help wondering how it turned out.

* * *

Notes for Book

Chapter 4 Weaving the Walls: Memory and Imagination

The walls enclose the space, creating the scope of the story and the lens. They define inside and outside, the designated world of the characters.

Walls that breathe challenge the limits and boundaries of fiction and reality as they respond to changing conditions.

The half-timbered house is both pre-modern (limited to the resources and knowledge available in the Middle Ages) and post-modern (adapting to the environment and cultural contexts of the Twentieth Century.) As a metaphor for writing, it is postmodern as it reveals the process of its own construction.

The weaving of the wicker sticks (the text) within the sections of the structure includes the threads of memory, experience, events, "facts" to set up the story, filled in with imagination, dreams, research, poetry. The warp and the weft of the writer's loom.

* * *

"I love my life right now." Clare often felt that way in those moments with Stefan, good coffee, and her favorite bread. She leaned over to kiss him on the mouth, lingering for a moment.

"Yup, it's pretty good, isn't it?" He went for another kiss, but she already held the mug to her mouth again.

"I just read another great Hannah Arendt quote. Something about loving life when you are away from home. You can create a new life because no one knows you and so you become more of a master of yourself than at any other time."

"After you get over the culture shock and the loneliness, that is."

"Right. Oh my god, like the shelf toilets! Remember how annoying and disgusting we found them our first time in Germany? A shelf to catch your poop so it's hard to flush down—what is wrong with these people? we said.

Like they needed to examine and appreciate their poop before they let it go."
They both laughed hard at the memory.

"Not to mention the *Wandpisserei*," Stefan added.

"I never had that experience."

"It was a wall with a drain instead of a urinal. A bunch of guys just pissing at a wall, as though we were in a back alley or something." They laughed some more at the images and their own early responses. The key to such humor, they knew, was the distance of time and the familiarity of experience they had shared. Those "quirks" of German culture had long ceased to seem foreign to them. In fact, other things that they had always taken for granted as normal in their home culture, felt strange when they returned.

July 1981

There were eight of them sharing a room in the maternity ward: four mothers and four babies. Clare lay awake listening to the sound of her daughter's breathing nearby. The nurses came in regularly to check them and help with the nursing. She wasn't supposed to get out of bed by herself that first night. She felt tired, but her body wouldn't let go. Stefan had gone home to be with Willy and her mom. Remembering the conversation with Willy on the phone brought a smile in the dark.

"Way to go, Mommy!" he had said. "You did it! I'm a big brother now and the soccer ball became my little sister." That made her laugh. Willy had talked to Gertrude many times, but he still liked to think of her as a soccer ball.

"At least she's not kicking goals in my belly anymore. Congratulations on being a big brother. And thanks for being my helper."

"You're welcome, Mom. Say hi to Anja for me. I can't wait to see her. When are you coming home?"

"We'll probably spend one more night here and then come home. I'll see you soon. And you know something? I love you so much, even more now that you are a big brother. You'll be a great one." *Did he just call me Mom?*

The next morning Clare got up to look at Anja sleeping in her little cradle. She felt a rush of affection and began to talk to her. "My sweet little love…" Suddenly she felt self-conscious. She had heard the other women coo over their babies in German and her words sounded hollow and strange in English. *"Meine Süße, mein kleines Liebchen…"* That felt better somehow. After living with German, Clare couldn't understand why people thought it was a harsh or cold language. There were so many possible sweet things to call your baby. One of them was *"Schnecke,"* but Clare could not bring herself to use that one. It just evoked images of dead slugs floating in beer.

The women had already formed a little community of new mothers. Meals were brought to them, and they would sit around a small table in the middle of the room to eat together. Each one would sit down awkwardly on the side where the episiotomy wasn't, smiling at each other in painful solidarity.

Clare told her mother that they would be coming home by the third day, after the milk came in. The baby was nursing well, and she was also fine, though it was still uncomfortable to sit. She was learning to re-center her balance with the big front pack mostly gone. She certainly felt lighter, but there was still that overstretched bag of muscles that hung there confused by its emptiness. That was what nursing was for. It would help the Gebärmutter get back to its original size and retreat to its hidden place and regular cycles of potential fertility. A pretty good system, Clare thought, though she hadn't been so sure of that during the "athletic event" of the day before.

Schwester Monika appeared by her bed. "How are you doing today?" she asked cheerfully.

"Great, thanks. But I have a question. Why does Anja have those red marks on her forehead?"

"Oh, those are *Storchbisse.*"

"What?"

"Stork bites, that's what we call them. Her head was probably pressed against your pelvic bones for a while."

"That's for sure. Will they go away?"

"Oh yeah, probably by the time she's old enough to vote… just kidding, don't worry," she added after seeing Clare's expression. "I'd say before she's a year old. I hear you are going home tomorrow. I'll stop by late afternoon to see how you are settling in. But before I go, let's get you started on a few exercises."

"Wow, so soon?"

"The sooner the better." They did some stretching and abdominal strengthening exercises and then walked down the hall and back. When they got back, Clare noticed that one of the mother-baby pairs had already left. Just as she got settled back in her bed, a nurse arrived pushing a new mother in a wheelchair, her bundled baby on her lap. Clare watched with curiosity, hardly remembering her own arrival the day before.

"Samira! *Salaan ka waran?* How are you?" Samira turned at the sound of Clare's voice and her tired face relaxed into a smile.

"I can't believe you are here. I thought you would have delivered before now. I'm so glad to see you!" Samira said, looking at the little bed next to Clare's.

"A girl. Her name is Anja. She did take her time getting here. Fifteen days late!"

Samira raised her left elbow to reveal the face of her bundle. "A boy. His name is Bashir. It means 'one who brings good news.'"

"I love that. Anja means 'grace.' I guess we are both hopeful with these babies."

"*Wiillkeyga yar ee macaan,*" Clare heard Samira whisper to her baby as the nurse took him to settle him in his bed. "My sweet little boy," she said, translating for Clare.

May 2001

May 10

The writing is going well. I love writing once it gets moving. It's so hard to get it going sometimes, especially with a big project. I guess you just start with big ideas and small pieces. You put something down to build on. It's odd how we distinguish creative writing from other writing. All writing is creative. I watch what Stefan does with the fragments he finds. With all that he has searched and researched to understand the context of Pastor Busch's life and times, in the end he has to construct the story out of those fragments and layers that he has found. The story that he writes will be his unique contribution to the modern understanding of the history of that past time.

"Creative writing" sounds like we create something out of nothing, but it also consists of fragments and layers of history, memory, experience, and research. The narrative that comes from our knowing (gnarus) is a construction that defines us as we define it.

The main difference that I see is that the writing of history needs to justify itself along the way, revealing its sources and building its analysis on the writing and thinking of others. Fiction frees us from doing that, but we know that the structures and sources are there underneath.

* * *

Notes For Book

Chapter 5 The Clay (Lehm): Creating the characters and stories.

Etymology of the word "fiction:" from the Latin verb *fingere:* to shape, form, feign; originally formed out of clay, mold with the hands. We create out of "clay" (the stuff of life, the basic material of God's art) the world of our stories and the beings that will inhabit it.

Walls (the containment field of the fictional story and world) are made of Lehm that breathes, responds to the environment, allows characters to grow in a world that is created by their own experience.

Jorge Luis Borges: The author as a god who dreams up an existence, while suffering the awareness that he might also be the product of the dream of a god above him, who in turn is also a creation. An endless chain of existential angst and irony. What happens if the top god wakes up? A metaphor for the self-consciousness of human existence and the mind that questions itself with itself.

The characters we create out of our metaphorical clay come to life and move in with us forever. It doesn't seem to matter whether they were molded around real people in our lives or from wholly imagined material. They all become immortal.

* * *

"*Hallo,* Johann. Sorry I'm late." He leaned towards her, offering his cheek for the kiss. "I got lost in—"

"The writing?" So, it's going well."

"Yes, it is. But sometimes it feels like whitewater kayaking. It's flowing so fast now, and I don't have a lot of control. All I can do is try to steer through it and avoid the rocks and whirlpools."

"You need to get stuff out of your head and on paper, right? Or a computer screen, I guess. So you can look at it more calmly later."

"Something like that. The good thing about computers is that you can go back and fill things in later, delete, change, rearrange, without losing anything or having to completely rewrite it."

"I wonder if that changes the way people write these days.

"Definitely. And maybe even the way we think."

"Hmm."

"Johann, I can't stop thinking about the story you told me. Your story."

"Sorry about that."

"No, no, it's a compelling story. It made me want to know more."

"What do you want to know?"

"Well, like about Mia. Did she ever go back to her Jewish roots?"

Johann smiled and lifted his gaze as though trying to see his daughter on some distant horizon. His voice changed as he began to narrate the story.

"Klara and I didn't talk with Mia about her past for the first few years, to keep her safe. We were trying to hide her in plain sight. She had to believe that she wasn't Jewish so that she could have the courage to live in the world and be convincing. We felt awful about it at first but then she just became our daughter and we forgot that we were pretending.

"I think we all erased ourselves to some extent during that time in order to survive." He paused. "Even the Nazis must have done that. It was...horrible." His voice cracked on the last word. Clare reached for his hand and squeezed it gently.

"Mia was only seven when her parents were taken. Later we began to talk to her about it little by little. By that time, it seemed unreal to her, a story about the past. It was a time that we all wanted to forget. We knew that wasn't healthy, but people weren't ready to face it. By the time Mia got to university, there was some public discussion, but it didn't really open up until the 1960s.

"We began to talk more about the war years and the Holocaust as Mia matured. We would light a menorah every year and remember her parents and my grandmother. We encouraged her to explore Judaism and try to connect with her lost past. We even considered joining the small Jewish community that began to gather after the war. But then she met Sam."

"The American?"

"Yes. He is a kind and generous guy. They married and moved to New York, to be near Sam's family. It was a whole new life. Mia met a couple young women there who invited her to visit their synagogue. It was a reform temple, and they were very welcoming of seekers, even agnostics who were interested in the secular values of the community. She had been cautious at first, confused about who she was and what she was seeking. But she found a home there and eventually Sam began attending as well. The kids were raised in that community, and they identify as Jewish, as do their own children. 'Jewish-lite,' they sometimes joke."

Johann sighed and looked at Clare as he returned to the present moment. "It brought us peace as well," he told her. "We never really found a church community for ourselves here, but it made us very happy that Mia did. And even though we had erased her past temporarily, for which we suffered great guilt in later years, she never doubted our love as her parents. When she turned eleven, the year after the Nazi regime had fallen, we had a special ceremony to honor her parents. We told her everything we knew about them and that they would have been very proud of her. We made a secret grave site and cried together over it."

"We can't change the past," Clare offered, "only ourselves and our relationship to it. I think you are a wonderful father," she added, realizing as she spoke the words how much she loved this man who had already become friends with the father she carried within her.

July 1981

The homecoming was joyful as they stepped out of the car. Jürgen had gone to pick them up and he grabbed the suitcase while Stefan cradled little Anja wrapped in a blanket. Willy ran to hug Clare and patted her soft belly.

"Looks like you lost the ball, Mom," he said solemnly. "Just kidding," he giggled. "Welcome home. I missed you."

"Sharon called to congratulate you and wish you luck settling in with the baby." Christina followed them up the stairs. "And Julia came by with some flowers. We put them in a vase on the table."

"They're beautiful," Clare said as she picked up a card next to the flowers.

> *"Congratulations to Clare, Stefan, Willy, and Anja,*
> *with love from Julia, Aleks and Zosia.*
> *P.S. Way to go, Gertrude!"*

They settled Anja in the cradle that Christina had lent them. There were hugs around and coffee, juice, and cookies. Willy and Jonas danced around the sleeping baby, not knowing what to do with their excitement. Lucas stood close and stared down at her, his eyes full of light and wonder. Clare put her hand on her middle, half expecting Gertrude to join in with her own little dance, but then she remembered. It would take a while to get used to the new emptiness inside her. The birth had been a wonderful relief and they had brought home a beautiful healthy daughter. But there was a faint sense of loss that lingered where Gertrude had been.

"I remember that feeling," her mother said, sensing by her gesture what Clare was experiencing. "It's the first stage of letting go."

Soon everyone cleared out to give Clare a chance to rest while the baby was still sleeping.

"It's good to be home," she said to Stefan, who had lain down next to her. "It seems like I've been gone forever." In those few short days, time had taken a big leap into a new era for them.

A knock woke them from a nap. Rosemary went downstairs to open the door and Clare heard Schwester Monika's voice. Stefan jumped up to greet her.

"Welcome, Schwester Monika. This is my mother-in-law, Rosemary Roney."

"Yes, she introduced herself at the door. It's so nice you can be here," Schwester Monika said, turning to Rosemary. "Nothing like having your mother with you when you have a baby."

"I'm delighted to be here. And it's so nice of you to make house calls," Rosemary responded with a smile.

"It's my pleasure and my job. So, how are you doing, Clare?" Schwester Monika walked over to the bed.

"Alright so far," Clare answered, still groggy. "I guess I fell asleep."

"That's a good thing, whenever you can." Schwester Monika smiled knowingly. Just then Anja woke up with whimpering noises that threatened to escalate quickly.

"Good timing," Schwester Monika said. "I always hate to disturb a sleeping baby to examine it."

Stefan handed the baby to Clare, and they entered that *Stillen* space together as Anja instinctively satisfied her hunger, at the same time relieving Clare's overflowing breasts.

"No problems with feeding I see," Schwester Monika said after watching them for a moment.

"Nope, the milk has clearly come in now and I'm a cow ready to be milked." When they finished, Anja lay limp and satisfied in her arms.

"I see you got a diaper service. That's a great plan."

"Yes, the increased *Kindergeld* just about covers it." Clare was still amazed that they got the monthly "child money," cash payments from the German government. You got a certain amount for the first kid and then that plus some for the second one. Anyone living in Germany received it, including immigrants and visitors. It amounted to a few hundred dollars a month and it really made a difference with expenses for the kids. "Such a civilized idea," they all agreed.

"Let's give her a quick bath and check the umbilical stub," Schwester Monika said, reaching for Anja. They went to the kitchen and cleared the counter next to the sink.

She undressed the baby gently, checking her over as she went.

"Everything seems fine. She looks like she had a few extra days in the spa."

"Yes, she certainly did take her time."

"Okay. Run the water and get it nice and warm but not hot. Test it on the inside of your wrist. Good, that seems about right." She balanced the baby on one forearm, which she maneuvered deftly under the running water.

"A little soap here and there but avoid direct contact with the umbilical stub. It will fall off in a few days. We don't want to immerse her in water until it's completely healed. There, we're done. Gentle but quick is the best, so she doesn't get cold."

Clare and her mother marveled at the woman's confidence and dexterity. Clare wondered if she would be able to do it.

"Don't worry, I'll be back tomorrow, and you can try it with me helping." Schwester Monika dressed the baby and handed her to Rosemary.

"Now, let's see how *you* are doing." She probed and kneaded Clare's belly. "A little massage for the Gebärmutter," she explained.

"She deserves it," Clare said, wincing a few times and marveling that her flabby womb could ever regain its shape after the service it had performed.

After a thorough checkup and some advice for Clare about care of her own body, Schwester Monika led her through a few exercises. No rest for the weary. Clare was stiff and sore from the episiotomy and lack of sleep made her grumpy.

"We often try to protect our pain and injuries," Schwester Monika explained, "when we really need to do the opposite. It's not about conquering pain; it's about giving it room to breathe freely and heal."

Easy to say when you aren't the one hurting and incredibly sleep deprived. But Clare grudgingly recognized the wisdom in it.

In the hospital the nurse had stressed the importance of another kind of movement when she handed Clare a small cup of rubbery plastic-like granules to swallow, *um den Darm zu bewegen.*

"*Darm?*" she asked.

The nurse patted her own belly and made a circular motion with her hand.

"Ah, the intestines, to move the bowels."

"Swallow these whole. Do NOT chew them!"

That sounded ominous. After she had swallowed the stuff and the nurse left, one of the other mothers said. "I forgot right away and began to chew them. It's some kind of compressed fiber. It quickly expanded in my mouth,

255

and I almost choked." The image made Clare grimace and she dreaded the imminent outcome of those little granules. It was bound to be painful.

"Movement is important," Schwester Monika went on. "And strengthening exercises. You need to retrain some muscles and help the Gebärmutter return to her original size." The word Gebärmutter happened to be grammatically feminine, so it was natural to refer to the womb as "she" and "her." And the expression "birthing mother" went beyond grammar to evoke an image of personhood. The way German seemed to personalize everything around the birthing process made Clare feel connected, as though her own body contained that community of women that Samira had talked about.

"There is a process beyond the birth that is part of pregnancy," Schwester Monika explained. "If you pay attention to how you move, what you eat and get the rest you need, you should bounce back just fine."

"Thanks so much, Schwester Monika. I'm glad I don't have to go back to work anytime soon. When Willy was born, we were working at a boarding school, and I was back to teaching a week later. Fortunately, the classroom was right next to our apartment."

"Well, rest when you can. You know that it takes a while for new babies to find a schedule and they won't respect yours. I brought you some raspberry leaf tea that helps to tone the Gebärmutter. And some *Stilltee*. It's great for supporting breastfeeding."

Clare read the ingredients: *Bockshornklee, Anis, Kümmel, Fenchel, Zitronenverbenenblätter*. She recognized anis, fennel, lemon verbena, but would have to look up the others.

"Fenugreek and caraway," Stefan found in the dictionary. "Sounds tasty. I might have to try it."

"Let me know if it works for you, I'd love some help with the breastfeeding." Clare grinned at him.

May 2001

The writing had gained momentum and Clare no longer had to force herself to open her laptop and get to work. It seemed like the ideas got together in secret conversation in her head, without her even being aware of it, like kids passing notes in class under the teacher's nose. She was eager each morning to sit down at the desk and see what would happen. It was a kind of intellectual journal that was no longer foreign to her daily experience; in fact, at times it was hard to separate the two.

* * *

Notes for Book

Chapter 6 Internal Structures: Plots and Twists, Conflict and conversation

Themes, internal spaces: internal monologues, dreams, thoughts, inner conflicts, leitmotifs

Dialogue to develop characters, backstories, growth, and movement. Conversation is the kitchen of writing. It brings the narrative to life, front and center, around the warmth of the stove.

Borges's Ficciones: stories of labyrinths and ironies, fiction that identifies itself as such as it questions reality. It reveals the underlying strangeness of the life we take for granted.

Julio Cortázar: short story *Continuidad de los parques,* "Continuity of Parks" The Chinese Box structure of a story within a story within a story that all lead back to the first outer story you are reading. Circular time entrapping the reader as part of the story.

Mikhail Bakhtin: "heteroglossia" —the novel as a polyphonic form, incorporating other genres and many voices. Diversity and stratification of language. The author cannot be found in any one of these levels or voices, but at the intersection of all of them.

"The outsider within" phenomenon – viewing the predominant culture from the perspective of "others" within that culture can add special insights. Literary characters can be the outsider voices that challenge and clarify the nature of the whole. Or a fictitious author / narrator who pretends to be outside the story but is very much inside it, merely inhabiting a wider circle of fiction.

* * *

"It's hard to choose. What are you going to order?" Samira looked to Clare for help. The list of desserts at Café Vetter was long and tempting and she was at a loss.

"Well, if you like chocolate I highly recommend the *Sachertorte* or the *Schwarzwälder Kirschtorte*. They are both to die for."

"To die...?"

"It's just an expression," Clare explained, shifting to German. "They are so delicious that you feel like you've died and gone to heaven."

Samira chuckled and shrugged her shoulders. "Okay, you choose one of them for me."

"How's Isra? I haven't seen her in a long time."

"She's doing well. There's more work at the lab now and she comes to the immigrant center often. It seems like she's finding her community. So how is Johann these days?"

"He is a dear man. We meet almost every day and talk about life and history, time, writing. He is wrestling with a difficult past."

"And what are you wrestling with these days? Besides writing, that is."

"Remember that I found out that Hannah's house used to be a birthing house? Well, now I am having midwife dreams."

"You are dreaming about the midwife?"

"Sort of. It's more like I *am* the midwife. It's strange."

July 1981

"Mom, I don't know how to thank you. It was so great having you here. All your help and support, your company and, well, your Mom-ness."

"I wouldn't have missed it," Rosemary said, "especially the weeks of card games." She winked at Clare, who understood both the irony and the special companionship they had shared during that long wait.

"I'm glad you got to meet Gertrude as well. And I think Anja was worth waiting for."

"You bet she was. *Meine süße Enkelin*," she said, kissing Anja on the cheek. "My sweet little granddaughter."

"And you are her *great* grandma," Willy said, And mine, too. *Meine tolle Oma*." He hugged her hard and grinned up at her.

Clare and Willy waved as Jürgen and Stefan drove off to take Rosemary to the airport.

"The house feels kind of empty, doesn't it?" Clare said as they sat down together.

Willy nodded.

"I guess we're on our own now, big brother."

After Rosemary left, they decided to move Anja's cradle to the back room. It had been convenient at first to have her close by, but Clare and Stefan hadn't slept well, hearing every little grunt and gurgle during the night. They all needed to get into a better routine. Anja would have to learn to communicate her needs and the parents had to learn to trust her to wake them from real sleep.

Clare began to appreciate those nightly feedings, despite her fatigue. She often awoke with milk leaking onto the sheets in anticipation of the call from the back room. They had a changing table at the end of the hall next to Anja's room. She would pick up the warm little bundle and change her diaper first, so she could go back to sleep undisturbed as soon as her belly was full. The stillness of the night and the Stillen between them was a time all its own, outside the flow of their days.

* * *

"You know, I never expected to have such a positive experience in childbirth, especially in Germany," Sharon said as they sipped their tea. Their "twin" babies had both been changed, fed, and were sleeping soundly on the bed. It was a rare moment for the two mothers to relax and chat.

"I know what you mean," Clare agreed. "They were so flexible, caring and responsive."

"And the midwife was really in charge of it all. I even asked a nurse at one point, and she confirmed that the rest of the team, even the doctor, followed the midwife's lead."

"It sounds like we had the same experience! Were you in a room with three other mothers and babies?"

"Yes, exactly." Sharon got up to put a blanket over the sleeping babies. "And we formed a little community among ourselves. It was a bit complicated because one woman had just had a miscarriage and we didn't know what to say to her. I felt like the rest of us were a cruel reminder of what she had just lost."

"Boy, do I know what you mean," Clare said as a melancholy image of her time in the hospital after the miscarriage flashed by briefly.

"And one of the women was from Afghanistan," Sharon went on. "She seemed lost and frightened. No one talked to her, and I felt sorry for her. I kept trying to communicate and I smiled at her a lot. She finally relaxed. Once when she didn't understand my German or English, I tried miming and that made her laugh. She held up her baby and said something I couldn't understand—maybe the baby's name. I nodded and did the same. Even if we didn't understand each other, it was communication, a gesture of friendship."

13
Jaunts and Journeys

May 2001

"So, how's your guy Busch doing these days?" Clare breathed in the aroma wafting up from her coffee cup.

"These days? You mean 240 years ago?"

"It's only time, something we humans don't understand anyway. Besides, he's been quite present in this house, wouldn't you say?" Clare raised her eyebrows over her coffee mug.

"You could say that. You know, I've come to respect the man. 'These days,' as you say, he's writing more about the scientific reasons that people die and maybe taking some of the pressure off God."

"Yeah, I think God has an awful lot on his plate."

"Or her plate?" That made Clare smile. Stefan continued. "Towards the end of his tenure Busch's sermons reflect a more modern perspective, though they are still steeped in biblical references. He focuses more on *why* people died, rather than *how* they died. He refers to life as a *Wanderschaft*, a pilgrimage."

"It's funny, I've been thinking of writing in that way recently. It's a journey, a process that we can control only partially. We head towards an end that we recognize when we get there, but we don't know just what or where it will be along the way. Even when we think we know where we're going from the beginning, it always changes, so we might as well enjoy the ride. Like life."

"Well said." Stefan raised his coffee mug to clink with hers.

"Stefan, I think we should invite Johann to dinner."

"Great idea. I was beginning to wonder if he really exists, outside your world of writing, that is."

"For some reason, I've been a bit nervous to bring him to this house of his memories. I wasn't sure how it would affect our special relationship. It feels so free and open there in the park, away from the reality of our lives."

"I promise I won't be the jealous husband and try to compete with him." Stefan's smile awakened the dimple in his left cheek that always charmed Clare, even when she was mad at him.

"And maybe even dial down the bad jokes?"

"Now that's asking a lot."

"I think I'll invite his sister Erika as well. And maybe Christina and Jürgen. Do you think we could give away a cat as a door prize?" A neighbor had taken the third kitten and the last one was now as big as its mother.

Clare and Stefan both liked to cook, and they enjoyed doing it together. They wanted to do something special, so they spent the morning coffee break the next day planning the menu.

* * *

"I'll get it," Stefan said, when they heard a knock. He took off his apron and opened the door to Jürgen and Christina who had brought a bottle of wine and a loaf of fresh bread.

A few minutes later, another knock. Clare hurried to the door.

"Please come in. I'm so happy you could come," she said, hugging Johann and then Erika. I guess you didn't have any trouble finding the place."

"I have a good memory," Johann said, winking at her. "I've often passed by here and wondered if it looked the same inside as my memory of it."

"Well, we'll just have to see." Clare had decided that her own childhood memories inhabited a special place that didn't change, no matter what happened to the actual places that evolved over time.

"We weren't sure what to bring, so I brought this for dessert." Johann held up his violin case.

"Oh, that's perfect, though I told you that you didn't need to bring anything," Clare said, taking his other hand and leading him into the living room. "I'd like you to meet our friends, Jürgen and Christina." They shook hands as Clare stood there beaming her love for them. Johann looked elegant in a crisp blue shirt and his thick white hair combed back. He seemed at ease as he looked around.

"Would you like to see the rest of the house?" Clare offered. They walked into the kitchen, where Stefan was cleaning up. "This is my husband, Stefan."

"*Es freut mich...*" Stefan said, as they shook hands. "Delighted to meet you. I've heard a lot about you."

"Uh oh, nothing bad I hope," Johann said with a mischievous smile.

"Oh, of course it was all good," Stefan assured him. "In fact, I've had to up my game as a husband, with your shining image out there."

"Wait 'till you hear him play his violin, then you'll really be jealous," Clare said to Stefan.

"This is Hannah's bedroom and the other one is where we sleep."

Johann stopped in the doorway of their small bedroom. His face got serious, and he seemed frozen in place. Clare waited and put her hand on his arm.

"This is the room," he said after a long silence. "This is the birthing room. It looks a lot like the way I remember it. I only came in for my mother's check-ups, but I knew this was where the babies were born. And there was a little..."

"It's right here," Clare said, opening a door to the small balcony.

"*Mein Gott*, so it is. I spent many moments sitting out here. I loved the purple flowers in the spring."

"Wisteria," Clare added. "I have always loved them as well."

"*Fast achtzig Jahre...*" Johann whispered. "Almost eighty years since I've been here. Where have all those years gone?"

The dinner was joyful. Delicious food with good wine, and comfortable new friendships. Johann was excited when he learned that Jürgen taught at the *Blindenschule* and they fell into deep discussion about it. Clare had always been impressed with how friendly Marburg was to the blind. Students came from all over to attend the school and she had noticed them walking through the city with confidence and autonomy.

Just recently Clare had seen a young man walking down the cobblestone streets of the Oberstadt. He was clearly intent on his path and swept his white stick back and forth vigorously as he navigated around obstacles and through the crowd with a dexterity that amazed her. She realized he had memorized the whole route: the outdoor seating, a slight hole here, a bump there. And people were so used to seeing the white sticks, they knew to step out of the way in time. It was a beautiful choreography that allowed for some people to wander along slowly, while others hurried by, and bicycles threaded their way through it all.

Jürgen talked about the challenges of teaching English to blind students. When he was first hired, the materials that the school had were outdated and unimaginative. He had ended up creating his own textbooks and devising new ways to respond to the students. He learned to read Braille on his own, memorizing the arrangements of bumps that signified the letters of the alphabet. He could read by sight the *Punktschrift*, the raised dots of Braille, that the students produced on special typewriters where the keys could be identified by touch.

"In the early years, I recorded my responses verbally on individual cassette tapes for each student. Now we work with computers."

Clare remembered hearing about Jürgen's work twenty years earlier and imagined that he had since developed new materials and strategies.

They were fascinated by his stories and the world in which he worked, humbled by all that they took for granted in their own lives.

"Jürgen, tell us about your amazing student, the one who went to Tibet." Clare was still dazzled by that story.

"Well, I had her in my English class and I could see right away that she was gifted with languages. She told me one day that she was interested in Tibetan culture, and she wondered if she could learn the language. I said that if she really wanted to, she could do it. It would take work and I didn't know what resources would be available to her. She found a way at the university and learned it rather quickly, along with some Mongolian and Chinese. Later she went to Tibet and started a school for blind children there. Those children had lived sad lives of isolation and near abandonment. There was no Punktschrift for blind people to read, and she had invented a Tibetan Braille alphabet for herself when she was first trying to learn the language. She even went on expeditions with Tibetan guides to find more blind children in need. She and her partner have recently founded an organization called Braille Without Borders."

"That is a remarkable story," Johann said and they all nodded.

The evening went by quickly in the soft light of candles, stories, and memories. Clare brought out a fruit torte with whipped cream and shaved chocolate on top. It was her favorite dessert to make, but she didn't do it often back home in her busy work life.

"I made a special *Nachtisch*, I hope you enjoy it." Clare loved the German word for dessert, the way it was described as an "after table" stage of the meal. She sometimes wondered if it meant you were supposed to retire to the living room to eat it. "And I can offer coffee or tea to go with it. But the real Nachtisch is something that Johann brought."

Clare smiled at him and nodded towards his violin case.

"Could you start with that piece you played for me?"

With the first notes, they all forgot the torte and put their forks down. The music filled the house and the hearts of that small audience. Clare couldn't explain it, but there was something about the tune that reached inside her and pulled. It was melancholy yet beautiful and it left a confusing mixture of sadness and loss with love and hope. She wondered if the music penetrated the walls of the house to the many stories contained there. Those in the room sighed in unison.

"Let's finish eating," she suggested, "and then we can move to more comfortable seats. Would you be willing, Johann, to play some more for us?"

"Well, I'm kind of out of practice, but I think there are a few more pieces in there. I'm counting on the violin to remember them."

They finished the dessert quickly and settled in the living room for the music. Clare noticed that the gray kitten had jumped into Erika's lap and was purring happily there.

When Johann picked up the violin again, Clare felt a swelling of love for this man she hardly knew. His hands were covered with old age spots and his fingers were knobby and twisted, but they found their grace as soon as they touched the strings. There was something intimate about the way he tucked the violin under his chin and coaxed the music out of it. Some pieces made them all want to dance and clap while others evoked nostalgia and tears.

"I haven't heard you play like that for many years," Erika said with a tender smile.

"That was a real gift, Johann," Clare whispered as she hugged him at the door. "And so are you."

July 1981

Willy liked to push the *Kinderwagen* that Christina and Jürgen had leant them. It was a nice size baby carriage, easy to maneuver, unlike some of the huge modern ones that Stefan called *Kinderpanzer*; "child tanks." Clare

265

especially liked walking to the Oberstadt. It was harder to push the Kinderwagen on the cobblestone streets, but the motion would jiggle the baby to sleep. One challenge was the aggressive *Omas*, who seemed to appear out of nowhere—self-appointed grandmothers who had an opinion about everything. "The baby needs to wear a hat, so she doesn't catch a draft." For a culture that championed fresh air and exercise as central to health, Clare never understood the seemingly universal horror of cool air on a baby.

"*Sie könnte einen Zug kriegen.*"

The first time Clare heard that expression, she couldn't understand what catching a train had to do with anything, but she let it go as one of those lost moments in communication. After hearing the expression several times, she asked Christina what it meant. *Zug* did mean "train," but it was also a "draft," as in a pull of air.

So Clare put a little hat on Anja before they went out. Then a different *Oma* would say "Oh, she is so sweet, but you cover her up too much, she'll get too hot and then sweat and she could catch a *Zug.*" Clare knew that they meant well, and it was a way to connect with otherwise reserved people, so she would smile and say "*Danke schön.*" Sometimes that would lead to a bit of conversation. Babies seemed to have the power to move people, to penetrate their otherwise carefully protected space. In Latin America, babies were equally treasured, but generally not seen as so fragile. They were in the middle of every activity. Clare thought maybe it was a climate thing.

Sometimes she went to see her friend Carmen, whose baby was born a few weeks after Anja. It had been a difficult birth that ended in a Cesarean, which left Carmen stuck at home for a while. Clare really appreciated their friendship, in part because they always spoke Spanish with each other. It was like a fresh mountain stream, so clear and easy for her to express herself. Clare's love affair with German was deepening every day, but it wasn't quite the inner force of nature that Spanish had become for her. She was fascinated by how she was a different person in each language.

That had become clear to her in teaching. Not only did she feel a unique cultural energy and dramatic expressiveness in the language, but she was also often "on stage" when she spoke it. "You have to turn up the volume of your personality," one of her teaching assistants had wisely explained to her students about learning Spanish. And that went double for the teacher in a classroom. You had to model that energy, make learning fun, and infuse the classroom and the students with a passion and confidence that got them to take risks, try things out, lose their inhibitions.

"This is your chance to try on a new personality," she would say to them. "It's a process and you won't be judged by your mistakes but by your ability to communicate. Learn to be creative and laugh a lot." She sometimes heard her own voice in her ear as she struggled with being a language student again herself.

"I think I'm finding my new persona in German now," Clare said to Stefan one day.

"Oh? I'd like to meet her."

"I feel more philosophical and thoughtful. And motherly. I am constantly charmed by the new words I meet. They make me see a new side of things I take for granted. Or, as Willy says, 'take for granite.' German is such a creative language. It's like linguistic *basteln*. You know, take whatever pieces you have and make something new out of it.

* * *

"*Ayyy*," Carmen groaned as her baby nursed. "They tell you that nursing is good for helping the uterus to contract, to recover its normal shape. What they don't tell you is that when you've had a cesarean—when, you know, they slice through the uterus itself as well as all your flesh—those contractions are not fun. "*Duele mucho,*" she said as she winced in pain again."

"*Pobrecita,*" Clare whispered as she stroked Carmen's arm. "Can I bring you some tea or something?" She had promised to stay a couple hours, while Carmen's husband, José, went to do some shopping. Clare almost felt guilty for the ease with which she lifted Anja out of the carriage and nursed her without pain. She remembered Schwester Monika saying, "You never know how it will go, so you need to be prepared for anything." By now, Gertrude was a legend of the past and the endless waiting had faded into insignificance with the present reality of Anja.

Clare picked up little Laia to change her diaper, leaving her friend to rest a while.

"*Gracias, amiga,*" Carmen said, before dozing off.

Notes for Book

Chapter 7 Scatology and Eschatology: Edits and Endings

In Spanish, the word *escatología* means both "scatology" and "eschatology." It's probably more a function of phonetics. (Spanish words don't begin with s + an occlusive consonant, as in sp-, sc-, st-, so there is always an "e" in front.) But it does suggest a relationship between the two words.

Scatology – the study of excrement and excretion (what is edited out, left unsaid, left behind, erased, censured.) Part of daily bodily life and human communication, self-understanding, medical and forensic science, paleontology.

Eschatology – the part of theology concerned with death, judgment, and the final destiny of the soul and of humankind (endings, end of the story, end of life, end of the book, physical end vs. narrative end, definition of time, death, transition, transcendence.)

The ending of a story determines the beginning and often sheds light on everything in between. For that reason, many stories, novels, and films begin with the ending. The chronological ending is not the same as the narrative ending. **Circular structures** can point to circular time, repetitive time, or just reinforce the importance of a moment that frames the story.

Friedrich Schlegel talked of historians as "prophets turned backwards." Most writing starts with an end (a relative present) vantage point and reconstructs the (hi)story from there. A translation of the past into present understanding.

* * *

Clare sat in front of a computer at the internet, sipping a cup of tea as she read the latest email from her mother. She had sensed for months that her mother's promise to visit would not be fulfilled, with postponements full of "maybe" and "not sure." Now it was clear and final. It didn't make sense for her to visit now anyway, so near the end of their year. They had each worked through their grief in their own way, and maybe their future time together wouldn't be so full of the shared loss.

July 1981

Willy liked to entertain Anja while her diapers were being changed. School was out and he was taking his big brother role seriously, when he wasn't playing outside with Jonas. He would stand beside her head and hold up a small black and white panda bear and make it dance. Sometimes he would talk to her behind it and other times he let it dance in silence. Anja noticed the little bear right away and began to turn her head to look for it first thing, even when Willy wasn't there.

"I don't believe what they say about babies not being able to focus in the first month or two. Anja clearly sees that panda and is curious about it." Clare said to Stefan. They also tried sticking out their tongues to see if she could imitate the action. She did at just a few weeks old, belying another supposed limitation of new babies.

"Of course, not every baby has Willy for a big brother," Stefan commented.

One morning, Anja woke up crying from her morning nap. Clare picked her up, checked her diaper and then walked around patting her back. She tried nursing her again. Nothing seemed to help, and the crying got louder and sharper.

"It sounds like she's in pain," she said to Christina, who held her while Clare called the doctor. Anja screamed louder. "The doctor says to come right away."

"I'm sorry that Jürgen is gone with the car. Is Stefan home?"

"No, he went to Frankfurt today to register Anja as an American citizen born in Germany and get her official birth certificate. Oh, and to check if her name is legally acceptable." There was a German law that restricted what you could name your child. It made Clare feel rebellious. She remembered the story about the singer Grace Slick naming her daughter "god," spelled with a small "g" because they wanted her to "be humble." It turned out to be a joke, but it had gotten a lot of coverage.

"It's not far to the doctor's office. I think I'll just put her in the carriage and jog there," Clare said, trying not to panic at the baby's shrill cries.

She trotted down the hill and around the curve. The crying intensified to a piercing stutter as they bounced along. *Stay calm, it's not far.* The doctor had said he would see them right away. When they arrived, Clare was out of breath, but Anja was quiet. A nurse came out to meet them.

"Frau Muller?" Clare nodded and they were escorted in ahead of a few waiting patients. She alternated between relief and extreme concern that the crying had stopped.

"She cried most of the way here," Clare explained after catching her breath. "It's been almost an hour. I've never heard her cry like that."

The doctor was kind and reassuring, though he looked concerned. He checked all the vitals of the calm and seemingly healthy baby. Clare was embarrassed, but still nervous.

"Everything looks good. But we should get a urine sample. It could be an infection."

"Really? Babies can get urinary infections?" One of the curses of the female anatomy, she thought. "But how do we do it?" She tried to imagine getting a baby to pee into a cup.

The nurse brought a little plastic bag with tape around the opening that she fixed on the tiny crotch while Clare held Anja in her lap.

"Just start nursing her, it shouldn't take long."

"I don't see any infection," the doctor said after examining the urine. "That's good news."

"She was screaming, doctor. It sounded like she was in serious pain."

"I believe you. Babies let you know what they are feeling. It was probably colic. That can be quite painful, though usually not dangerous. Try eliminating garlic, onions, cabbage from your diet for a while and see if that helps. Some babies are very sensitive to things that come through the milk. Also give her these drops every few hours. You can squeeze about half a dropper directly into her mouth. Don't worry, it's just chamomile oil. It can't hurt her. Come back again if that doesn't help." He showed her how as he gave her the first dose.

Clare was relieved as she pushed the carriage back up the hill. The doctor was a pediatrician who also practiced homeopathic medicine. It seemed a good balance. Anja slept all the way home.

Stefan had been doing most of the cooking and he loved garlic. He would have to give it up for a while.

May 2001

Notes for Book

Chapter 8 Archives and Archeology: Hidden History and Fairy Tales

Social history (and fiction) as archeology. Finding pieces of stories buried in the past, connecting written fragments to create a narrative. The history of a point in time is not only the accumulation of events, artifacts, customs, and writings up to that time, but also a kaleidoscopic view of all that was in play to produce each of those things.

The author (and authority) of a text is connected to the circumstances—the context—in which that text is produced. "Context" from Latin *contextus: con* (together) + *texere* (to weave). Not just the background but the actual weaving together of elements about the time, the place, the language, the events, the people that created, influenced, and informed the resources that remain. Also important is the authority of the producers of those texts and for what audience and purpose they were produced. How were they read in their time?

The original sources that are preserved and later uncovered are in a sense not original, but rather texts that are already responding to many other texts and traditions. Added to that is the "rewriting" of those texts as they are read and interpreted in each subsequent time.

History is a process of investigation and inquiry, preserved in a narrative of complex patterns of stories and assumptions.

History vs. fiction

History is more "objective" than fiction because the emphasisis more on the "object" narrated (the past) than on the narration itself.

Fiction is more "subjective," because the emphasis is on the "subject" of the narration (the writer) and his/her art of narrating. But history is also subjective, and fiction has objective value.

Literary texts as history: fairy tales are documents of traditional storytelling (with questions of context, changing authorship and authority), also with their own history of editing, rewriting, repurposing, and evolving reception.

* * *

"*Hallo, Johann.* How are you today?"

"*Grüß dich, Clare.* I'm doing okay. It was lovely to be in your house last night and meet your husband and your friends. By the way, Erika says to tell you she would be happy to take the cat."

"That's great! Johann, it was wonderful to have you in our house, in Hannah's house. Your music was a big hit." She sat down next to her friend and turned to look at him for a moment. "Are you sure you're alright?"

"*Ja, ja,* I'm fine. Lots of memories recently. I'm trying to sort it all out."

"To be honest, I was a bit worried about that. It can be hard to visit memories from our childhood in places that have since changed. It can destabilize our mental pictures of past moments that are important to who we are now."

"*Ne, ne,* that wasn't a problem. My childhood memories are okay. But there's lots of other stuff I put away in a closet for many years."

"The war?" She put her hand on his.

"*Ja,* I don't like the person I was then. I still can't seem to forgive him."

"I think that the Johann I know would be kind to him now." His face softened with a smile, but his eyes still held the sadness.

"I should have died back then. I was resigned to it. There was no other way out."

Clare waited, holding her breath.

272

"It was horrific; we were all trying to survive. For some that meant succumbing to the evil and becoming Nazis and for others, well, we tried to hide."

She released her breath slowly. "Was it possible to hide from the Nazis?"

"No. What I mean is we tried to hide from evil…and from ourselves. It was constant compromise and collaboration no matter what we did. To resist was to die. To not resist was to die in another way. But human nature makes us try to survive at any cost. My violin saved my life more than once and I felt that I was at least giving something good, even if it was sometimes to the Nazis. It gave me hope when I was playing, but at the same time I came to hate the music because it was a coward's way to survive. I had to pretend to be something I wasn't without becoming what I was pretending to be. I'm not sure who I was in the end.

"By 1941, things had escalated to an insane level. If the killing had been random, it might have been easier to bear. But it wasn't. It made me desperate. One day I grabbed my violin and ran. I didn't have a plan or a place to go and they found me after a few days. I turned to face them, knowing they would shoot me. I felt an explosive pain in my gut when the bullet hit. I was almost grateful. The officer in charge of the unit was ready to finish me off and I was ready to die. But another officer intervened when he saw my violin. 'We need his music,' he explained. For a long time, I was angry at being alive."

Clare listened in silence, her eyes fixed on the ground in front of her.

"Even in the worst situations in life, we sometimes still find kindness and beauty. There were days I could remember that and other days I considered ending it all myself. In a way I did die, at least part of me did. But I got out of the army. I think the Nazi officer who saved my life probably hated who he was as well, but he loved music. He convinced the other officer to spare me so that I could dedicate my musical talent to 'the glory of The Third Reich.' I doubt he believed that. It was just what he needed to say.

"I went home and did my best to disappear. I took over the little shop that my mother had been trying to keep going after my father's death. Many small shop owners had swallowed the Nazi propaganda in those times— preserving traditional German values, resisting change and the big department stores that were owned by Jews. We tried to hide under that image, without going along with it. It was a delicate dance.

"The irony of trying to be thought of as Nazis so we could protect our little Jewish daughter was stressful and absurd. But we had many moments of joy together. Life can be stubborn, you know. Even during the darkest times, it tries to sustain itself with light."

"And love," Clare added.

"Yes, Klara is the one who saved me with her love."

"How did you meet her?"

"She was a nurse at the hospital where I was sent to convalesce. There were many makeshift hospitals in Marburg to deal with the thousands of wounded—so many, that Marburg became known as a "hospital city," and for that reason it was mostly spared the bombings that destroyed other cities.

"Klara was a compassionate nurse and a courageous woman. She found Mia wandering in the streets and risked her own life to rescue her, hiding her in her apartment while she went to work. During the weeks of my recovery, a great love grew between us and Klara finally trusted me enough to share her secret. When we got married, we pretended that Mia was her illegitimate daughter and we officially adopted her.

"In the years that followed Klara continued to help me heal. She saw the parts of me that were still alive and nourished like those old trees, where the trunk falls and a new one sprouts from the dead part. That's what happened to me, though I tried to forget that the dead wood was always still there underneath me. My dear, dear, Klara."

"It's a beautiful story. You are a good man, Johann, with a heavy burden to bear and great gifts to share. Your music speaks to all that. Please don't give it up. I am honored that you have told me your story, and I won't ever forget it." Clare had known in some small measure the guilt of complicity in her own life. "There are so many destructive forces in the world, some beyond our reach or even our knowledge, yet we still contribute to them."

Johann nodded. "Here in Germany, it has taken a couple of generations to even be able to face our past. Some families just never talked about it."

"You know, we have suffered from long-term amnesia in the United States as well. We are just beginning to acknowledge and understand the atrocities we have committed. What we protect our children from today can leave them more vulnerable to it tomorrow." Clare wondered how many times she had erred on one side or the other with her own children. Those decisions often felt like a shot in the dark.

"Yes, I suppose so. And when we try to protect *ourselves* from it, it becomes another monster in the closet."

"Well, one thing I do know; it's always good to keep joy alive. And art. It may be the only thing that can save us."

They hugged for a long time, dampening each other's shoulders with their tears.

"Ein Stein ist mir vom Herzen gefallen," he whispered. "A stone has fallen from my heart."

August 1981

They needed to get a passport picture for Anja for a trip to Berlin. Stefan had suggested the trip to visit friends of the family and get a chance to see "that magnificent city." Clare was worried about traveling with such a young baby, but Stefan convinced her that it was the easiest time to travel with them, since they sleep so much of the time.

"I think they do passport photos at Ahrens. I'll check." Clare started thinking of all the things they would need to pack just for Anja. "I must remember to pack some things for myself," she said out loud. She was already in that mother mode where the mother comes last on the list if she even makes it there.

Clare invited Sharon to go with her to Ahrens, since her daughter needed a passport as well. Their babies had been due about a week apart, but with Laura three weeks early and Anja two weeks late, they ended up six weeks apart in age, but about the same size. They sometimes called them "the twins."

"You won't believe this," Clare reported to Stefan when she got home. "They insisted that the baby must be alone in the photo. It was ridiculous! I had to crouch down behind the little table and reach under the tablecloth to steady her. She was in one of those baby recliners, but it was way too big for her, so she kept slumping to one side. They told me to move this way and that until they couldn't see me at all. Anja wasn't happy about it, but we got it done just before she let loose with her opinion of the whole thing. A baby mugshot. Sharon had the same experience with Laura."

"Oh well, all babies look alike at that age anyway."

"Only a man would say that."

They were off to Berlin. Willy was happy to be on a train again and they all enjoyed the scenery. Anja seemed content with the gentle rocking motion of the train, and it was easy to feed her on demand. Clare seemed to have an endless supply of milk. The greater the demand, the more was produced. The only problem was when the baby's appetite lessened. Then it could be painful.

The train stopped at the East German border. Clare felt tense about the border crossing. She'd seen too many spy movies. Three men in army-like uniforms boarded, looking like they had just walked off the set of one of those movies. They were intensely serious and formal as they stopped at each seat to check passports and official papers. Clare had their four passports ready.

"*Reisepass und andere Dokumente,*" the official said curtly, and he stuck out his hand in front of Clare. She went to hand him all four passports. "*Nur Sie zuerst,*" he said. "Just you first." He examined Clare's, Stefan's and then Willy's carefully, as though matters of national security were at stake. We're not spies, Clare wanted to say. Then the official looked at Anja and Clare thought for sure he would expect the baby to hand over her own documents. Clare gave him the baby mugshot passport, thinking Anja looked guilty of something by the expression on her face. Or maybe just defiant. He looked at Anja, then at the photo, at Anja again and at both parents. Clare thought maybe he would at least smile at the absurdity of such formality for a tiny baby, but he just nodded and gave her back the passport.

"Did he think she was a spy? Or that we were smuggling a baby?" she whispered to Stefan.

"Shhh," he whispered back to her. "They take this stuff very seriously."

It was strange to travel through East Germany briefly and then into West Berlin—a West German island in the middle of the city.

* * *

They were welcomed warmly by the family in Berlin and glad to be settled in their house. The next day they saw some sights and then went to the Berlin zoo. Their hosts had found a baby carriage to lend them, which made things much easier. It was a beautiful summer day. Willy was thrilled with the zoo and Anja slept through most of it. After a lovely evening of conversation and good food, they went to bed early. Stefan, Clare, and Willy fit comfortably on a large mattress on the floor of a guest room, with Anja in the baby carriage next to them. They were all tired and fell asleep quickly.

"Mom! Mom!!" The urgency of Willy's voice set off an alarm in Clare's body as she awoke suddenly. Before she could make sense of the situation, she recognized the swoosh of the contents of a stomach being expelled. "Mommy…" Willy whimpered miserably.

"Okay, it's okay. Let's get you cleaned up." She took off his pajama top and replaced it with the shirt he had worn that day. They mopped up the vomit from the bed and placed a towel over it. Another round in the bathroom and he settled into bed comfortably.

"Maybe it's something he ate," Stefan offered. Clare had just dozed off when an uneasiness stirred in her middle. She tried to ignore it and go back to sleep.

"Oh no," she whispered when it became clear what was next. She ran to the bathroom and made it just in time for a similarly explosive projection. At least she hadn't messed up the bed again. Her body wasn't as efficient as Willy's had been, so she camped out on the bathroom floor for a couple of hours. Finally stable enough to crawl back into bed, she sighed loudly as her head hit the pillow.

"Are you okay?" Stefan asked groggily.

"I think so." Just then Anja's hungry cry changed her mind. "Well, not so much. Could you bring her to me?"

The next morning, Clare managed to eat a little oatmeal and then go back to bed with Anja. Their plans for the second day in Berlin went from unlikely to impossible, as they realized how shaky Clare and Willy were. The important thing was to get strong enough for the train trip home the following day.

The sick ones rallied enough to manage the trip and they were all glad to be back home. Clare felt well enough to eat something and went to bed grateful that it hadn't been worse. But the night had other plans. She awoke with overwhelming nausea and ran to the bathroom. Things got steadily worse, and she could barely even sip water. At one point she heard Willy vomit as well and Stefan got up to help him.

Anja seemed unaffected and wanted her meals as usual. Clare was getting worried about her milk supply. It was one thing to not be able to eat, but it was crucial to drink enough. The next morning, she couldn't get out of bed. *Herr Hexe* came upstairs with one of his herbal remedies. "This will help," he assured her.

She sipped the tea gratefully, hoping it would settle her stomach. But she soon realized it had the opposite effect. It was in such revolution that she was nearly propelled onto the floor as she leaned over the bed.

Stefan had prepared a bottle with some formula that they hoped Anja would take. So far, their daughter had made it clear that it was a poor substitute for the real thing. It was a long and violent morning, even though Clare's stomach was completely empty by then. But finally, gradually, she settled into sleep, occasionally interrupted by Anja's cries. Stefan worked valiantly with the bottle, getting her to drink a little before she would get angry at it.

Jürgen came to check on her later and explained that he had given her *Schafgarbe*, a kind of yarrow that can be used as an antibacterial, astringent, and antispasmodic infusion. "It cleans out your stomach and then helps settle it." She was quite sure that it had done at least the first part.

* * *

"Mom. Mom." She felt Willy's hand shaking her shoulder. "Mom, Dad's getting sick now." The sounds from the bathroom convinced her.

"What are we going to do?" she moaned, immediately regretting having said it out loud when she saw Willy's face. "Don't worry, we'll get through it."

They did get through it, but it was a long haul.

"*Die Grippe*," Jürgen said, as they headed into the second phase of the illness. "It seems like a bad flu." The symptoms had moved up to head and chest and fever. They felt helpless and were immensely grateful to their downstairs neighbors for taking care of them.

"I think it has a "grippe" on our family," Stefan said weakly, unable to resist the pun.

"But we don't want you to get it," Clare said to Christina when she offered to bring them food.

"Don't worry, we'll just set things on the stairs for you. Oh, and there's a pot of soup that Julia brought for you."

Even Jürgen was being more careful. Willy recovered sooner and was proud to play nurse to his parents, making scrambled eggs and tea for them.

Clare's illness dragged on the longest, turning into an infection that left her pale and drained. She finally went to see the doctor.

"I know you are a pediatrician, but also a homeopath. I wanted someone who would think about the baby as well. I don't want to take anything that could go through the milk and be bad for her."

"Yes, that's very wise. This may sound strange, but I'm going to prescribe tiny doses of arsenic for a couple days to reduce the swelling and congestion of your respiratory passages. It is safe in those amounts. And then, I want you to take this bee venom three times a day for a month. It has anti-microbial and anti-inflammatory properties and supports your immune system without harming your gut. I also recommend some *Brust- und Husten Tee*, chest and cough tea. That will help your whole system as well."

"How did it go?" Stefan asked when she got home.

"Well, I've got poison, bee venom and cough tea. We'll see what happens."

June 2001

Notes for Book

Chapter 9 Symbols and Synchronicity: Everything can also mean something else.

(We mean more than we say and say more than we know.)

All language is symbolic, but cultures and their religions and mythologies establish special powerful symbols that can contain a whole story that undergirds the structure of social meaning. A common language for a community, a kind of shorthand. Writers use symbols and synchronicity to weave a **deeper narrative structure** with poetic and temporal associations.

Co-incidence, events that occur at the same time, can create connections beyond what they appear to mean. Symbols and metaphorical comparisons use an economy of words to point to a bigger story and create more colorful scenarios. The reader can see both at the same time – the symbol and what stands behind it.

"Synchronic" from Greek *syn* (together) + *khronos* (time) = occurring at the same time. Postmodern fiction often uses **synchronic timelines,** to keep several simultaneous stories moving forward and provide multiple, even contradictory perspectives.

Fictional narrative often also **interweaves different temporal lines** that presumably can't co-exist, yet they do in many ways in human experience. **Diachronic** = occurring across time. Memory, dreams, traumas, inherited culture, past relationships, perspectives, foreshadowing, omens, premonitions – all important tools of fictional narrative that is, by its nature, a condensed construction to suggest and sketch a larger story. It reaches out across time, looking backward, and at the same time forward to a future time of reading.

* * *

"More coffee? You seem lost in your thoughts. Everything okay?"

"I can't stop thinking about my conversation with Johann yesterday. He shared more of his story. It's just so painful. And all these years later he still finds it hard to forgive himself. I guess he will always bear that scar."

"That's the thing about scars. They are physical memory, whether they are visible or not."

"Why is it so hard to be a person?"

Stefan laughed. "That sounds like a Willy question."

Clare smiled and sipped her coffee thoughtfully. "I guess we are always children in this life, trying to understand the contradictions of being human."

"Hmmm."

"It's amazing how a few can always whip up the fears of many and convince them to swallow a poison in the name of purification."

"Fascism always thrives on fear and disinformation. It builds a kind of insanity through mass hypnosis." Stefan knew more than he would like about the Holocaust and history of fascism. He often recognized signs of it in current times.

"And it's incremental, like tiny doses of arsenic." Clare was still amazed that a doctor had prescribed that for her. "At first it seems to help, but in the long term it will kill you. By the way, did you know that the name "Marburg" means "Frontier Fortress?"

"I think I read that once. It belonged to the Landgraves of Thuringia, starting sometime in the twelfth century."

"In those days a stone wall could keep out the enemy. Now, 'the enemy' is everywhere."

"A great philosopher once said, 'We have met the enemy and he is us.'"

"You mean Pogo?" Clare laughed, remembering the cartoon figure of her childhood who had become a voice of reason for the times. She stood up and put her coffee cup in the sink.

"Are you off to see your outside man?"

"I guess I'd better. It's getting harder to imagine leaving him soon."

"He's a good man. Give him my regards."

14
Grace

August 1981

"You seem chipper this morning." Stefan handed Clare a plate of scrambled eggs and toast.

"Thanks. The thing about illness is that it makes you so grateful when you get back to even the minimum level of wellness. I do have more energy. Maybe those bees did spin some magic."

"That's good. Feel like a stroll after breakfast?"

"It's raining."

"We have a cover for the Kinderwagen, and Willy would love to put on his rain boots and splash through puddles."

They were off, with Willy leading the way. "Can I go barefoot?" he asked. "Since we're walking on Barfüßerstraße. 'Barefoot Street' should mean I get to go barefoot."

"Nice try, little guy, but it's not a good idea," Stefan responded. "Besides, you have such cool yellow boots that make a nice splashing sound." Willy nodded and went on splashing contentedly.

As they walked, Clare felt like she was in Pennsylvania, west of Philadelphia, where she grew up. The grand old maple and beech trees, lindens and oaks, ivy growing on old stone buildings and walls; it all seemed like they were from her own past.

"This part of the street is called Barfüßertor," Stefan explained, "because it led up to the gate into the old city. *Tor* means 'gate.' I'll show you where the wall around the city used to be. That's where it changes to Barfüßerstraße."

"But it's still barefoot all the way," Willy asserted. "Why did they call it that? Did everybody go barefoot back then?"

"That must have been before they invented shoes." Willy looked at Stefan for a moment and then laughed. His senses were becoming tuned to his dad's teasing. "Look, a little gate!" He pointed to iron bars that allowed a window through a moss-covered stone wall. "It opens!" Willy exclaimed, already stepping into a small cemetery that had rested there for centuries.

"I'm not sure we should…" Clare began, but father and son were already exploring. A plaque read that the cemetery had been established in the mid 1500s. Old headstones and crosses weathered by time, moss, and lichen, stood amidst the bright green of living grass.

"I think this is near where the gate to the old city was." Stefan said. "This cemetery was probably just outside the wall."

Anja slept on peacefully in the carriage, lulled by the soft patter of rain on the plastic cover.

They walked on and soon arrived at the Marktplatz. Clare loved the community that formed there around the Saturday market, a spontaneous gathering of strangers, who greeted each other like old friends. It was an impressionist painting with bright colored umbrellas in the street, raincoats, bicycles, carriages, and cut flowers for sale. Everything was slightly blurred by the light rain, the colors freshly washed.

Clare liked to look at people as she walked through the crowd. Each person lived at the center of their own story, and she was just one of the crowd for them, as they were for her. She enjoyed shifting her perspective in that way, a profound and dizzying flip of her worldview, her *Weltanschauung*. With her mental camera she would frame the weathered face of an old woman and try to imagine seeing through her eyes. Or a young couple walking arm in arm, the bushy eyebrows of a man with a cane, a small girl with dark curling eyelashes damp with rain. A baby in a carriage sucking on a pacifier, protected from the rain by a transparent plastic cover, just like theirs. Clare collected such impressions and tucked them into an album in her memory to take home with her. She wondered how much little Anja would absorb of these experiences, though she would clearly not remember them.

June 2001

Clare sat down at the writing desk and moved her laptop aside. It had taken center stage for a while, she realized. She picked up her journal and opened it in front of her, wiping the page with her hand as though to clear cobwebs from it.

Jun 15

I haven't written for a long time, Hannah. I'm not sure why. I guess my book has gained momentum and taken over my time. You have been part of my writing, you know. I don't mean you, Hannah Baumgartner, whom I have not yet actually met. But your house, this room, your mother's desk, this space in my life. I will always be grateful for that. I still dream every night, of course. It is often a jumble of things, a meeting of so many different times, places, and people in the bed of this room.

Clare put down her pencil and folded the gilded edged flap over the dark brown leather of the journal. It was a familiar gesture, a definitive closing the door of her inner explorations to move on with the day. Before going downstairs to join Stefan for their writing break, she went out to sit on the balcony for a moment. She had also abandoned that space in her daily routine. The wisteria bloom was past, but the vines were still thick with green leaves and new tendrils. She felt immediately the peace of that private retreat space and wondered why she had forgotten about it for so long.

The sweet dark aroma of coffee drew her out of her reverie and down the stairs. She was always amazed how it could penetrate both interior and exterior walls.

* * *

"Yum, did you just buy this bread? It's still warm."

"*Ja, Schatzi, ein leckeres Bauernbrot.* Scrumptious, huh?"

"Mmm. Farmer's bread. Speaking of farmers, I was perusing those pages you gave me from your Death Register document. I got curious about people's occupations in those days."

"They were mostly farmers in this area—subsistence farming."

"Yeah, I saw lots of references to herdsmen and shepherds, sometimes just 'a poor man.' But also, blacksmiths, soldiers, church elders, court assessors, cooks, innkeepers…"

"And weavers: wool weavers and linen weavers."

284

"Tailors, saltpeter miner, schoolmaster, cabinet maker, brew master, wagonmaker, sheriff, pastor, treasurer, doctor. Just seeing the variety of occupations gives a picture of their community life."

"And don't forget the 'wellborn.' The nobles."

"The first one on the list is 'whore.'"

"Yup, they were there, too. The oldest profession, as they say. And midwives, of course."

"A weaver. I think I would have been a weaver."

"Not a writer?"

"Kind of the same thing. I am beginning to understand your fascination with Busch's records of that past time. Even in a death register there are more hidden stories than one would expect."

"We know so much more about death today, medically that is, but it is still a mystery."

"According to your Busch, it seems people mostly died either 'a blissful and honorable death' or from dysentery, consumption, stroke, smallpox, chest illness or apoplexy, whatever that is." Clare had heard the word "apoplectic" used in modern times to express intense anger or rage.

"Apoplexy referred to any death that began with a sudden collapse, loss of consciousness and quick death—usually a stroke."

"I guess that's where religion comes in. Busch often identifies people as either Catholic or Reformed Church. What is that precisely?"

"That means Lutheran basically, about 200 years after the Protestant Reformation. Most in the parish were protestant, called *Evangelisch* in German."

"And whoever they were, whatever their occupation, social status or religion, they all died."

"Life is one hundred percent fatal, as they say."

August 1981

Clare stopped folding laundry to watch Willy lying on the big bed next to Anja, his head propped on his hand. He was whispering something to her.

"It's like he's telling her about life, preparing her to grow up in this world," Stefan said as he joined Claire.

"She seems to be listening." They stood there smiling at the scene from afar; the earnest expression on their son's face and the trusting look of their baby daughter as she watched him talk. Clare wanted to take a picture, but she didn't dare move and break the spell. She would just have to hope that the moment would live on as a memory.

"What will she know of these early months of her life? And of this year of her gestation. I should have kept a journal."

"Just keep singing to her in German," Stefan reassured her.

Clare smiled, remembering the baby blanket her mother had made, with the words to *Wiegenlied* embroidered on it in different colors. That would be a treasure for the future, a reminder to her daughter that she had been born in Germany.

* * *

"Willy, time to get your stuff ready. We need to leave soon for your last soccer game." He came out of his room already dressed and carrying his shoes and shin guards.

"Wow, good job, kiddo."

"I'm kinda 'cited about it. But I'm sad, too."

"Why are you sad?"

"'Cuz I prolly won't ever see them again and they'll forget me."

"I know, Schatzi, I'll be sad to leave, too. But they won't forget you. And we'll take lots of good memories back with us, right?"

"I guess so. But it won't be the same."

* * *

They came home tired but happy. It had been a good game and Willy was proud of having shot a goal.

"And you made a couple of assists as well," Stefan said, giving him a high five. "Those are just as important," his coach-dad reminded him.

"The best part was this." Willy held up the soccer ball the team had given him after the game. The kids and the coach had all signed it and they had cheered for him as he held it up over his head. "This will be my memory," he said, hugging the ball. It slept next to him in bed every night after that.

June 2001

"Guten Tag, Muller."

"Clare, wie geht's? Hier ist Hannah."

"Hannah, how are you? It's nice to hear from you."

"I'm doing fine. I'm coming home soon."

"Really? That's great! When will you arrive?"

"Well, I'm going to visit my daughter for a while first. I was wondering if it would be okay to stay in the house with you for a couple of days before you leave."

"Of course! It's your house. And we'd love to meet you in person. There's so much I want to ask you and tell you."

"Super! I look forward to meeting you as well. I'll keep in touch when I get back to Germany."

"Hannah, do you like cats?"

"I love them. My beloved Mitzi died last year. I didn't want to get another one when I was going to be gone for so long."

"Oh, that's sad. I was just wondering. See you soon."

"Tschuß."

* * *

June 17

I can't believe you'll be home soon, Hannah. I'm excited, but also a bit nervous to meet the real you. The one who traveled far away will probably be quite different from the one who lived with me here in your house.

* * *

Notes for Book

Chapter 10 Author and text: The story of the story

The windows of the house—view from the outside into the fictional world of the house, the work observing itself and its own creation. Also, the fictional world offers windows out to the "real" world, with stories, images, references, and metaphors that comment on that world in which it was created as well as an "outside world" of the imagination.

Mikhail Bakhtin: Novelists, like ventriloquists, speak indirectly through the mouths of others… Narrative, whether fiction, history, or political propaganda, is always a weaving together (*textura*) of words and intentions of others with the voice of the author. The word in language is always half someone else's.

Roland Barthes: "The Death of the Author." The "author-god" who in the past preceded the text and dictated a single message, has yielded to the modern writer who is born simultaneously with the text. **Barthes'** *écriture,* an introspective writing that examines its own creative process. Relationship between artistic creation and society, where the artists portray themselves as part of that society.

What is the **role of the author** in the creation of a literary work? Who is the author of the text? Is it the person who has created the story or the presence created in and through that story?

Luis Costa Lima: Fiction as a refraction of the "I" of the author. The reader as a poet in reverse, an analyst who can sense the author's self behind the writing.

How much can we know about the author of a text from his or her fingerprints left on the narrative?

* * *

"I dreamed about teaching last night, Stefan."

"Good dream or nightmare?"

"Sort of both. I was back at the university, but I felt lost. I knew I had to teach a class, but I didn't know what it was supposed to be. 'What am I doing here? Do I know how to teach?' I asked myself."

"Sounds like a nightmare to me. A classic one. The imposter syndrome."

"Yeah, well, so I went to the classroom early and sat down at the desk to try to think. I couldn't remember what I used to do, who I was as a professor. It was a mess in my mind, and I couldn't sort through it all. I just sat and waited."

"I feel like I've had that dream. Or maybe it was real life."

"The students arrived one at a time. Each one came up to me, told me their story and then went and sat down. After I had met all of them, I stood up and said, 'Okay, let's make a class.'"

August 1981

School started again, and even though they were going to leave soon, Willy wanted to go.

"*Ich will meine Freunde wiedersehen.*" He wanted to see his friends again. Willy loved the fact that expressing his desires started with something that sounded like his name. "*Ich will...weil ich Willy bin,*" he would say and laugh. "I want...because I am Willy." Clare had to laugh as well. There was some truth in it. He was a kid who went after life with his arms wide open, ready to embrace adventure and all its rich possibilities. But he was also seven years old, which explained most of it.

Clare asked if he wanted someone to go with him the first day.

"*Mom,* I'm a big kid now. I can go by myself."

"Okay, but remember—"

"To come straight home. I know, I know."

That afternoon he came striding up the hill right on time. Clare had planned to be hanging out some laundry at just that moment, so she could greet him.

"How was school?"

"Fine. I'm a second grader now."

"Wow!" Clare exclaimed as though it was news.

"We have to write in small script, and you need to buy me a *Füller.*"

"A *Füller.* A fountain pen? Really? That seems..."

"My teacher said. *Damit wir elefant schreiben können.* She said so we can write elephant, I mean elegant."

"...ly. Elegantly. That's impressive!"

"Mom, I saw an elephant today on the bus."

"An elephant on the bus?"

"No, I mean I was on the bus, and I saw an elephant in the street."

"An elephant in the street? That sounds crazy."

"I just saw it riding by, and a giraffe and a zebra and—"

"Wait a minute. You saw them riding by? On bicycles or what?" Clare had been used to Willy's wild fantasies a few years ago, but not at age seven. "Are you teasing me?" she asked, with hands on hips.

"No, honest, I saw them going by my bus, but I couldn't see what they were on."

"Okay, let's go upstairs and get a snack and then maybe we can run to town to find a fountain pen."

Clare got Anja ready and loaded her in the front pack, while Willy ate his snack. As they were leaving, they met Stefan coming up the stairs.

"You'll never guess what I just saw."

"An elephant? A giraffe?" Willy guessed.

"Well, yes! How did you know?"

"I saw them, too, didn't I Mom?"

"I guess so," she answered, perplexed.

"There's a traveling circus in town. Apparently, they parade the animals through the streets first, with them riding on open platforms to attract attention. We should find out where they will camp so we can go see them."

"It seems a bit cruel to me. But sure, let's go," she conceded, seeing the excitement in Willy's face.

"And don't forget my fountain pen. I hafta write something for tomorrow."

June 2001

June 22

I had a terrifying nightmare—that the Nazis had come back. There was propaganda everywhere about gypsies, Jews, and communists and how they were destroying German culture and its fine traditions. Words like "freedom," "morality," "purity," were thrown around. Innocent words used with a violent purpose. It reminded me of Orwell's "1984." Like "Goodspeak," the language of political tyranny. It was confusing and chaotic, and people were afraid. Everyone just wanted to be left alone. Anyone who challenged the Nazis was called anti-German. Foreigners were not welcome. "But I love this country!" I shouted. "I don't want to leave!"

* * *

Notes for Book

Chapter 11   The Reader in the Mirror: a creative partner.

Roland Barthes: A new **partnership between writer and reader.** "Writerly" texts that require the participation of the reader to complete them. A kind of 'pre-text' that forces us to notice, pay attention, find connections, and fill in the holes. In a sense fiction has always required that. The reader unconsciously accepts leaps in time, lack of description in some areas and deep detail in others. Much of the story is merely suggested or implied.

The reading of a text can never duplicate the writing of it—i.e. the author's intentions or unconscious associations and experiences. But writing does depend on a reader and the work can only be completed by the reading of it. Otherwise, it is just marks on a page sleeping between the book covers. In a sense, the work is rewritten with every reading.

Wolfgang Iser: We cannot identify the literary work with either the text or the realization of the text; it must lie half-way between the two. Reading is an active and creative process. It is reading which brings the text to life, which unfolds its inherently dynamic character.

Jacques Derrida: **The problem of language.** There is a complex relationship between the text and the reading, a word and its meaning.

The **historical context** of a text's creation also weighs in: the construction process, the readers of its time, the ancient foundations, cultural references, myths, values, language, literary heritage, personal history and psychology of the author and of the current reader.

And the **future history of the work** - the stories that saturate the walls of the house over time. The many readings, each in its own time and social-historical context, the infinite possible receptions (inhabitants?) of the work as it interacts with other times and places.

* * *

"I've been thinking a lot about language recently." Clare set her coffee cup down. "Remember how in graduate school I used to complain about all the literary theory we had to study? It was a love-hate relationship that shifted according to my own state of mind."

"Like whether you'd had your coffee yet or not?" There was that dimple again.

"Something like that," she smiled. "I was often intrigued, but it was just so darn hard to grasp. Sometimes I felt like those writers were trying to screw with your mind, just for fun. Every time we managed to get some handle on a philosophical or psychoanalytical perspective, they would throw another one at us. We used to joke about 'Derridiacy' and 'semi-idiotics.'"

"As in Derrida and semiotics, I presume."

"Exactly. But I must admit that each one does add something to the soup. The theories are too rigid and totalizing to accept as truths, but somehow the whole kaleidoscopic picture of them seems to give us something."

"Even Derrida?"

"Well, he makes me dizzy if I dive in too deeply, but there is something there. I understand the instability of language. I mean, even you and I, married for…for—"

"Thirty years?"

"Well, maybe twenty-eight. But yes, even after twenty-eight years of marriage and theoretically speaking the same language, we often don't understand each other. I mean, we have individual experiences, perspectives, and connections for every word we speak. Communication is always an approximation."

"Really? You mean to say that you don't understand every word I say perfectly? I am disillusioned. Well, one thing I know, though, is that I love you. Approximately, that is." Stefan grinned. Clare made a face at him for a moment and went on.

"Anyway, back to Derrida. What I like about him is how he questioned what he called the 'violent hierarchies' of oppositional differences contained in words. You know how we say that things are as different as day and night, or night and day. The problem is these things are comparisons that only work in their extremes and they are defined by each other."

"Like man/woman?"

"Yes. Does being female mean just not male? And vice-versa? Does true mean not false? Or maybe also real, complete, perfect, God-given, or just accepted. Did you know that Turkish is a gender-neutral language? It doesn't reflect gender in pronouns, for example. Isra told me that. She thought it was ironic that such a language would accompany a culture that adheres to rigid social norms of gender.

"Then there is the whole mind/body thing, but that is a complex story."

"More coffee? I mean, speaking of mind/body…"

"Thanks. One more cup and then I'm going for a walk."

"To meet Johann, I assume."

"No, he's not feeling well. I saw Erika and the dog in the park yesterday and she told me. I called today and he's doing better now, but not up for walking yet. I'm meeting Christina and Samira."

September 1981

Ever since Anja was born, Stefan often came home for lunch. They enjoyed eating out on the little balcony to savor the pleasant days of late summer. A few trees had turned colors and mottled the hillside view in front of them. Anja lay in the middle of the big bed, where they could watch her through the window. Walks to the Marktplatz had become a Saturday custom for them and the day before Willy had come home with a sparkly helium balloon in the shape of a heart.

"It's for Anja," he announced, and he tied it to her wrist so she could watch it bounce when she moved her arm. "Look, she loves it!" Willy exclaimed as the balloon caught her attention. They decided to try it on her again. It looked like pure joy, the balloon bouncing in the air as she moved.

"I don't know if she realizes that she can affect its motion, but the more it bounces, the more excited she gets and then the more it bounces," Clare observed as they went inside to check on her.

"Look how bright her eyes are and how her whole body wiggles."

"But listen to how she's breathing harder now. I think it may be too much stimulation, an endless feedback loop." Clare went to untie the balloon. She decided they would limit it to small doses, wondering at what point that joyful experience for a tiny baby could turn into a runaway train.

"You know, we only have a few more weeks here together." Stefan took Clare's hand. "We should think about what we want to do with the time left before you leave. I wish I didn't have to stay longer, but I still have a lot of things to wrap up before I go."

"There are things we haven't seen and some places I'd like to go again. But we're finally getting a good schedule with Anja, so I don't want to mess that up too much. Let's see what's on Willy's list."

July 2001

Notes for Book

Conclusion??? Something to wrap up all of this? Does the house need a roof or a back door?

* * *

Clare walked into the kitchen and kissed Stefan on the back of the neck. "Hannah called this morning to say that she'd like to come next week, if it's okay with us."

"It's her house. How could we say no? Besides, I look forward to meeting her."

"That's what I said. It will be fascinating and strange to meet someone that I feel I already know. And yet, I don't know her at all. I'm a bit nervous about it, to be honest."

"Don't overthink it. Just be yourself."

* * *

Clare had finished rough drafts for each of the chapters of her book. But she had no idea about the conclusion yet. Usually when she was writing, she knew where she was going and then worked on how to get there. This time had been way more open ended.

"Maybe you really can't write a conclusion until the very end," Stefan suggested. "You could wait until you get home; get some distance and a new perspective on the whole thing."

"I'll keep at it as long I can. I'd like to have an ending of some kind, even a rough one, before I leave Germany."

Clare had been thinking about Stefan's writing as she worked on her last chapter. In some ways, as a social historian he was a postmodern reader of past texts. He had Busch's accounts and notes: a combination of data, pieces of sermons, biblical passages, and his changing commentary on death. It was a collection of fragments, identified in time and place. All that suggested a lot, but there was no master narrative.

"You, as the reader, create that narrative," she told him, "trying to be faithful to the author (Busch) while also having a broader perspective than he did on the co-texts and contexts of his time. In some ways, you are reading him back to life."

"Interesting. That's part of the field of historiography, the writing of history. It is about how we see the past, understand it, and construct our narratives about it. None of that will change the past, but it changes our conception of it and our resulting identities. Not only are original sources part of history, but they also become part of the later texts written about them, which in turn become historical documents themselves."

"Fictional texts are part of history, too. They are original sources, in a sense, artifacts of their time. No wonder it's so hard to figure out who we are."

* * *

"*Hallo, Johann.* How are you today? Are you feeling better? Did you have a nice visit with your family? Nephew's family, wasn't it?"

"I'm fine and *ja,* the visit was very nice."

"I've missed you, just these few days. What will I do when I go back to America?"

"I will surely miss you as well. We'll just have to keep in touch. Who knows, maybe I'll find the courage to travel again and visit my family, which includes you now, you know." Clare smiled and patted his hand.

"I heard from Hannah today, the owner of the house. She'll be coming back soon. I have so many questions for her."

"I believe I have met her before, but it was some time ago. What kind of questions do you have?"

"I want to know more about the midwife, like how long she worked, stories about her practice and the house."

"It's my impression that by the late 1920s many women had stopped using midwives, especially in the cities," Johann explained. They believed that hospitals were safer. I think this midwife kept working privately the whole time. In the 1930s, midwifery was encouraged again and openly supported by the Nazis. It was part of a campaign to promote good health and more births, 'to improve the German race.' It was a horrific time for

295

medicine. Midwives and nurses were forced to take part in the eugenics campaign, indirectly at least."

"I'm afraid to ask."

"It was a program of selective breeding. Nurses and midwives were to identify mothers who were disabled or mentally incapacitated, or with any kind of inheritable condition, to weed them out. Midwives had to keep careful records of every birth and report all babies born with any kind of disability or disfigurement. They were rewarded if they did and punished if they didn't. The unsuitable babies were later eliminated as 'lives not worthy of life.'"

"Oh God. Couldn't people just refuse? Or quit? Or..or…I don't know."

"Well, there was *Die Weiße Rose.*"

"The White Rose?"

"*Ja.* That was a small group of medical students and a couple professors at the university of Mainz. They resisted and began to spread pamphlets and graffiti against the Nazi regime. They stood up and spoke out. A friend of mine from school was a student there and he told me about it. I think he was ready to join them."

"What happened? Did it make a difference?"

"I would say it was an important voice of morality and reason in a time of insanity. But it didn't last long. They were all arrested, and most were eventually killed."

Clare thought about her college years when there was a lot of resistance to the war in Vietnam. Some had been arrested or left the country. Most people she knew thought it was an unjust war. Stefan had been a conscientious objector. But it had never gone as far as what Germany had faced. She had heard and read about the Holocaust and the war years. It was nothing new to her, but somehow being in Germany and meeting people who had seen it, made it more real. And yet, it was still unimaginable.

"How can a country and its people ever recover from something like that?" she asked in despair.

Johann nodded and they sat in silence.

September 1981

"Willy, you know we are leaving in a couple weeks. We should start thinking about what we want to do before we leave."

"Let's go feed Die Enten. We haven't done that for a long time. Do you think they will remember us?"

"We'll be sure to take some breadcrumbs and it won't matter. They'll be glad to see us. I was thinking it might be fun to go out in the pedal boats. What do you think?"

"*Ja!!!* That would be *toll!!* Can we do that Mom? Maybe we could invite Zosia."

As they counted down the days, Clare filled the calendar, feeling suddenly like the time was too short for all the things left to do. She wanted to do something special with their downstairs family. She would really miss them.

"Mom, what will happen to German?"

"What do you mean?"

"When we go home. We won't speak it anymore. What will happen to it?"

"Well, we'll forget some of the words, but we won't forget what it feels like to speak them. You'll have lots of memories with words attached to them, so you won't ever forget—"

"Die Enten or Schokoladenkremegebäck! And I could come back, and the kids would teach me the other words again."

"Yes, I hope we can come back. And don't worry, you would learn everything again quickly. Probably faster than I would."

* * *

Nick and Sharon had already left. That was the first goodbye. Clare had a baby stroll date with Carmen and Samira that week and the next weekend was pedal boats on the river.

They went to feed the ducks. It was still peaceful to see them gliding towards shore, pulling gentle V-shaped ripples on the water behind them. They were old friends, among Willy's first words in German.

"How did this year go by so fast?" Clare wondered.

"It just kept going like the river." Willy put his hand in hers and they stood watching the minutes flow gently by.

15
Writing Back

July 2001

July 9

Another nightmare. I seem to have lots of them these days. I was Elizabetha again. My alter-ego from the past. A woman from the neighborhood had just given birth and she and the baby were resting upstairs. I poured myself some tea and began to record the details in my book. Her baby had a twisted foot. I thought it was something that could be corrected in time, but I had to record everything officially. The authorities would come by periodically to check. I couldn't bear the thought of condemning this poor baby to death, but what could I do? The punishment for resisting was severe. I pounded my fist on the table, crying "No, no, no..." but I knew I would do it.

I woke up in the night, still saying "No, no..." Stefan put his arm around my shoulder to calm my breathing. Oh Hannah, how could people survive such cruelty?

* * *

"Stefan, have you heard about *Die Weiße Rose?* It's something Johann told me about."

"Yes, of course. The White Rose. It was a resistance movement that started among medical students, I think."

"It seems like it's so often up to the young to protest and remind us of the values we say we have. What a burden for them to bear."

Clare had to know more. She was intrigued by the bravery of a few, especially the young ones. The next day she went to the library and found a biography of Sophie Scholl, one of the university students in the White Rose movement. She immediately became engrossed in the story, moved by the young woman's courage and commitment against the seemingly unstoppable momentum of the Nazi movement. Sophie was twenty-one.

In 1942, Sophie, along with her brother, Hans, three other students and a professor named Kurt Huber, began producing pamphlets of resistance to The Third Reich, naming their movement *Die Weiße Rose*.

> Our current 'state' is the dictatorship of evil...gradually
> robbing you of one right after another—they wrote.

They were a small group, but they created a wide network of supporters and eventually distributed thousands of pamphlets all over Germany.

"Stand up for what you believe in, even if you are standing alone," Sophie was quoted as saying.

Clare felt admiration and compassion for this young woman, barely older than Anja. Where did she find such courage and wisdom?

In 1943, Sophie and Hans were arrested by the Gestapo. At first, Sophie was believed to be innocent, but she took full responsibility in order to protect others in the movement. Sophie and Hans were both executed, along with another student, by guillotine. Shortly before the execution, she was reported to have said,

> "It is such a splendid sunny day and I have to go. But how
> many have to die on the battlefield in these days, how many
> young, promising lives? What does my death matter, if by
> our acts thousands are warned and alerted?"

Clare stopped reading and took a deep breath as she wiped a tear from her cheek. How could people throw away such precious young lives? "Why can't we all stand up sooner?" People near her in the library looked up and she realized she had said it aloud.

September 1981

Clare put Anja in the front pack and started towards the university. It was a beautiful day to walk by the river and she wanted to say good-bye to the professors she had gotten to know. They had been welcoming to her as a visitor, letting her participate in their classes without being officially registered. She wanted to introduce them to Anja, who was no longer the mysterious and sometimes athletic Gertrude they had known.

When she arrived on the university campus, Clare noticed some hand painted banners on the walls inside and outside the buildings.

NO MORE SILENCE!
WE NEED TO KNOW!

WE CAN'T BUILD A FUTURE IF WE PRETEND
THE PAST DIDN'T HAPPEN!

WHY DIDN'T YOU TALK TO US?

Clare assumed this was about Hitler, the Holocaust, the war, though none of that was mentioned specifically. As Germany began to recover from the trauma and devastation of the Nazi era and the war, people wanted to forget. Reconstruction took years. The chaos and confusion, poverty, destruction of homes and infrastructure were the visible scars of the war. But the moral wounds were hidden and deep. Clare sensed them whenever "The War" was mentioned.

The loss of lives and identity was unfathomable. Six million Jews, two thirds of the pre-war Jewish population in Europe, had been killed, along with Roma and Sinti—often known as gypsies—homosexuals, communists, resisters, and any others considered undesirable by the Nazi regime. Many others had died as soldiers or victims of bombings in the war.

After the war, German Jewish survivors returned to their homeland and lived together with other Germans in camps for displaced persons, forming improbable communities of victims. Some had barely survived starvation and the erasure of their humanity. Others lived on with shame for having surrendered their own humanity through collaboration or non-resistance to the horrors of Hitler's Third Reich. All had suffered a daily diet of brutality and fear and lived to try to imagine a future.

Clare's father had shared stories of working with Quaker humanitarian efforts after the war. He was part of a food distribution effort in Germany. Although he had known poverty himself as the son of a tenant farmer in Kansas, he was overwhelmed by the misery and rubble, the hunger and desperation that he saw. Children, dazed and starving, wandered in the streets. It was truly a nightmare. Parents didn't want to relive that past or burden their children and grandchildren with it. But the generations that followed wanted and demanded to know. Students had started pressuring for that in the 1960s, but the society then was still reluctant to look back.

All this Clare had known already. She had heard about it here and there during her lifetime and had been haunted by a couple books she had read. The banners brought it all together in a present-day Germany that was still waking up from the nightmare. Clare shook her head, trying to erase from her mind the images she had seen in her father's pictures and the books about the concentration camps. She hugged her little baby to her chest and walked into the university building, still burdened by the pain that so many had suffered in this country she had come to love.

July 2001

"It's funny how once you become aware of something, you notice connections to it everywhere," Clare commented over breakfast one morning. "It's as though each topic, each theme of our lives, is connected by an underground root system that we never notice."

Stefan looked up with an amused expression on his still sleepy face. "That's an interesting statement. Are you saying that you just noticed how wonderful I am in so many ways?"

"Really? No, I hadn't noticed that yet," she said, fielding his teasing with a quick return. "But seriously, ever since I found out about Elizabetha, I've been dreaming about her, hearing about midwifery, meeting people who were born in this house. Recently I read about the first birthing house in Marburg. It was a ghastly place in the late 18th and early 19th century; unsanitary, with miserable conditions and high mortality rates for both mothers and babies. Thousands of women died. Only unmarried mothers or the very poor went to these birthing houses, having been rejected by their families or kicked out by employers. These houses were the only option for such women to avoid heavy fines or imprisonment for their 'crime.'"

"Yes, those were not the best of times for women," Stefan interjected.

"I'm learning more than I ever wanted to know about that those days. The Marburg birthing house had been one of the first in Germany and part of a movement towards the medicalization of the long tradition of

302

midwifery. A profession that had been in the hands of highly trained and skilled women for centuries, even millennia, was taken over by men who claimed that their "lying in" hospitals and advances of science would save women's lives.

"The ancient practice of *Geburtshilfe* was turned into the field of *Geburtsmedizin*. Young male doctors needed hands-on training as part of their education. The women desperate enough to go to these birthing houses were used as objects of observation and practice. A large audience of young male students would watch and participate in the event, handling the body of the mother, alive or dead, one after the other, while the midwives stood by as helpless handmaidens. The original Marburg Geburtshaus building is still standing, though long since used for something else."

"Wow, you *have* been reading."

Clare nodded and sighed. It was such a stark contrast to the wonderful experience she and Stefan had in 1981.

"I wonder what it's like for midwives today?" Clare was surprised that with all the past stories of midwives she had heard, even about the very house in which they were living, it had not occurred to her before to ask that question.

The next day she went to the Internet Café and did some research. She found stories of famous midwives of the past since the 1600s. Marie Boivin's story was the most spectacular one. A renowned French midwife of the early nineteenth century, she had helped to establish a school of obstetrics in Versailles, discovered cures for several gynecological diseases and conditions that could cause miscarriages. She invented new medical tools for obstetrical practice, performed surgeries and published articles and a gynecological textbook. In 1827 Madam Boivin was awarded a Doctor of Medicine degree from the University in Marburg.

Another story that caught Clare's attention was a more recent one. Berta Hamel began her career as a midwife in 1940 in Romrod, a small town in central Hesse, and its surrounding communities. Midwives who served rural areas and small towns often had to travel significant distances to the homes of their clients. When Berta's husband died during the war and left her with three children to support, her sister stepped in to care for the children while Berta expanded her practice. By 1949 she was able to obtain a motorbike, and she was known to arrive through *"Wind und Wetter"* to her clients ever farther afield. A motorcycle midwife. Clare loved the image.

Although the use of midwives declined gradually from the 1950s, Berta attended a total of 1188 births during her thirty-eight years of practice. Clare admired the fortitude of the famous motorcycle woman who managed to raise three children while traveling far and wide to help other mothers give birth at home.

There was one other story of a famous midwife that stood out for Clare. She wished she hadn't read it. Nanna Conti was named the Nazi director of midwifery during the Third Reich. The profession was raised to a position of high regard and German women who met all the requirements of the eugenics program of the Reich were encouraged to have as many babies as possible. If the parents were of German blood, "hereditarily healthy, decent and morally impeccable," a mother could receive a badge of honor called the *Mutterkreuz*, the "mother cross," for her contribution to The Reich. If she had four or five children, she received a bronze cross, six or seven warranted a silver cross, and eight or more a gold one. Hitler compared the birthing bed to a battlefield and the mothers were heroic soldiers. The midwives had the status of officers directing a battle. They were sometimes called "the mother of mothers," or "officers in the birthing war." This web of propaganda accompanied the increasing marginalization of women in the public sector of German society, while "purifying the race."

* * *

"Did you know that midwives were entangled at the center of the Nazi ideology and propaganda?" Clare asked Stefan at breakfast the next morning. "It was all part of an Aryan cult of motherhood."

"Yes, I am aware of that. It was a very dark time."

"It seems that it was also a way to control women, to brainwash them and keep them out of the way by making them feel patriotic."

"Yup, pretty much."

"I wonder how many midwives resisted."

"I think in rural areas they could get away with it more easily. But it was still very risky."

"I know this isn't news, but I've never seen it so clearly before. Fascist societies need to control their women, for they are the most dangerous revolutionaries. Women are the ones who incubate the future and the ongoing story."

"Yeah. Fascism seeks the end of history."

* * *

Clare had also found out about a modern birthing house in Marburg, and she decided to visit it. The Marburger Geburtshaus was founded in 1985, and it was the opposite of the first one from the 18th century. When she walked into the place, it felt like a dream. The atmosphere was warm and welcoming, family centered and educational. The furnishings and the friendly staff inspired calm and trust. It wasn't just a birthing house, it also included guidance throughout the pregnancy and well beyond the birth. The midwives offered a variety of classes from prenatal yoga to postnatal baby massage. It was a modern adaptation of an ancient tradition that seemed to honor the best of both worlds. Far from being passive bodies or patients, the mothers (and often the fathers) were active, educated participants in a collaborative process.

The emphasis was on a natural process of giving birth, rather than a medical procedure to relieve a condition: *die Entbindung,* it had come to be called—the "unbinding." In the new Geburtshaus, they made it clear that there were times when medical intervention was necessary, but that didn't erase the many benefits and opportunities of midwifery. There was a sign on the wall near the entrance that read "Midwives see with their fingers and hear with their hearts."

In the past, Clare read, midwives had an ongoing relationship to the families, often delivering all their babies. The family midwife would be consulted early in a pregnancy, and she would visit the mother and baby often after the birth. It was common for her to become the godmother who played a key role in baptisms and other important family rituals for children. She was respected for her knowledge and experience as a professional and loved for her compassion and commitment to the community.

On the way home Clare decided to visit the building where the first birthing house had been from 1823-1866, though it was founded in 1792.

"You know, that old birthing house is now the Department of Geography of the university," Stefan had said casually one day. "It's right behind the Elizabethkirche."

"How do you know that? Why didn't you tell me before?"

305

"Anja and I saw it in January. I didn't think to mention it then. It didn't seem that important."

Clare expected to feel a residue of the horror she had read about as she entered the beautiful Fachwerk building. It was startling how normal it felt—just a dignified old university building. No ghosts in the walls or distant screams of pain. No plaques to remember all the women who had died in the name of science. Maybe conditions had improved by the time it moved to that building.

"When you think about it, so much of the normalcy of our lives is built on such stories; buried, forgotten, and painted over by years of respectability. It's tragic."

Stefan nodded. "Forgetting seems to be a well-used strategy to cope with a shameful past. People just want to move on with their lives and leave that past behind. It's dangerous, but very human."

September 1981

"Schwester Monika!" Clare recognized the midwife's bright and cheerful face amid other shoppers in the grocery store. It seemed incongruous to run into her in the everyday world, as though health professionals only lived in their place of work.

"Hallo, Frau..."

"Muller, Clare Muller," Clare jumped in to help her out, realizing suddenly that despite the closeness she had felt to the midwife, the relationship was probably not mutual. She had been just one of so many cases.

"Yes, of course. A daughter. Anja? Was that her name?"

Clare grinned and pulled aside the cloth of the front pack to reveal her baby's sleeping face. "I'm impressed that you remember."

"Well, I did see her before you did, you know. I never forget that first glimpse, when a baby opens its eyes to a new world. It's a magical moment. Every time."

"Are you in a hurry? Could I invite you to *Kaffee und Kuchen* in the café?" Clare asked, wondering if it would seem awkward to Schwester Monika. Was there some taboo about socializing with your medical professional?

"Sure, that would be lovely." Schwester Monika responded with the same reassuring smile that had cheered Clare on during her experience in the hospital.

They fell into an easy conversation, two women chatting over coffee and cake. Clare asked Schwester Monika how she had become a midwife and the story unfolded, beginning with her childhood in a nearby small town. Her mother had been a midwife, attending home births for women in neighboring towns as well. Monika had grown up in the background of that profession, sometimes accompanying her mother to the births. As a teenager, she began to assist her mother with easy support tasks, occasionally stepping in to do more if there was no one else to help.

"I liked being included in the adult world of women," Schwester Monika shared. "It made me feel important to be able to help. My favorite part was getting to clean up the newborn baby and wrap it in a warm blanket, while my mother attended to the rest of the birthing process. I was moved by being able to hold the tiny person in the first moments of new life and then hand it, safe and snug, to its mother.

"I don't remember when I formally decided to become a midwife," Monika continued, resting her chin thoughtfully on her hand. "It was such a part of my life, that I think I always knew. But I realized that I needed to choose a different path than my mother did. Although home births continued some in rural areas, by the time I was an adult, most births were in hospitals. I trained as a nurse-midwife and dedicated my service to the Diakonie."

"And we're so glad you did. Could I ask one more question?"

"Of course."

"Why are you called "Sister? The Diakonie organization is Protestant, isn't it?"

"Yes, we are not really nuns, but we do dedicate our lives to Christian service. We are allowed to marry and live on our own if we want to, but we are always connected to the Diakonie community. Also, all nurses are referred to as Schwester. It's just part of our professional title."

Ah, yes, Clare remembered. The word for "nurse" in German was *Krankenschwester*. Sister to the sick.

"I'm so glad we could have this conversation today," Clare said as they parted with a hug. "I have been wanting to thank you again for your guidance during our birthing experience. I will never forget it."

"I was honored to be there. I mean that."

Clare waited at the bus stop, her bags of groceries at her feet.

"*Die Welt ist verrückt, es dreht sich nur,*" Clare heard a woman's voice behind her. "The world is crazy; it just goes around and around."

Clare waited to hear a response, not wanting to intrude on someone else's conversation. There was no reply, so she turned to see if the person was addressing her. She recognized Die Nachtigall in her usual black suit and derby hat.

"No one knows how," the woman said. Clare could hear despair in her voice.

She smiled and Die Nachtigall looked at her, encouraged by having a listener.

"They just keep going and going and nobody stops them." Clare nodded as the woman pointed at the cars in the street.

"It's nice to see you again." Clare reached out to touch the woman's arm. "How *are* you?"

"It's dark, too dark. No one listens. They don't remember. We need to tell stories, lots of stories and sing songs. Sing to everything to stop the spinning."

"Yes," Clare said softly. "Yes, we do."

The nightingale-woman moved closer and patted the bundle strapped to Clare's front. "You sing to her, don't you," she said in a declarative tone.

"Yes, every day."

"Good." The woman walked off, singing lightly as she went.

July 2001

Clare walked along, enjoying the summer morning that hadn't yet reached the full heat of July days. She was lost in thoughts of midwives and birthing houses and almost tripped over a woman kneeling on the sidewalk.

"Oh, *Entschuldigung,* I'm so sorry…" Clare stammered as she caught her balance. The woman was busy scrubbing something and looked up, surprised by Clare's presence.

"They were our neighbors," the woman said, as though the two of them had been in mid conversation. It still happened to Clare occasionally, that she found herself understanding the words but had somehow missed the context.

"I'm sorry, I don't understand," she confessed.

The woman sat back and pointed to a small cluster of square metal plates inlayed in the sidewalk. Some of them shone with the yellow-gold patina of brass and others were still dulled by the tarnish of time and elements. Clare kneeled next to the woman and saw that each small plaque had something written on it.

Here lived
ANITA WOLF
born De Jonge
year 1916.

Deported 1941
murdered in
Auschwitz.

"These are *Stolpersteine*, the woman explained. "They commemorate people who were taken away by the Nazis: Jews, mostly, but also gays, gypsies, communists, anti-Nazi resisters and others. They are installed in front of the residence of the victims, to remind us that they were individuals living their lives like the rest of us, not just faceless numbers. We must not forget that."

Anita was only twenty-five, Clare realized as she ran her fingers over the plaque. Next to it was another one to Hans Martin Wolf, born in 1914. He must have been her husband, she thought, seeing that Wolf was Anita's married name.

"Who made them?" Clare asked.

"A German artist started the program some years ago and there are now many thousands around the country. Each one is made individually. Churches, schools, and other community groups take on the project of doing the research and funding the making of new ones. These 'stumbling stones' are scattered about the city where our neighbors lived. We come across them as we go about our lives and 'stumble,' mentally at least, over them as reminders of that awful past that we all must bear. We clean them now and then, to keep their names alive. People are only forgotten when their names are forgotten."

Clare sat back on her heels and bowed her head for a moment, trying to picture those two young people and the rest of their family or neighbors who had disappeared with them. The shock and terror of the moment was so present for her, that her breath caught as her chest contracted in a spasm. She wondered if they'd had any idea of the greater horrors that awaited them. Clare looked at the woman kneeling next to her, whose expression was calm but focused. She had clearly faced this vision many times, perhaps daily, and she had turned her own shock and pain into determination. It was a small but powerful gesture, a kind of prayer.

"Thank you," was all that Clare could say, as they stood up. She hugged the woman in silence and then walked on, her eyes clouded with tears but her mind painfully clear. On the surface, it had been an inappropriate action to hug a stranger, but the moment and the past it had invoked had gone far beyond the rules of social etiquette.

September 1981

They were four women; mothers who had left their children and babies at home for a walk in the woods. Their husbands had arranged to give them a few hours together out of the flow of time and the traffic of family and work. It was a strange kind of freedom and they each felt naked, like a peeled away self, missing its outer layers. The space of motherhood was defined not only by the walls of the home, but by the radar of responsibility that extended as far as the children wandered. At least until they, the ones on duty, were relieved by a clear changing of the guard.

Clare sometimes found herself swaying gently back and forth when she stood alone waiting for a bus. The rocking motion to calm a baby had become ingrained in her own body and associated with any period of waiting. It was as though she had taken in permanently a baby that would always need soothing. She felt silly when she caught herself in the act, but the habit was stronger than her self-awareness.

The four friends followed the *"Trimm Dich Pfad*, the "Trim Yourself Path," a fitness network of clean, paved paths that cut through well-managed old forest and green undergrowth. Wooden structures for strengthening and cardio exercises were placed strategically along the way.

But the women were not on a fitness mission as much as a friendship one. They needed time and space to talk, reminisce, and begin their good-byes. Clare would be returning to the U.S. soon, and she was sad to think of leaving her friends behind. They walked in silence for a while and then Clare stopped suddenly and turned to face the other women. Julia, Christina, and Samira stopped as well, startled by her abruptness.

"Will we ever see each other again?" she asked, with a tremor in her voice. "I know that we say we will, that we'll keep in touch. But we will each follow our own paths and who knows where they will lead."

"I know we will meet again," Christina's voice was bright and confident. "I'm sure I will still be here, so you will just have to come back to Marburg. We could plan a reunion."

"I'm really not sure about the future," Samira sighed. "It's hard to tell where we will end up. We hope to go back to Somalia, but things are chaotic there right now."

Julia agreed, there was too much uncertainty. "We aren't sure we want to stay in Germany, though we won't be going back to Poland. Some days it really gets me down. "But we will stay here for a while, at least." She hesitated and then smiled as she patted her belly.

Clare opened her mouth in surprise and Julia nodded. "I'm pregnant," she said.

"That's a good thing, right?" Clare asked cautiously.

"Yes, it is. It was part of the plan."

They all moved in to hug and congratulate Julia.

"Oh, my dear friend, I will miss seeing your baby. I do hope I get to meet this new member of your family before he or she goes off to college!"

* * *

Clare knew that she would be jumping back into classes and teaching as soon as they got back home to Iowa, barely having time to settle in. She and the kids would stay with her parents until Stefan returned, and then they would also visit his parents along the way. They were excited to introduce the new baby to her grandparents and share the still fresh experiences of their year in Germany. But she knew that the photographs, memories, and the language that had taken center stage in her mind would soon be packed away in a dusty corner of the past, lost in the swirl of life that would sweep them towards an unknown future.

July 2001

Clare sat in front of her open laptop. She needed a conclusion for her book, and she was running out of time. She looked at some notes she had written the day before—scattered thoughts and a few good quotes.

Notes for Book

Chapter 12   End of the story?

Friedrich Nietzsche: Only through art can we transcend our existence to be able to see ourselves better.

Frank Kermode: Fictions are for finding things out, and they change as the needs of sense-making change. Myths are the agents of stability; fictions are the agents of change.

What responsibility do we bear for our myths and fictions, our collaborations—whether intentional or inadvertent? Are we unknowing midwives to evil?

The danger of myths that can drive a Holocaust. **The promise of fiction** that can shine a light on our tragedies and imagine a world where we overcome them. Words can destroy and words can rebuild. As writers, we put our words down on paper, open the door to our house and invite others in.

Mayan conceptions of time as a closed circle, a succession of cycles without beginning or end. Time was believed to be divine and would repeat infinitely. An event can be both a past and a future, depending on your viewpoint. How do we come to terms with our past so that it won't be our future the next time around? How do we structure our writing?

Aztec philosophy – emphasis on balance. How can humans maintain their balance upon the slippery earth? (I picture humans sliding off the smooth curve of a globe!) Humans must conduct every aspect of their lives wisely.

"The slippery earth" could be a metaphor for the complexity of ethical questions on which we try to build the foundations of our societies.

* * *

"Guten Tag, Muller."

"Hi Clare, it's Samira. *Setahay?* How are you?"

"Doing well, thanks. Hey, guess what? Hannah is coming home early, so we get to meet her. I think I'll have a party. I'd love for you and Omar to be there."

"Of course. I'll put it on my calendar. Are we still meeting tomorrow?"

"Yes, let's. The last lunch at Café Barfuß. See if Isra wants to come, too."

September 1981

Willy came walking up the hill slowly, stopping twice to look back. It had been his last bus ride after his last day of school. All the kids and the teacher had signed a card for him, and they had cupcakes at the end of the day.

"How was school?" Clare asked as she gave him a hug. Willy showed her the card.

"Wow, that was so sweet of them! You must be a very special person."

"I'm sad," he said. I'm going to miss the kids. And the teacher. She's cool."

"I know, Sweetie, it's hard to leave." She gave him another hug. They sat in the yard for a few minutes listening to the sounds of the afternoon.

"How about we go in and sort through your clothes and see if there is anything that is worn out or that you have grown out of? We need to fit everything into the suitcases that we brought, so we'll want to get rid of some things."

"I'm a lot bigger now," Willy said proudly, forgetting his sadness for a moment. They made a pile of clothes to discard.

"What about my Legos? They won't all fit in my bag. I can't throw any away."

"Hmmm. That's a good question. What do you think we should do?"

"Maybe I could give some to Zosia. She would take good care of them."

"That's a wonderful idea! How about we take a little trip tomorrow to visit her."

* * *

Clare let Willy lead the way to the bus stop.

"This is it. This is our bus," he said with authority. "You have to show them your ticket when we get on."

"Okay, *Herr Willy*, thanks for the reminder."

"It's not crowded today, so we can sit wherever we want. Let's sit right here in the front." Willy sat next to the window and narrated, pointing out familiar landmarks along the way.

"There's my school! Good-bye, school."

Clare showed an enthusiastic interest in Willy's tour, already missing the life they hadn't yet left behind. A premature nostalgia.

"Wir könnten die Bäckerei besuchen...," Willy said hopefully, just as Clare said the same thing in English. "We could visit the bakery..." They laughed.

"What would you like, Mom? I will treat you," Willy said, pulling out a handful of change from his pocket. She chose the same thing that she knew he would order.

"Ich hätte gerne zwei Stück Schokoladencremegebäck," he said with confidence in polite German. "I would like..." The woman behind the counter handed Willy the two chocolate cream pastries and then his change. He counted it carefully and then nodded. *"Danke schön."*

"You're welcome," the woman said, smiling at Clare as she turned to follow her son out the door.

"Mmmm, *lecker,"* Clare said as she bit into the pastry. "Thanks for the yummy treat, Willy. That was very generous of you."

His smile was ringed by a chocolate and cream smear of delight.

Julia answered the door and invited them in.

"Is Zosia here?" Willy asked with urgency.

"Zosia!" Julia called, and the girl came in from the balcony.

"Have you ever noticed how much they look alike?" Clare whispered to Julia as the two kids talked. "They could be siblings."

Julia nodded and smiled. "They do seem like brother and sister in many ways—their blond hair, blue eyes, and easy friendship in German."

"*Ich habe dir Legos mitgebracht.* I brought you Legos," Willy said, handing Zosia a box. German was still their only common language. "I thought you could keep these to play with since I have too many to take home. Do you still like to play with them?"

"Oh yes, I do! But we never bought any for me. I will take good care of them."

"Good. I'm gonna miss you, Zosia."

"Me too." They stood looking at each other in solemn silence. The Legos were serious business. The good-byes were too much for the moment.

Clare and Julia hugged for longer than usual. "I'll miss you, my dear friend. And you, too," she whispered looking at Julia's still flat abdomen.

"Yes, same here." Julia said. "I'm not ready to think about it. Let's not say good-bye yet. Hey, where is Gertr-, I mean Anja?"

"She's at home with her dad."

"I need to give her a good-bye kiss."

"Yes, we'll get together before we leave."

"*Auf Wiedersehen!* See you later," they all said as Willy and Clare headed back to the bus.

"And thanks for the Legos!" Zosia's voice followed them.

July 2001

The stories of midwives had become an obsession for Clare. She brought it up nearly every time she and Stefan were together in the kitchen.

"I read that the Jewish neighborhoods in the cities often had their own midwife who could perform the traditional rituals before and after the birth as well." Clare shared her latest discovery.

"Yes, that makes sense. In rural areas, they would have depended on the local midwife, who was likely Christian, but probably with another Jewish woman present to oversee the important rituals."

"And in the concentration camps, I can't even imagine."

"I think many women who were pregnant were killed directly, or they were worked to death. If they did manage to give birth, it was probably alone or with the help of another prisoner."

There was a knock on the door.

Clare went to see who it was. A woman stood with a suitcase in each hand. The face was familiar, but it took Clare a minute to react.

"Hannah!!" It was the face from the photograph. They looked at each other and then hugged like old friends. "Please come in. I mean, it's your house. Welcome home! We're so glad to see you and finally meet you." It was confusing.

"I'm sorry I'm a bit early, but I was excited to meet you, too. My daughter dropped me off and I didn't have a chance to call first."

"It's perfect timing, Hannah."

They sat down at the table while Stefan made fresh coffee. There was so much to talk about. First in bits and pieces, a chaotic collage of getting to know each other. Clare wanted to know everything about Hannah's life. Hannah told about her work as a schoolteacher, helping young kids with special needs, especially Roma, Sinti, and immigrant children.

"Those kids were eager to learn but they weren't ready to be in regular school yet. They were overwhelmed by so much at once," Hannah explained. "I tried to make the learning fun and help them gain confidence in themselves. More than anything they needed to be treated with patience and kindness. The rest would come in time. We sang and danced and learned about each other's lives. Soon they were talking and playing together. I loved my work and I loved them. I just retired last year before I left for Bali."

Clare talked about teaching college students, some of whom still needed extra patience and kindness as they were leaving home for the first time. There were others, even students who had come from afar across national and language boundaries, who were already well prepared for the challenge. She tried to meet them all where they were and help them learn together and from each other.

"We often sing and dance as well, especially in beginning language classes. I need to make it fun and lively to get the students to relax and interact in different ways. Sometimes it feels like kindergarten."

The two women walked around the yard and through the house.

"You certainly took good care of the garden and the house feels happy and lived in."

"It's been good to us, Hannah. Tending the flowers and house plants helped me settle in. I can't begin to express how much living here has meant to me. By the way, we're planning a party in a couple days. You will be the guest of honor. Well, not really a guest...I hope you don't mind. Just a few good friends, including Christina and Jürgen, whom you already know."

"I look forward to it," Hannah said giving Clare's hand a squeeze.

Clare felt the cat rub against her legs and she leaned down to pick her up. "Oh and Hannah...I have a present for you."

* * *

"I have so many questions," Clare said the next morning after breakfast. "Like anything you could tell me about Elizabetha and midwives in general. The more I learn about their stories, the more curious I get."

"Well, I didn't know Elizabetha personally, but I can tell you what I heard through the years. I had often wondered how long she had worked in this house, since I didn't live in Ockershausen during that time. When older people told me they had been born here in this house, I figured she must have started in the early 1900s. But then I heard people talk about a midwife many years later and it didn't seem possible that it could be the same one.

"One day I met someone who had given birth in the house in the 1970s and she explained that her midwife was the daughter. Elizabetha Emilia was born maybe around 1880, and her daughter, Elizabetha Angelina worked with her for a while in the later years and then took over the practice. The daughter was called Lina by people close to her. I think she worked until around 1980, still going out occasionally for home births. By then it was getting harder to be an independent midwife. Insurance premiums were high and malpractice suits were scaring women away from the profession."

"What do you know about the Nazi era?"

"Well, it was a strange paradox. In 1939, Hitler declared a *Hebammengesetz*, a 'midwife law' that required that all German births be

317

attended by a German midwife. He wanted to create the image of a healthy folk culture and women happily having many babies naturally. It gave a boost to the profession, which was greatly diminished by that time. They say that the Nazis were notorious penny pinchers, so it was also a way to reduce costs for the Nazi run hospitals."

"Oh my God, that must have put midwives in terrible ethical binds."

"Certainly. They were already inadvertently cooperating with the Nazi agenda, just by doing their jobs. But either way, babies were being born and midwives were needed. A few willingly participated in the ideology but most just did their best to help people, one birth at a time. Some resisted reporting the babies, but I don't know how many. It must have been very dangerous. People watched each other and some people turned in their neighbors and even their own family members. It was a culture of fear in those days. You know, after finding out about the history of this house, I became curious about midwives myself, and learned more than I ever wanted to know."

"What happened to the babies that were turned in?" Clare asked, remembering her dream.

"The ones that were declared 'unfit' or 'undesirable' were either done away with by doctors or they were sent to a 'hospital,' a house where they were allowed to waste away. It would then be declared a 'natural death.'"

"That is unimaginable," Clare said as the image invaded her imagination anyway.

"There was a Polish midwife who had worked in the resistance and ended up a prisoner at Auschwitz. Her name was Stanislawa Leszczyńska, and she became famous for her work at the camp. Though also a prisoner herself, she delivered over three thousand babies during the years she was there, refusing the orders she was given to murder them. Most of them would be snatched away and drowned in a barrel in the next room. Some were kidnapped, if they looked Aryan enough, and given to Nazi families. But Stanislawa's personal mission was to try to save the mothers and give the babies at least a dignified birth."

Clare took a deep breath and slumped back in her chair. The story was beyond the horror she had imagined. "What happened to Stanislawa?" she asked in a whisper.

"It was kind of a miracle. She survived and continued with her work as a midwife after the war. Her children did, too, and they grew up to be physicians."

They sat in silence. Clare wondered how that woman could get up each day to face such a job and then see other people destroy the lives she had saved. At least she could go to bed at night with her hands clean, in the moral sense. Clare shuddered as she felt a cold wind rage inside her.

"We don't any of us know how we would respond to such a nightmare," Hannah said softly. "I would like to think I could be as strong as Stanislawa was. She honored the Hippocratic oath to do no harm, even in impossible circumstances. She did what she could, knowing it could never be enough."

September 1981

Willy stood on the balcony, leaning on the rails as he looked out over the town. Clare walked out to join him.

"What are you thinking about?"

"I was just wondering what it will be like to go home."

"Yeah, me too."

"Mom?"

"Yes Willy?"

"Will I get a little brother sometime?"

"Well, uh, I don't know. We aren't planning on it right now."

"I think you should. I'm getting used to being a big brother."

July 2001

Notes for Book

Chapter 13 In Conclusion or Inconclusive?

Our stories have no ending. When we set them free, we don't know what they will become, how they will be read or rewritten. We write as midwives and entrust our fictions to an uncertain world. Once they are out there, they no longer belong to us.

319

Philosophers try to reduce complex reality to simple structures and language. Their theories are great for exploring big questions, but they don't seem to fit the messy contours of the real world. How could some of those great explorers of meaning end up as Nazi supporters? Or let their words become appropriated as prisons for humanity?

Language in its essence is like a newborn baby. It can be loved and nurtured, or it can be abused and abandoned. Innocent words can be transformed into instruments of horror.

The word "philosophy" comes from Greek *philo* (loving) plus *sophia* (knowledge or wisdom.) Philosophers are lovers of wisdom. The word *wisdom* in English comes from Old English *wis* (certain) and *dom* (judgement.) So, philosophers are also lovers of certain judgement. But those judgements, like the theological and political ones through the ages, all seem so limited by myopic self-interest.

Iris Murdoch was an Irish-British writer and philosopher. Her philosophy centered around the notion of goodness as a process of seeking the truth and paying "just and loving attention" to the world and to others. Such a simple idea, yet so radical in these times. She wrote about the importance of the inner life to moral action and a process of "un-selfing," a way of seeing others as equally real as oneself. I like that. Is it possible?

So how to conclude this book?

Maybe the "roof" is the back cover of the book, a door that is always ajar. And like the Oberstadt of Marburg; the site of its beginnings, the Upper Story of Hannah's house is where my writing begins and ends—in the birthing room. The story of the writing is difficult to separate from the rest of the house and all the history it contains. When we contemplate our lives, we can only do it from within those very lives. We try to understand ourselves with a part of our own body, yet at the same time step out of ourselves to see more clearly. The act of writing helps us to see, but it doesn't liberate us from ourselves. On the contrary, it weaves us inextricably into the texts and grounds us in time, at least for a moment.

A conclusion puts a lock on the back door, philosophically and morally enclosing the questions in a defined space. But we cannot close the past. It is ever evolving, chasing our heels even as we flee it.

September 1981

It was their last night together before Clare, Willy and Anja would fly home. They sat around a small table on the balcony enjoying ice cream for dessert. The golden light of the early autumn evening gave a soft glow to their faces. Anja dozed in the carriage.

Stefan sat back with a satisfied "Ahh." "So, kiddo, what do you think about this year in Germany?"

"Whadya mean?" Willy asked while licking his bowl clean.

"Well, what will you take home with you? What new things did you learn this year?"

Willy thought for a moment, wiping the back of his hand over the ice cream drips on his chin.

"I learned that German has long words with pieces like Legos. Um…and babies take a very long time to be born. Plants help us breathe…blind people can see with their canes, sometimes people are nice to you even when they don't know you. And you can use The Force to help them be nice to you."

"That's a great list, Willy." Clare picked up Anja and bounced her on her lap.

"And grownups don't know everything."

"Really? And I always thought we did!" Stefan made an exaggerated expression of surprise and Willy laughed.

"And…and…we have new friends everywhere. We just hafta find them."

"Well said, *Herr Villy*, well said."

They all listened as the crickets sang of nightfall and the turning of the seasons.

16
Auf Wiedersehen

July 2001

Clare stood in the doorway listening to the sounds of summer. A bicycle went bumping down the stone street. An older woman trudged up the hill with a bag of groceries. Three teenage girls walked arm in arm farther on down, their lighthearted voices gradually swallowed by the distance.

Hannah and Stefan were busy in the kitchen with the food for the party. Clare was posted at the door to greet the guests. Christina and Jürgen arrived first, offering to help with preparations. They both wandered into the kitchen as Clare waved to Samira and Omar walking up the hill. She glanced at the living room, which looked festive with freshly cut flowers from Hannah's garden.

"*Soo dhawaada sxb,*" Clare said as she hugged Samira and then Omar. "Welcome friends."

Isra and Esin soon followed, with arms around each other's waist. Clare noted that Esin was a little taller and her hair was not as dark as Isra's. But they looked like they could be sisters.

"I'm so glad you could come," she greeted them, wishing she had learned something in Turkish. Hugs would have to do. "Please come in."

The food was on the table and the guests were mingling comfortably and nibbling on the food. Clare kept glancing at the door as she chatted with her friends.

"I wonder where Johann and Erika are?" she worried.

A few minutes later a knock at the door reassured her. "Hallo?" she heard Johann's deep voice and went to give him a hug and a kiss on the cheek. Erika was right behind him and they hugged and held hands for a moment.

"*Willkommen* to both of you."

"Sorry we're late. I had to finish something," Johann said breathlessly.

Clare was happy to see that he had brought his violin. "Let me introduce you to a few folks you haven't met yet."

"So, you are the famous Johann." Samira smiled as she took his hand and held it for a moment. "I am so glad to meet you."

Johann bowed slightly and placed his other hand on top of hers. "Delighted to meet you as well."

Clare tugged on his arm to meet Omar and then Isra and Esin, who stood nearby. Erika followed and they chatted briefly with each one.

Jürgen and Christina came out of the kitchen to join the group, greeting the new arrivals with friendly familiarity.

It was a joyful gathering, charged with the energy of good friends and their full lives.

"Have you finished your book?" Samira asked.

"Almost. I'm still working on the ending. I have a very inconclusive conclusion."

"Give it time."

"Yes, it's a first draft. There will be lots of editing."

"May I have your attention please?" Clare said as she tapped a glass with a fork. "Stefan, Hannah, please come join us. We can clean up the kitchen later!"

As the room quieted, she looked around and already felt the pangs of missing her friends—the warm-up contractions of separation.

"Thank you all for coming. It means so much to have you here together in our house, which is Hannah's house. So first, I want to introduce you to this dear friend I have just met, but who has been with us this whole year—Hannah Baumgartner.

"Hannah, I can't find the words to express what living in this house has meant to me, to us. Of course, you already know Christina and Jürgen, and we are so grateful to them as well for this opportunity."

Clare hugged Hannah and took her around to meet the others in the party. They moved the table to one side and Clare asked them all to sit down in the circle of chairs around the room. She had invited each one to share something.

"Hannah, how about you tell us some stories about your year, the house, the midwife—whatever you want.

"*Mal sehen,*" she began. "Let's see. I went to Bali to stay with my cousin for a year. She is an artist, who visited there some years ago to learn about their traditional arts. She fell in love with the island and decided to retire there. It is a beautiful place full of diverse art forms, music, dance, and other performing arts. Despite layers of Dutch colonization, Japanese occupation, the increasing invasion of tourism, they have managed to maintain a strong cultural identity. It was a wonderful year for me as well. I was a schoolteacher and I had never had a chance to travel. So as soon as I retired, I decided to take this opportunity.

"The house. Well, I don't know exactly how old it is, but at least several hundred years. I bought it from the daughter of a midwife, whose grandmother had also been a midwife. They were both named Elizabetha and they were *the* midwives of Ockershausen."

Johann and Erika smiled and nodded.

"This is a very special house," Hannah continued. "I believe that Clare and Stefan have learned much about it during their stay here."

Hannah turned to Clare and asked, "Have you met any of the ghosts? Or heard a baby cry?"

Clare's mouth dropped as she relived her feelings of the presence of other beings, the distant cry of a baby, the intense scenes of her dreams. It had all mixed together in the night and she had given up trying to sort it out.

"The birthing room where you sleep holds many stories—births, a few deaths, abortions, the moral and financial struggles of a midwife during difficult times. Especially the Nazi era. I imagine the first Elizabetha broke the rules a few times, probably risking her life to do so. During the Nazi regime, there was not only heavy surveillance, but neighbors sometimes informed on each other. In all their years of practice, the Elizabethas helped to bring many healthy babies into this world and gave the mothers loving support before and after the birth. This house was very important to the community of Ockershausen."

"Thank you, Hannah. We are so grateful to become part of the story of this house."

Everyone clapped. "Hooray for Hannah!" a few shouted, and then they settled into silence.

Samira stood up, smiled at Hannah, and began to sing in Somali.

"*Anigaa iska leh…*" They were all entranced with the music and the sounds of words that they couldn't understand. Clare glanced at Omar, who was smiling as his wife sang.

Samira let the last note fade gradually and then took a breath. "That was a poem I wrote recently. It follows our tradition of women's poetry. Our poems are usually performed, often sung, and they relate to issues of women's lives.

"I have translated it into German and English, trying to preserve the feeling and the rhyme of the original. In German, it is called *Mein Eigenes Ich.*"

> *Mein Kopf unbedeckt*
> *Mein Geist befreit....*

It was the same tune, but it felt like a different song as they understood the words and the familiar sounds of German.

"And now in English: 'My Own I.'"

> My head is bare
> my mind is free
> to receive and share
> what Allah may grant me.
>
> My womb has bloomed
> with two lives I hold dear
> but I won't be consumed
> by a birth every year.
>
> My tongue misses its mother.
> amid sounds from many lands
> while the stories of others
> unfold in my hands.
>
> My soul has fled
> a tyranny that would bind
> and my heart has bled
> for all I left behind.
>
> Now my arms open wide.
> to meet hope and despair
> for all who decide
> to seek comfort there.

They all applauded and cheered.

Clare had to clear her throat to speak. "Thank you, Samira. That was wonderful. The versions felt so different, yet your poem was at home in each language. You are amazing!"

Samira walked over to hand Clare a paper with her song in the three languages. At the bottom, she had written by hand.

> *We are many things: our language, our culture, faith and family,*
> *the paths we choose to take and the ones we leave behind.*
> *We come together and find a new home in each other.*
> *Assalaam- u- Alaikum saaxib.*
> *May peace be upon you, my friend.*
> *-Love, Samira*

Clare was so moved that she could only nod at her friend across the room as she placed both hands over her heart. Again, a moment of silence.

Then Isra jumped up to put a cd in Hannah's player.

"Esin and I are going to show you a traditional Turkish line dance."

She put on the music and both women lifted their arms out to the side with palms up. They moved gracefully with simple steps as they bounced on the balls of their feet and then twirled around.

"Come join us now," Isra said, taking the hands of a couple people as Esin did the same. "Just take small steps and let yourself feel the music."

Soon they were all on their feet bouncing, stepping, and twirling. Then they held hands and formed a circle. Esin stepped into the middle to do some more intricate steps, kicking her feet and then kneeling on one knee as she turned with the circle. A few others took a turn to improvise in the center. Clare was shocked to see Stefan jump in. He had always claimed he couldn't dance, but the spirit moved him in the moment. When it was Clare's turn, she held out both hands in front of her and turned around slowly in a gesture of thanks to each of the dancers.

The music stopped and they sat down breathless and laughing. Pulses slowed as they caught their breath. Clare closed her eyes and waited with her hands in her lap. She felt the trusting openness of a Quaker meeting, wrapped in the warm embrace of friendship. Time stopped and the moment hung in the quiet like a drop of water about to fall.

Christina stood up and began to speak in her gentle voice about the many moments they had enjoyed together and the special community that had grown around Clare and Stefan.

"Jürgen and I are grateful to you two as well for this year and the past we have shared. So many memories. I have pictures of some of them that I have collected for you." She handed Clare a photo album that began in 1980, full of children and family events and ended in recent weeks. She thumbed through and waves of memories washed over her.

"How did you…" Clare began to ask and paused.

"We made copies of the old pictures in our albums and Jürgen managed to sneak other shots here and there."

"He *is* sneaky," Clare agreed. "I didn't even notice him doing it."

"And there is one more thing," Jürgen added as he stood up, "I thought you might like to take this old friend home with you."

"Oh my," Clare said as she opened the gift, trying to hold back internal waters that threatened to overflow. "Oh. It's perfect. Did you paint this? How did you know?"

"A little bird told me," Jürgen said, winking at Christina. "It's your muse, isn't it?"

It was a painting of a window with a small bird perched on the sill outside. The play of light and shadows and a palette of soft colors created for the viewer the sense of being in the room looking out while also embodying the gaze of the bird looking in. The glass that separated them was suggested in light watercolor shades of blue and purple, but it seemed to dissolve in the middle where outside and inside met. A ray of morning sunlight shone in through the window and warmed part of an adjacent wall.

"It's my little friend," Clare said, nodding to Jürgen. "Yes, she was there for me when I needed her. Such precious gifts. We will always treasure them."

They passed the album and the painting around as the party loosened and people went to refill their plates and drinks.

"I'm counting on you to play for us," Clare whispered to Johann as she passed.

"I promise," he said, reaching for her hand and kissing it lightly. "My violin is ready."

"Hey, everyone, are you ready for the Nachtisch? I believe Johann has a dessert for us." Clare felt her already full emotions stir in anticipation of his music as she sat down.

Johann took out his violin and stood. With the instrument hanging from one hand and the bow from the other, he looked around slowly at each face and then smiled.

"I have just finished composing a piece that I want to dedicate to all of you, but especially to Clare. It is called *Die Saiten Meiner Seele,* The Strings of My Soul. Clare is the one who has awakened those strings from a long sleep and helped me to retune them."

Johann lifted the instrument to his chin and held the bow above the strings. A darkness washed over him as his hand trembled and a shiver ran through his body. He stood frozen in an endless moment of the past.

"I'm sorry." He dropped his hands and bowed his head.

Clare was about to jump up to embrace her friend, but something stopped her. She closed her eyes and waited. After what seemed an eternity, the music emerged from a deep and faraway silence. The tune had the same melancholy beauty of the first piece he had played for her. Gradually the notes began to spin into intricate musical threads with occasional underlying harmonies. For a moment, they were caught in churning waters, an intense emotional eddy. But as the tempo picked up and the texture of the music opened, there was a sense of movement towards something. Clare smiled with tears streaming down her face.

The music climbed and Johann's fingers moved up the neck of his violin, nearing his chin that held the body of the instrument to his shoulder. The tempo slowed as his fingers rocked gently on the strings and a tear rolled down the side of his nose. It was an intimate dance of vulnerability and love, uncertainty and hope. The last high notes hung in the air with a soft vibrato that faded into the twilight.

September 1981

They had said their goodbyes and packed their bags. Stefan would have another month there, so it was up to him to deal with the last stages of leaving the apartment. Frau Holzer had already been notified about when to pick up the furniture.

"I'm glad I don't have to be here at the end," Clare confessed to Stefan. "I don't want to see the apartment wiped clean of all traces of our year here." She walked from room to room, thanking each one for the memories they held.

"Guess we'd better get moving, so we can get to the airport with plenty of time to spare," Stefan said as he loaded the last of their bags in the car. Jürgen waited by the open car door on the driver's side.

They stood around the car, trying to stretch out the last minutes before leaving. Clare was grateful that Jürgen would be driving them to the airport, not only for the convenience but also to postpone one of the goodbyes. It was hard to look at Christina, whose watery eyes mirrored her own. They hugged long and hard, a wordless conversation that they both understood. Quick hugs for the kids, and they were off, waving out the window behind them. Clare held Anja up to the window, waving her little hand for her.

"*Auf Wiedersehen!*" Willy called with his last wave.

The airport was busy as usual. Clare focused on getting to her gate. Stefan and Jürgen accompanied her as far as they were allowed. Anja was strapped in the front pack and Willy had his backpack full of Legos. Clare shifted her emotional gears to neutral and gave her last hugs. A "see you soon" one for Stefan, and a "I can't even think about it" one for Jürgen.

They found their seats on the plane at the front of the coach fare cabin. There was a baby hammock bed hanging from the wall in front of her seat. She placed Anja gently in the little bed, immensely grateful for the luxury. She and Willy buckled up and waited for the take-off.

"Here we go," Willy said softly.

Clare leaned over and kissed his forehead.

Soon they were in the air, in that in between space that belonged to no one, chasing time backwards across the ocean.

July 2001

They sat at the little round table in the kitchen, eating their last German breakfast. Stefan had made omelets to go with their favorite bread and his specialty coffee. Hannah commented on how good the coffee was and Stefan launched into his short version of the art of making coffee with a French press.

"I would love to leave this for you, Hannah, if you would like it."

"That would be great!" Hannah responded with appropriate enthusiasm. They ate in silence for a while, enjoying the food and the company. Stefan got up to clear the dishes away.

"It was a wonderful party," Hannah said, reaching over to place her palm gently on Clare's cheek. The same eyes that had watched over Clare's writing looked at her now, their warmth and understanding intact.

"Yes, it was. It was perfect."

Clare had tried to see people off quickly after the party the night before. She didn't want lots of drama. It would be easier to act as though she would see them again soon and let them go easily. The German "goodbye" was helpful that way. It had less finality to it. *Auf Wiedersehen*—literally "on seeing (you) again." But with Johann, it had been harder. She had hugged him at the door and couldn't let go.

"Johann, I..I don't know how..."

He touched her mouth lightly with his hand. "Shhh. I know, I know. We let go and we hang on at the same time. *Meine liebe Clare,* this moment is forever. I will always play the music for you, and you will hear it in your heart." With that, he kissed her on the cheek, took Erika's arm and walked off into the night.

Clare sat down and cried. She bent over and hugged her own chest. How can this small heart stretch across an ocean? Will I ever see these dear people again? Then she got up and started cleaning.

"I think we need to sing something," Hannah said as she walked into the living room still wearing an apron. "Stefan, come sing with us."

The three of them had sat around singing together into the night. They were surprised at how many songs they had in common, both in German and English. Then Hannah put on a cd of German waltzes to cheer them while they finished cleaning. Stefan grabbed Clare and waltzed her around the room. He twirled her three times and eased her into a chair. Then he turned to bow to Hannah with a hand outstretched. Hannah looked surprised but she couldn't resist, so off they went. Clare watched them through her tears, with the house still spinning around her. What a year it had been!

* * *

Their bags were stacked neatly by the door. Clare kissed her journal and tucked it in a carry-on bag.

"Thanks, Dad," she whispered as she zippered it in next to her laptop.

Stefan began to sing. It was a three-part round that they had tried out the night before. The same words bounced through three different melody lines that wove together in an uplifting counterpoint.

Alles ist eitel, du aber bleibst, und wen du ins Buch des Lebens schreibst.

All is vain, you alone remain, and whomever you write
in the book of life.

* * *

Clare gave Hannah one final hug. "I feel like we've known each other forever."

"We have."

Stefan loaded the car and Hannah went out to give him a jar of their favorite jam to take home with them. Clare looked around the house once more, her hand on the open door.

"Thanks, Hannah," she said. "Thanks for everything." She meant all of them: the woman in the photo, the one who listened in her journal, the friend she had only just met. And most of all, the house that had given her a new life.

"Auf Wiedersehen," she whispered as she closed the door.

Acknowledgements

The idea for this novel was conceived when we lived in Marburg, Germany briefly in 2001 and I reflected on our experiences from an earlier longer stay in 1982-83. I felt such a strong sense of place in that town, and the memories, friendships and challenges came back to me so vividly; it was as if they had just paused there, waiting for me to return and reactivate them. The intersection of language, stories, and layers of history as rich as the chocolate cakes Germany is famous for, seemed like a novel waiting to be written. But life rushed on and the idea was left behind in a seemingly unretrievable past.

Then one day not too long ago, I was talking to a writer friend and I told her of that lost opportunity. "Why don't you write it now?" she asked. At first, I couldn't imagine it. For so long it had been part of the anthology of *The Stories I Didn't Write*.

"Just do it," she said.

So I did.

I am grateful to Laurel McHargue for that nudge. And to Linda Taylor, who was my developmental editor. She pushed me, asked hard questions, suggested ideas, and paid attention to detail while cheering me on. Marita Metz-Becker provided valuable resources on the history of midwives in Germany. Ilgin Yorukoglu's writing gave me some ideas for developing the character of Isra.

Much of the early timeline is based on my own experiences in Marburg, remembered and reimagined with the freedom that fiction allows. I thank my dear friends and family who were part of that wonderful time and who consented to leading a double life as fictional characters. Their contributions to the writing were invaluable. I am also grateful to the imagined characters who found me. They have enriched my life and moved in with me forever.

Heartfelt thanks to my wonderful beta readers: Leslie Bishop, Majka Jankowiak, Adrienne Hoskins, Aletha Stahl, and dear friends Jochen and Maria, for their helpful feedback and suggestions. And special thanks to Barbara Jurasek for her insights and corrections as I read an early draft aloud to her on a delightful nostalgia trip to Marburg that we shared. She was my mobile German dictionary and guide to the nuances of German culture and philosophy. Later she was also a careful reader and copy editor for the book, for which I am most grateful. I owe a debt as well to serendipity, and to the real *Das Haus* and its owner. Our stay there was magical and it provided the initial inspiration for this novel.

My husband Peter Taylor, played an important supporting role in so many aspects of this book: as partner in life and imagination, cheerleader, student and then professor of German History, whose research took us to Marburg in the first place. He was my resource for many historical questions, my companion through the challenges, joys, and frustrations of writing. He was also an attentive listener as I read the manuscript aloud to him, offering corrections, additions, and suggestions for the backstories of characters, especially Johann. To my beloved children: Jordy, my wise and innocent little Jedi companion, who gave me joy and courage in our new adventure; and Ani, my inner body mate, a source of hope and wonder as she grew towards the light and the gift of her birth in Marburg. They are both mature adults now, but the little boy and the baby are immortal for me.

Miranda Pratt and Chris Wells, dear friends and companions in many of our life adventures, also gave substantial support and encouragement to this venture.

And finally, to my father, Dan Wilson, who inspired me to dream, imagine and write:

Thanks, Dad.

About The Author

Kathy Taylor is a writer and musician and a retired professor of Spanish literature, linguistics, and creative writing. A passionate polyglot, she loves languages and their cultures and is fascinated by language in general. She has lived in Mexico, Nicaragua, Ireland, Curaçao and Germany and has written songs in Spanish, Portuguese, German, and Papiamentu (a Caribbean Creole language), as well as in English.

Kathy has published in English, Spanish and Papiamentu: poetry, short stories, essays, translations, a bilingual ethnographic novel on Mexican taxi drivers, and literary and linguistic theory. Her recent short story collection *Trees and Other Witnesses* features tales of migration and struggle, cultural conflict and adaptation in the U.S., Mexico, and Central America. It was a 2022 finalist for the Colorado Author's League award in the category of literary/mainstream fiction. She lives off the grid with her husband in the mountains of Colorado.

Discussion Questions

1. Discuss the narrative structure of *The Birthing House*. What different kinds of texts are there and what is their function? What is the effect of the two alternating timelines on the story and the reader?

2. Clare's fascination with words and languages is a theme throughout the book. How does this affect her experience in Germany and the friendships that develop?

3. What is the symbolic importance of Willy's Legos?

4. What is the importance of the "Notes For Book" sections?

5. How does *Das Haus* serve as an important metaphor in the novel? What is the relationship between *The House of Fiction* and *The Birthing House*?

6. Discuss the references to blindness and seeing in the novel. How does this interplay affect Clare's character development?

7. How do the themes of loss, pregnancy and birth help to structure the novel in the two timelines?

8. Discuss the tension in the book between how cultures create and preserve community and how they can also imprison or exclude.

9. What sacrifices and obstacles do the immigrants in this novel face? How does their identity evolve as they find new community? Clare shares their experience as foreigners, yet it is different for her. How?

10. Johann's story is full of painful ironies and traumatic experiences. Discuss the role of music and the two Claras (Klara/Clare) in his survival and recovery.

11. There are several metaphors for writing that appear in the book: the author as weaver, midwife, architect, spinner, wordsmith, listener. Others? Discuss how the writing process is presented in *The Birthing House* and how the reader becomes an active participant.